WHO IS
THE
JACKAL?

A tall, blond Englishman with opaque gray eyes
. . . A killer at the top of his grisly profession . . .
A man unknown to any Secret Service in the
world . . . An assassin with a contract to kill the
world's most heavily guarded man . . .
As *THE DAY OF THE JACKAL* unfolds, you
will follow this mysterious Englishman on his
murderous mission. His icy, calculating mind
masters every detail of death-by-gunfire. Each act
is intricately planned; no stone is left unturned to
achieve perfection in his design for death.
The Jackal will take you along the route that
his target will travel on the last day of his life.
And finally, you will watch as the Jackal perfects
the split-second timing that will bring his un-
knowing victim between the crosshairs of his
high-powered gun.
"So plausible has Mr. Forsyth made his im-
plausible villain . . . so excitingly does he lead
him on his murderous mission against impossible
odds, that even saintly readers will be hard put
not to cheer this particular villain along his devious way." —Stanley Ellin, *The New York
Times Book Review*

THE CRITICS AGREE—

"YOU WON'T STOP TURNING PAGES TILL THE LAST SHOT EXPLODES."

—*Book World*

"A masterpiece tour de force of crisp, sharp, suspenseful writing. *THE DAY OF THE JACKAL* marks the emergence of a major new suspense-adventure writer, one of the happy few in the fine tradition of Geoffrey Household, Lionel Davidson, and John Le Carré. It's an awful cliché to say that 'you won't be able to put this book down,' but cliché or not, it's the truth."

—*The Wall Street Journal*

"I was held spellbound, riveted to this chilling, superbly researched story . . . A superb piece of mystery."

—Peter Harvey, *The Guardian*

"So chillingly real that it makes this novel a notable suspense story—skillfully contrived, rushing along with such passion that the reader himself seems to be traveling with 'The Jackal.' One of the best books of its type in a long time."

—*Newsday*

"What distinguishes this tale is the excellent writing, meticulous detail and the persuasively authentic background."

—*Minneapolis Star*

THE DAY OF
THE JACKAL
Frederick Forsyth

*This low-priced Bantam Book
has been completely reset in a type face
designed for easy reading, and was printed
from new plates. It contains the complete
text of the original hard-cover edition.*
NOT ONE WORD WAS OMITTED.

THE DAY OF THE JACKAL

*A Bantam Book / published by arrangement with
The Viking Press*

PRINTING HISTORY
Viking edition published August 1971

Bantam edition / September 1972

2nd printing .. September 1972	10th printing . September 1973
3rd printing .. September 1972	11th printing .. January 1974
4th printing .. September 1972	12th printing ..... April 1975
5th printing ..... March 1973	13th printing .... August 1975
6th printing .... June 1973	14th printing . November 1975
7th printing .... June 1973	15th printing .. January 1976
8th printing .... June 1973	16th printing . February 1976
9th printing .... July 1973	17th printing . February 1977

ISBN 0-553-10857-3

Published simultaneously in the United States and Canada

Bantam Books are published by Bantam Books, Inc. Its trademark, consisting of the words "Bantam Books" and the portrayal of a bantam, is registered in the United States Patent Office and in other countries. Marca Registrada. Bantam Books, Inc., 666 Fifth Avenue, New York, New York 10019.

PRINTED IN THE UNITED STATES OF AMERICA

The Day of
the Jackal

PART ONE

Anatomy of a Plot

It is cold at 6:40 in the morning of a March day in Paris, and seems even colder when a man is about to be executed by firing squad. At that hour on March 11, 1963, in the main courtyard of the Fort d'Ivry a French Air Force colonel stood before a stake driven into the chilly gravel as his hands were bound behind the post, and stared with slowly diminishing disbelief at the squad of soldiers facing him twenty metres away.

A foot scuffed the grit, a tiny release from tension, as the blindfold was wrapped around the eyes of Lieutenant-Colonel Jean-Marie Bastien-Thiry, age thirty-five, blotting out the light for the last time. The mumbling of the priest was a helpless counterpoint to the crackling of twenty rifle bolts as the soldiers charged and cocked their carbines.

Beyond the walls a Berliet truck blared for a passage as some smaller vehicle crossed its path towards the centre of the city; the sound died away, masking the "Take your aim" order from the officer in charge of the squad. The crash of rifle fire, when it came, caused no ripple on the surface of the waking city, other than to send a flutter of pigeons skywards for a few moments. The single "whack" seconds later of the coup-de-grace was lost in the rising din of traffic from beyond the walls.

The death of the officer, leader of a gang of Secret Army Organisation killers who had sought to shoot the

3

President of France, was to have been an end—an end to further attempts on the President's life. By a quirk of fate it marked a beginning, and to explain why, it is first necessary to explain why a riddled body came to hang from its ropes in the courtyard of the military prison outside Paris on that March morning. . . .

The sun had dropped at last behind the palace wall, and long shadows rippled across the courtyard bringing a welcome relief. Even at 7 in the evening of the hottest day of the year the temperature was still twenty-five degrees centigrade. Across the sweltering city the Parisians piled querulous wives and yelling children into cars and trains to leave for the weekend in the country. It was August 22, 1962, the day a few men waiting beyond the city boundaries had decided that the President, General Charles de Gaulle, should die.

While the city's population prepared to flee the heat for the relative cool of the rivers and beaches, the cabinet meeting behind the ornate façade of the Elysée Palace continued. Across the tan gravel of the front courtyard, now cooling in welcome shadow, sixteen black Citroen DS sedans were drawn up nose to tail, forming a circle round three quarters of the area.

The drivers, lurking in the deepest shade close to the west wall where the shadows had arrived first, exchanged the inconsequential banter of those who spend most of their working days waiting on their masters' whims.

There was more desultory grumbling at the unusual length of the Cabinet's deliberations, until a moment before 7:30 a chained and bemedalled usher appeared behind the plate glass doors at the top of the six steps of the palace and gestured towards the guards. Among the drivers, half-smoked Gauloises were dropped and ground into the gravel. The security men and guards stiffened in their boxes beside the front gate and the massive iron grilles were swung open.

The chauffeurs were at the wheels of their limousines when the first group of ministers appeared behind the plate glass. The usher opened the doors and the members of the Cabinet straggled down the steps exchanging a few last-minute wishes for a restful weekend. In order of precedence the sedans eased up to the base of the steps, the usher opened the rear door with a bow, the Ministers climbed into their respective cars and were driven away past the salutes of the Garde Républicaine and out into Faubourg Saint Honoré.

Within ten minutes they were gone. Two long black DS 19 Citroens remained in the yard, and each slowly cruised to the base of the steps. The first, flying the pennant of the President of the French Republic, was driven by François Marroux, a police driver from the training and headquarters camp of the Gendarmerie Nationale at Satory. His silent temperament had kept him apart from the joking of the ministerial drivers in the courtyard; his ice-cold nerves and ability to drive fast and safely kept him de Gaulle's personal driver. Apart from Marroux, the car was empty. Behind it the second DS 19 was also driven by a gendarme from Satory.

At 7:45 another group appeared behind the glass doors, and again the men on the gravel stiffened to attention. Dressed in his habitual double-breasted charcoal grey suit and dark tie, Charles de Gaulle appeared behind the glass. With old-world courtesy he first ushered Madame Yvonne de Gaulle through the doors, then took her arm to guide her down the steps to the waiting Citroen. They parted at the car, and the President's wife climbed into the rear seat of the front vehicle on the left-hand side. The General got in behind her from the right.

Their son-in-law, Colonel Alain de Boissieu, then chief-of-staff of the Armoured and Cavalry units of the French Army, checked that both rear doors were safely shut, then took his place in the front beside Marroux.

In the second car two others from the group of functionaries who had accompanied the presidential couple down the steps took their seats. Henri d'Jouder, the hulking bodyguard of the day, a Kabyle from Algeria, took the front seat beside the driver, eased the heavy revolver under his left armpit, and slumped back. From then on his eyes would flicker incessantly, not over the car in front, but over the pavements and street corners as they flashed past. After a last word to one of the duty security men to be left behind, the second man got into the back alone. He was Commissaire Jean Ducret, chief of the Presidential Security Corps.

From beside the west wall two white-helmeted motorcyclists gunned their engines into life and rode slowly out of the shadows towards the gate. Before the entrance they stopped ten feet apart and glanced back. Marroux pulled the first Citroen away from the steps, swung towards the gate, and drew up behind the motorcycle outriders. The second car followed. It was 7:50 p.m.

Again the iron grille swung open, and the small cortege swept past the ramrod guards into the Faubourg

Saint Honoré and from there into the Avenue de Marigny. From under the chestnut trees a young man in
a white crash helmet astride a scooter watched the
cortege pass, then slid away from the kerb and followed. Traffic was normal for an August weekend, and
no advance warning of the President's departure had
been given. Only the whine of the motorcycle sirens
told traffic cops on duty of the approach of the convoy, and they had to wave and whistle frantically to
get the traffic stopped in time.

The convoy picked up speed in the tree-darkened
avenue and erupted into the sunlit Place Clemenceau,
heading straight across towards the Pont Alexandre
III. Riding in the slipstream of the official cars, the
scooterist had little difficulty in following. After the
bridge Marroux followed the motorcyclists into the
Avenue General Gallieni and thence into the broad
Boulevard des Invalides. The scooterist at this point
had his answer—the route de Gaulle's convoy would
take out of Paris. At the junction of the Boulevard des
Invalides and the rue de Varennes he eased back the
screaming throttle and swerved towards a corner cafe.
Inside, taking a small metal token from his pocket, he
strode to the back of the cafe where the telephone was
situated and placed a local call.

Lieutenant-Colonel Jean-Marie Bastien-Thiry waited
in the suburb of Meudon. He was married, with three
children, and he worked in the Air Ministry. Behind
the conventional façade of his professional and family
life, he nurtured a deep bitterness towards Charles de
Gaulle, who, he believed, had betrayed France and the
men who in 1958 had called him back to power by
yielding Algeria to the Algerian nationalists.

He personally had lost nothing through the loss of Algeria, and it was not personal consideration that motivated him. In his own eyes he was a patriot, a man convinced that he would be serving his beloved country by slaying the man he thought had betrayed her. Many thousands shared his views at that time, but few in comparison were fanatical members of the Secret Army Organisations, which had sworn to kill de Gaulle and bring down his government. Bastien-Thiry was such a man.

He was sipping a beer when the call came through. The barman passed him the phone, then went to adjust the television set at the other end of the bar. Bastien-Thiry listened for a few seconds, muttered, "Very good, thank you," into the mouthpiece, and set it down. His beer was already paid for. He strolled out of the bar onto the pavement, took a rolled newspaper from under his arm, and carefully unfolded it twice.

Across the street a young woman let drop the lace curtain of her first floor flat, and, turning to the twelve men who lounged about the room, she said, "It's route number two." The five youngsters, amateurs at the business of killing, stopped twisting their hands and jumped up.

The other seven were older and less nervous. Senior among them in the assassination attempt and second-in-command to Bastien-Thiry was Lieutenant Alain Bougrenet de la Tocnaye, an extreme right-winger from a family of landed gentry. He was thirty-five, married, with two children.

The most dangerous man in the room was Georges Watin, aged thirty-nine, a bulky-shouldered, square-jowled OAS fanatic, originally an agricultural engineer from Algeria, who in two years had emerged again as one of the OAS's most dangerous trigger-men. From an old leg-wound he was known as "the Limp."

When the girl announced the news, the twelve men trooped downstairs via the back of the building to a side street where six vehicles, all stolen or hired, had been parked. The time was 7:55.

Bastien-Thiry had personally spent days preparing the site of the assassination, measuring angles of fire, speed and distance of the moving vehicles, and the degree of firepower necessary to stop them. The place he had chosen was a long straight road called the Avenue de la Libération, leading up to the main cross-roads of Petit-Clamart. The plan was for the first group containing the marksmen with their rifles to open fire on the President's car some two hundred yards before the cross-roads. They would shelter behind an Estafette van parked by the roadside, beginning their fire at a very shallow angle to the oncoming vehicles.

By Bastien-Thiry's calculations, 150 bullets should pass through the leading car by the time it came abreast of the van. With the presidential car brought to a stop, the second OAS group would sweep out of a side road to blast the security police vehicle at close range. Both groups would spend a few seconds finishing off the presidential party, then spring for the three getaway vehicles in another side street.

Bastien-Thiry himself, the thirteenth of the party, would be the lookout man. By 8:05 the groups were in position. A hundred yards on the Paris side of the ambush, Bastien-Thiry stood idly by a bus stop with his newspaper. Waving the newspaper would give the signal to Serge Bernier, leader of the first commando, who would be standing by the Estafette. He would pass the order to the gunmen spreadeagled in the grass at his feet. Bougrenet de la Tocnaye would drive the car to intercept the security police, with Watin the Limp beside him clutching a submachine gun.

As the safety catches flicked off beside the road at Petit-Clamart, General de Gaulle's convoy cleared the heavier traffic of central Paris and reached the more open avenues of the suburbs. Here the speed increased to nearly sixty miles per hour.

As the road opened out, François Marroux flicked a glance at his watch, sensed the testy impatience of the old General behind him, and pushed the speed up even higher. The two motorcycle outriders dropped back to take up station at the rear of the convoy. De Gaulle never liked such ostentation sitting out in front and dispensed with them whenever he could. In this manner the convoy entered the Avenue de la Division Leclerc at Petit-Clamart. It was 8:17 p.m.

A mile up the road Bastien-Thiry was experiencing the effects of his big mistake. He would not learn of it until told by the police as he sat months later in Death Row. Investigating the timetable of his assassination, he had consulted a calendar to discover that dusk fell on August 22 at 8:35, seemingly plenty late enough even if de Gaulle was late on his usual schedule, as indeed he was. But the calendar the Air Force colonel had consulted related to 1961. On August 22, 1962, dusk fell at 8:10. Those twenty-five minutes were to change the history of France. At 8:18 Bastien-Thiry discerned the convoy hurtling down the Avenue de la

Libération towards him at seventy miles per hour. Frantically he waved his newspaper.

Across the road and a hundred yards down, Bernier peered angrily through the gloom at the dim figure by the bus stop. "Has the colonel waved his paper yet?" he asked of no one in particular. The words were hardly out of his mouth when he saw the shark-nose of the President's car flash past the bus stop and into vision. "Fire," he screamed to the men at his feet. They opened up as the convoy came abreast of them, firing with a ninety-degree lay-off at a moving target passing them at seventy miles per hour.

That the car took twelve bullets at all was a tribute to the killers' marksmanship. Most of those hit the Citroen from behind. Two tires shredded under the fire, and although they were self-sealing tubes the sudden loss of pressure caused the speeding car to lurch and go into a front-wheel skid. That was when François Marroux saved de Gaulle's life.

While the ace marksman, ex-legionnaire Varga, cut up the tires, the remainder emptied their magazines at the disappearing rear window. Several slugs passed through the bodywork, and one shattered the rear window, passing within a few inches of the presidential nose. In the front seat Colonel de Boissieu turned and roared, "Get down," at his parents-in-law. Madame de Gaulle lowered her head towards her husband's lap. The General gave vent to a frosty "What, again?" and turned to look out of the back window.

Marroux held the shuddering steering wheel and gently turned into the skid, easing down the accelerator as he did so. After a momentary loss of power the Citroen surged forward again towards the intersection with the Avenue du Bois, the side-road where the second commando of OAS men waited. Behind Marroux the security car clung to his tail, untouched by any bullets at all.

For Bougrenet de la Tocnaye, waiting with engine running in the Avenue du Bois, the speed of the approaching cars gave him a clear choice: to intercept and commit suicide as the hurtling metal cut him to pieces, or let the clutch in a half-second too late. He chose the latter. As he swung his car out of the side road and into line with the presidential convoy, it was not de Gaulle's car he came alongside, but that of the marksman bodyguard d'Jouder and Commissaire Ducret.

Leaning from the right-hand side window, outside the car from the waist up, Watin emptied his submachine gun at the back of the DS in front, in which he could see de Gaulle's haughty profile through the smashed glass.

"Why don't those idiots fire back?" de Gaulle asked querulously. D'Jouder was trying to get a shot at the OAS killers across ten feet of air between the two cars, but the police driver blocked his view. Ducret shouted to the driver to stick with the President, and a second later the OAS were left behind. The two motorcycle outriders, one having nearly been unseated by de la Tocnaye's sudden rush out of the side road, recovered and closed up. The whole convoy swept into the roundabout and road-junction, crossed it, and continued towards Villacoublay.

At the ambush site the OAS men had no time for recriminations. They were to come later. Leaving the three cars used in the operation, they leapt aboard the getaway vehicles and disappeared into the descending gloom.

From his car-borne transmitter Commissaire Ducret called Villacoublay and told them briefly what had happened. When the convoy arrived ten minutes later, General de Gaulle insisted on driving straight to the apron where the helicopter was waiting. As the car stopped, a surge of officers and officials surrounded it, pulling open the doors to assist a shaken Madame de Gaulle to her feet. From the other side the General emerged from the debris and shook glass splinters from his lapel. Ignoring the panicky solicitude of the surrounding officers, he walked round the car to take his wife's arm.

"Come, my dear, we are going home," he told her, and finally gave the Air Force staff his verdict on the OAS: "They can't shoot straight." With that he guided his wife into the helicopter and took his seat beside her. He was joined by d'Jouder, and they took off for a weekend in the country.

On the tarmac François Marroux sat ashen-faced behind the wheel. Both tires along the right-hand side of the car had finally given out, and the DS was riding on its rims. Ducret muttered a quiet word of congratulations to him, then went on with the business of clearing up.

While journalists the world over speculated on the assassination attempt and for lack of anything better filled their columns with personal conjectures, the French police, headed by the Sûreté Nationale and backed up by the Secret Service and the Gendarmerie, launched the biggest police operation in French history. Soon it was to become the biggest manhunt the country had yet known, only later to be surpassed by the manhunt for another assassin whose story remains unknown but who is still listed in the files by his code-name, the Jackal.

They got their first break on September 3, and, as is so often the case with police work, it was a routine check that brought results. Outside the town of Va-lence, south of Lyons on the main road from Paris to Marseilles, a police roadblock stopped a private car containing four men. They had stopped hundreds that day to examine identity papers, but in this case one of the men in the car had no papers on him. He claimed he had lost them. He and the other three were taken to Valence for routine questioning.

At Valence it was established that the other three in the car had nothing to do with the fourth, apart from having offered him a lift. They were released. The fourth man's fingerprints were taken and sent to Paris, just to see if he was who he said he was. The answer came back twelve hours later: the fingerprints were those of a twenty-two-year-old deserter from the For-eign Legion, who faced charges under military law. But the name he had given was quite accurate—Pierre-Denis Magade.

Magade was taken to the headquarters of the Ser-vice Régional of the Police Judiciaire at Lyons. While waiting in an anteroom for interrogation, one of the police guarding him playfully asked, "Well, what about Petit-Clamart?"

Magade shrugged helplessly. "All right," he an-swered, "what do you want to know?"

As stunned police officers listened to him and ste-nographers' pens scratched across one notebook after another, Magade "sang" for eight hours. By the end he had named every one of the participants of Petit-Clamart, and nine others who had played smaller roles in the plotting stages or in procuring the equipment. Twenty-two in all. The hunt was on, and this time the police knew whom they were looking for.

In the end only one escaped, and has never been caught to this day. Georges Watin got away and is presumed to be living in Spain along with most of the other OAS chiefs.

The interrogation and preparation of the charges against Bastien-Thiry, Bougrenet de la Tocnaye, and the other leaders of the plot were finished by December, and the group went on trial in January 1963.

While the trial was on, the OAS gathered its strength for another all-out attack on the Gaullist government, and the French Secret Service fought back tooth and claw. Under the pleasant norms of Parisian life, beneath the veneer of culture and civilisation, one of the bitterest and most sadistic underground wars of modern history was fought out.

The French Secret Service is called the Service de Documentation Extérieure et de Contre-Espionage, known for short as SDECE. Its duties are both those of espionage outside France and counter-espionage within, though each service may overlap the other's territory on occasion. Service One is pure intelligence, subdivided into bureaux known by the initial R for Renseignement (Information). These subdivisions are R 1, Intelligence Analysis; R 2, Eastern Europe; R 3, Western Europe; R 4, Africa; R 5, Middle East; R 6, Far East; R 7, America/Western Hemisphere. Service Two is concerned with counter-espionage. Three and

Four comprise the Communist Section in one office, Six is Finance, and Seven, Administration.

Service Five has a one-word title—Action. This office was the core of the anti-OAS war. From the headquarters in a complex of nondescript buildings off the Boulevard Mortier, close to the Porte des Lilas, a dingy suburb of northeast Paris, the hundred toughs of the Action Service went out to war. These men, mainly Corsicans, were trained to a peak of physical fitness, then taken to Satory camp, where a special section shut off from the rest taught them everything known about destruction. They became experts in fighting with small arms and in unarmed combat—Karate and Judo. They underwent courses in radio communication, demolition and sabotage, interrogation with and without the use of torture, kidnapping, arson, and assassination.

Some spoke only French, others were fluent in several languages and at home in any capital in the world. They had the authority to kill in the course of duty and often used it.

As the activities of the OAS became more violent and brutal, the Director of the SDECE, General Eugène Guibaud, finally took the muzzle off these men and let them loose on the OAS. Some of them enlisted in the OAS and infiltrated its highest councils. From here they were content to provide information on which others could act, and many OAS emissaries on missions into France or other areas where they were vulnerable to the police were picked up on information provided by Action Service men inside the terrorist organization. On other occasions wanted men could not be inveigled into France and were ruthlessly killed outside the country. Many relatives of OAS men who simply disappeared believed ever after that the men had been liquidated by the Action Service.

Not that the OAS needed lessons in violence. They hated the Action Service men (known as the Barbouzes, or Bearded Ones, because of their undercover role) more than any policeman. In the last days of the struggle for power between the OAS and the Gaullist authorities inside Algiers, the OAS captured seven Barbouzes alive. The bodies were later found hanging from balconies and lamp-posts minus ears and noses. In this manner the undercover war went on, and the complete story of who died under torture at whose hands in which cellar will never be told.

The remainder of the Barbouzes stayed outside the OAS at the beck and call of the SDECE. Some of them had been professional thugs from the underworld before being enlisted, kept up their old contacts, and on more than one occasion enlisted the aid of their former underworld friends to do a particularly dirty job for the government. It was these activities that gave rise to talk in France of a "parallel" (unofficial) police, supposedly at the orders of one of President de Gaulle's right-hand men, M. Jacques Foccart. In truth no "parallel" police existed; the activities attributed to them were carried out by the Action Service strong-arms or temporarily enlisted gang-bosses from the "milieu."

Corsicans, who dominated both the Paris and Marseilles underworld and the Action Service, know a thing or two about vendettas, and after the slaying of the seven Barbouzes of Mission C in Algiers, a vendetta was declared against the OAS. In the same manner as the Corsican underworld helped the Allies during the landings in the South of France in 1944 (for their own ends; they later cornered most of the vice trade along the Côte d'Azur as a reward), so in the early sixties the Corsicans fought for France again in a vendetta with the OAS. Many of the OAS men who were *pieds-noirs* (Algerian-born Frenchmen) had the same characteristics as the Corsicans, and at times the war was almost fratricidal.

As the trial of Bastien-Thiry and his fellows wore on, the OAS campaign also got under way. Its guiding light, the behind-the-scenes instigator of the Petit-Clamart plot, was Colonel Antoine Argoud. A product of one of France's top universities, the Ecole Polytechnique, Argoud had a good brain and dynamic energy. As a lieutenant under de Gaulle in the Free French, he had fought for the liberation of France from the Nazis. Later he commanded a regiment of cavalry in Algiers. A short, wiry man, he was a brilliant but ruthless soldier, and by 1962 he had become operations chief for the OAS in exile.

Experienced in psychological warfare, he understood that the fight against Gaullist France had to be conducted on all levels, by terror, diplomacy, and public relations. As part of the campaign he arranged for the head of the National Resistance Council, the political wing of the OAS, former French Foreign Minister Georges Bidault, to give a series of interviews to newspapers and television across Western Europe to explain the OAS's opposition to General de Gaulle in "respectable" terms.

Argoud was now putting to use the fine intellect that had once made him the youngest colonel in the French Army and now made him the most dangerous man in the OAS. He set up for Bidault a series of interviews with major networks and newspaper correspondents, during which the old politician was able to put a cloak of sober rectitude over the less acceptable activities of the OAS thugs.

The success of Bidault's Argoud-inspired propaganda operation alarmed the French government as much as the terror tactics and the wave of plastic bombs exploding in cinemas and cafes all over France. Then on February 14 another plot to assassinate General de Gaulle was uncovered. The following day he was due to give a lecture at the Ecole Militaire on the Champ de Mars. The plot was that on entering the hall he was to be shot in the back by an assassin perched among the eaves of the adjacent block.

Those who later faced trial for the plot were Jean Bicnon, a captain of artillery named Robert Poinard, and an English-language teacher at the Military Academy, Madame Paule Rousselet de Liffiac. The triggerman was to have been Georges Watin, but once again the Limp got away. A rifle with sniperscope was found at Poinard's flat, and the three were arrested. It was stated at their later trial that, seeking a way to spirit Watin and his gun into the Academy, they had consulted Warrant Officer Marius Tho, who had gone straight to the police. General de Gaulle duly attended the military ceremony at the appointed time on the 15th but made the concession of arriving in an armour-plated car, to his great distaste.

As a plot, it was amateurish beyond belief, but it annoyed de Gaulle. Summoning Interior Minister Frey the next day, he hammered the table and told the

Minister responsible for national security, "This assassination business has gone far enough."

It was decided to make an example of some of the top OAS conspirators to deter the others. Frey had no doubts about the outcome of the Bastien-Thiry trial still going on in the Supreme Military Court, for Bastien-Thiry was at pains to explain from the dock why he thought Charles de Gaulle should die. But something more in the way of a deterrent was needed.

On February 22 a copy of a memorandum which the director of Service Two of SDECE had sent to the Interior Minister landed on the desk of the head of the Action Service. Here is an extract:

"We have succeeded in ascertaining the whereabouts of one of the main ringleaders of the subversive movement, namely ex-Colonel of the French Army Antoine Argoud. He has fled to Germany and intends, according to information from our Intelligence Service there, to remain for several days. . . .

"This being so, it should be possible to get at Argoud and perhaps seize him. As the request made by our official counter-espionage service to the competent German security organisations has been refused, and these organisations now expect our agents to be on the heels of Argoud and other OAS leaders, the operation must, insofar as it is directed against the person of Argoud, be carried out with maximum speed and discretion."

The job was handed over to the Action Service.

In the midafternoon of February 25 Argoud arrived back in Munich from Rome where he had been meeting other OAS leaders. Instead of going straight to Unertlstrasse he took a taxi to the Eden-Wolff Hotel, where he had booked a room, apparently for a meeting. He never attended it. In the hall he was accosted by two men who spoke to him in faultless German. He presumed they were German police and reached into his breast pocket for his passport.

He felt both arms grabbed in a vice-like grip, his feet left the ground, and he was whisked outside to a waiting laundry van. He lashed out and was answered with a torrent of French oaths. A horny hand chopped across his nose, another slammed him in the stomach, a finger felt for the nerve spot below the ear, and he went out like a light.

Twenty-four hours later a telephone rang in the Brigade Criminelle of the Police Judiciaire at 36, Quai des Orfèvres in Paris. A hoarse voice told the answering desk sergeant that he was speaking for the OAS and that Antoine Argoud, "nicely tied up," was in a van parked behind the building. A few minutes later the door of the van was jerked open and Argoud stumbled out into a circle of dumbfounded police officers.

His eyes, bandaged for twenty-four hours, would not focus. He had to be helped to stand. His face was covered with dried blood from a nose-bleed, and his mouth ached from the gag which the police pulled out of it. When someone asked him, "Are you Colonel Antoine Argoud?" he mumbled, "Yes." Somehow the Action Service had spirited him across the frontier during the previous night, and the anonymous phone call to the police about the parcel waiting them in their own parking lot was just their private sense of humour at work. Argoud was held until June 1968, and then released.

But one thing the Action Service men had not counted on: in removing Argoud, despite the enormous demoralisation this caused in the OAS, they had paved the way for his shadowy deputy, the little known but equally astute Lieutenant Colonel Marc Rodin, to assume command of operations aimed at assassinating de Gaulle. In many ways it was a bad bargain.

On March 4 the Supreme Military Court delivered its verdict on Jean-Marie Bastien-Thiry. He and two others were sentenced to death, as were a further three still at large including Watin the Limp. On March 8 General de Gaulle listened for three hours in silence to appeals for clemency by the lawyers of the condemned men. He commuted two of the death sentences to life imprisonment, but Bastien-Thiry's condemnation stood.

That night his lawyer told the Air Force colonel of the decision.

"It is fixed for the eleventh," he told his client, and when the latter continued to smile disbelievingly, blurted out, "You are going to be shot."

Bastien-Thiry kept smiling and shook his head.

"You don't understand," he told the lawyer, "no squad of Frenchmen will raise their rifles against me."

He was wrong. The execution was reported on the 8 a.m. news of Radio Europe Number One in French. It was heard in most parts of Western Europe by those who cared to tune in. In a small hotel room in Austria the broadcast was to set off a train of thoughts and actions that brought General de Gaulle nearer to death than at any time in his career. The room was that of Colonel Marc Rodin, new operations chief of the OAS.

two

Marc Rodin flicked off the switch of his transistor radio and rose from the table, leaving the breakfast tray almost untouched. He walked over to the window, lit another in the endless chain of cigarettes and gazed out at the snow-encrusted landscape, which the late-arriving spring had not yet started to dismantle.

"Bastards." He murmured the word quietly and with great venom, following up with another sotto voce string of nouns and epithets that expressed his feelings towards the French President, his government, and the Action Service.

Rodin was unlike his predecessor in almost every way. Tall and spare, with a cadaverous face hollowed by the hatred within, he usually masked his emotions with an un-Latin frigidity. For him there had been no Ecole Polytechnique to open doors to promotion. The son of a cobbler, he had escaped to England by fishing boat in the halcyon days of his late teens when the Germans overran France, and had enlisted as a private soldier under the banner of the Cross of Lorraine.

Promotion through sergeant to Warrant Officer had come the hard way, in bloody battles across the face of North Africa under Koenig and later through the hedgerows of Normandy with Leclerc. A field commission during the fight for Paris had got him the officer's chevrons his education and breeding could never have obtained, and in post-war France the

choice had been between staying in the Army or re-
verting to civilian life.

But revert to what? He had no trade but that of
cobbler which his father had taught him, and he found
the working class of his native country dominated by
Communists, who had also taken over the Resistance
and the Free French of the Interior. So he stayed in
the Army, later to experience the bitterness of an officer from the ranks who saw a new young generation
of educated boys graduating from the officer schools,
earning in theoretical lessons carried out in classrooms
the same chevrons he had sweated blood for. As he
watched them pass him in rank and privilege, the bitterness started to set in.

There was only one thing left to do, and that was
join one of the colonial regiments, the tough crack
soldiers who did the fighting while the conscript army
paraded round drill squares. He managed a transfer to
the colonial paratroops.

Within a year he had been a company commander
in Indochina, living among other men who spoke and
thought as he did. For a young man from a cobbler's
bench, promotion could still be obtained through combat, and more combat. By the end of the Indochina
campaign he was a major, and after an unhappy and
frustrating year in France he was sent to Algeria.

The French withdrawal from Indochina and the
year he spent in France had turned his latent bitterness into a consuming loathing of politicians and Communists, whom he regarded as one and the same thing.
Not until France was ruled by a soldier could she ever
be pried loose from the grip of the traitors and lick-

spittles who permeated her public life. Only in the Army were both breeds extinct.

Like most combat officers who had seen their men die and occasionally buried the hideously mutilated bodies of those unlucky enough to be taken alive, Rodin worshipped soldiers as the true salt of the earth, the men who sacrificed themselves in blood so that the bourgeoisie could live at home in comfort. To learn from the civilians of his native land after his eight years of combat in the forests of Indochina that most of them cared not a fig for the soldiery, to read the denunciations of the military by the Left-wing intellectuals for mere trifles like the torturing of prisoners to obtain vital information, had set off inside Marc Rodin a reaction which, combined with the native bitterness stemming from his own lack of opportunity, had turned into zealotry.

He remained convinced that given enough backing by the civil authorities on the spot and the Government and people back home, the Army could have beaten the Viet-Minh. The cession of Indochina had been a massive betrayal of the thousands of fine young men who had died there—seemingly for nothing. For Rodin there would be, could be, no more betrayals. Algeria would prove it. He left the shore of Marseilles in the spring of 1956 as near a happy man as he would ever be, convinced that the distant hills of Algeria would see the consummation of what he regarded as his life's work, the apotheosis of the French Army in the eyes of the world.

Within two years of bitter and ferocious fighting little happened to shake his convictions. True, the rebels were not as easy to put down as he had thought at first. However many fellagha he and his men shot, however many villages were razed to the ground, however many FLN terrorists died under torture, the rebellion spread until it enveloped the land and consumed the cities.

What was needed, of course, was more help from the Métropole. Here at least there could be no question of a war in a far-flung corner of the Empire. Algeria was France, a part of France, inhabited by three million Frenchmen. One would fight for Algeria as for Normandy, Brittany, or the Alpes-Maritimes. When he got his lieutenant-colonelcy Marc Rodin moved out of the *bled* and into the cities, first Bone then Constantine.

In the *bled* he had been fighting the soldiers of the FLN, irregular soldiers but still fighting men. His hatred of them was as nothing to what consumed him as he entered the sneaking, vicious war of the cities, a war fought with plastic bombs planted by cleaners in French-patronised cafes, supermarkets, and play-parks. The measures he took to cleanse Constantine of the filth who planted these bombs among French civilians earned him in the Casbah the title of Butcher.

All that was lacking for the final obliteration of the FLN and its army, the ALN, was more help from Paris. Like most fanatics, Rodin could blind himself to facts with sheer belief. The escalating costs of the war, the tottering economy of France under the burden of a war becoming increasingly unwinnable, the demoralisation of the conscripts, were a bagatelle.

In June 1958 General de Gaulle returned to power as Prime Minister of France. Efficiently disposing of the corrupt and tottering Fourth Republic, he founded the Fifth. When he spoke the words whose utterance in the mouths of the Generals had brought him back to the Matignon and then in January 1959 to the Elysée, "Algérie Française," Rodin went to his room and cried. When de Gaulle visited Algeria, his presence was for Rodin like that of Zeus coming down from Olympus. The new policy, he was sure, was on the way. The Communists would be swept from their offices, Jean-Paul Sartre must surely be shot for treason, the trade unions would be brought into submission, and the final wholehearted backing of France for her kith and kin in Algeria and for her Army protecting the frontiers of French civilisation would be forthcoming.

Rodin was as sure of this as the rising of the sun in the east. When de Gaulle started his measures to restore France his own way, Rodin thought there must be some mistake. One had to give the old man time. When the first rumours of preliminary talks with Ben Bella and the FLN filtered through, Rodin could not believe it. Although he sympathised with the revolt of the settlers led by Big Joe Ortiz in 1960, he still felt the lack of progress in smashing the fellagha once and for all was simply a tactical move by de Gaulle. Le Vieux, he felt sure, must know what he was doing. Had he not said it, the golden words "Algérie Française"?

When the proof came finally and beyond any doubt that Charles de Gaulle's concept of a resuscitated France did not include a French Algeria, Rodin's world disintegrated like a china vase hit by a train. Of faith and hope, belief and confidence, there was nothing left. Just hate. Hate for the system, for the politicians, for the intellectuals, for the Algerians, for the trade unions, for the journalists, for the foreigners; but most of all, hate for That Man. Apart from a few wet-eared ninnies who refused to come, Rodin led his entire battalion into the military putsch of April 1961.

It failed. In one simple, depressingly clever move de Gaulle foiled the putsch before it could get off the ground. None of the officers had taken more than a passing notice when thousands of simple transistor radios were issued to the troops in the weeks before the final announcement that talks were being started with the FLN. The radios were regarded as a harmless comfort for the troops, and many officers and senior NCO's approved the idea. The pop music that came over the air from France was a pleasant distraction for the boys from the heat, the flies, the boredom.

The voice of de Gaulle was not so harmless. When the loyalty of the Army was finally put to the test, tens of thousands of conscripts spread out in barracks across Algeria turned on their radios for the news. After the news they heard the same voice that Rodin himself had listened to in June 1940. Almost the same message. You are faced with a choice of loyalties. I am France, the instrument of her destiny. Follow me. Obey me.

Some battalion commanders woke up with only a handful of officers and most of their sergeants left.

The mutiny was broken like the illusions—by radio. Rodin had been luckier than some. One hundred and twenty of his officers, NCO's, and rankers remained with him. This was because he commanded a unit with a higher proportion of old sweats from Indochina and the Algerian *bled* than most. Together with the

other putschistes they formed the Secret Army Organisation, pledged to overthrow the Judas of the Elysée
Palace.

Between the triumphant FLN and the loyal Army
of France, there was little left out time for an orgy of
destruction. In the last seven weeks, as the French
settlers sold their life's work for a song and fled the
war-torn coast, the Secret Army exacted one last hid-
eous revenge on what they had to leave behind. When
it was over there remained only exile for the leaders
whose names were known to the Gaullist authorities.

Rodin became deputy to Argoud as operations chief
of the OAS in exile in the winter of 1961. Argoud's was
the flair, the talent, the inspiration behind the offensive
the OAS launched on Metropolitan France from then
on; Rodin's was the organisation, the cunning, the
shrewd common sense.

Had he merely been a tough fanatic, he would have
been dangerous but not exceptional. There were many
others of that calibre toting guns for the OAS in the
early sixties. But he was more. The old cobbler had
sired a boy with a good thinking brain, never developed by formal education or army service. Rodin had
developed it on his own, in his own way.

When faced with his own concept of France and the
honour of the Army, Rodin was as bigoted as the rest;
but when faced with a purely practical problem, he
could bring to bear a pragmatic and logical concentration that was more effective than all the volatile enthusiasm and senseless violence in the world.

This was what he brought on the morning of March
11 to the problem of killing Charles de Gaulle. He was
not fool enough to think the job would be easy; on the

contrary, the failures of Petit-Clamart and the Ecole Militaire would make it much harder. Killers alone were not hard to find; the problem was to find a man or a plan that had one single factor built in that would be sufficiently unusual to penetrate the wall of security now built up in concentric rings round the person of the President.

Methodically he listed in his mind the problems. For two hours, chain-smoking before the window until the room became cloudy with a blue haze, he set them up, then devised a plan to demolish or circumvent them. Each plan seemed feasible under most of the critical examination to which he submitted them; each then disintegrated under the final test. Out of this train of thought one problem emerged as virtually insurmountable—the question of security.

Things had changed since Petit-Clamart. The penetration of the Action Service into the ranks and cadres of the OAS had increased to an alarming degree. The recent abduction of his own superior, Argoud, indicated the lengths to which the Action Service was prepared to go to get at and interrogate the leaders of the OAS. Even a blazing row with the German Government was not avoided.

With Argoud already fourteen days under interrogation, the whole OAS leadership had had to go on the run. Bidault had suddenly lost his taste for publicity and self-exposure; others of the CNR had fled panicking to Spain, America, Belgium. There had been a rush for false papers, tickets to far places.

Watching this, the lower ranks had suffered a staggering setback to morale. Men inside France previously prepared to help, to shelter wanted men, to carry packages of arms, to pass messages, even to provide information, were hanging up the phone with a muttered excuse.

Following the failure of Petit-Clamart and the interrogation of the prisoners, three whole networks inside France had had to be closed down. With inside information the French police had raided house after house, uncovered cache after cache of weapons and stores; two other plots to kill de Gaulle had been swamped with police as the conspirators sat down to their second meeting.

While the CNR made speeches in committee and burbled about the restoration of democracy in France, Rodin grimly faced the facts of life as exposed in the bulging briefcase by his bed. Short of funds, losing national and international support, membership and credibility, the OAS was crumbling before the onslaught of the French Secret Service and police.

Arriving at the end of his own argument, Rodin muttered, "A man who is not known . . ." He ran through the list of men whom he knew would not flinch from assassinating a president. Every one had a file thick as the Bible in French police HQ. Why else would he, Marc Rodin, be hiding in a hotel in an obscure Austrian mountain village?

The answer came to him just before noon. He dismissed it for a while, but was drawn back to it with insistent curiosity. If such a man could be found . . . if only such a man existed. Slowly, laboriously, he built another plan around such a man, then subjected it to all the obstacles and objections. The plan passed them all, even the question of security.

Just before the lunch-hour struck Marc Rodin

shrugged into his greatcoat and went downstairs. At the front door he caught the first blast of the wind along the icy street. It made him flinch, but cleared the dull headache caused by the cigarettes in the overheated bedroom. Turning left he crunched away towards the post office in the Adlerstrasse and sent a series of brief telegrams, informing his colleagues, scattered under aliases across southern Germany, Austria, Italy, and Spain, that he would not be available for a few weeks because he was going on a mission.

It occurred to him, as he trudged back to the humble rooming house, that some might think he too was chickening out, disappearing from the threat of kidnap or assassination by the Action Service. He shrugged to himself. Let them think what they wished, the time for lengthy explanations was over.

He lunched at the boarding house Stammkarte, the meal of the day being pot roast and noodles. Although years in the jungle and the wilderness of Algeria had left him little discrimination about food, he had difficulty cramming it down. By midafternoon he was gone, bags packed, bill paid, departed on a lonely mission to find a man, or more precisely a type of man he was not sure existed.

As he boarded his train, a BOAC Comet 4B drifted down the flight path towards runway Zero-Four at London Airport. It was inbound from Beirut. Among the passengers filing through the arrivals lounge was a tall, blond Englishman. His face was healthily tanned by the Middle East sun. He felt relaxed and fit after two months of enjoying the undeniable pleasures of the Lebanon and the, for him, even greater pleasure of supervising the transfer of a handsome sum of money from a bank in Beirut to another in Switzerland.

Far behind him in the sandy soil of Egypt, long since buried by the baffled and furious Egyptian police, each with a neat bullet hole through the spine, were the bodies of two German missile engineers. Their departure from life had set back the development of Nasser's Al Goumhouria rocket by several years, and a Zionist millionaire in New York felt his money had been well spent. After passing easily through customs, the Englishman took a hire car to his flat in Mayfair.

It was ninety days before Rodin's search was over, and what he had to show for it was three slim dossiers, each encased in a manila file which he kept with him permanently in his brief-case. It was in the middle of June that he arrived back in Austria and checked into a small boarding house, the Pension Kleist in the Brucknerallee in Vienna.

From the city's main post office he sent off two crisp telegrams, one to Bolzano in northern Italy, the other to Rome. Each summoned his two principal lieutenants to an urgent meeting in his room in Vienna. Within twenty-four hours the men had arrived. René Montclair came by hired car from Bolzano, André Casson flew in from Rome. Each travelled under false name and papers, for both in Italy and Austria the resident officers of the SDECE had both men top-listed on their files and by this time were spending a lot of money buying agents and informers at border checkpoints and airports.

André Casson was the first to arrive at the Pension

Kleist, seven minutes before the appointed time of eleven o'clock. He ordered his taxi to drop him at the corner of the Brucknerallee and spent several minutes adjusting his tie in the reflection of a florist's window before walking quickly into the hotel foyer. Rodin had as usual registered under a false name, one of twenty known only to his immediate colleagues. Each of the two he had summoned had received a cable the previous day signed by the name of Schulze, Rodin's code-name for that particular twenty-day period.

"*Herr Schulze, bitte?*" Casson enquired of the young man at the reception desk. The clerk consulted his registration book.

"Room sixty-four. Are you expected, sir?"

"Yes, indeed," replied Casson and headed straight up the stairs. He turned the landing to the first floor and walked along the passage looking for Room 64. He found it halfway along on the right. As he raised his hand to knock, it was gripped from behind. He turned and stared up into a heavy blue-jowled face. The eyes beneath a thick single band of black hair that passed for eyebrows gazed down at him without curiosity. The man had fallen in behind him as he passed an alcove twelve feet back and despite the thinness of the cord carpet Casson had not heard a sound.

"*Vous désirez?*" said the giant as if he could not have cared less. But the grip on Casson's right wrist did not slacken.

For a moment Casson's stomach turned over as he imagined the speedy removal of Argoud from the Eden-Wolff Hotel four months earlier. Then he recognized the man behind him as a Polish Foreign Legionnaire from Rodin's former company in Indochina and Vietnam. He recalled that Rodin occasionally used Viktor Kowalski for special assignments.

"I have an appointment with Colonel Rodin, Viktor," he replied softly. Kowalski's brows knotted even closer together at the mention of his own and his master's name. "I am André Casson," he added. Kowalski seemed unimpressed. Reaching round Casson he rapped with his left hand on the door of Room 64.

A voice from inside replied, *"Oui."*

Kowalski approached his mouth to the wooden panel of the door.

"There's a visitor here," he growled, and the door opened a fraction. Rodin gazed out, then swung the door wide.

"My dear André. So sorry about this." He nodded to Kowalski. "All right, corporal, I am expecting this man."

Casson found his wrist freed at last, and stepped into the bedroom. Rodin had another word with Kowalski on the threshold, then closed the door again. The Pole went back to stand in the shadows of the alcove.

Rodin shook hands and led Casson over to the two armchairs in front of the gas fire. Although it was mid-June, the weather outside was a fine chill drizzle, and both men were used to the warmer sun of North Africa. The gas fire was full on. Casson stripped off his raincoat and settled before the fire.

"You don't usually take precautions like this, Marc," he observed.

"It's not so much for me," replied Rodin. "If anything should happen I can take care of myself. But I

might need a few minutes to get rid of the papers."
He gestured to the writing desk by the window where
a thick manila folder lay beside his briefcase. "That's
really why I brought Viktor. Whatever happened he
would give me sixty seconds to destroy the papers."

"They must be important."

"Maybe, maybe." There was nevertheless a note of
satisfaction in Rodin's voice. "But we'll wait for René.
I told him to come at eleven-fifteen so the two of you
would not arrive within a few seconds of each other
and upset Viktor. He gets nervous when there is too
much company around whom he does not know."

Rodin permitted himself one of his rare smiles at
the thought of what would ensue if Viktor became
nervous with the heavy Colt under his left armpit.
There was a knock at the door. Rodin crossed the
room and put his mouth to the wood. *"Oui?"*

This time it was René Montclair's voice, nervous
and strained.

"Marc, for the love of God . . ."

Rodin swung open the door. Montclair stood there
dwarfed by the giant Pole behind him. Viktor's left
arm encircled him, pinning both the accountant's arms
to his side.

"Ça va, Viktor," murmured Rodin to the bodyguard,
and Montclair was released. He entered the room
thankfully and grimaced at Casson, who was grinning
from the chair by the fire. Again the door closed, and
Rodin made his excuses to Montclair.

Montclair came forward and the two shook hands.
He had taken off his overcoat to reveal a rumpled
dark-grey suit of poor cut which he wore badly. Like

most ex-army men accustomed to a uniform, both he
and Rodin had never worn suits well.

As host, Rodin saw the other two seated, in the bedroom's two easy chairs. He kept for himself the upright
chair behind the plain table that served him for a desk.
From the bedside cabinet he took a bottle of French
brandy and held it up enquiringly. Both his guests
nodded. Rodin poured a generous measure into each
of three glasses and handed two to Montclair and Casson. They drank first, the two travellers letting the hot
liquor get to work on the chill inside them.

René Montclair, leaning back against the bedhead,
was short and stocky, like Rodin a career officer from
the Army. But unlike Rodin he had not had a combat
command. Most of his life he had been in the administrative branches, and for the previous ten years in the
pay-accounts branch of the Foreign Legion. By the
spring of 1963 he was treasurer of the OAS.

André Casson was the only civilian. Small and precise, he dressed still like the bank manager he had
been in Algeria. He was the coordinator of the OAS-
CNR underground in Metropolitan France.

Both men were, like Rodin, hardliners even among
the OAS, albeit for different reasons. Montclair had
had a son, a nineteen-year-old boy who had been doing his National Service in Algeria three years previously while his father was running the pay-accounts
department of the Foreign Legion base outside Marseilles. Major Montclair never saw the body of his son;
it had been buried in the *bled* by the Legion patrol
that took the village where the young private had been
held a prisoner by the guerrillas. But he heard the details of what had been done to the young man after-

wards. Nothing remains secret for long in the Legion.
People talk.

André Casson was more involved. Born in Algeria,
he had devoted his entire life to his work, his flat, and
his family. The bank for which he worked had its
headquarters in Paris, so even with the fall of Algeria
he would not have been out of work. But when the
settlers rose in revolt in 1960 he had been with them,
one of the leaders in his native Constantine. Even after
that he had kept his job, but realised as account after
account closed and the businessmen sold out to move
back to France that the heyday of French presence in
Algeria was over. Shortly after the Army mutiny, in-
censed by the new Gaullist policy and the misery of
the small-time farmers and traders of the region, fleeing ruined to a country many of them had hardly seen
across the water, he had helped an OAS unit to rob
his own bank of 30,000,000 old francs. His complicity
had been noticed and reported by a junior cashier, and
his career with the bank was over. He sent his wife
and two children to live with his in-laws at Perpignan,
and joined the OAS. His value to them was his personal knowledge of several thousand OAS sympathisers now living inside France.

Marc Rodin took his seat behind his desk and surveyed the other two. They gazed back with curiosity
but no questions.

Carefully and methodically Rodin began his briefing, concentrating on the growing list of failures and
defeats the OAS had sustained at the hands of the
French Secret Service over the past few months. His
guests stared gloomily into their glasses.

"We simply must face facts. In the past four months

we have taken three severe blows. I don't need to go into the details, you know them all as well as I do.

"Despite Antoine Argoud's loyalty to the cause, there can be no doubt that with modern methods of interrogation, probably including drugs, used on him, the whole organisation stands in jeopardy from the security standpoint. We have to start again, almost from scratch. But even starting from scratch would not be so bad if it were a year ago. Then we could call on thousands of volunteers full of enthusiasm and patriotism. Now that is not so easy. I do not blame our sympathisers too much. They have a right to expect results, not words."

"All right, all right. What are you getting at?" said Montclair. Both listeners knew Rodin was right. Montclair realised better than any that the funds gained in robbing banks across Algeria were expended on the costs of running the organisation, and that the donations from Right-wing industrialists were beginning to dry up. More recently his approaches had been met with ill-concealed disdain. Casson knew his lines of communications with the underground in France were becoming more tenuous by the week, his safe-houses were being raided, and since the capture of Argoud many had withdrawn their support. The execution of Bastien-Thiry could only accelerate this process. The résumé given by Rodin was the truth, but no more pleasant to hear for all that.

Rodin continued as though there had been no interruption.

"We have now reached a position where the prime aim of our cause to liberate France, the elimination of Grand Zohra, without which all further plans must

inevitably abort, has become virtually impossible by
the traditional means. I hesitate, gentlemen, to commit more patriotic young men to plans which stand
little chance of remaining unrevealed to the French
Gestapo for more than a few days. In short, there are
too many squealers, too many backsliders, too many
recusants.

"Taking advantage of this, the Secret Police have
now so completely infiltrated the movement that the
deliberations of even our highest councils are being
leaked to them. They seem to know, within days of
the decision being taken, what we intend, what are our
plans, and who are our personnel. It is undeniably unpleasant to have to face this situation, but I am convinced that if we do not face it we shall continue to
live in a fool's paradise.

"In my estimation there is only one method remaining to accomplish our first objective, the killing of
Zohra, in a manner that will by-pass the whole network of spies and agents, leave the Secret Police
stripped of its advantages, and face them with a situation not only of which they are unaware but which
they could hardly frustrate even if they knew about it."

Montclair and Casson looked up quickly. There was
dead silence in the bedroom, broken only by the occasional clatter of rain against the windowpane.

"If we accept that my appreciation of the situation
is, unfortunately, accurate," continued Rodin, "then
we must also accept that all of those we now know as
being both prepared and capable of doing the job of
eliminating Grand Zohra are equally known to the
Secret Police. None of them can move inside France
as other than a hunted animal, not only pursued by

the conventional police forces but betrayed from behind by the Barbouzes and the stool-pigeons. I believe,
gentlemen, that the only alternative left to us is to engage the services of an outsider."

Montclair and Casson gazed at him first in amazement, then dawning comprehension.

"What kind of outsider?" asked Casson at length.

"It would be necessary for this man, whoever he is,
to be a foreigner," said Rodin. "He would not be a
member of the OAS or the CNR. He would not be
known to any policeman in France, nor would he exist
on any file. The weakness of all dictatorships is that
they are vast bureaucracies. What is not on file does
not exist. The assassin would be an unknown and
therefore non-existent quantity. He would travel under
a foreign passport, do the job, and disappear back to
his own country while the people of France rose to
sweep away the remnants of de Gaulle's treasonable
rabble. For the man to get out would not in any case
be vastly important, since we would in any case liberate him after taking power. The important thing is
that he be able to get in, unspotted and unsuspected.
That is something which at the moment not one of us
can do."

Both his listeners were silent, each gazing into his
private thoughts as Rodin's plan took shape in their
minds also.

Montclair let out a low whistle.

"A professional assassin, a mercenary."

"Precisely," replied Rodin. "It would be quite un-
reasonable to suppose that an outsider is going to do
such a job for the love of us or for patriotism or for
the hell of it. In order to get the level of skill and of

nerve necessary for this kind of operation, we must engage a true professional. And such a man would only work for money, a lot of money," he added, glancing quickly at Montclair.

"But how do we know we can find such a man?" asked Casson.

Rodin held up his hand.

"First things first, gentlemen. Evidently there is a mass of detail to be worked out. What I wish to know first of all is if you agree in principle to the idea."

Montclair and Casson looked at each other. Both turned to Rodin and nodded slowly.

"*Bien.*" Rodin leaned back as far as the upright chair would allow him. "That then is the first point disposed of—agreement in principle. The second concerns security and is fundamental to the whole idea. In my view there are increasingly few who can be regarded as absolutely beyond suspicion as the possible source of a leak of information. That is not to say I regard any of our colleagues either in the OAS or the CNR as traitors to the cause, not as such. But it is an old axiom that the more people know a secret, the less sure that secret becomes. The whole essence of this idea is absolute secrecy. Consequently, the fewer who are aware of it the better.

"Even within the OAS there are infiltrators who have achieved responsible positions and who yet report our plans to the Secret Police. These men's time will come one day, but for the moment they are dangerous. Among the politicians of the CNR there are those either too squeamish or too gutless to realise the full extent of the project they are supposed to have become committed to. I would not wish to put the

life of any man in danger by gratuitously and unnecessarily informing such men of his existence.

"I have summoned you, René, and you, André, here
because I am utterly convinced of your loyalty to the
cause and your ability to retain a secret. Moreover,
for the plan I have in mind, the active cooperation of
you, René, as treasurer and paymaster is necessary to
meet the hire that any professional assassin will undoubtedly demand. Your cooperation, André, will be
necessary to assure such a man of the assistance inside France of a small handful of men loyal beyond
doubt in case he should have to call on them.

"But I see no reason why details of the idea should
go further than we three. I am therefore proposing to
you that we form a committee of ourselves to take the
entire responsibility for this idea, its planning, execution, and subsidisation."

There was another silence. At length Montclair said,
"You mean we cut out the entire council of the OAS,
the whole of the CNR? They won't like that."

"Firstly, they won't know about it," replied Rodin
calmly. "If we were to put the idea to them all, it
would require a plenary meeting. This alone would
attract attention and the Barbouzes would be active
to find out what the plenary meeting was called for.
There may even be a leak on one of the two councils.
If we visited each member in turn, it would take weeks
even to get preliminary approval in principle. Then
they would all want to know the details as each planning stage was reached and passed. You know what
these bloody politicians and committeemen are like.
They want to know everything just for the sake of
knowing it. They do nothing, but each one can put the

whole operation in jeopardy with a word spoken in drunkenness or carelessness.

"Secondly, if the agreement of the entire council of the OAS and the CNR could be obtained to the idea, we would be no further forward, and nearly thirty people would know about it. If, on the other hand, we go ahead, take the responsibility, and it fails, we shall be no further back than we are now. There will be recriminations no doubt, but nothing more. If the plan succeeds we shall be in power and no one will start arguing at that time. The exact means of achieving the destruction of the dictator will have become an academic point. In brief, then, do you two agree to join me as sole planners, organisers, and operators of the idea I have expounded to you?"

Again Montclair and Casson looked at each other, turned to Rodin, and nodded. It was the first time they had met with him since the snatching of Argoud three months earlier. When Argoud had taken the chair, Rodin had kept quietly in the background. Now he had emerged as a leader in his own right. The chief of the underground and the purse were impressed.

Rodin looked at them both, exhaled slowly, and smiled.

"Good," he said, "now let us get down to details. The idea of using a professional mercenary assassin first occurred to me on the day I heard over the radio that poor Bastien-Thiry had been murdered. Since that time I have been searching for the man we want. Obviously such men are hard to find; they do not advertise themselves. I have been searching since the middle of March, and the outcome can be summed up in these."

He held up the three manila folders that had been lying on his desk. Montclair and Casson exchanged glances again, eyebrows raised, and remained silent. Rodin resumed.

"I think it would be best if you studied the dossiers, then we can discuss our first choice. Personally, I have listed all three in terms of preference in case the first-listed either cannot or will not take the job. There is only one copy of each dossier, so you will have to exchange them."

He reached into the manila folder and took out three slimmer files. He handed one to Montclair and one to Casson. The third he kept in his own hand, but did not bother to read it. He knew the contents of all three files intimately.

There was little enough to read. Rodin's reference to a "brief" dossier was depressingly accurate. Casson finished his file first, looked up at Rodin and grimaced.

"That's all?"

"Such men do not make details about themselves easily available," replied Rodin. "Try this one." He handed down to Casson the file he held in his hand.

A few moments later Montclair also finished and passed his file back to Rodin, who gave him the dossier Casson had just finished. Both men were again lost in reading. This time it was Montclair who finished first. He looked up at Rodin and shrugged.

"Well . . . not much to go on, but surely we have fifty men like that. Gunslingers are two a penny—"

He was interrupted by Casson.

"Wait a minute, wait till you see this one." He flicked over the last page and ran his eyes down the three remaining paragraphs. When he had finished he closed the file and looked up at Rodin. The OAS chief gave away nothing of his own preferences. He took the file Casson had finished and passed it to Montclair. To Casson he passed the third of the folders. Both men finished their reading together four minutes later.

Rodin collected the folders and replaced them on the writing desk. He took the straight-backed chair, reversed it, and drew it towards the fire, sitting astride it with his arms on the back. From this perch he surveyed the other two.

"Well, I told you it was a small market. There may be more men about who do this kind of work, but without access to the files of a good Secret Service, they are damned hard to find. And probably the best ones aren't even on any files at all. You've seen all three. For the moment let us refer to them as the German, the South African, and the Englishman. André?"

Casson shrugged, "For me there is no debate. On his record, if it is true, the Englishman is out ahead by a mile."

"René?"

"I agree. The German is a bit old for this kind of thing now. Apart from a few jobs done for the surviving Nazis against the Israeli agents who pursue them, he doesn't seem to have done much in the political field. Besides his motivations against Jews are probably personal, therefore not completely professional. The South African may be all right chopping up nigger politicians like Lumumba, but that's a far cry from putting a bullet through the President of France. Besides, the Englishman speaks fluent French."

Rodin nodded slowly. "I didn't think there would be much doubt. Even before I had finished compiling those dossiers, the choice seemed to stand out a mile."

"Are you sure about this Anglo-Saxon?" Casson asked. "Has he really done those jobs?"

"I was surprised myself," said Rodin. "So I spent extra time on this one. As regards absolute proof, there is none. If there were, it would be a bad sign. It would mean he would be listed everywhere as an undesirable immigrant. As it is, there is nothing against him but rumour. Formally, his sheet is white as snow. Even if the British have him listed, they can put no more than a question mark against him. That does not merit filing him with Interpol. The chances that the British would tip off the SDECE about such a man, even if a formal enquiry were made, are slim. You know how they hate each other. They even kept silent about Georges Bidault being in London last January. No, for this kind of job the Englishman has all the advantages but one—"

"What's that?" asked Montclair quickly.

"Simple. He will not be cheap. A man like him can ask a lot of money. How are the finances, René?"

Montclair shrugged. "Not too good. Expenditure has gone down a bit. Since the Argoud affair all the heroes of the CNR have gone to ground in cheap hotels. They seem to have lost their taste for the three-star palaces and the television interviews. On the other hand, income is down to a trickle. As you said there must be some action, or we shall be finished for lack of funds. One cannot run this kind of thing on love and kisses."

Rodin nodded grimly. "I thought so. We have to raise some money from somewhere. On the other hand, there would be no point in getting into that kind of action until we know how much we shall need—"

"Which presumes," cut in Casson smoothly, "that the next step is to contact the Englishman and ask him if he will do the job and for how much."

"Yes, well, are we all agreed on that?" Rodin glanced at both men in turn. Both nodded. Rodin glanced at his watch. "It is now just after one o'clock. I have an agent in London whom I must telephone now and ask him to contact this man to ask him to come. If he is prepared to fly to Vienna tonight on the evening plane, we could meet him here after dinner. Either way, we will know when my agent phones back. I have taken the liberty of booking you both into adjoining rooms down the corridor. I think it would be safer to be together protected by Viktor than separated but without defenses. Just in case, you understand."

"You were pretty certain, weren't you?" asked Casson, piqued at being predicted in this manner.

Rodin shrugged. "It has been a long process getting this information. The less time wasted from now on the better. If we are going to go ahead, let us now move fast."

He rose and the other two got up with him. Rodin called Viktor and told him to go down to the hall to collect the keys for rooms 65 and 66, and to bring them back up. While waiting he told Montclair and Casson, "I have to telephone from the main post office. I shall take Viktor with me. While I am gone, would you both stay together in one room with the door locked. My signal will be three knocks, a pause, then two more."

The sign was the familiar three-plus-two that made up the rhythm of the words *Algérie Française* that Parisian motorists had hooted on their car horns in previous years to express their disapproval of Gaullist policy.

"By the way," continued Rodin, "does either of you have a gun?"

Both men shook their heads. Rodin went to the escritoire and took out a chunky MAB 9 mm. that he kept for his private use. He checked the magazine, snapped it back, and charged the breech. He held it out towards Montclair. "You know this *flingue?*" Montclair nodded. "Well enough," he said, and took it.

Viktor returned and escorted the pair of them to Montclair's room. When he returned, Rodin was buttoning his overcoat.

"Come, corporal, we have work to do."

The BEA Vanguard from London to Vienna that evening glided into Schwechat Airport as the dusk deepened into night. Near the tail of the plane the blond Englishman lay back in his seat near the window and gazed out at the lead-in lights as they flashed past the sinking aircraft. It always gave him a feeling of pleasure to see them coming closer and closer until it appeared certain the plane must touch down in the grass of the undershoot area. At the very last minute the dimly lit blur of grass, the numbered panels by the vergeside, and the lights themselves vanished, to be replaced by black-slicked concrete, and wheels touched down at last. The precision of the business of landing appealed to him. He liked precision.

By his side the young Frenchman from the French Tourist Office in Piccadilly glanced at him nervously. Since the telephone call during the lunch-hour he had been in a state of nerves. Nearly a year ago on leave in Paris he had offered to put himself at the disposal of the OAS but since then had been told simply to stay at his desk in London. A letter or telephone call, addressed to him in his rightful name, but beginning "Dear Pierre . . ." should be obeyed immediately and precisely. Since then, nothing, until today, June 15.

The operator had told him there was a person-to-person call for him from Vienna, and had then added "In Austria" to distinguish it from the town Vienne in France. Wonderingly he had taken the call, to hear a voice call him "my dear Pierre." It had taken him several seconds to remember his own code-name.

Pleading a bout of migraine after his lunch-hour, he had gone to the flat off South Audley Street and given the message to the Englishman who answered the door. The latter had evinced no surprise that he should be asked to fly to Vienna in three hours. He had quietly packed an overnight case, and the pair of them had taken a taxi to Heathrow Airport. The Englishman had calmly produced a roll of notes enough to buy two return tickets for cash after the Frenchman had admitted he had not thought of paying cash and had only brought his passport and a checkbook.

Since then they had hardly exchanged a word. The Englishman had not asked where they were going in Vienna, or whom they were to meet, or why, which was just as well because the Frenchman did not know. His instructions had merely been to telephone back from London airport and confirm his arrival on the BEA flight, at which he was told to report to General Information on arrival at Schwechat. All of which made him nervous, and the controlled calm of the

Englishman beside him, far from helping, made things worse.

At the information desk in the main hall he gave his name to the pretty Austrian girl, who searched in a rack of pigeon-holes behind her, then passed him a small buff message form. It said simply "Ring 61.44.03, ask for Schulze." He turned and headed towards the bank of public phones along the back of the main hall. The Englishman tapped him on the shoulder and pointed at the booth marked *Wechsel*.

"You'll need some coins," he said in fluent French. "Not even the Austrians are that generous."

The Frenchman blushed and strode towards the money-change counter, while the Englishman sat himself comfortably in the corner of one of the upholstered settees against the wall and lit another king-size English filter. In a minute his guide was back with several Austrian bank-notes and a handful of coins. The Frenchman went to the telephones, found an empty booth, and dialled. At the other end Herr Schulze gave him clipped and precise instructions. It took only a few seconds, then the phone went dead.

The young Frenchman came back to the settee, and the blond man looked up at him.

"*On y va?*" he asked.

"*On y va.*" As he turned to leave, the Frenchman screwed up the message form with the telephone number and dropped it on the floor. The Englishman picked it up, opened it out, and held it to the flame of his lighter. It blazed for an instant and disappeared in black crumbs beneath the elegant suede boot. They walked in silence out of the building and hailed a taxi.

The centre of the city was ablaze with lights and

choked with cars, so it was not until forty minutes later that the taxi arrived at the Pension Kleist.

"This is where we part. I was told to bring you here, but to take the taxi somewhere else. You are to go straight up to Room Sixty-four. You are expected."

The Englishman nodded and got out of the car. The driver turned enquiringly to the Frenchman. "Drive on," he said, and the taxi disappeared down the street. The Englishman glanced up at the old Gothic writing on the street name-plate, then the square roman capitals above the door of the Pension Kleist. Finally he threw away his cigarette, half smoked, and entered.

The clerk on duty had his back turned, but the door creaked. Without giving any sign of approaching the desk, the Englishman walked towards the stairs. The clerk was about to ask what he wanted when the visitor glanced in his direction, nodded casually as to any other menial, and said firmly, *"Guten Abend."*

"Guten Abend, mein Herr," replied the clerk automatically, and by the time he had finished the blond man was gone, taking the stairs two at a time without seeming to hurry. At the top he paused and glanced down the only corridor available. At the far end was Room 68. He counted back down the corridor to what must be 64, although the figures were out of sight.

Between himself and the door of 64 were twenty feet of corridor, the walls being studded on the right by two other doors before 64, and on the left a small alcove partially curtained with red velours hanging from a cheap brass rod.

He studied the alcove carefully. From beneath the curtain, which cleared the floor by four inches, the toe of a single black shoe emerged slightly. He turned and walked back to the foyer. This time the clerk was ready. At least he managed to get his mouth open.

"Get me Room Sixty-four, please," said the Englishman. The clerk looked him in the face for a second, then obeyed. After a few seconds he turned back from the small switchboard, picked up the desk phone, and passed it over.

"If that gorilla is not out of the alcove in fifteen seconds I am going back home," said the blond man, and put the phone down. Then he walked back up the stairs.

At the top he watched the door of 64 open and Colonel Rodin appeared. He stared down the corridor for a moment at the Englishman, then called softly, "Viktor." From the alcove the giant Pole emerged and stood looking from one to the other. Rodin said, "It's all right. He is expected." Kowalski glowered. The Englishman started to walk.

Rodin ushered him inside the bedroom. It had been arranged like an office for a recruiting board. The escritoire served for the chairman's desk and was littered with papers. Behind it was the single upright chair in the room. But two other uprights brought in from adjacent rooms flanked the central chair, and these were occupied by Montclair and Casson, who eyed the visitor curiously. There was no chair in front of the desk. The Englishman cast an eye around, selected one of the two easy chairs, and spun it around to face the desk. By the time Rodin had given fresh instructions to Viktor and closed the door, the Englishman was comfortably seated and staring back at Casson and Montclair. Rodin took his seat behind the desk.

For a few seconds he stared at the man from London. What he saw did not displease him, and he was an expert in men. The visitor stood above six feet tall, apparently in his early thirties, and with a lean, athletic build. He looked fit, the suntanned face had regular but not remarkable features, and the hands lay quietly along the arms of the chair. To Rodin's eye he looked like a man who retained control of himself. But the eyes bothered him. He had seen the soft, moist eyes of weaklings, the dull, shuttered eyes of psychopaths, and the watchful eyes of soldiers. The eyes of the Englishman were open and stared back with frank candor. Except for the irises, which were of flecked grey so that they seemed smoky like the hoar mist on a winter's morning. It took Rodin a few seconds to realise that they had no expression at all. Whatever thoughts did go on behind the smokescreen, nothing came through, and Rodin felt a worm of unease. Like all men created by systems and procedures, he did not like the unpredictable and therefore the uncontrollable.

"We know who you are," he began abruptly. "I had better introduce myself. I am Colonel Marc Rodin—"

"I know," said the Englishman, "you are chief of operations of the OAS. You are Major René Montclair, treasurer, and you are Monsieur André Casson, head of the underground in the Métropole." He stared at each of the men in turn as he spoke, and reached for a cigarette.

"You seem to know a lot already," interjected Casson as the three watched the visitor light up. The Englishman leaned back and blew out the first stream of smoke.

"Gentlemen, let us be frank. I know what you are,

and you know what I am. We both have unusual oc-
cupations. You are hunted while I am free to move
where I will without surveillance. I operate for money,
you for idealism. But when it comes to practical details, we are all professionals at our jobs. Therefore we
do not need to fence. You have been making enquiries
about me. It is impossible to make such enquiries without the news of them soon getting back to the man
being asked about. Naturally I wished to know who
was so interested in me. It could have been someone
seeking revenge or wishing to employ me. It was important to me to know. As soon as I discovered the
identity of the organisation interested in me, two days
among the French newspaper files in the British Museum were enough to tell me about you and your organisation. So the visit of your little errand boy this
afternoon was hardly a surprise. *Bon.* I know who you
are, and whom you represent. What I would like to
know is what you want."

There was silence for several minutes. Casson and
Montclair glanced for guidance at Rodin. The para-
troop colonel and the assassin stared at each other.
Rodin knew enough about violent men to understand
the man facing him was what he wanted. From then
on Montclair and Casson were part of the furniture.

"Since you have read the files available, I will not
bore you with the motivations behind our organisation,
which you have accurately summed up as idealism.
We believe France is now ruled by a dictator who has
polluted our country and prostituted its honour. We
believe his regime can only fall and France be restored
to Frenchmen if he first dies. Out of six attempts by
our supporters to eliminate him, three were exposed

in the early planning stages, one was betrayed the day before the attempt, and two took place but misfired.

"We are considering, but at this stage only considering, engaging the services of a professional to do the job. However we do not wish to waste our money. The first thing we would like to know is if it is possible."

Rodin had played his cards shrewdly. The last sentence, to which he already knew the answer, brought a flicker of expression to the grey eyes.

"There is no man in the world who is proof against an assassin's bullet," said the Englishman. "De Gaulle's exposure rate is very high. Of course, it's possible to kill him. The point is that the chances of escape would not be too high. A fanatic prepared to die himself in the attempt is always the most certain method of eliminating a dictator who exposes himself to the public. I notice," he added with a touch of malice, "that despite your idealism you have not yet been able to produce such a man. Both Pont-de-Seine and Petit-Clamart failed because no one was prepared to risk his own life to make absolutely certain."

"There are patriotic Frenchmen prepared even now —" began Casson hotly, but Rodin silenced him with a gesture. The Englishman did not even glance at him.

"And as regards a professional?"—prompted Rodin.

"A professional does not act out of fervour and is therefore more calm and less likely to make elementary errors. Not being idealistic, he is not likely to have second thoughts at the last minute about who else might get hurt in the explosion, or whatever method, and being a professional he has calculated the risks to the last contingency. So his chances of success on schedule are surer than anyone else, but he will not even enter into operation until he has devised a plan that will enable him not only to complete the mission, but to escape unharmed."

"Do you estimate that such a plan could be worked out to permit a professional to kill Grand Zohra and escape?"

The Englishman smoked quietly for a few minutes and stared out of the window. "In principle, yes," he replied at length. "In principle, it is always possible with enough time and planning. But in this case it would be extremely difficult. More so than with most other targets."

"Why more than others?" asked Montclair.

"Because de Gaulle is forewarned—not about the specific attempt but about the general intention. All big men have bodyguards and security men, but over a period of years without any serious attempt on the life of the big man, the checks become formal, the routines mechanical, and the degree of watchfulness is lowered. The single bullet that finishes the target is wholly unexpected and therefore provokes panic. Under cover of this the assassin escapes. In this case there will be no lowering of the level of watchfulness, no mechanical routines, and if the bullet were to get to the target, there would be many who would not panic but would go for the assassin. It could be done, but it would be one of the hardest jobs in the world at this moment. You see, gentlemen, your own efforts have not only failed but have queered the pitch for everyone else."

"In the event that we decide to employ a professional assassin to do this job—" began Rodin.

"You have to employ a professional," cut in the Englishman quietly.

"And why, pray? There are many men still who would be prepared to do the job out of purely patriotic motives."

"Yes, there are still Watin and Curutchet," replied the blond man. "And doubtless there are more Degueldres and Bastien-Thirys around somewhere. But you three men did not call me here for a chat in general terms about the theory of political assassination, nor because you have a sudden shortage of trigger-fingers. You called me here because you have belatedly come to the conclusion that your organisation is so infiltrated by the French Secret Service agents that little you decide remains secret for long, and also because the faces of every one of you is imprinted on the memory of every cop in France. Therefore you need an outsider. And you are right. If the job is to be done, an outsider has to do it. The only questions that remain are who, and for how much. Now, gentlemen, I think you have had long enough to examine the merchandise, don't you?"

Rodin looked sideways at Montclair and raised an eyebrow. Montclair nodded. Casson followed suit. The Englishman gazed out of the window without a shred of interest.

"Will you assassinate de Gaulle?" asked Rodin at last. The voice was quiet, but the question filled the room. The Englishman's glance came back to him, and the eyes were blank again.

"Yes, but it will cost a lot of money."

"How much?" asked Montclair.

"You must understand this is a once-in-a-lifetime

job. The man who does it will never work again. The chances of remaining not only uncaught but undiscovered are very small. One must take enough for this job both to be able to live well for the rest of his days and to acquire protection against the revenge of the Gaullists—"

"When we have France," said Casson, "there will be no shortage—"

"Cash," said the Englishman. "Half in advance and half on completion."

"How much?" asked Rodin.

"Half a million."

Rodin glanced at Montclair, who grimaced. "That's a lot of money, half a million new francs—"

"Dollars," said the Englishman.

"Half a million dollars?" shouted Montclair, rising from his seat. "You are crazy?"

"No," said the Englishman calmly, "but I am the best, and therefore the most expensive."

"We could certainly get cheaper estimates," sneered Casson.

"Yes," said the blond man without emotion, "you would get men cheaper, and you would find they took your fifty-per-cent deposit and vanished or made excuses later as to why it could not be done. When you employ the best you pay. Half a million dollars is the price. Considering you expect to get France itself, you value your country very cheap."

Rodin, who had remained quiet through this exchange, took the point.

"*Touché.* The point is, monsieur, we do not have half a million dollars cash."

"I am aware of that," replied the Englishman. "If

you want the job done you will have to make that sum
from somewhere. I do not need the job, you understand. After my last assignment I have enough to live
well for some years. But the idea of having enough to
retire is appealing. Therefore I am prepared to take
some exceptionally high risks for that price. Your
friends here want a prize even greater—France herself.
Yet the idea of risks appals them. I am sorry. If you
cannot acquire the sum involved, then you must go
back to arranging your own plots and seeing them destroyed by the authorities one by one."

He half-rose from his chair, stubbing out his cigarette in the process. Rodin rose with him.

"Be seated, monsieur. We shall get the money." Both
sat down.

"Good," said the Englishman, "but there are also
conditions."

"Yes?"

"The reason you need an outsider in the first place
is because of constant security leaks to the French authorities. How many people in your organisation know
of this idea of hiring any outsider at all, let alone me?"

"Just the three of us in this room. I worked out the
idea the day after Bastien-Thiry was executed. Since
then I have undertaken all the enquiries personally.
There is no one else in the know."

"Then it must remain that way," said the Englishman. "All records of all meetings, files, and dossiers
must be destroyed. There must be nothing available
outside your three heads. In view of what happened
in February to Argoud, I shall feel myself free to call
off if any of you three are captured. Therefore you

should remain somewhere safe and under heavy guard until the job is done. Agreed?"

"*D'accord*. What else?"

"The planning will be mine, as with the operation. I shall divulge the details to no one, not even to you. In short, I shall disappear. You will hear nothing from me again. You have my telephone number in London and my address, but I shall be leaving both as soon as I am ready to move.

"In any event you will only contact me at that place in an emergency. For the rest there will be no contact at all. I shall leave you the name of my bank in Switzerland. When they tell me the first two hundred and fifty thousand dollars has been deposited, or when I am fully ready, whichever is the later, I shall move. I will not be hurried beyond my own judgement, nor will I be subject to interference. Agreed?"

"*D'accord*. But our undercover men in France are in a position to offer you considerable assistance in the way of information. Some of them are highly placed."

The Englishman considered this for a moment. "All right, when you are ready send me by mail a single telephone number, preferably in Paris so that I can ring that number direct from anywhere in France. I will not give anyone my own whereabouts, but simply ring that number for latest information about the security situation surrounding the President. But the man on the end of that telephone should not know what I am doing in France. Simply tell him that I am on a mission for you and need his assistance. The less he knows, the better. Let him be simply a clearing house for information. Even his sources should be confined uniquely to those in a position to give valuable inside information, not rubbish that I can read in the newspapers. Agreed?"

"Very well. You wish to operate entirely alone, without friends or refuge. Be it on your own head. How about false papers? We have two excellent forgers at our disposal."

"I will acquire my own, thank you."

Casson broke in. "I have a complete organisation inside France similar to the Resistance during the German occupation. I can put this entire structure at your disposal for assistance purposes."

"No thank you. I prefer to bank on my own complete anonymity. It is the best weapon I have."

"But supposing something should go wrong, you might have to go on the run—"

"Nothing will go wrong, unless it comes from your side. I will operate without contacting or being known to your organisation, M. Casson, for exactly the same reason I am here in the first place: because the organisation is crawling with agents and stool-pigeons."

Casson looked fit to explode. Montclair stared glumly at the window trying to envisage raising half a million dollars in a hurry. Rodin stared thoughtfully back at the Englishman across the table.

"Calm, André. Monsieur wishes to work alone. So be it. That is his way. We do not pay half a million dollars for a man who needs the same amount of molly-coddling our own shooters need."

"What I would like to know," muttered Montclair, "is how we can raise so much money so quickly."

"Use your organisation to rob a few banks," suggested the Englishman lightly.

"In any case, that is our problem," said Rodin. "Before our visitor returns to London, are there any further points?"

"What is to prevent you from taking the first quarter of a million and disappearing?" asked Casson.

"I told you, messieurs, I wanted to retire. I do not wish to have half an army of ex-paras gunning for me. I would have to spend more protecting myself than the money I have made. It would soon be gone."

"And what," persisted Casson, "is to prevent us waiting until the job is done and then refusing to pay you the balance of the half million?"

"The same reason," replied the Englishman smoothly. "In that event I should go to work on my own account. And the target would be you three gentlemen. However, I don't think that will occur, do you?"

Rodin interrupted. "Well, if that is all, I don't think we need detain our guest any longer. Oh . . . there is one last point. Your name. If you wish to remain anonymous you should have a code name. Do you have any ideas?"

The Englishman thought for a moment. "Since we have been speaking of hunting, what about the Jackal? Will that do?"

Rodin nodded. "Yes, that will do fine. In fact I think I like it."

He escorted the Englishman to the door and opened it. Viktor left his alcove and approached. For the first time Rodin smiled and held out his hand to the assassin. "We will be in touch in the agreed manner as soon as we can. In the meantime could you begin planning in general terms so as not to waste too much time? Good. Then *bonsoir, Monsieur Chacal.*"

The Pole watched the visitor depart as quietly as

he had come. The Englishman spent the night at the airport hotel and caught the first plane back to London in the morning.

Inside the Pension Kleist Rodin faced a barrage of belated questions and complaints from Casson and Montclair, who had both been shaken by the three hours between nine and midnight.

"Half a million dollars," Montclair kept repeating. "How on earth do we raise half a million dollars?"

"We may have to take up Chacal's suggestion and rob a few banks," answered Rodin.

"I don't like that man," said Casson. "He works alone, without allies. Such men are dangerous. One cannot control them."

Rodin closed the discussion. "Look, you two, we devised a plan, we agreed on a proposal, and we sought a man prepared to and capable of killing the President of France for money. I know a bit about men like that. If anyone can do it, he can. Now we have made our play. Let us get on with our side and let him get on with his."

three

During the second half of June and the whole of July in 1963 France was rocked by an outbreak of violent crime against banks, jewellers' shops, and post offices that was unprecedented at the time and has never been repeated since. The details of this crime wave are now a matter of record.

From one end of the country to the other, banks were held up with pistols, sawn-off shotguns, and submachine guns on an almost daily basis. Smash and grab raids at jewellers' shops became so common throughout that period that local police forces had hardly finished taking depositions from the shaken and often bleeding jewellers and their assistants than they were called away to another similar case within their own district.

Two bank clerks were shot in different towns as they tried to resist the robbers, and before the end of July the crisis had grown so great that the men of the Corps Républicain de Sécurité, the anti-riot squads known to every Frenchman simply as the CRS, were called in and for the first time armed with submachine guns. It became habitual for those entering a bank to have to pass one or two of the blue-uniformed CRS guards in the foyer, each toting a loaded submachine carbine.

In response to pressure from the bankers and jewellers, who complained bitterly to Government about this crime wave, police checks on banks at night were increased in frequency, but to no avail, since the robbers were not professional cracksmen able to open a bank vault skilfully during the hours of darkness, but simply thugs in masks, armed and ready to shoot if provoked in the slightest way.

The danger hours were in daylight, when any bank or jeweller shop throughout the country could be surprised in the middle of business by the appearance of two or three armed and masked men, and the peremptory cry *"Haut les mains."*

Three robbers were wounded towards the end of July in different hold-ups, and taken prisoner. Each turned out to be either a petty crook known to be using the existence of the OAS as an excuse for general anarchy or a deserter from one of the former colonial regiments who soon admitted he was an OAS man. But despite the most diligent interrogations at police headquarters, none of the three could be persuaded to say why this rash of robberies had suddenly struck the country, other than that they had been contacted by their *patron* (gang boss) and given a target in the form of a bank or jewel-shop. Eventually the police came to believe that the prisoners did not know what the purpose of the robberies was; they had each been promised a cut of the total, and being small fry had done what they were told.

It did not take the French authorities long to realise that the OAS was behind the outbreak and that for some reason the OAS needed money in a hurry. But it was not until the first fortnight of August, and then in a quite different manner, that the authorities discovered why.

Within the last two weeks of June the wave of crime against banks and other places where money or gems could be quickly and unceremoniously acquired had become sufficiently serious to be handed over to the Commissaire Maurice Bouvier, the much-revered chief of the Brigade Criminelle of the Police Judiciaire. In his surprisingly small, work-strewn office at the headquarters of the PJ at 36, Quai des Orfèvres along the banks of the Seine a chart was prepared showing the cash or, in the case of jewellery, approximate re-sale value of the stolen money and gems. By the latter half of July the total was well over two million new francs, or 400,000 dollars. Even with a reasonable sum deducted for the expenses of mounting the various robberies, and more for paying the hoodlums and deserters who carried them out, that still left, in the Commissaire's estimation, a sizeable sum of money that could not be accounted for.

In the last week of June a report landed on the desk of General Guibaud, the head of the SDECE, from the chief of his permanent office in Rome. It was to the effect that the three top men of the OAS, Marc Rodin, René Montclair, and André Casson, had taken up residence together on the top floor of a hotel just off the Via Condotti. The report added that despite the obvious cost of residing in such an exclusive quarter, the three had taken the entire top floor for themselves, and the floor below for their bodyguards. They were being guarded night and day by no less than eight extremely tough ex-members of the Foreign Legion and were not venturing out at all. At first it was thought they had met for a conference, but as the days passed SDECE came to the view that they were simply taking exceptionally heavy precautions to ensure that they were not the victims of another kidnapping as

had been inflicted on Antoine Argoud. General Guibaud permitted himself a grim smile at the sight of
the top men of the terrorist organisation themselves
now cowering in a hotel in Rome, and filed the report
in a routine manner. Despite the bitter row still fester-
ing between the French Foreign Ministry at the Quai
d'Orsay and the German Foreign Ministry in Bonn
over the infringement of German territorial integrity
at the Eden-Wolff Hotel the previous February, Guibaud had every reason to be pleased with his Action
Service men who had carried out the coup. The sight
of the OAS chiefs running scared was reward enough
in itself. The General smothered a small shadow of
misgiving as he surveyed the file of Marc Rodin and
nevertheless asked himself why a man like Rodin
should scare that easily. As a man with considerable
experience in his own job and an awareness of the re-
alities of politics and diplomacy, he knew he would
be most unlikely ever to obtain permission to organise
another snatch-job. It was only much later that the
real significance of the precautions the three OAS men
were taking for their own safety became clear to him.

In London the Jackal spent the last fortnight of June
and the first two weeks of July in carefully controlled
and planned activity. From the day of his return he
set himself among other things to acquire and read
almost every word written about or by Charles de
Gaulle. By the simple expedient of going to the local
lending library and looking up the most recent books
on de Gaulle he compiled a comprehensive bibliogra-
phy about his subject.

After that he wrote off to various well-known bookshops, using a false name and a forwarding address in Praed Street, Paddington, and acquired the necessary books by post. These he scoured until the small hours each morning in his flat, building up in his mind a most detailed picture of the incumbent of the Elysée Palace from his boyhood until the time of reading. Much of the information he gleaned was of no practical use, but here and there a quirk or character trait would emerge that he noted in a small exercise book. Most instructive concerning the character of the French President was the third volume of the General's memoirs, *The Edge of the Sword* (*Le Fil de l'Epée*), in which Charles de Gaulle was at his most illuminating about his own personal attitude to life, his country, and his destiny as he saw it.

The Jackal was neither a slow nor a stupid man. He read voraciously and planned meticulously, and possessed the faculty to store in his mind an enormous amount of factual information on the offchance that he might later have a use for it.

But although his reading of the works of Charles de Gaulle, and the books about him by the men who knew him best, provided a full picture of the proud and disdainful President of France, it still did not solve the main question that had been baffling him since he accepted the assignment in Rodin's bedroom in Vienna on June 15. By the end of the first week in July he still had not worked out the answer to this question—when, where, and how should the "hit" take place? As a last resort he went down to the reading room of the British Museum and, after signing his application for permission to do research with his habitual false name, started to work his way through the back copies of France's leading daily newspaper, *Le Figaro*.

Just when the answer came to him is not exactly known, but it is fair to presume it was within three days from July 7. Within those three days, starting with the germ of an idea triggered by a columnist writing in 1962, cross-checking back through the files covering every year of de Gaulle's presidency since 1945, the assassin managed to answer his own question. He decided within that time precisely on what day, come illness or bad weather, totally regardless of any considerations of personal danger, Charles de Gaulle would stand up publicly and show himself. From that point on, the Jackal's preparations moved out of the research stage and into that of practical planning.

It took long hours of thought, lying on his back in his flat staring up at the cream painted ceiling and chain-smoking his habitual king-size filter cigarettes, before the last detail had clicked into place.

At least a dozen ideas were considered and rejected before he finally hit on the plan he decided to adopt, the "how" that had to be added to the "when" and "where" that he had already decided.

The Jackal was perfectly aware that in 1963 General de Gaulle was not only the President of France; he was also the most closely and skilfully guarded figure in the western world. To assassinate him, as was later proved, was considerably more difficult than to kill President John F. Kennedy of the United States. Although the English killer did not know it, French security experts who had through American courtesy been given an opportunity to study the precautions

taken to guard the life of President Kennedy had returned somewhat disdainful of those precautions as
exercised by the American Secret Service. The French
experts' rejection of the American methods was later
justified when in November 1963 John Kennedy was
killed in Dallas by a half-crazed amateur while Charles
de Gaulle lived on, to retire in peace and eventually
to die in his own house.

What the Jackal did know was that the security men
he was up against were at least among the best in the
world, that the whole security apparatus around de
Gaulle was in a state of permanent forewarning of
the likelihood of some attempt being made on their
charge's life, and that the organisation for which he
worked was riddled with security leaks. On the credit
side he could reasonably bank on his own anonymity
and on the choleric refusal of his victim to cooperate
with his own security forces.

On the chosen day, the pride, the stubbornness, and
the absolute contempt for personal danger of the French
President would force him to come out into the open
for a few seconds no matter what the risks involved.

The SAS airliner from Kastrup, Copenhagen, made
one last swing into line in front of the terminal building at London, trundled forward a few feet, and
halted. The engines whined on for a few seconds, then
they also died away. Within a few minutes the steps
were wheeled up, and the passengers started to file
out and down, nodding a last goodbye to the smiling
stewardess at the top. On the observation terrace the
blond man slipped his dark glasses upwards onto his
forehead and applied his eyes to a pair of binoculars.

The file of passengers coming down the steps was the sixth that morning to be subjected to this kind of scrutiny, but as the terrace was crowded in the warm sunshine with people waiting for arriving passengers and trying to spot them as soon as they emerged from their aircraft, the watcher's behaviour aroused no interest.

As the eighth passenger emerged into the light and straightened up, the man on the terrace tensed slightly and followed the new arrival down the steps. The passenger from Denmark was a priest or pastor, in a clerical grey suit with a dog-collar. He appeared to be in his late forties from the iron-grey hair cut at medium length that was brushed back from the forehead, but the face was more youthful. He was a tall man with wide shoulders, and he looked physically fit. He had approximately the same build as the man who watched him from the terrace above.

As the passengers filed into the arrivals lounge for passport and customs clearance, the Jackal dropped the binoculars into the leather brief-case by his side, closed it, and walked quietly back through the glass doors and down into the main hall. Fifteen minutes later the Danish pastor emerged from the customs hall holding a grip and a suitcase. There appeared to be nobody to meet him, and his first call was made to the Barclays Bank counter to change money.

From what he told the Danish police when they interrogated him six weeks later, he did not notice the blond young Englishman standing beside him at the counter, apparently waiting his turn in the queue but quietly examining the features of the Dane from behind dark glasses. At least he had no memory of such a man. But when he came out of the main hall to board the BEA coach to the Cromwell Road terminal, the Englishman was a few paces behind him holding his brief-case, and they must have travelled into London on the same coach.

At the terminal the Dane had to wait a few minutes while his suitcase was unloaded from the luggage trailer behind the coach, then wend his way past the checking-in counters to the exit signs marked with an arrow and the international word "Taxis." While he did so, the Jackal strode round the back of the coach and across the floor of the coach-park to where he had left his car in the staff car-park. He hefted the brief-case into the passenger seat of the open sports model, climbed in, and started up, bringing the car to a halt close to the left-hand wall of the terminal from where he could glance to the right down the long line of waiting taxis under the pillared arcade. The Dane climbed into the third taxi, which cruised off into the Cromwell road, heading towards Knightsbridge. The sports car followed.

The taxi dropped the oblivious priest at a small but comfortable hotel in Half Moon Street, while the sports car shot past the entrance and within a few minutes had found a spare parking metre on the far side of Curzon Street. The Jackal locked the brief-case in the trunk, bought a midday edition of the *Evening Standard* at the newsagent in Shepherd Market, and was back in the foyer of the hotel within five minutes. He had to wait another twenty-five before the Dane came downstairs and handed back his room key to the receptionist. After she hung it up, the key swayed for a few seconds from the hook, and the man in one of the foyer arm chairs apparently waiting for a friend, who lowered his newspaper as the Dane passed into the restaurant, noted that the number of the key was 47. A few minutes later, as the receptionist bobbed back into the rear office to check a theatre booking for one of the guests, the man in the dark glasses slipped quietly and unnoticed up the stairs.

A two-inch-wide strip of flexible mica was not enough to open the door of Room 47, which was rather stiff, but the mica strip stiffened by a whippy little artist's palette knife did the trick, and the spring lock slipped back with a click. As he had only gone downstairs for lunch, the pastor had left his passport on the bedside table. The Jackal was back in the corridor within thirty seconds, leaving the folder of traveller's cheques untouched in the hopes that without any evidence of a theft the authorities would try to persuade the Dane that he had simply lost his passport somewhere else. And so it proved. Long before the Dane had finished his coffee, the Englishman had departed unseen, and it was not until much later in the afternoon, after a thorough and mystified search of his room, that the pastor mentioned the disappearance of his passport to the manager. The manager also searched the room, and after pointing out that everything else including the wallet of traveller's cheques was intact, brought all his advocacy to bear to persuade his bewildered guest that there was no need to bring the police to his hotel since he had evidently lost his passport somewhere in transit. The Dane, being a kindly man and not too sure of his ground in a foreign country, agreed despite himself that this was what must have happened. So he reported the loss to the Danish Consulate-General the next day, was issued with travel

documents with which to return to Copenhagen at the
end of his fortnight's stay in London, and thought no
more about it. The clerk at the Consulate-General who
issued the travel documents filed the loss of a passport
in the name of Pastor Per Jensen of Sankt Kjeldskirke
in Copenhagen, and thought no more about it either.
The date was July 14.

Two days later a similar loss was experienced by an
American student from Syracuse, New York. He had
arrived at the Oceanic Building of London Airport
from New York, and he produced his passport in order
to change the first of his traveller's cheques at the
American Express counter. After changing the cheque
he placed the money in an inside pocket of his jacket,
and the passport inside a zipped pouch which he
stuffed back into a small leather hand-grip. A few minutes later, trying to attract the attention of a porter,
he put the grip down for a moment and three seconds
later it was gone. At first he remonstrated with the porter, who led him to the Pan American enquiries desk,
which directed him to the attention of the nearest terminal security police officer. The latter took him to an
office where he explained his dilemma.

After a search had ruled out the possibility that the
grip might have been taken by someone else accident-
ally in mistake for his own, a report was filed listing
the matter as a deliberate theft.

Apologies were made and regrets were expressed to
the tall and athletic young American about the activities of pickpockets and bagsnatchers in public places,
and he was told of the many precautions the airport
authorities took to try to curb their thefts from incoming foreigners. He had the grace to admit that a friend

of his was once robbed in a similar manner in Grand Central Station.

The report was eventually circulated in a routine manner to all the divisions of the London Metropolitan Police, together with a description of the missing grip, its contents, and the papers and passport in the pouch. This was duly filed, but as weeks passed and no trace was found of either the grip or its contents, no more was thought of the incident.

Meanwhile Marty Schulberg went to his consulate in Grosvenor Square, reported the theft of his passport, and was issued with travel documents enabling him to fly back to the United States after his month's vacation touring the highlands of Scotland with his exchange-student girl friend. At the consulate the loss was registered, reported to State Department in Washington, and duly forgotten by both establishments.

It will never be known just how many incoming passengers at London Airport's two overseas arrivals passenger buildings were scanned through binoculars from the observation terraces as they emerged from their aircraft and headed down the steps. Despite the difference in their ages, the two who lost their passports had some things in common. Both were around six feet tall, had broad shoulders and slim figures, blue eyes, and a fairly close facial resemblance to the unobtrusive Englishman who had followed and robbed them. Otherwise, Pastor Jensen was aged forty-eight, with grey hair and gold-rimmed glasses for reading; Marty Schulberg was twenty-five, with chestnut brown hair and heavy-rimmed executive glasses which he wore all the time.

These were the faces the Jackal studied at length

on the writing bureau in his flat off South Audley Street. It took him one day and a series of visits to theatrical costumiers, opticians, a man's clothing store in the West End specializing in garments of American type and mainly made in New York to acquire a set of blue-tinted clear-vision contact lenses; two pairs of spectacles, one with gold rims and the other with heavy black frames, and both with clear lenses; a complete outfit consisting of a pair of black leather loafers, T-shirt and underpants, off-white slacks and a sky-blue nylon windbreaker with a zip-up front and collars and cuffs in red and white wool, all made in New York; and a clergyman's white shirt, starched dog-collar, and black bib. From each of the last three the maker's label was carefully removed.

His last visit of the day was to a men's wig and toupee emporium in Chelsea run by two homosexuals. Here he acquired a preparation for tinting the hair a medium grey and another for tinting it chestnut brown, along with precise and coyly delivered instructions on how to apply the tint to achieve the best and most natural-looking effect in the shortest time. He also bought several small hairbrushes for applying the liquids. Otherwise, apart from the complete set of American clothes, he did not make more than one purchase at any one shop.

The following day, July 18, there was a small paragraph at the bottom of an inside page of *Le Figaro*. It announced that in Paris the Deputy Chief of the Brigade-Criminelle of the Police Judiciaire, Commissaire Hippolyte Dupuy, had suffered a severe stroke in his office at the Quai des Orfèvres and had died on his way to hospital. A successor had been named. He was Commissaire Claude Lebel, Chief of the Homicide Division, and in view of the pressure of work on all the departments of the Brigade during the summer months, he would take up his new duties forthwith. The Jackal, who read every French newspaper available in London each day, read the paragraph after his eye had been caught by the word "Criminelle" in the headline, but thought nothing of it.

Before starting his daily watch at London Airport, he had decided to operate throughout the whole of the forthcoming assassination under a false identity. It is one of the easiest things in the world to acquire a false British passport. The Jackal followed the procedure used by most mercenaries, smugglers, and others who wish to adopt an alias for passing national boundaries. First he took a car trip through the Home Counties of the Thames Valley looking for small villages. Almost every English village has an attractive little church, and a graveyard nestling in its shadow. In the third cemetery he visited the Jackal found a gravestone to suit his purpose, that of Alexander Duggan who died at the age of two and a half years in 1931. Had he lived, the Duggan child would have been a few months older than the Jackal in July 1963. The elderly vicar was courteous and helpful when the visitor presented himself at the vicarage to announce that he was an amateur genealogist engaged in attempting to trace the family tree of the Duggans. He had been informed that there had been a Duggan family that had settled in the village in years past. He wondered, somewhat diffidently, if the parish records might be able to help him in his search.

The vicar was kindness itself, and on their way over to the church a compliment on the beauty of the little Norman building and a contribution to the donations box for the restoration fund improved the atmosphere yet more. The records showed that both the Duggan parents had died over the past seven years, and, alas, their only son Alexander had been buried in this very churchyard over thirty years before. The Jackal idly turned over the pages in the parish register of births, marriages, and deaths for 1929, and for the month of April the name of Duggan, written in a crabbed and clerkly hand, caught his eye.

Alexander James Quentin Duggan, born April 3, 1929, in the Parish of Saint Mark's, Sambourne Fishley.

He noted the details, thanked the vicar profusely, and left. Back in London he presented himself at the Central Registry of Births, Marriages and Deaths, where a helpful young assistant accepted without query his visiting card showing him to be a partner in a firm of solicitors of Market Drayton, Shropshire, and his explanation that he was engaged in trying to trace the whereabouts of the grandchildren of one of the firm's clients who had recently died and left her estate to her grandchildren. One of these grandchildren was Alexander James Quentin Duggan, born at Sambourne Fishley, in the parish of Saint Mark's on April 3, 1929.

Most civil servants in Britain do their best to be helpful when confronted by a polite enquiry, and in this case the assistant was no exception. A search of the records showed that the child in question had been registered precisely according to the enquirer's information, but had died on November 8, 1931, as the result of a road accident. For a few shillings the Jackal received a copy of both the birth and death certificates. Before returning home he stopped at a branch office of the Ministry of Labour and was issued with a passport application form, at a toyshop where for fifteen shillings he bought a child's printing set, and at a post office for a one-pound postal order.

Back in his flat he filled in the application form in Duggan's name, giving exactly the right age, date of birth, etc., but his own personal description. He wrote in his own height, colour of hair and eyes, and for profession put down simply "businessman." The full names of Duggan's parents, taken from the child's birth certificate, were also filled in. For the reference he filled in the name of Reverend James Elderly, vicar of Saint Mark's, Sambourne Fishley, to whom he had spoken that morning, and whose full name and title of LLD had obligingly been printed on a board outside the church gate. The vicar's signature was forged in a thin hand in thin ink with a thin nib, and from the printing set he made up a stamp reading:

> SAINT MARK'S PARISH CHURCH
> SAMBOURNE FISHLEY

which was placed firmly next to the vicar's name. The copy of the birth certificate, the application form, and the postal order were sent off to the Passport Office in Petty France. The death certificate he destroyed. The brand new passport arrived at the accommodation address by post four days later as he was reading that morning's edition of *Le Figaro*. He picked it up after lunch. Late that afternoon he locked the flat and drove to London Airport, where he boarded the flight to Copenhagen, paying in cash again to avoid using a cheque book. In the false bottom of his suitcase, in a compartment barely thicker than an ordinary magazine and almost undetectable except to the most thorough search, was two thousand pounds, which he had drawn earlier that day from his private deed box in the vaults of a firm of solicitors in Holborn.

The visit to Copenhagen was brisk and businesslike. Before leaving Kastrup Airport, he booked himself on the next afternoon's Sabena flight to Brussels. In the Danish capital it was far too late to go shopping, so he booked in at the Hotel D'Angleterre on Kongens Nytorv, ate like a king at the Seven Nations, had a mild flirtation with two Danish blondes while strolling through the Tivoli gardens, and was in bed by one in the morning.

The next day he bought a lightweight clerical grey suit at one of the best known men's outfitters in central Copenhagen, a pair of sober black walking shoes, a pair of socks, a set of underwear, and three white shirts with collars attached. In each case he bought only what had the Danish maker's name on a small cloth tab inside. In the case of the three white shirts, which he did not need, the point of the purchase was simply to acquire the tabs for transference to the clerical shirt, dog-collar, and bib that he had bought in London while claiming to be a theological student on the verge of ordination.

His last purchase was a book in Danish on the notable churches and cathedrals of France. He lunched off a large cold collation at a lakeside restaurant in the Tivoli Gardens, and caught the 3:15 plane to Brussels.

four

Why a man of the undoubted talents of Paul Goossens should have gone wrong in middle age was something of a mystery even to his few friends, his rather more numerous customers, and the Belgian police. During his thirty years as a trusted employee of the Fabrique Nationale at Liège he had established a reputation for unfailing precision in a branch of engineering where precision is absolutely indispensable. Of his honesty also there had been no doubt. He had also during those thirty years become the company's foremost expert in the very wide range of weapons that that excellent company produces, from the tiniest lady's automatic to the heaviest of machine guns.

His war record had been remarkable. Although he had continued after the Occupation to work in the arms factory run by the Germans for the Nazi war effort, later examination of his career had established beyond doubt his undercover work for the Resistance, his participation in private in a chain of safe-houses for the escape of downed Allied airmen, and at work his leadership of a sabotage ring that ensured a fair proportion of the weapons turned out by Liège either never fired accurately or blew up at the fiftieth shell, killing the German crews. All this, so modest and unassuming was the man, had been wormed out of him later by his defence lawyers and triumphantly produced in court on his behalf. It had gone a long way to mitigating his sentence, and the jury had also been impressed by his own halting admission that he had never revealed his activities during the war because post-liberation honours and medals would have embarrassed him.

By the time in the early fifties that a large sum of money had been embezzled from a foreign customer in the course of a lucrative arms deal, and suspicion had fallen upon him, he was a departmental chief in the firm, and his own superiors had been loudest in informing the police that their suspicions with regard to the trusted M. Goossens were ridiculous.

Even at the trial his managing director spoke for him. But the presiding judge took the view that to betray a position of trust in such a manner was all the more reprehensible, and he had been given ten years in prison. On appeal it was reduced to five. With good conduct he had been released after three and a half.

His wife had divorced him and taken the children with her. The old life of the suburban dweller in a neat flower-rimmed detached house in one of the prettier outskirts of Liège (there are not many) was over, a thing of the past. So was his career with F.N. He had taken a small flat in Brussels, later a house further out of town, as his fortunes prospered from his private business as the source of illegal arms to half the underworld in Western Europe.

By the early sixties he had the nickname l'Armurier, the Armourer. Any Belgian citizen can buy a lethal weapon—revolver, automatic, or rifle—at any sports or gun shop in the country on production of a national identity card proving Belgian nationality. Goossens never used his own, for at each sale of the weapon and subsequent ammunition the sale is noted in the gunsmith's log-book, along with the name and I.D. card of the purchaser. Goossens used other people's cards, either stolen or forged.

He had established close links with one of the city's top pickpockets, a man who, when not languishing in prison as a guest of the state, could remove any wallet from any pocket at ease. These he bought outright for cash from the thief. He also had at his disposal the services of a master forger who, having come badly unstuck in the late forties over the production of a large amount of French francs in which he had inadvertently left the "u" out of "Banque de France" (he was young then), had finally gone into the false passport business with much greater success. Lastly, when Goossens needed to acquire a firearm for a customer, the client who presented himself at the gunsmith's with a neatly forged I.D. card was never himself but always an out-of-work and out-of-jail petty crook or an actor resting between conquests of the stage.

Of his own "staff" only the pickpocket and the forger knew his real identity. So also did some of his customers, notably the top men in the Belgian underworld, who not only left him alone to his devices but also offered him a certain amount of protection in refusing to reveal when captured where they had got their guns, simply because he was so useful to them.

This did not stop the Belgian police being aware of a portion of his activities, but it did prevent them ever being able to catch him with the goods in his possession or being able to get testimony that would stand up in court and convict him. They were aware of and highly suspicious of the small but superbly equipped forge and workshop in his converted garage, but repeated visits had revealed nothing more than the paraphernalia for the manufacture of wrought-metal medallions and souvenirs of the statues of Brussels. On their last visit he had solemnly presented the Chief Inspector with a figurine of the Manneken-Pis as a token of his esteem for the forces of law and order.

He felt no qualms as he waited on the morning of July 21, 1963, for the arrival of an Englishman who had been guaranteed to him over the phone by one of his best customers, a former mercenary in the services of Katanga from 1960 to 1962 who had since masterminded a protection business among the whorehouses of the Belgian capital.

The visitor turned up at noon, as promised, and M. Goossens showed him into his little office off the hall.

"Would you please remove your glasses?" he asked when his visitor was seated and, as the tall Englishman hesitated, added, "You see I think it is better that we trust each other insofar as we can while our business association lasts. A drink, perhaps?"

The man whose passport would have announced him as Alexander Duggan removed his dark glasses and stared quizzically at the little gunsmith as two beers were poured. M. Goossens seated himself behind his desk, sipped his beer, and asked quietly, "In what way may I be of service to you, monsieur?"

"I believe Louis rang you earlier about my coming?"

"Certainly," M. Goossens nodded. "Otherwise you would not be here."

"Did he tell you what is my business?"

"No. Simply that he knew you in Katanga, that he could vouch for your discretion, that you needed a firearm, and that you would be prepared to pay in cash, sterling."

The Englishman nodded slowly. "Well, since I know what your business is, there is little reason why you should not know mine. Besides which, the weapon I need will have to be a specialist gun with certain unusual attachments. I—er—specialise in the removal of men who have powerful and wealthy enemies. Evidently, such men are usually powerful and wealthy themselves. It is not always easy. They can afford specialist protection. Such a job needs planning and the right weapon. I have such a job on hand at the moment. I shall need a rifle."

M. Goossens again sipped his beer, nodded benignly at his guest.

"Excellent, excellent. A specialist like myself. I think I sense a challenge. What kind of rifle had you in mind?"

"It is not so much the type of rifle that is important. It is more of a question of the limitations that are imposed by the job, and of finding a rifle which will perform satisfactorily under those limitations."

M. Goossens eyes gleamed with pleasure.

"A one-off," he purred delightedly. "A gun that will be tailor-made for one man and one job under one set of circumstances, never to be repeated. You have come to the right man. I sense a challenge, my dear monsieur. I am glad that you came."

The Englishman permitted himself a smile at the Belgian's professorial enthusiasm. "So am I, monsieur."

"Now tell me, what are these limitations?"

"The main limitation is of size, not in length but in the physical bulk of the working parts. The chamber and breech must be no bulkier than that—" He held up his right hand, the tip of the middle finger touching the end of the thumb in the form of a letter o less than two and a half inches in diameter.

"That seems to mean it cannot be a repeater, since a gas chamber would be larger than that, nor can it have a bulky spring mechanism for the same reason," said the Englishman. "It seems to me it must be a bolt-action rifle."

M. Goossens was nodding at the ceiling, his mind taking in the details of what his visitor was saying, making a mental picture of a rifle of great slimness in the working parts.

"Go on, go on," he murmured.

"On the other hand it cannot have a bolt with a handle that sticks out sideways like the Mauser seven-ninety-two or the Lee Enfield three-o-three. The bolt must slide straight back towards the shoulder, gripped between forefinger and thumb for the fitting of the bullet into the breech. Also there must be no trigger guard, and the trigger itself must be detachable so that it can be fitted just before firing."

"Why?" asked the Belgian.

"Because the whole mechanism must pass into a tubular compartment for storage and carrying, and the compartment must not attract attention. For that it must not be larger in diameter than I have just shown, for reasons I shall explain. It is possible to have a detachable trigger?"

"Certainly, almost all is possible. Of course, one could design a single-shot rifle that breaks open at the back for loading like a shotgun. That would dispense with the bolt completely, but it would involve a hinge, which might be no saving. Also it would be necessary to design and manufacture such a rifle from scratch, milling a piece of metal to make the entire breech and chamber. Not an easy task in a small workshop, but possible."

"How long would that take?" asked the Englishman.

The Belgian shrugged and spread his hands. "Several months, I am afraid."

"I do not have that amount of time."

"In that case it will be necessary to take an existing rifle purchasable in a shop and make modifications. Please go on."

"Right. The gun must also be light in weight. It need not be of heavy calibre, the bullet will do the work. It must have a short barrel, probably not longer than twelve inches—"

"Over what range will you have to fire?"

"This is still not certain, but probably not more than a hundred and thirty metres."

"Will you go for a head or chest shot?"

"It will probably have to be head. I may get a shot at the chest, but the head is surer."

"Surer to kill, yes, if you get a good hit," said the Belgian. "But the chest is surer to get a good hit. At least, when one is using a light weapon with a short barrel over a hundred and thirty metres with possible obstructions. I assume," he added, "from your uncertainty on this point of the head or the chest that there may be someone passing in the way?"

"Yes, there may be."

"Will you get the chance of a second shot, bearing in mind that it will take several seconds to extract the spent cartridge and insert a fresh one, close the breech, and take aim again?"

"Almost certainly not. I just might get a second if I use a silencer and the first shot is a complete miss which is not noticed by anyone nearby. But even if I get a first hit through the temple, I need the silencer to effect my own escape. There must be several minutes of clear time before anyone nearby realises even roughly where the bullet has come from."

The Belgian continued nodding, by now staring down at his deskpad.

"In that case, you had better have explosive bullets. I shall prepare a handful along with the gun. You know what I mean?"

The Englishman nodded. "Glycerine or mercury?"

"Oh mercury, I think. So much neater and cleaner. Are there any more points concerning this gun?"

"I'm afraid so. In the interests of slimness, all the woodwork on the handgrip beneath the barrel should be removed. The entire stock must be removed. For firing it must have a frame-stock like a Sten gun, each of the three sections of which, upper and lower members and shoulder-rest, must unscrew into three separate rods. Lastly, there must be a completely effective silencer and a telescopic sight. Both of these too must be removable for storage and carrying."

The Belgian thought for a long time, sipping his beer until it was drained. The Englishman became impatient.

"Well, can you do it?"

M. Goossens seemed to emerge from his reverie. He smiled apologetically.

"Do forgive me. It is a very complex order. But yes, I can do it. I have never failed yet to produce the required article. Really, what you have described is a hunting expedition in which the equipment must be carried past certain checks in such a manner as to arouse no suspicion. A hunting expedition supposes a hunting rifle, and that is what you shall have. Not as small as a twenty-two calibre, for that is for rabbits and hares. Nor as big as a Remington three hundred, which would never conform to the limitations of size you have demanded.

"I think I have such a gun in mind, and easily available here in Brussels at some sports shops. An expensive gun, a high-precision instrument. Very accurate, beautifully tooled, and yet light and slim. Used a lot for chamois and other small deer, but with explosive bullets just the thing for bigger game. Tell me, will the —er—gentleman be moving slowly, fast, or not at all?"

"Stationary."

"No problems then. The fittings of a frame-stock of three separate steel rods and the screw-in trigger are mere mechanics. The tapping of the barrel for the silencer and the shortening of the barrel by eight inches I can do myself. One loses accuracy as one loses eight inches of barrel. Pity, pity. Are you a marksman?"

The Englishman nodded.

"Then there will be no problem with a stationary human being at a hundred and thirty metres with a telescopic sight. As for the silencer, I shall make it myself. They are not complex, but difficult to obtain

as a manufactured article, particularly long ones for
rifles which are not usual in hunting. Now, monsieur,
you mentioned earlier some tubular compartments for
carrying the gun in its broken-down form. What had
you in mind?"

The Englishman rose and crossed to the desk, towering over the little Belgian. He slipped his hand inside
his jacket, and for a second there was a flicker of fear
in the smaller man's eyes. For the first time he noticed
that whatever expression was on the killer's face, it
never touched his eyes, which appeared clouded by
streaks of grey like wisps of smoke covering all expression that might have touched them. But the Englishman produced only a silver propelling pencil.

He spun round M. Goossens's note pad and sketched
rapidly for a few seconds.

"Do you recognize that?" he asked, turning the pad
back to the gunsmith.

"Of course," replied the Belgian after giving the
precisely drawn sketch a glance.

"Right. Well now, the whole thing is composed of
a series of hollow aluminum tubes which screw together. This one"—tapping with the point of the pencil at a place on the diagram—"contains one of the
struts of the rifle stock. This here contains the other
strut. Both are concealed within the tubes that make
up this section. The shoulder-rest of the rifle is this—
here—in its entirety. This is therefore the only part
which doubles up with two purposes without changing in any way.

"Here"—tapping at another point on the diagram
as the Belgian's eyes widened in surprise—"at the
thickest point is the largest diameter tube which con-

tains the breech of the rifle with the bolt inside it. This tapers to the barrel without a break. Obviously, with a telescopic sight being used there need be no foresight, so the whole thing slides out of this compartment when the assemblage is unscrewed. The last two sections—here and here—contain the telescopic sight itself and the silencer. Finally the bullets. They should be inserted into this little stump at the bottom. When the whole thing is assembled it must pass for precisely what it looks. When unscrewed into its seven component parts, the bullets, silencer, telescope, rifle, and the three struts that make up the triangular frame stock can be extracted for reassembly as a fully operational rifle. OK?"

For a few seconds longer the little Belgian looked at the diagram. Slowly he rose, then held out his hand.

"Monsieur," he said with reverence, "it is a conception of genius. Undetectable. And yet so simple. It shall be done."

The Englishman was neither gratified nor displeased.

"Good," he said. "Now, the question of time. I shall need the gun in about fourteen days, can that be arranged?"

"Yes. I can acquire the gun within three. A week's work should see the modifications achieved. Buying the telescopic sight presents no problems. You may leave the choice of the sight to me, I know what will be required for the range of a hundred and thirty metres you have in mind. You had better calibrate and zero the settings yourself at your own discretion. Making the silencer, modifying the bullets, and constructing the outer casing . . . yes, it can be done within the time allowed if I burn the candle at both ends. However, it would be better if you could arrive back here with a day or two in hand, just in case there are some last minute details to talk over. Could you be back in twelve days?"

"Yes, any time between seven and fourteen days from now. But fourteen days is the deadline. I must be back in London by August the fourth."

"You shall have the completed weapon with all last details arranged to your satisfaction on the morning of the fourth if you can be here yourself on August first for final discussions and collection, monsieur."

"Good. Now for the question of your expenses and fee," said the Englishman. "Have you an idea how much they will be?"

The Belgian thought for a while. "For this kind of job, with all the work it entails, for the facilities available here and my own specialised knowledge, I must ask a fee of one thousand English pounds. I concede that is above the rate for a simple rifle. But this is not a simple rifle. It must be a work of art. I believe I am the only man in Europe capable of doing it justice, of making a perfect job of it. Like yourself, monsieur, I am in my field the best. For the best, one pays. Then on top there would be the purchasing price of the weapon, bullets, telescope, and raw materials . . . say, the equivalent of another two hundred pounds."

"Done," replied the Englishman without argument. He reached into his breast pocket again and extracted a bundle of five-pound notes. They were bound in lots of twenty. He counted out five wads of twenty notes each.

"I would suggest," he went on evenly, "that in order

to establish my bona fides I make you a down payment as an advance and to cover costs of five hundred pounds. I shall bring the remaining seven hundred on my return in eleven days. Is that agreeable to you?"

"Monsieur," said the Belgian skilfully pocketing the notes, "it is a pleasure to do business both with a professional and a gentleman."

"There is a little more," went on his visitor as though he had not been interrupted. "You will make no further attempt to contact Louis or ask him or anyone else who I am or what is my true identity. Nor will you seek to enquire for whom I am working, nor against whom. In the event that you should try to do so it is certain I shall hear about the enquiries. In that event you will die. On my return here, if there has been any attempt to contact the police or to lay a trap, you will die. Is that understood?"

M. Goossens was pained. Standing in the hallway he looked up at the Englishman, and an eel of fear wriggled in his bowels. He had faced many of the tough men of the Belgian underworld when they came to him for special or unusual weapons, or simply a run-of-the-mill snub-nosed Colt Special. These were hard men. But there was something distant and implacable about the visitor from across the Channel who intended to kill an important and well-protected figure. Not another gangland boss, but a big man, perhaps a politician. He thought of protesting or expostulating, then decided better.

"Monsieur," he said quietly. "I do not want to know about you, anything about you. The gun you will receive will bear no serial number. You see, it is of more importance to me that nothing you do should

ever be traced back to me than that I should seek to
know more than I do about you. *Bonjour, monsieur."*

The Jackal walked away into the bright sunshine
and two streets away found a cruising taxi to take him
back to the city centre and the Hotel Amigo.

He suspected that in order to acquire guns Goossens
would have to have a forger in his employ somewhere,
but preferred to find and use one of his own. Again
Louis, his contact from the old days in Katanga, helped
him. Not that it was difficult. Brussels has a long tradition as the centre of the forged identity-card industry, and many foreigners appreciate the lack of formalities with which assistance in this field can be
obtained. In the early sixties Brussels had also become
the operations base of the mercenary soldier, for this
was before the emergence in the Congo of the French
and South African/British units who later came to
dominate the business. With Katanga gone, over three
hundred out of work "military advisers" from the old
Tshombe regime were hanging around the bars of
the red-light quarter, many of them in possession of
several sets of identity papers.

The Jackal found his man in a bar off the rue Neuve
after Louis had arranged the appointment. He introduced himself, and the pair retired to a corner alcove. The Jackal produced his driving licence, which
was in his own name, issued by the London County
Council two years earlier and with some months still
to run.

"This," he told the Belgian, "belonged to a man now
dead. As I am banned from driving in Britain, I need
a new front page in my own name."

He put the passport in the name of Duggan in front

of the forger. The man opposite glanced at the passport first, took in the newness of the passport, the
fact that it had been issued three days earlier, and
glanced shrewdly at the Englishman.

"*En effet*," he murmured, then flicked open the little
red driving licence. After a few minutes he looked up.

"Not difficult, monsieur. The English authorities
are gentlemen. They do not seem to expect that official
documents might perhaps be forged, therefore they
take few precautions. This paper"—he flicked the small
sheet gummed onto the first page of the licence, which
carried the licence number and the full name of the
holder—"could be printed by a child's printing set.
The watermark is easy. This presents no problems.
Was that all you wanted?"

"No, there are two other papers."

"Ah. If you will permit my saying so, it appeared
strange that you should wish to contact me for such
a simple task. There must be men in your own London
who could do this within a few hours. What are the
other papers?"

The Jackal described them to the last detail. The
Belgian's eyes narrowed in thought. He took out a
packet of Bastos, offered one to the Englishman, who
declined, and lit one for himself.

"That is not so easy. The French identity card, not
too bad. There are plenty about from which one can
work. You understand, one must work from an original to achieve the best results. But the other one.
I do not think I have seen such a one. It is a most unusual requirement."

He paused while the Jackal ordered a passing waiter

to refill their glasses. When the waiter had gone he
resumed.

"And then the photograph. That will not be easy.
You say there must be a difference in age, in hair
colouring and length. Most of those wishing for a
false document intend that their own photograph shall
be on the document, but with the personal details
falsified. But to devise a new photograph which does
not even look like you as you now appear this com-
plicates things."

He drank off half of his beer, still eyeing the Englishman opposite him. "To achieve this it will be
necessary to seek out a man of the approximate age
of the bearer of the cards, who also bears a reasonable similarity to yourself, at least as far as the head
and face is concerned, and cut his hair to the length
you require. Then a photograph of this man would
be put onto the cards. From that point on it would
be up to you to model your subsequent disguise on
this man's true appearance, rather than the reverse.
You follow me?"

"Yes," replied the Jackal.

"This will take some time. How long can you stay
in Brussels?"

"Not long," said the Jackal. "I must leave fairly soon,
but I could be back on August first. From then I could
stay another three days. I have to be returning to London on the fourth."

The Belgian thought again for a while, staring at
the photograph in the passport in front of him. At last
he folded it closed and passed it back to the Englishman after copying onto a piece of paper from his
pocket the name Alexander James Quentin Duggan.

He pocketed both the piece of paper and the driving license.

"All right. It can be done. But I have to have a good portrait photograph of yourself as you are now, full-face and profile. This will take time. And money. There are extra expenses involved . . . it may be necessary to undertake an operation into France itself with a colleague adept in picking pockets in order to acquire the second of these cards you mention. Obviously, I shall ask around Brussels first, but it may be necessary to go to these lengths—"

"How much?" cut in the Englishman.

"Twenty thousand Belgian francs."

The Jackal thought for a moment. "About a hundred and fifty pounds sterling. All right. I will pay you a hundred deposit and the remainder on delivery."

The Belgian rose. "Then we had better get the portrait photos taken. I have my own studio."

They took a taxi to a small basement flat more than a mile away. It turned out to be a seedy and run-down photographer's studio, with a sign outside indicating that the premises were run as a commercial establishment specialising in passport photographs developed while the customer waited. Inevitably stuck in the window were what a passer-by must have presumed to be the high-points of the studio owner's past work—two portraits of simpering girls, hideously retouched, a marriage photo of a couple sufficiently unprepossessing to deal a nasty blow to the whole concept of wedlock, and two babies. The Belgian led the way down the steps to the front door, unlocked it, and ushered his guest inside.

The session took two hours, in which the Belgian

showed a skill with the camera that could never have been possessed by the author of the portraits in the window. A large trunk in one corner, which he unlocked with his own key, revealed a selection of expensive cameras and flash equipment, besides a host of facial props including hair tints and dyes, toupees, wigs, spectacles in great variety, and a case of theatrical cosmetics.

It was halfway through the session that the Belgian hit on the idea that obviated the necessity to seek out a substitute to pose for the real photograph. Studying the effect of thirty minutes working on the Jackal's face with makeup, he suddenly dived into the chest and produced a wig.

"What do you think of this?" he asked.

The wig was of hair coloured iron-grey and cut *en brosse.*

"Do you think that your own hair, cut to this length and dyed this colour, could look like this?"

The Jackal took the wig and examined it. "We can give it a try and see how it looks in the photo," he suggested.

And it worked. The Belgian came out of the developing room half an hour after taking six photos of his customer with a sheaf of prints in his hand. Together they pored over the desk. Staring up was the face of an old and tired man. The skin was an ashen gray and there were dark rings of fatigue or pain beneath the eyes. The man wore neither beard nor moustache, but the grey hair on his head gave the impression he must have been in his fifties at least, and not a robust fifty at that.

"I think it will work," said the Belgian at last.

"The problem is," replied the Jackal, "that you had to work on me with cosmetics for half an hour to achieve this effect. Then there was the wig. I cannot emulate all that by myself. And here we were under lights, whereas I shall be in the open air when I have to produce these papers I have asked for."

"But this is precisely not the point," reposted the forger. "It is not so much that you will not be a dead image of the photograph, but that the photograph will not be a dead likeness of you. This is the way the mind of a man examining papers works. He looks at the face first, the real face, then asks for the papers. Then he sees the photograph. He already has the image of the man standing beside him in his mind's eye. This affects his judgement. He looks for points of similarity, not the opposite.

"Secondly, this photograph is twenty-five by twenty centimetres. The photograph in the identity card will be three by four. Thirdly, a too precise likeness should be avoided. If the card was issued several years previously, it is impossible that a man should not change a bit. In the photograph here we have you in open-necked striped shirt with collar attached. Try to avoid that shirt for example, or even avoid an open-necked shirt at all. Wear a tie, or a scarf, or a turtle-necked sweater.

"Lastly, nothing that I have done to you cannot be easily simulated. The main point of course is the hair. It must be cut *en brosse* before this photo is presented, and dyed grey, perhaps even greyer than in the photograph, but not less so. To increase the impression of age and decrepitude, grow two or three days of beard stubble. Then shave with a cut-throat razor, but badly,

nicking yourself in a couple of places. Elderly men
tend to do this. As for the complexion, this is vital.
To extract pity it must be grey and tired, rather waxy
and ill-looking. Can you get hold of some pieces of
cordite?'"

The Jackal had listened to the exegesis of the forger
with admiration, though nothing showed on his face.
For the second time in a day he had been able to contact a professional who knew his job thoroughly. He
reminded himself to thank Louis appropriately—after
the job was done.

"It might be arranged," he said cautiously.

"Two or three small pieces of cordite, chewed and
swallowed, produce within half an hour a feeling of
nausea, uncomfortable but not disastrous. They also
turn the skin a grey pallor and cause facial sweating.
We used to use this trick in the Army to simulate illness and avoid fatigue and route marches."

"Thank you for the information. Now for the rest,
do you think you can produce the documents in time?"

"From the technical standpoint, there is no doubt
of it. The only remaining problem is to acquire an
original of the second French document. For that I
may have to work fast. But if you come back in the
first few days of August, I think I can have them all
ready for you. You—er—had mentioned a down payment to cover expenses—"

The Jackal reached into his inside pocket and produced a single bundle of twenty five-pound notes,
which he handed the Belgian.

"How do I contact you?" he asked.

"I would suggest by the same way as tonight."

"Too risky. My contact man may be missing, or out

of town. Then I would have no way of finding you."

The Belgian thought for a minute. "Then I shall wait from six until seven each evening in the bar where we met tonight on each of the first three days of August. If you do not come, I shall presume the deal is off."

The Englishman had removed the wig and was wiping his face with a towel soaked in removing spirit. In silence he slipped on his tie and jacket. When he was finished he turned to the Belgian.

"There are certain things I wish to make clear," he said quietly. The friendliness was gone from the voice and the eyes stared at the Belgian as bleak as a Channel fog. "When you have finished the job, you will be present at the bar as promised. You will return to me the new license and the page removed from the one you now have. Also the negatives and all prints of the photographs we have just taken. You will also forget the names of Duggan and of the original owner of that driving licence. The name of the two French documents you are going to produce you may select yourself, providing it is a simple and common French name. After handing them over to me you will forget that name also. You will never speak to anyone of this commission again. In the event that you infringe any of these conditions, you will die. Is that understood?"

The Belgian stared back for a few moments. Over the past three hours he had come to think of the Englishman as a run-of-the-mill customer who simply wished to drive a car in Britain and masquerade for his own purposes as a middle-aged man in France. A smuggler, perhaps, running dope or diamonds from a lonely Breton fishing port into England.

"It is understood, monsieur."

A few seconds later the Englishman was gone into the night. He walked for five blocks before taking a taxi back to the Amigo, and it was midnight when he arrived. He ordered cold chicken and a bottle of Moselle in his room, bathed thoroughly to get rid of the last traces of make-up, then slept.

The following morning he checked out of the hotel and took the Brabant Express to Paris. It was July 22.

The head of the Action Service of the SDECE sat at his desk on that same morning and surveyed the two pieces of paper before him. Each was a copy of a routine report filed by agents of other departments. At the head of each piece of blue flimsy was a list of department chiefs entitled to receive a copy of the report. Opposite his own designation was a small tick. Both reports had come in that morning and in the normal course of events Colonel Rolland would have glanced at each, taken in what they had to say, stored the knowledge somewhere in his fearsome memory, and had them filed under separate headings. But there was one word that cropped up in each of the reports, a word that intrigued him.

The first report that arrived was an interdepartmental memo from R 3 (Western Europe) containing a synopsis of a despatch from their permanent office in Rome. The despatch was a straight-forward report to the effect that Rodin, Montclair, and Casson were still holed up in their top floor suite and were still being guarded by their eight guards. They had not moved out of the building since they established themselves there on June 18. Extra staff had been drafted from R 3 Paris to Rome to assist in keeping the hotel under round-the-clock surveillance. Instructions from Paris remained unchanged: not to make any approach but simply to keep watch. The men in the hotel had established a routine for keeping in touch with the outside world three weeks previously ("see R 3 Rome report of June 30"), and this was being maintained. The courier remained Viktor Kowalski. End of message.

Colonel Rolland flicked open the buff file lying on the right of his desk next to the sawn-off 105 mm. shell case that served for a copious ashtray and was even by then half-full of Disque Bleue stubs. His eyes strayed down the R 3 Rome report of June 30 till he found the paragraph he wanted.

Each day, it said, one of the guards left the hotel and walked to the head post office of Rome. Here a Poste Restante pigeonhole was reserved in the name of one Poitiers. The OAS had not taken a postal box with a key, apparently for fear it might be burgled. All mail for the top men of the OAS was addressed to Poitiers and was kept by the clerk on duty at the Poste Restante counter. An attempt to bribe the original such clerk to hand over the mail to an agent of R 3 had failed. The man had reported the approach to his superiors and had been replaced by a senior clerk. It was possible that mail for Poitiers was now being screened by the Italian security police, but R 3 had instructions not to approach the Italians to ask for cooperation. The attempt to bribe the clerk had failed, but it was felt the initiative had to be taken. Each day the mail arriving overnight in the post office was handed to the guard, who had been identified as one

Viktor Kowalski, formerly a corporal of the Foreign
Legion and a member of Rodin's original company in
Indochina. Kowalski seemingly had adequate false
papers identifying him to the post office as Poitiers,
or a letter of authority acceptable to the post office.
If Kowalski had letters to post, he waited by the post
box inside the main hall of the building until five minutes before collection time, dropped the mail through
the slit, then waited until the entire box-full was collected and taken back into the heart of the building
for sorting. Attempts to interfere with the process of
either collection or despatch of the OAS chief's mail
would entail a degree of violence, which had already
been precluded by Paris. Occasionally Kowalski made
a telephone call, long-distance, from the Overseas Calls
telephone counter, but here again attempts either to
learn the number asked for or to overhear the conversation had failed. End of message.

Colonel Rolland let the cover of the file fall back
on the contents and took up the second of the two
reports that had come in that morning. It was a police
report from the Police Judiciaire of Metz stating that
a man had been questioned during a routine raid on
a bar and had half-killed two policemen in the ensuing
fight. Later at the police station he had been identified by his fingerprints as a deserter from the Foreign
Legion by the name of Sandor Kovacs, Hungarian by
birth and a refugee from Budapest in 1956. Kovacs,
a note from PJ Paris added at the end of the information from Metz, was a notorious OAS thug long wanted
for his connection with a series of terror murders of
loyalist notables in the Bone and Constantine areas
of Algeria during 1961. At that time he had operated

as partner of another OAS gunman still at large, former Foreign Legion corporal Viktor Kowalski. End of message.

Rolland pondered the connection between the two men yet again, as he had done for the previous hour. At last he pressed a buzzer in front of him and replied to the *"Oui, mon colonel"* that came out of it.

"Get me the personal file on Viktor Kowalski. At once."

He had the file up from archives in ten minutes, and spent another hour reading it. Several times he ran his eye over one particular paragraph. As other Parisians in less demanding professions hurried past on the pavement below to their lunches, Colonel Rolland convened a small meeting consisting of himself, his personal secretary, a specialist in handwriting from the documentation department three floors down, and two strong-arm men from his private Praetorian Guard.

"Gentlemen," he told them, "with the unwilling but inevitable assistance of one not here present, we are going to compose, write, and despatch a letter."

five

The Jackal's train arrived at the Gare du Nord just before lunch, and he took a taxi to a small but extremely comfortable hotel in the rue de Suresne, leading off from the Place de la Madeleine. While it was not a hotel in the same class as the D'Angleterre of Copenhagen or the Amigo of Brussels, he had reasons for wishing to seek a more modest and less known place to stay while in Paris. For one thing his stay would be longer, and for another there was far more likelihood of running into somebody in Paris in late July who might have known him fleetingly in London under his real name than in either Copenhagen or Brussels. Out on the street he was confident that the wraparound dark glasses he habitually wore, and which in the bright sunshine of the boulevards were completely natural, would protect his identity. The possible danger lay in being seen in a hotel corridor or foyer. The last thing he wished at this stage was to be halted by a cheery "Well, fancy seeing you here," and then the mention of his name within the hearing of a desk clerk who knew him as Mr. Duggan.

Not that his stay in Paris had anything about it to excite attention. He lived quietly, taking his breakfast of croissants and coffee in his room. From the delicatessen across the road from his hotel he bought a jar of English marmalade to replace the black currant jam provided on the breakfast tray, and asked the hotel staff to include the jar of marmalade on his tray each morning in place of the jam.

He was quietly courteous to the staff, spoke only a few words of French with the Englishman's habitually atrocious pronunciation of the French language, and smiled politely when addressed. He replied to the management's solicitous enquiries by assuring them that he was extremely comfortable and thank you.

"*M. Duggan,*" the hotel proprietress told her desk clerk one day, "*est extrêmement gentil. Un vrai* gentleman." There was no dissent.

His days were spent out of the hotel in the pursuits of the tourists. On his first day he bought a street map of Paris, and from a small notebook marked off on the map the places of interest he most wanted to see. These he visited and studied with remarkable devotion, even bearing in mind the architectural beauty of some of them or the historical association of the others.

He spent three days roaming round the Arc de Triomphe or sitting on the terrace of the Café de l'Elysée scanning the monument and the rooftops of the great buildings that surround the Place de l'Etoile. Anyone who had followed him in those days (and no one did) would have been surprised that even the architecture of the brilliant M. Haussmann should have attracted so devoted an admirer. Certainly no watcher could have divined that the quiet and elegant English tourist stirring his coffee and gazing at the buildings for so many hours was mentally working out angles of fire, distances from the upper stories to the Eternal Flame flickering beneath the Arc, and the chances of a man fleeing down a rear fire escape unnoticed into the milling crowds.

After three days he left the Etoile and visited the ossuary of the martyrs of the French Resistance at Montvalérien. Here he arrived with a bouquet of flowers, and a guide, touched by the gesture of the Englishman to the guide's one-time fellow Resistants, gave him an exhaustive tour of the shrine and a running commentary. He was hardly to perceive that the visitor's eyes kept straying away from the entrance to the ossuary towards the high walls of the prison which cut off all direct vision into the courtyard from the roofs of the surrounding buildings. After two hours he left with a polite "thank-you" and a generous but not extravagant *pourboire*.

He also visited the Place des Invalides, dominated on its southern side by the Hôtel des Invalides, home of Napoleon's tomb and shrine to the glories of the French Army. The western side of the enormous square, formed by the rue Fabert, interested him most, and he sat for a morning at the corner cafe where the rue Fabert adjoins the tiny triangular Place de Santiago du Chili. From the sixth or seventh floor of the building above his head, 146, rue de Grenelle, where that street joins the rue Fabert at an angle of ninety degrees, he estimated that a gunman would be able to dominate the front gardens of the Invalides, the entrance to the inner courtyard, most of the Place des Invalides, and two or three streets. A good place for a last stand, but not for an assassination. For one thing, the distance from the upper windows to the gravelled path leading from the Invalides Palace to where cars would be drawn up at the base of the steps between the two tanks was over two hundred metres. For another, the view downwards from the windows of number 146 would be partly obscured by the topmost branches of the dense lime trees growing in the Place de Santiago and from which the pigeons dropped their off-white tributes onto the shoulders of the uncomplaining statue of Vauban. Regretfully, he paid for his Vittel Menthe and left.

A day was spent in the precincts of Notre Dame cathedral. Here amid the rabbit warren of the Ile de la Cité were back stairways, alleys, and passageways, but the distance from the entrance to the cathedral to the parked cars at the foot of the steps was only a few metres, and the rooftops of the Place du Parvis were too far away, while those of the tiny abutting Square Charlemagne were too close and easy for security forces to infest with watchers.

His last visit was to the square at the southern end of the rue de Rennes. He arrived on July 28. Once called the Place de Rennes, the square had been renamed when the Gaullists took power in the City Hall, and was now called Place du 18 Juin 1940. The Jackal's eyes strayed to the shining new name plate on the wall of the building and remained there. Something of what he had read the previous month returned to him. June 18, 1940, the day when the lonely but lofty exile in London had taken the microphone to tell the French that if they had lost a battle, they had not lost the war.

There was something about this square, with the crouching bulk of the Gare Montparnasse on its southern side, full of memories for the Parisians of the war generation, that caused the assassin to stop. Slowly he surveyed the expanse of tarmac, crisscrossed now by a maelstrom of traffic pounding down the Boulevard de Montparnasse and joined by other streams from the rue d'Odessa and the rue de Rennes. He looked round at the tall, narrow-fronted buildings on each side of the rue de Rennes that also overlooked the square. Slowly he wended his way round the square to the southern side and peered through the railings into the courtyard of the station. It was a-buzz with cars and taxis bringing or taking away tens of thousands of commuter passengers a day, one of the great mainline stations of Paris. By that winter it would become a silent hulk, brooding on the events, human and historical, that had taken place in its steely, smoky shadow. The station was destined for demolition in 1964, when a new station was to be built five hundred yards along the railway line.

The Jackal turned with his back to the railings and looked down the traffic artery of the rue de Rennes. He was facing the Place du 18 Juin 1940, convinced that this was the place the President of France would come one last time, on the appointed day. The other places he had examined during the past week were possibles; this one, he felt sure, was the certainty. Within a short time there would be no more Gare Montparnasse, the columns that had looked down on so much would be smelted for suburban fences, and the forecourt that had seen Berlin humiliated and Paris preserved would be just another executives' cafeteria. But before that happened, he, the man with the kepi and two gold stars, would come once again. But in the meantime the distance from the top floor of the corner house on the western side of the rue de Rennes and the centre of the forecourt was about 130 metres.

The Jackal took in the landscape facing him with a practised eye. Both corner houses on the rue de Rennes where it debouched into the square were obvious choices. The first three houses up the rue de Rennes were possibles, presenting a narrow firing angle into the forecourt. Beyond them the angle became too narrow. Similarly, the first three houses that fronted the Boulevard de Montparnasse running straight through the square east to west were possibles. Beyond them the angles became too narrow again, and the distance too great. There were no other buildings that dominated the forecourt that were not too far away, other than the station building itself. But this would be out of bounds, its upper office windows overlooking the forecourt crawling with security men. The Jackal decided to study the three corner houses on the western side of the rue de Rennes first, and sauntered over to a cafe on the corner at the eastern side, the Café Duchesse Anne.

Here he sat on the terrace a few feet from the roaring traffic, ordered a coffee, and stared at the houses across the street. He stayed for three hours. Later he lunched at the Hansi Brasserie Alsacienne on the far side, and studied the eastern façades. For the afternoon he sauntered up and down, looking at closer quarters into the front doors of the blocks of apartments he had picked out as possibles.

He moved on eventually to the houses that fronted the Boulevard de Montparnasse itself, but here the buildings were offices, newer and more briskly busy.

The next day he was back again, sauntering past the façades, crossing the road to sit on a pavement bench under the trees and toying with a newspaper while he studied the upper floors. Five or six floors of stone façade, topped by a parapet, then the steeply sloping black-tiled roofs containing the attics, pierced by mansard windows, once the quarters of the servants, now the homes of the poorer pensionnaires. The roofs, and possibly the mansards themselves, would certainly be watched on the day. There might even be watchers on the roofs, crouching among the chimney stacks, their field glasses on the opposite windows and roofs. But the topmost floor below the attics would be high enough, providing one could sit well back into the darkness of the room not to be visible from across the street. The open window, in the sweltering heat of a Paris summer, would be natural enough.

But the further back one sat inside the room, the narrower would be the angle of fire sideways down into the forecourt of the station. For this reason the Jackal ruled out the third house into the rue de Rennes on each side of the street. The angle would be too narrow. That left him four houses to choose from. As the time of day he expected to fire would be the midafternoon, with the sun moving towards the west, but still high enough in the sky to shine over the top of the station roof into the windows of the houses on the east side of the street, he eventually chose those two on the west side. To prove it, he waited until four o'clock on July 29 and noticed that on the west side the topmost windows were receiving only a slanting ray from the sun, while it still fiercely lit the houses on the east.

The next day he noticed the concierge. It was his

third day sitting either at a cafe terrace or on a pavement bench, and he had chosen a bench a few feet from the doorways of the two blocks of flats that still interested him. Within a few feet, behind him and separated by the pavement down which pedestrians scurried endlessly, the concierge sat in her doorway and knitted. Once, from a nearby cafe, a waiter strolled over for a chat. He called the concierge Madame Berthe. It was a pleasant scene. The day was warm, the sun bright, reaching several feet into the dark doorway while it was still in the southeast and south, high in the sky over the station roof across the square.

She was a comfortable grandmotherly soul, and from the way she chirped *"Bonjour, monsieur"* to the people who occasionally entered or left her block, and from the cheerful *"Bonjour, Madame Berthe"* that she received each time in return, the watcher on the bench twenty feet away judged that she was well-liked. A good-natured body, and with compassion for the unfortunate of this world. For shortly after two in the afternoon a cat presented itself and within a few minutes, after diving into the dark recesses of her loge at the rear of the ground floor, Madame Berthe was back with a saucer of milk for the creature she referred to as her little Minet.

Shortly before four she bundled up her knitting, put it into one of the capacious pockets of her pinafore, and shuffled on slippered feet down the road to the bakery. The Jackal rose quietly from his bench and entered the apartment block. He chose the stairs rather than the lift and ran silently upwards.

The stairs ran round the lift shaft, and at each curve on the rear of the building, the stairs halted

to make room for a small half-landing. On each second
floor this landing gave access through a door in the
rear wall of the block to a steel fire escape. At the
sixth and top floor, apart from the attics, he opened
the rear door and looked down. The fire escape led
to an inner courtyard, around which were the rear
entrances to the other blocks that made up the corner
of the square behind him. On the far side of the courtyard the hollow square of buildings was penetrated
by a narrow covered alleyway leading towards the
north.

The Jackal closed the door quietly, replaced the
safety bar, and mounted the last half-flight to the
sixth floor. From here, at the end of the passage, a
humbler staircase led to the upper attics. There were
two doors in the passage giving access to flats overlooking the inner courtyard and two others for flats on
the front of the building. His sense of direction told
him either of these front flats contained windows looking down into the rue de Rennes, or half-sideways
onto the square and beyond it the forecourt of the
station. These were the windows he had been observ-
ing for so long from the street below.

One of the name plates next to the bell pushes of
the two front flats he now confronted bore the inscrip-
tion "Mlle Béranger." The other bore the name "M. et
Mme Charrier." He listened for a moment but there
was no sound from either of the flats. He examined the
locks; both were embedded in the woodwork, which
was thick and strong. The tongues of the locks on the
far side were probably of the thick bar of steel type so
favoured by the security-conscious French, and of the
double-locking variety. He would need keys, he real-

ised, of which Mme Berthe would certainly have one for each flat somewhere in her little loge.

A few minutes later he was running lightly down the stairs the way he had come. He had been in the block less than five minutes. The concierge was back. He caught a glimpse of her through the frosted glass pane in the door of her cubbyhole, then he had turned and was striding out of the arched entrance.

He turned left up the rue de Rennes, passed two other blocks of apartments, then the façade of a post office. At the corner of the block was a narrow street, the rue Littre. He turned into it, still following the wall of the post office. Where the building ended there was a narrow covered alleyway. The Jackal stopped to light a cigarette and while the flame flickered glanced sideways down the alley. It gave access to a rear entrance into the post office for the telephone exchange switchboard night staff. At the end of the tunnel was a sunlit courtyard. On the far side he could make out in the shadows the last rungs of the fire escape of the building he had just left. He had found his escape route.

At the end of the rue Littre he turned left again into the rue de Vaugirard and walked back to where it joined the Boulevard de Montparnasse. He had reached the corner and was looking up and down the main street for a free taxi, when a police motorcyclist swept into the road junction, jerked his machine onto its stand, and in the center of the junction began to halt the traffic. By shrill blasts on his whistle he stopped all the traffic coming out of the rue de Vaugirard, as well as that heading down the Boulevard from the direction of the station. The cars coming up the Boulevard from Duroc were imperiously waved into the right hand side of the road. He had barely got them all stopped when the distant wail of police sirens was heard from the direction of Duroc. Standing on the corner looking down the length of the Boulevard de Montparnasse, the Jackal saw five-hundred yards away a motorcade sweep into the Duroc junction from the Boulevard des Invalides and start to head towards him.

In the lead were two black-leather-clad motorcyclists, white helmets gleaming in the sun, sirens blaring. Behind them appeared the shark-like snouts of two DS 19 Citroens in the line astern. The policeman in front of the Jackal stood bolt upright facing away from him, left arm gesturing rigidly down towards the Avenue du Maine on the southern side of the junction, right arm bent across the chest, palm downwards, indicating priority passage for the approaching motorcade.

Heeling over to the right, the two motorcyclists swept into the Avenue du Maine, followed by the two limousines. In the back of the first one, sitting upright behind the driver and the A.D.C., staring rigidly in front of himself, was a tall figure in a charcoal-grey suit. The Jackal had a fleeting glimpse of the uptilted head and the unmistakable nose before the convoy was gone. The next time I see your face, he silently told the departed image, it will be in closer focus through a telescopic sight. Then he found a taxi and was taken back to his hotel.

Farther down the road, near the exit from the Duroc Métro station from which she had just emerged, another figure had watched the passing of the President with more than usual interest. She had been about to cross the road when a policeman had waved her back. Seconds later the motorcade swept out of the Boulevard des Invalides across the expanse of cobbles and into the Boulevard de Montparnasse. She too had seen the distinctive profile in the back of the first Citroen, and her eyes had glowed with a passionate fervour. Even when the cars had gone, she stared after them, until she saw the policeman looking her up and down. Hastily she had resumed her crossing of the road.

Jacqueline Dumas was then twenty-six years old and of considerable beauty, which she knew how to show off to its best advantage, for she worked as a beautician in an expensive salon behind the Champs Elysées. On the evening of July 30 she was hurrying home to her little flat off the Place de Breteuil to get ready for her evening's date. Within a few hours she knew she would be naked in the arms of the lover she hated, and she wanted to look her best.

A few years earlier the thing that mattered most in her life was her next date. Hers was a good family, a tight-knit group with her father working as a respectable clerk in a banking house, mother being a typical middle-class French housewife and Maman, she finishing her beautician's course, and Jean-Claude doing his National Service. The family lived in the outer suburb of Le Vésinet, not in the best part, but a nice house all the same.

The telegram from the Ministry of the Armed Forces had come one day at breakfast towards the end of 1959. It said that the Minister was required with infinite regret to inform Monsieur and Madame Armand Dumas of the death in Algeria of their son Jean-Claude, private soldier in the First Colonial Paratroops. His personal effects would be returned to the bereaved family as soon as possible.

For some time Jacqueline's private world disintegrated. Nothing seemed to make sense, not the quiet security of the family at Le Vésinet or the chatter of the other girls at the salon on the charms of Yves Montand or the latest dance craze imported from America, le Rock. The only thing that seemed to pound through her mind was that little Jean-Claude, her darling baby brother, so vulnerable and gentle, hating war and violence, wanting only to be alone with his books, scarcely more than a boy whom she loved to spoil, had been shot dead in a battle in some God-forsaken *wadi* in Algeria. She began to hate. It was the Arabs, the loathsome, dirty, cowardly "melons" who had done it.

Then François came. Quite suddenly one winter morning he turned up at the house on a Sunday when the parents were away visiting relatives. It was December, there was snow in the avenue and crusted onto the garden path. Other people were pale and pinched, and François looked tanned and fit. He asked if he could speak to Mademoiselle Jacqueline. She said, *"C'est moi-même"* and what did he want? He replied he commanded the platoon in which one Jean-Claude Dumas, private soldier, had been killed, and he bore a letter. She asked him in.

The letter had been written some weeks before Jean-Claude died, and he had kept it in his inside pocket during the patrol in the *djebel* looking for a

band of fellagha who had wiped out a settler family.
They had not found the guerrillas, but had run into a
battalion of the ALN, the trained troops of the Algerian national movement, the FLN. There had been
a bitter skirmish in the half light of dawn and Jean-
Claude had taken a bullet through the lungs. He gave
the letter to the platoon commander before he died.

Jacqueline read the letter and cried a little. It said
nothing of the last weeks, just chatter about the barracks at Constantine, the assault courses, and the disci-
pline. The rest she learned from François: the pull-back
through the scrub for four miles while the outflanking
ALN closed in, the repeated calls on the radio for air
support, and at eight o'clock the arrival of the fighter-
bombers with their screaming engines and thundering
rockets. And how her brother, who had volunteered
for one of the toughest regiments to prove he was a
man, had died like one, coughing blood over the knees
of a corporal in the lee of a rock.

François had been very gentle with her. As a man
he was hard as the earth of the colonial province in
whose four years of war he had been forged as a professional soldier. But he was very gentle with the sister of one of his platoon. She liked him for that and
accepted his offer to dine in Paris. Besides, she feared
her parents would return and surprise them. She did
not want them to hear how Jean-Claude had died, for
both had managed to numb themselves to the loss in
the intervening two months and somehow carry on as
usual. Over dinner she swore the lieutenant to silence
and he agreed.

But for her the curiosity became insatiable, to know
about the Algerian war, what really happened, what

it really stood for, what the politicians were really
playing at. General de Gaulle had come to the presidency from the premiership the previous January,
swept into the Elysée on a tide of patriotic fervour as
the man who would finish the war and still keep Algeria French. It was from François that she first heard
the man her father adored referred to as a traitor to
France.

They spent François's leave together, she meeting
him every evening after work in the salon to which
she had gone in January 1960 from the training school.
He told her of the betrayal of the French Army, of the
Paris government's secret negotiations with the im-
prisoned Ahmed Ben Bella, leader of the FLN, and of
the pending handover of Algeria to the melons. He
had returned to his war in the second half of January,
and she had snatched a brief time alone with him
when he managed to get a week's leave in August in
Marseilles. She had waited for him, building him in
her private thoughts into the symbol of all that was
good and clean and virile in French young manhood.
She had waited throughout the autumn and winter of
1960, with his picture on her bedside table throughout
the day and evening, pushed down her nightdress and
clasped to her belly while she slept.

In his last leave of the spring of 1961 he had come
again to Paris, and when they walked down the boulevards, he in uniform, she in her prettiest dress, she
thought he was the strongest, broadest, handsomest
man in the city. One of the other girls at work had
seen them, and the next day the salon was a-buzz with
news of Jacqui's beautiful "para." She was not there;

she had taken her annual holiday to be with him all the time.

François was excited. There was something in the wind. The news of the talks with the FLN was public knowledge. The Army, the real Army, would not stand for it much longer, he promised. That Algeria should remain French was, for both of them, the combat-hardened twenty-seven-year-old officer and the adoring twenty-three-year-old mother-to-be, an article of faith.

François never knew about the baby. He returned to Algeria in March 1961 and on April 21 several units of the French Army mutinied against the Metropolitan government. The First Colonial Paras were in the mutiny almost to a man. Only a handful of conscripts scuttled out of barracks and made rendezvous at the Prefet's office. The professionals let them go. Fighting broke out between the mutineers and the loyal regiments within a week. Early in May François was shot in a skirmish with a loyalist Army unit.

Jacqueline, who had expected no letters from April onwards, suspected nothing until she was told the news in July. She quietly took a flat in a cheap suburb of Paris and tried to gas herself. She failed because the room had too many gas leaks, but lost the baby. Her parents took her away with them for their August annual holidays, and she seemed to have recovered by the time they returned. In December she became an active underground worker for the OAS.

Her motives were simple: François, and after him Jean-Claude. They should be avenged, no matter by what means, no matter what the cost to herself or anyone else. Apart from this passion, she was without an ambition in the world. Her only complaint was that she could not do more than run errands, carry messages, occasionally a slab of plastic explosive stuffed into a loaf in her shopping bag. She was convinced she could do more. Did not the "flics" on the corners, carrying out snap searches of passers-by after one of the regular bombings of cafes and cinemas, inevitably let her pass after one flutter of her long dark eyelashes, one pout of her lips?

After the Petit-Clamart affair one of the would-be killers had spent three nights at her flat off the Place de Breteuil while on the run. It had been her big moment, but then he had moved on. A month later he had been caught, but had said nothing of his stay with her. Perhaps he had forgotten. But to be on the safe side, her cell leader instructed her to do no more work for the OAS for a few months, until the heat wore off. It was January 1963 when she began carrying messages again.

And so it went on, until in July a man came to see her. He was accompanied by her cell leader, who showed him great deference. He had no name. Would she be prepared to undertake a special job for the Organisation? Of course. Perhaps dangerous, certainly distasteful? No matter.

Three days later she was shown a man emerging from a block of flats. They were sitting in a parked car. She was told who he was, and what was his position. And what she had to do.

By mid-July they had met, apparently by chance, when she sat next to the man in a restaurant and smiled shyly at him while asking for the loan of the salt cellar on his table. He had spoken, she had been reserved, modest. The reaction had been the right one. Her demureness interested him. Without seeming to, the conversation blossomed, the man leading, she docilely following. Within a fortnight they were having an affair.

She knew enough about men to be able to judge the basic types of appetites. Her new lover was accustomed to easy conquests, experienced women. She played shy, attentive, but chaste, reserved on the outside with just a hint now and again that her superb body was one day not to be completely wasted. The bait worked. For the man the ultimate conquest became a matter of top priority.

In late July her cell leader told her their cohabitation should begin soon. The snag was the man's wife and two children, who lived with him. On July 29 they left for the family's country house in the Loire Valley, while the husband was required to stay on in Paris for his work. Within a few minutes of his family's departure he was on the phone to the salon to insist that Jacqueline and he should dine alone at his flat the following night.

Once inside her flat, Jacqueline Dumas glanced at her watch. She had three hours to get ready, and although she intended to be meticulous in her preparations, two hours would suffice. She stripped and showered, drying herself in front of the full-length mirror on the back of the wardrobe door, watching the towel run over her skin with unfeeling detachment, raising her arms high to lift the full, rose-nippled breasts with none of the feeling of anticipatory delight she used to feel when she knew they would soon be caressed in François's palms.

She thought dully of the coming night, and her belly tightened with revulsion. She would, she vowed, she would go through with it, no matter what kind of loving he wanted. From a compartment in the back of the bureau she took her photo of François, looking out of the frame with the same old ironic half-smile he had always smiled when he saw her flying the length of the station platform to meet him. The picture's soft brown hair, the cool buff uniform with the hard-muscled pectorals beneath, against which she loved once long ago to rest her face, and the steel paratrooper's wings, so cool on a burning cheek. They were all still there—in celluloid. She lay on the bed and held François above her looking down as he did when they made love, asking superfluously, *"Alors, petite, tu veux? . . ."* She always whispered, *"Oui, tu sais bien . . ."* And then it happened.

When she closed her eyes she could feel him inside her, hard and hot and throbbing strength, and hear the softly growled endearments in her ear, the final stifled command *"Viens, viens . . ."* which she never disobeyed.

She opened her eyes and stared at the ceiling, holding the warmed glass of the portrait to her breasts. "François," she breathed, "help me, please help me tonight."

On the last day of the month the Jackal was busy. He spent the morning at the Flea Market, wandering from stall to stall with a cheap holdall by his side. He bought a greasy black beret, a pair of well-scuffed shoes, some not-too-clean trousers, and, after much searching, a long once-military greatcoat. He would have preferred one of lighter material, but military greatcoats are seldom tailored for midsummer and in the French Army are made of Duffel. But it was long enough, even on him, stretching to well below the knee, which was the important thing.

As he was on his way out, his eye was caught by a stall full of medals, mostly stained with age. He bought a collection, together with a booklet describing French military medals with faded colour pictures of the ribbons and captions telling the reader for which campaigns or for what kind of acts of gallantry the various medals were awarded.

After lunching lightly at Queenie's on the rue Royale he slipped round the corner to his hotel, paid his bill, and packed. His new purchases went into the bottom of one of his two expensive suitcases. From the collection of medals and with the help of the guide-book he made up a bar of decorations starting with the Médaille Militaire for courage in the face of the enemy, and adding the Médaille de la Libération and five campaign medals awarded to those who fought in the Free French Forces during the Second World War. He awarded himself decorations for Bir Hakeim, Libya, Tunisia, D-Day, and the Second Armoured Division of General Philippe Leclerc.

The rest of the medals, and the book, he dumped separately into two waste paper baskets attached to lamp posts up the Boulevard Malesherbes. The hotel desk clerk informed him there was the excellent Etoile du Nord express for Brussels leaving the Gare du Nord at 5:15. This he caught, and dined well, arriving in Brussels in the last hours of July.

six

The letter for Viktor Kowalski arrived in Rome the following morning. The giant corporal was crossing the foyer of the hotel on his return from picking up the daily mail from the post office when one of the bell-hops called after him, "*Signor, per un favore . . .*"

He turned, as surly as ever. The wop was one he did not recognise, but there was nothing unusual in that. He never noticed them as he bulled his way across the floor of the foyer towards the lift. The dark-eyed young man held a letter in his hand as he came to Kowalski's side.

"*E una lettera, signor. Per un Signor Kowalski . . . non cognosco questo signor. . . . E forse un francese . . .*"

Kowalski did not understand a word of the babble of Italian, but he got the sense and he recognised his own name, badly pronounced though it was. He snatched the letter from the man's hand and stared at the scrawled name and address. He was registered under another name, and not being a reading man had failed to notice that five days earlier a Paris newspaper had had a scoop announcing that three of the top men of the OAS were now holed up on the top floor of the hotel.

So far as he was concerned, no one was supposed to know where he was. And yet the letter intrigued him. He did not often receive letters, and as with most simple people the arrival of one was an important event. He had cottoned from the Italian, now standing with spaniel eyes by his side staring up as if he, Kowalski, was the fount of human knowledge who would solve the dilemma, that none of the desk staff had heard of a guest of that name and did not know what to do with the letter.

Kowalski looked down. *"Bon. Je vais demander,"* he said loftily. The Italian's brow did not uncrease.

"Demander, demander," repeated Kowalski, pointing upwards through the ceiling.

The Italian saw the light. *"Ah, sì. Domandare. Prego, Signor. Tante grazie . . ."*

Kowalski strode away leaving the Italian gesticulating his gratitude. Taking the lift to the eighth floor, he emerged to find himself confronted by the desk-duty man in the corridor, automatic drawn and cocked. For a second the two stared at each other. Then the other slipped on the safety catch and pocketed the gun. He could see only Kowalski, no one else in the lift. It was purely routine, happening every time the lights above the lift doors indicated that the ascending lift was coming beyond the seventh floor.

Apart from the desk-duty man, there was another facing the fire escape door at the end of the corridor and another at the head of the stairs. Both the stairs and the fire escape were booby-trapped, although the management did not know this, and the booby-traps could be rendered harmless only when the current to the detonators was cut off from a switch under the desk in the corridor.

The fourth man on the day shift was on the roof above the ninth floor where the chiefs lived, but in case of attack there were three others now asleep in their rooms down the corridor who had been on night shift, but who would awake and be operational in a few seconds if anything happened. On the eighth floor the lift doors had been welded closed from the outside, but even if the light above the lift on the eighth floor indicated the lift was heading right for the top it was a sign for a general alarm. It had only happened once and then by accident, when a bell-hop delivering a tray of drinks had pressed the button for "Nine." He had been quickly discouraged from this practice.

The desk man telephoned upstairs to announce the arrival of the mail, then signalled to Kowalski to go up. The ex-corporal had already stuffed the letter addressed to himself into his inside pocket while the mail for his chiefs was in a steel case chained to his left wrist. Both the lock for the chain and for the flat case were spring-loaded, and only Rodin had the keys. A few minutes later the OAS colonel had unlocked both, and Kowalski returned to his room to sleep before relieving the desk man in the late afternoon.

In his room back on the eighth floor he finally read his letter, starting with the signature. He was surprised that it should be from Kovacs, whom he had not seen for a year and who hardly knew how to write, as Kowalski had some difficulty in reading. But by dint of application he deciphered the letter. It was not long.

Kovacs began by saying that he had seen a newspaper story on the day of writing, which a friend had read aloud to him, saying that Rodin, Montclair, and Casson were hiding at that hotel in Rome. He had supposed his old friend Kowalski would be with them, hence was writing on the offchance of reaching him.

Several paragraphs followed to the effect that things were getting tough in France these days, with the *flics* everywhere asking for papers, and orders still coming through for smash-and-grab raids on jewellers. He had personally been in four, said Kovacs, and it was no joke, particularly when one had to hand over the proceeds. He had done better in Budapest in the good old days, even though these had only lasted for a fortnight.

The last paragraph recounted that Kovacs had met Michel some weeks before, and Michel had said that he had been talking to JoJo, who had said little Sylvie was sick with Luke-something; anyway it was to do with her blood having gone wrong, but that he Kovacs hoped she would soon be all right and Viktor should not worry.

But Viktor did worry. It worrried him badly to think that little Sylvie was ill. There was not a great deal that had ever penetrated into the heart of Viktor Kowalski in his thirty-six violent years. He had been twelve years old when the Germans invaded Poland and one year older when his parents were taken away in a dark van. Old enough to know what his sister was doing in the big hotel behind the cathedral that had been taken over by the Germans and was visited by so many of their officers, which so upset his parents that they protested to the military governor's office. Old enough to join the partisans. He had killed his first German at fifteen. He was seventeen when the Russians came, but his parents had always hated and feared them, and told him terrible tales about what

they did to Poles, so he left the partisans, who were
later executed on orders of the commissar, and went
westwards like a hunted animal towards Czechoslo-
vakia. Later it was Austria and a Displaced Persons
camp for the tall raw-boned gangling youth who spoke
only Polish and was weak from hunger. They thought
he was another of the harmless flotsam of post-war
Europe. On American food his strength returned. He
broke out one spring night in 1946 and hitched south
towards Italy, and thence into France in company
with another Pole he had met in DP camp who spoke
French. In Marseilles he broke into a shop one night,
killed the proprietor, who disturbed him, and was on
the run again. His companion left him, advising Viktor
there was only one place to go—the Foreign Legion.
He signed on the next morning and was in Sidi-Bel-
Abbes before the police investigation in war-torn Marseilles was really off the ground. The Mediterranean
city was still a big import-base for American foodstuffs, and murders committed for these foodstuffs
were not uncommon. The case was dropped in a few
days when no immediate suspect came to light. By
the time he learned this, however, Kowalski was a
legionnaire.

He was nineteen and at first the old sweats called
him *"petit bonhomme."* Then he showed them how
he could kill, and they called him Kowalski.

Six years in Indochina finished off what might have
been left in him of a normally adjusted individual,
and after that Kowalski was sent to Algeria. In between he had a posting to a weapons training course
for six months outside Marseilles. There he met Julie,
a tiny but vicious scrubber in a dockside bar, who had

been having trouble with her mec. Kowalski knocked the man six metres across the bar and out cold for ten hours with one blow. The man enunciated oddly for years afterwards, so badly was the lower mandible shattered.

Julie liked the enormous legionnaire, and for several months he became her "protector" by night, escorting her home after work to the sleazy attic in the Vieux Port. There was a lot of lust, particularly on her side, but no love between them, and even less when she discovered she was pregnant. The child, she told him, was his, and he may have believed it because he wanted to. She also told him she did not want the baby, and knew an old woman who would get rid of it for her. Kowalski clouted her and told her if she did that he would kill her. Three months later he had to return to Algeria. In the meantime he had become friendly with another Polish ex-legionnaire, Josef Grzybowski, known as JoJo the Pole, who had been invalided out of Indochina and had settled with a jolly widow running a snack-stall on wheels up and down the platforms at the main station. Since their marriage in 1953 they had run it together, JoJo limping along behind his wife taking the money and giving out the change while his wife dispensed the snacks. On the evenings when he was not working, JoJo liked to frequent the bars haunted by the legionnaires from the nearby barracks to talk over old times. Most of them were youngsters, recruits since his own days at Tourane, Indochina, but one evening he ran into Kowalski.

It was to JoJo that Kowalski had turned for advice

about the baby. JoJo agreed with him. They had both
been Catholics once.

"She wants to have the kid done in," said Viktor.

"*Salope*," said JoJo.

"Cow," agreed Viktor. They drank some more, staring moodily into the mirror at the back of the bar.

"Not fair to the kid," said Viktor.

"Not right," agreed JoJo.

"Never had a kid before," said Viktor after some
thought.

"Nor me, even being married and all," replied JoJo.

Somewhere in the small hours of the morning, very
drunk, they agreed on their plan and drank to it with
the solemnity of the truly intoxicated. The next morning JoJo remembered his pledge, but could not think
how to break the news to Madame. It took him three
days. He skated warily round the subject once or
twice, then blurted it out while he and the missis were
in bed. To his amazement, Madame was delighted.
And so it was arranged.

In due course Viktor returned to Algeria, then to
rejoin Major Rodin, who now commanded the battalion, and to a new war. In Marseilles JoJo and his wife,
by a mixture of threats and cajolement, supervised
the pregnant Julie. By the time Viktor left Marseilles
she was already four months gone and it was too late
for an abortion, as JoJo menacingly pointed out to the
pimp with the broken jaw who soon came hanging
around. This individual had become wary of crossing
legionnaires, even old veterans with gammy legs, so
he obscenely foreswore his former source of income
and looked elsewhere.

Julie was brought to bed in late 1955 and produced

a girl, blue-eyed and golden-haired. Adoption papers
were duly filed by JoJo and his wife, with the concurrence of Julie. The adoption went through. Julie
went back to her old life, and the JoJos had themselves
a daughter, whom they named Sylvie. They informed
Viktor by letter, and in his barracks bed he was
strangely pleased. But he did not tell anyone. He had
never actually owned anything within his memory
that, if revealed, had not been taken away from him.

Nevertheless, three years later, before a long combat mission in the Algerian hills, the chaplain had
proposed to him that he might like to make a will.
The idea had never even occurred to him before. He
had never had anything to leave behind for one thing,
since he spent all his accumulated pay in the bars and
whorehouses of the cities when given his rare periods
of leave, and what he had belonged to the Legion.
But the chaplain assured him that in the modern Legion a will was perfectly in order, so with considerable assistance he made one, leaving all his worldly
goods and chattels to the daughter of one Josef Grzybowski, former legionnaire, presently of Marseilles.
Eventually a copy of this document, along with the
rest of his dossier, was filed with the archives of the Ministry of the Armed Forces in Paris. When Kowalski's
name became known to the French security forces in
connection with the Bone and Constantine terrorism
in 1961, this dossier was unearthed along with many
others and came to the attention of Colonel Rolland's
Action Service at the Porte des Lilas. A visit was paid
to the Grzybowskis, and the story came out. Kowalski
never learned this.

He saw his daughter twice in his life, once in 1957

after taking a bullet in the thigh and being sent on convalescent leave to Marseilles, and again in 1960 when he came to the city when on escort duty for Lieutenant Colonel Rodin, who had to attend a court martial as a witness. The first time the little girl was two, the next time four and a half. Kowalski arrived laden with presents for the JoJos and toys for Sylvie. They got on very well together, the small child and her bear-like Uncle Viktor. But he never mentioned her to anyone else, not even Rodin.

And now she was sick with Luke-something, and Kowalski worried a lot throughout the rest of the morning. After lunch he was upstairs to have the steel etui for the mail chained to his wrist. Rodin was expecting an important letter from France containing further details of the total sum of money amassed by the series of robberies, and he wanted Kowalski to pay a second visit to the post office for the afternoon mail arrivals.

"What," the corporal suddenly blurted out, "is Luke-something?"

Rodin, attaching the chain to his wrist, looked up in surprise.

"I've never heard of him," he replied.

"It's a malady of the blood," explained Kowalski.

From the other side of the room where he was reading a glossy magazine Casson laughed.

"Leukaemia, you mean," he said.

"Well, what is it, monsieur?"

"It's cancer," replied Casson, "cancer of the blood."

Kowalski looked at Rodin in front of him. He did not trust civilians.

"They can cure it, the *toubibs, mon colonel?*"

"No, Kowalski, it's fatal. There's no cure. Why?"

"Nothing," mumbled Kowalski, "just something I read."

Then he left. If Rodin was surprised that his bodyguard who had never been known to read anything more complex than standing orders of the day had come across that word in a book, he did not show it and the matter was soon swept from his mind. For the afternoon's mail brought the letter he was waiting for, to say that the combined OAS bank accounts in Switzerland now contained over $250,000.

Rodin was satisfied as he sat down to write and despatch the instructions to the bankers transferring that sum to the account of his hired assassin. For the balance he had no qualms. With President de Gaulle dead, there would be no delay before the industrialists and bankers of the extreme Right-wing, who had financed the OAS in its earlier and more successful days, produced the other $250,000. The same men who had replied to his approaches for a further advance of cash only a few weeks earlier with mealy-mouthed excuses that the "lack of progress and initiative shown over recent months by the forces of patriotism" had decreased their chances of ever seeing a return on previous investments, would be clamouring for the honour of backing the soldiers who shortly afterwards would become the new rulers of a re-born France.

He finished the instructions to the bankers as darkness fell, but when he saw the orders Rodin had written instructing the Swiss bankers to pay over the money to the Jackal, Casson objected. He argued that one vitally important thing they had all three promised their Englishman was that he would have a

contact in Paris capable of supplying him constantly
with the latest accurate information about the move-
ments of the French President, along with any changes
in the security routines surrounding him that might
occur. These could, indeed probably would, be of vital importance to the assassin. To inform him of the
transfer of the money at this stage, Casson reasoned,
would be to encourage him to go into action prema-
turely. Whenever the man intended to strike was obviously his own choice, but a few extra days would
make no difference. What might very well make a
difference between success and another, certainly the
last, failure would be the question of information provided to the killer.

He, Casson, had received word that very morning
in the mail that his chief representative in Paris had
succeeded in placing an agent very close to one of
the men in de Gaulle's immediate entourage. A few
days more would be necessary before this agent was
in a position to acquire consistently reliable information as to the General's whereabouts and above all his
travelling intentions and his public appearances,
neither of which were being publicly announced in
advance any more. Would Rodin therefore please stay
his hand for a few more days until Casson was in a
position to supply the assassin with a telephone number in Paris from which he could receive the information that would be vital to his mission?

Rodin reflected long over Casson's argument, and
eventually agreed that he was right. Neither man could
be aware of the Jackal's intentions, and in fact the
transmission of the instructions to the bankers, followed later by the letter to London containing the

Paris telephone number, would not have caused the assassin to alter any detail of his schedule. Neither terrorist in Rome could know that the killer had already chosen his day and was proceeding with his planning and contingency precautions with clockwork precision.

Sitting up on the roof in the hot Roman night, his bulky form merging into the shadow of the air conditioner ventilation stack, the Colt 45 resting easily in a practised hand, Kowalski worried about a little girl in a bed in Marseilles with Luke-something in her blood. Shortly before dawn he had an idea. He remembered that the last time he had seen JoJo in 1960, the ex-legionnaire had talked of getting a telephone in his flat.

On the morning that Kowalski received his letter, the Jackal left the Amigo hotel in Brussels and took a taxi to a corner of the street where M. Goossens lived. He had rung the armourer over breakfast in the name of Duggan, which was how Goossens knew him, and the appointment was for 11 a.m. He arrived at the corner of the street at 10:30 and spent half an hour surveying the street from behind a newspaper on a kerbside bench in the little public gardens at the end of the street.

It seemed quiet enough. He presented himself at the door at 11 sharp, and Goossens let him in and led him to the little office off the hallway. After the Jackal had passed, M. Goossens carefully locked the front door and put it on the chain. Inside the office the Englishman turned to the armourer.

"Any problems?" he asked. The Belgian looked embarrassed.

"Well, yes, I am afraid so."

The assassin surveyed him coldly, with no expression on his face, the eyes half closed and sullen.

"You told me that if I came back on August 1 I could have the gun by August 4 to take home with me," he said.

"That's perfectly true, and I assure you the problem is not with the gun," said the Belgian. "Indeed the gun is ready, and frankly I regard it as one of my masterpieces, a beautiful specimen. The trouble has been with the other product, which evidently had to be made from scratch. Let me show you."

On top of the desk lay a flat case about two feet long by eighteen inches broad four inches deep. M. Goossens opened the case and the Jackal looked down on it as the upper half fell back to the table.

It was like a flat tray, divided into carefully shaped compartments, each exactly the shape of the component of the rifle that it contained.

"It was not the original case, you understand," explained M. Goossens. "That would have been much too long. I made the case myself. It all fits."

It fitted very compactly. Along the top of the open tray was the barrel and breech, the whole no longer than eighteen inches. The Jackal lifted it out and examined it. It was very light, and looked rather like a submachine gun barrel. The breech contained a narrow bolt which was closed shut. It ended at the back with a knurled grip no larger than the breech into which the rest of the bolt was fitted.

The Englishman took the knurled end of the bolt

between forefinger and thumb of the right hand, gave it a sharp turn anti-clockwise. The bolt unlocked itself and rolled over in its groove. As he pulled, the bolt slid back to reveal the gleaming tray into which the bullet would lie, and the dark hole at the rear end of the barrel. He rammed the bolt back home and twisted it clockwise. Smoothly it locked into place.

Just below the rear end of the bolt an extra disc of steel had been expertly welded onto the mechanism. It was half an inch thick but less than an inch round, and in the top part of the disc was a cutout crescent to allow free passage backwards of the bolt. In the centre of the rear face of the disc was a single hole half an inch across; the inside of this hole had been threaded as if to take a screw.

"That's for the frame of the stock," said the Belgian quietly.

The Jackal noticed that where the wooden stock of the original rifle had been removed no trace remained except the slight flanges running along the underside of the breech where the woodwork had once fitted. The two holes made by the retaining screws that had secured the wooden stock to the rifle had been expertly plugged and blued. He turned the rifle over and examined the underside. There was a narrow slit beneath the breech. Through it he could see the underside of the bolt that contained the firing pin which fired the bullet. Through both slits protruded the stump of the trigger. It had been sawn off flush with the surface of the steel breech.

Welded to the stump of the old trigger was a tiny knob of metal, also with a threaded hole in it. Silently M. Goossens handed him a small sliver of steel, an

inch long, curved and with one end threaded. He
fitted the threaded end into the hole and twiddled it
quickly with forefinger and thumb. When it was tight
the new trigger protruded below the breech.

By his side the Belgian reached back into the tray
and held up a single narrow steel rod, one end of it
threaded.

"The first part of the stock assembly," he said.

The assassin fitted the end of the steel rod into a
hole at the rear of the breech and wound it till it was
firm. In profile the steel rod seemed to emerge from
the back of the gun and cant downwards at thirty degrees. Two inches from the threaded end, up near the
mechanism of the rifle, the steel rod had been lightly
flattened, and in the centre of the flattened portion a
hole had been drilled at an angle to the line of the
rod. This hole now faced directly backwards. Goossens held up a second and shorter steel rod.

"The upper strut," he said.

This too was fitted into place. The two rods stuck
out backwards, the upper one at a much shallower
angle to the line of the barrel so that the two rods
separated from each other like two sides of a narrow
triangle with no base. Goossens produced the base. It
was curved, about five or six inches long, and heavily
padded with black leather. At each end of the shoulder guard, or butt of the rifle, was a small hole.

"There's nothing to screw here," said the armourer,
"just press it onto the ends of the rods."

The Englishman fitted the end of each steel rod
into the appropriate hole and smacked the butt home.
The rifle now, when seen in profile, looked more normal, with a trigger and a complete stock sketched in

outline by the upper and lower strut and the base plate. The Jackal lifted the butt-plate onto his shoulder, left hand gripping the underside of the barrel, right forefinger round the trigger, left eye closed, and right eye squinting down the barrel. He aimed at the far wall and squeezed the trigger. There was a soft click from inside the breech.

He turned to the Belgian, who held what looked like a ten-inch long black tube in each hand.

"Silencer," said the Englishman. He took the proffered tube and studied the end of the rifle barrel. It had been finely "tapped" or threaded. He slipped the wider end of the silencer over the barrel and wound it quickly round and round until it would go no more. The silencer protruded off the end of the barrel like a long sausage. He held his hand out from his side and M. Goossens slipped the telescopic sight into it.

Along the top of the barrel were a series of pairs of grooves gouged into the metal. Into these the sprung clips on the underside of the telescope fitted, ensuring the telescopic sight and the barrel were exactly parallel. On the right hand side and on the top of the telescope were tiny grub screws for adjusting the crossed hairs inside the sight. Again the Englishman held up the rifle and squinted as he took aim. To a casual glance he might have been an elegant, check-suited English gentleman in a Piccadilly gunshop trying out a new sporting gun. But what had been ten minutes before a handful of odd-looking components was no sporting gun any more; it was a high-velocity, long-range, fully silenced assassin's rifle. The Jackal put it down. He turned to the Belgian and nodded, satisfied.

"Good," he said, "very good. I congratulate you. A beautiful piece of work."

M. Goossens beamed.

"There still remains the question of zeroing the sights and firing some practise shots. Do you have any shells?"

The Belgian reached into the drawer of the desk and pulled out a box of a hundred bullets. The seals of the packet had been broken, and six shells were missing.

"These are for practice," said the armourer. "I have taken six others out for converting them to explosive tips."

The Jackal poured a handful of the shells into his hand and looked at them. They seemed terribly small for the job one of them would have to do, but he noticed they were the extra long type of that calibre, the extra explosive charge giving the bullet a very high velocity and consequently increased accuracy and killing power. The tips too were pointed, where most hunting bullets are snub-nosed, and where hunting bullets have a dull leaden head, these were tipped with cupronickel. They were competition rifle bullets of the same calibre as the hunting gun he held.

"Where are the real shells?" asked the assassin.

M. Goossens went to the desk again and produced a screw of tissue paper.

"Normally, of course, I keep these in a very safe place," he explained, "but since I knew you were coming, I got them out."

He undid the screw of paper and poured the contents out onto the white blotter. At first glance the bullets looked the same as those the Englishman was pouring from his cupped hand back into the cardboard box. When he had finished he took one of the bullets off the blotter and examined it closely.

From a small area around the extreme tip of the bullet the cupronickel had been finely sanded away to expose the lead inside. The sharp tip of the bullet had been slightly blunted, and into the nose a tiny hole had been drilled down the length of the nose-cap for a quarter of an inch. Into this aperture a droplet of mercury was poured, then the hole was tamped with a drop of liquid lead. After the lead had hardened, it too was filed and papered until the original pointed shape of the bullet tip had been exactly re-created.

The Jackal knew about these bullets, although he had never had occasion to use one. Far too complex to be used en masse except if factory-produced, banned by the Geneva Convention, more vicious than the simple dum-dum, the explosive bullet would go off like a small grenade when it hit the human body. On firing, the droplet of mercury would be slammed back in its cavity by the forward rush of the bullet, as when a car passenger is pressed into his seat by a violent acceleration. As soon as the bullet struck flesh, gristle, or bone, it would experience a sudden deceleration.

The effect on the mercury would be to hurl the droplet forwards towards the plugged front of the bullet. Here its onward rush would rip away the tip of the slug, splaying the lead outwards like the fingers of an open hand or the petals of a blossoming flower. In this shape the leaded projectile would tear through nerve and tissue, ripping, cutting, slicing, leaving fragments of itself over an area the size of a tea-saucer. Hitting the head, such a bullet would not emerge, but would demolish everything inside the cranium, forcing the bone-shell to fragment.

The assassin put the bullet carefully back on the tissue paper. Beside him the mild little man who had designed it was looking up at him quizzically.

"They look all right to me. You are evidently a craftsman, M. Goossens. What then is the problem?"

"It is the other, monsieur. The tubes. These have been more difficult to fabricate than I had imagined. First I used aluminum as you suggested. But please understand I acquired and perfected the gun first. That is why I only got around to doing the other things a few days ago. I had hoped it would be relatively simple, with my skill and the machinery I have in my workshop.

"But in order to keep the tubes as narrow as possible, I bought very thin metal. It was too thin. When threaded on my machine for later assembly piece by piece, it was like tissue paper. It bent when the slightest pressure was put upon it. In order to keep the inside measurements big enough to accommodate the breech of the rifle at its widest part, and yet get thicker-metalled tubes, I had to produce something that simply would not look natural. So I decided on stainless steel.

"It was the only thing. It looks just like aluminum, but slightly heavier. Being stronger, it can be thinner. It can take the thread and still be tough enough not to bend. Of course, it is a harder metal to work, and it takes time. I began yesterday . . ."

"All right. What you say is logical. The point is, I need it, and I need it perfect. When?"

The Belgian shrugged. "It is difficult to say. I have all the basic components, unless other problems crop up. Which I doubt. I am certain the last technical problems are licked. Five days, six days. A week perhaps . . ."

The Englishman showed no signs of his annoyance. The face remained impassive, studying the Belgian as he completed his explanations. When he finished, the other was still thinking.

"All right," he said at last. "It will mean an alteration of my travelling plans. But perhaps not as serious as I thought the last time I was here. That depends to a certain degree on the results of a telephone call I shall have to make. In any event, it will be necessary for me to acclimatise myself to the gun, and that may as well be done in Belgium as anywhere else. But I shall need the gun and the undoctored shells, plus one of the doctored ones. Also, I shall need some peace and quiet in which to practise. Where would one pick in this country to test a new rifle in conditions of complete secrecy? Over a hundred and thirty to a hundred and fifty metres in the open air?"

M. Goossens thought for a moment. "In the forest of the Ardennes," he said at length. "There are great reaches of forest there where a man may be alone for several hours. You could be there and back in a day. Today is Thursday, the weekend starts tomorrow and the woods might be too full of people picnicking. I would suggest Monday, the fifth. By Tuesday or Wednesday, I hope to have the rest of the job finished."

The Englishman nodded, satisfied.

"All right. I think I had better take the gun and the

ammunition now. I shall contact you again on Tuesday or Wednesday next week."

The Belgian was about to protest when the customer forestalled him.

"I believe I still owe you some seven hundred pounds. Here"—he dropped another few bundles of notes onto the blotter—"is a further five hundred. The outstanding two hundred pounds you will receive when I get the rest of the equipment."

"*Merci, monsieur*," said the armourer, scooping the five bundles of twenty five-pound notes into his pocket. Piece by piece he disassembled the rifle, placing each component carefully into its green baize-lined compartment in the carrying case. The single explosive bullet the assassin had asked for was wrapped in a separate piece of tissue paper and slotted into the case beside the cleaning rags and brushes. When the case was closed, he proffered it and the box of shells to the Englishman, who pocketed the shells and kept the neat attaché case in his hand.

M. Goossens showed him politely out.

The Jackal arrived back at his hotel in time for a late lunch. First he placed the case containing the gun carefully in the bottom of the wardrobe, locked it, and pocketed the key.

In the afternoon he strolled unhurriedly into the main post office and asked for a call to a number in Zurich, Switzerland. It took half an hour for the call to be put through and another five minutes until Herr Meier came on the line. The Englishman introduced himself by quoting a number and then giving his name.

Herr Meier excused himself and came back two

minutes later. His tone had lost the cautious reserve it had previously had. Customers whose accounts in dollars and Swiss francs grew steadily merited courteous treatment. The man in Brussels asked one question, and again the Swiss banker excused himself, this time to be back on the line in less than thirty seconds. He had evidently had the customer's file and statement brought out of the safe and was studying it.

"No, *mein Herr,*" the voice crackled into the Brussels phone booth. "We have here your letter of instruction requiring us to inform you by letter express airmail the moment any fresh in-payments are made, but there have been none over the period you mention."

"I only wondered, Herr Meier, because I have been away from London for two weeks and it might have come in my absence."

"No, there has been nothing. The moment anything is paid in, we shall inform you without delay."

In a flurry of Herr Meier's good wishes, the Jackal put the phone down, settled the amount charged, and left.

He met the forger in the bar off the rue Neuve that evening, arriving shortly after 6. The man was there already, and the Englishman spotted a corner seat still free, ordered the forger to join him with a jerk of his head. A few seconds after he had sat down and lit a cigarette, the Belgian joined him.

"Finished?" asked the Englishman.

"Yes, all finished. And very good work, even if I do say so myself."

The Englishman held out his hand.

"Show me," he ordered. The Belgian lit one of his Bastos and shook his head.

"Please understand, monsieur, this is a very public place. Also one needs a good light to examine them, particularly the French cards. They are at the studio."

The Jackal studied him coldly for a moment, then nodded.

"All right. We'll go and have a look at them in private."

They left the bar a few minutes later and took a taxi to the corner of the street where the basement studio was situated. It was still a warm, sunny evening, and though the street was narrow and no sun percolated, the Englishman wore the wraparound dark glasses to avoid recognition. One old man passed them coming the other way, but he was bent with arthritis and shuffled with his head to the ground.

The forger led the way down the steps and unlocked the door from a key on his ring. Inside the studio it was almost as dark as if it were night outside. A few shafts of dullish daylight filtered between the ghastly photographs stuck to the inside of the window beside the door, so that the Englishman could make out the shapes of the chair and table in the outer office. The forger led the way through the two velvet curtains into the studio and switched on the centre light.

From inside his pocket he drew a flat brown envelope, tipped it open, and spread the contents on the small round mahogany table that stood to one side, a prop for the taking of portrait photographs. The table he then lifted over to the centre of the room and placed it under the centre light. The twin arc lamps above the tiny stage at the far back of the studio remained unlit.

"Please, monsieur." He smiled broadly and gestured towards the three cards lying on the table. The Englishman picked the first up and held it under the light. It was his driving licence, the first page covered by a stuck-on tab of paper. This informed the reader that Mr. Alexander James Quentin Duggan of London W.1. is hereby licensed to drive motor vehicles of Groups 1a, 1b, 2, 3, 11, 12, and 13 only from 10 DEC 1960 until 9 DEC 1963 inclusive. Above this was the licence number (an imaginary one of course) and the words "London County Council" and "Road Traffic Act 1960." Then, "DRIVING LICENCE" and "Fee of 15/— received." So far as the Jackal could tell, it was a perfect forgery, certainly good enough for his purposes.

The second card was simply a French *carte d'identité* in the name of André Martin, aged fifty-three, born at Colmar and resident in Paris. His own photograph, aged by twenty years, with iron-grey hair cut *en brosse,* muzzy and embarrassed, stared out of a tiny corner of the card. The card itself was stained and dog-eared, a working man's card.

The third specimen drew his closest attention. The photograph on it was slightly different from the one on the I.D. card, for the date of issue of each card was different by several months, since the renewal dates would probably not have coincided precisely, had they been real. The card bore another portrait of himself that had been taken nearly two weeks earlier, but the shirt seemed to be darker and there was a hint of stubble round the chin of the photo on the card he now held. This effect had been achieved by skilful retouching, giving the impression of two different photographs of the same man, taken at different times and in different clothes. In both cases the draughtsmanship of the forger was excellent. The Jackal looked up and pocketed the cards.

"Very nice," he said. "Just what I wanted. I congratulate you. There is fifty pounds outstanding, I believe."

"That is true, monsieur. *Merci.*" The forger waited expectantly for the money. The Englishman drew a single wad of ten five-pound notes from his pocket but held them extended between forefinger and thumb. He said, "I believe there is something more, no?"

The Belgian tried unsuccessfully to look as if he did not comprehend.

"Monsieur?"

"The genuine front page of the driving licence. The one I said I wanted back."

There could be no doubt now that the forger was acting. He raised his eyebrows in extravagant surprise, as if the thought had just occurred to him, and turned away. He walked several paces one way, head bowed as if deep in thought, hands held behind his back. Then he turned and walked back.

"I thought we might be able to have a little chat about that piece of paper, monsieur."

"Yes?" The Jackal's tone gave nothing away. It was flat, without expression, apart from a slight interrogative. The face said nothing either, and the eyes seemed half shrouded as if they stared only into their own private world.

"The fact is, monsieur, that the original front page of the driving licence, with, I imagine, your real name on it, is not here. Oh, please, please"—he made an elaborate gesture as if to reassure one seized by anxiety, which the Englishman gave no sense of being—"it is in a very safe place. In a private deed box in a bank, which can be opened by no one but me. You see, monsieur, a man in my precarious line of business has to take precautions, take out, if you like, some form of insurance."

"What do you want?"

"Now, my dear sir, I had hoped that you might be prepared to do business on the basis of an exchange of ownership of that piece of paper, business based on a sum somewhat above the last figure of a hundred and fifty pounds which we mentioned in this room."

The Englishman sighed softly, as if slightly puzzled by the ability of man to complicate unnecessarily his own existence on this earth. He gave no other sign that the proposal of the Belgian interested him.

"You are interested?" asked the forger, coyly. He was playing his part as if he had rehearsed it at length; the oblique approach, the supposedly subtle hints. It reminded the other of a bad B-picture.

"I have met blackmailers before," said the Englishman, not an accusation, just a flat statement in a flat voice. The Belgian was shocked.

"Ah, monsieur, I beg you. Blackmail? Me? What I propose is not blackmail, since that is a process that repeats itself. I propose simply a trade. The whole package for a certain sum of money. After all, I have in my deed box the original of your licence, the developed plates, and all the negatives of the photographs I took of you, and, I am afraid"—he made a regretful grimace to show he was afraid—"one other picture taken of you very quickly while you were standing under the arc lights without your makeup. I am sure these documents, in the hands of the British and French authorities, could cause you some inconvenience. You are evidently a man accustomed to paying in order to avoid the inconveniences of life—"

"How much?"

"One thousand pounds, monsieur."

The Englishman considered the proposition, nodding quietly as if it was of mild academic interest only.

"It would be worth that amount to me to recover those documents," he conceded.

The Belgian grinned triumphantly. "I am most glad to hear it, monsieur."

"But the answer is no," went on the Englishman as if he were still thinking hard. The Belgian's eyes narrowed.

"But why? I do not understand. You say it is worth a thousand pounds to you to have them back. It is a straight deal. We are both used to dealing in desirable property and being paid for it."

"There are two reasons," said the other mildly. "Firstly, I have no evidence whatever that the original negatives of the photographs have not been copied, so that the first demand would not be succeeded by others. Nor have I any evidence that you have not given the documents to a friend, who, when asked to produce them will suddenly decide that he no longer has them, unless he too is sweetened to the tune of another thousand pounds."

The Belgian looked relieved. "If that is all that worries you, your fears are groundless. It would be in my interest not to entrust the documents to any partner, for fear that he might not produce them. I do not imagine you would part with a thousand pounds without receiving the documents. So there is no reason for me to part with them. I repeat, they are in a bank deposit box.

"From the point of view of repeated requests for money, that would not make sense. A photostat copy of the driving licence would not impress the British authorities, and even if you were caught with a false driving licence, it would only cause you some inconvenience, but not enough to justify several payments of money to me. As for the French cards, if the French authorities were informed that a certain Englishman were masquerading as a non-existent Frenchman called André Martin, they might indeed arrest you if you passed in France under that name. But if I were to make repeated requests for money, it would become worth your while to throw the cards away and get another forger to make you a new set. Then you would no longer need to fear exposure while in France as André Martin, since Martin would have ceased to exist."

"Then why cannot I do that now?" asked the Englishman, "since another complete set would cost me probably no more than an extra hundred and fifty pounds?"

The Belgian gestured with hands apart, palms upwards.

"I am banking on the fact that convenience and the time element to you are worth money. I think you need those André Martin papers and my silence in not too long a time. To get another set made would involve a lot more time, and they would not be as good. Those you have are perfect. So you want the papers, and my silence, and both now. The papers you have. My silence costs a thousand pounds."

"Very well, since you put it like that. But what makes you think I have a thousand pounds right here in Belgium?"

The forger smiled tolerantly, as one who knows all the answers but has no rooted objections to exposing them to satisfy the whims of a close friend.

"Monsieur, you are an English gentleman. It is clear to all. Yet you wish to pass for a middle-aged French working man. Your French is fluent and almost without accent. That is why I put the birthplace of André Martin as Colmar. You know, Alsatians speak French with a trace of accent like your own. You pass through France disguised as André Martin. Perfect, a stroke of genius. Who would ever think of searching an old man like Martin? So whatever you are carrying on you must be valuable. Drugs perhaps? Very fashionable in certain smart English circles these days. And Marseilles is one of the main supply centres. Or diamonds? I do not know. But the business you are in is profitable. English milords do not waste their time with picking pockets on racecourses. Please, monsieur, we stop playing games, *hein?* You telephone your friends in London and ask them to cable a thousand pounds to you at the bank here. Then tomorrow night we exchange packages and—hop—you are on your way, not so?"

The Englishman nodded several times, as if in rueful contemplation of a past life full of errors. Suddenly he raised his head and smiled engagingly at the

Belgian. It was the first time the forger had seen him smile, and he felt enormously relieved that this quiet Englishman had taken the matter so calmly without the usual twisting around to seek an outlet. But in the long run no problems. The man had come around. He felt the tension drain out of him.

"Very well," said the Englishman, "you win. I can have a thousand pounds here by noon tomorrow. But there is one condition."

"Condition?" At once the Belgian was wary again.

"We do not meet here."

The forger was baffled. "There is nothing wrong with this place. It is quiet, private—"

"There is everything wrong with this place from my point of view. You have just told me that you took a clandestine picture of me here. I do not wish our little ceremony of handing over our respective packages to be interrupted by the quiet click of a camera from some concealed point where one of your friends has thoughtfully hidden himself . . ."

The Belgian's relief was visible. He laughed aloud.

"You need have no fear of that, *cher ami.* This place is mine, very discreet, and nobody comes in here unless they are invited in by me. One has to be discreet, you understand, for I make a sideline from here in taking pictures for the tourists, you know, very popular but not quite the kind of work one does in a studio on the Grand' Place."

He held up his left hand, the forefinger and thumb forming the letter O, and ran the extended forefinger of the right hand through the circular aperture several times to indicate the sex act in progress.

The Englishman's eyes twinkled. He grinned wide,

then started to laugh. The Belgian laughed too at the joke. The Englishman clapped his hands against the Belgian's upper arms, and the fingers tightened on the biceps muscles, holding the forger steady, his hands still going through their erotic gestures. The Belgian was still laughing when he got the impression that his private parts had been hit by an express train.

The head jerked forward, the hands discontinued their mime and dropped downwards to the crushed testicles from which the man who held him had withdrawn his right knee, and the laugh turned to a screech, a gurgle, a retch. Half unconscious, he slithered to his knees, then tried to roll forwards and sideways to lie on the floor and nurse himself.

The Jackal let him slip quite gently to his knees. Then he stepped round and over the fallen figure, straddling the exposed back of the Belgian. His right hand slipped round and past the Belgian's neck and with it he gripped his own left biceps. The left hand was placed against the back of the forger's head. He gave one short, vicious twist to the neck, backwards, upwards, and sideways.

The crack as the cervical column snapped was probably not very loud, but in the quiet of the studio it sounded like a small pistol going off. The forger's body gave one last contraction, then slumped as limp as a rag doll. The Jackal held on for a moment longer before letting the body fall face down on the floor. The dead face twisted sideways, hands buried beneath the hips still clutching the privates, tongue protruding slightly between the clenched teeth, half bitten through, eyes open and staring at the faded pattern of the linoleum.

The Englishman walked quickly across to the curtains to make sure they were closed completely, then went back to the body. He turned it over and patted the pockets, finding the keys eventually in the left-hand side of the trousers. In the far corner of the studio stood the large trunk of props and make-up trays. The fourth key he tried opened the lid, and he spent ten minutes removing the contents and piling them in untidy heaps on the floor.

When the trunk was quite empty, the killer lifted the body of the forger by the armpits and hefted it over to the trunk. It went in quite easily, the limp limbs buckling to conform with the contours of the interior of the trunk. Within a few hours rigor mortis would set in, jamming the corpse into its adopted position at the bottom of the case. The Jackal then started replacing the articles that had come out. Wigs, women's underwear, toupees, and anything else that was small and soft were stuffed into the crevices between the limbs. On top went the several trays of make-up brushes and tubes of grease. Finally the jumble of remaining pots of cream, two negligees, some assorted sweaters and jeans, a dressing-gown, and several pairs of black fishnet stockings was placed on top of the body, completely covering it and filling the trunk to the brim. It took a bit of pressure to make the lid close, but then the hasp went home and the padlock was shut.

Throughout the operation the Englishman had handled the pots and jars by wrapping his hand in a piece of cloth from inside the case. Using his own handkerchief he now wiped off the lock and all outer surfaces of the trunk, pocketed the bundle of five-pound notes that still lay on the table, wiped that too, and replaced it against the wall where it had stood when he came in. Finally he put out the light, took a seat on one of the occasional chairs against the wall, and settled down to wait until darkness fell. After a few minutes he took out his box of cigarettes, emptied the remaining ten into one of the side pockets of his jacket, and smoked one of them, using the empty box as the ashtray and carefully preserving the used stub by putting it into the box when it was finished.

He had few illusions that the disappearance of the forger could remain undetected forever but thought there was a likelihood that a man like that would probably have to go underground or travel out of town at periodic intervals. If any of his friends remarked on his sudden failure to appear at his normal haunts, they would probably put the fact down to that. After a while a search would start, first of all among the people connected with the forging or pornographic photo business. Some of these might know about the studio and visit it, but most would be deterred by the locked door. Anyone who did penetrate into the studio would have to ransack the place, force the lock on the trunk, and empty it before finding the body.

A member of the underworld, doing this, would probably not report the matter to the police, he reasoned, thinking the forger had fallen foul of a gangland boss. No maniac customer interested in pornography alone would have bothered to hide the body so meticulously after a killing in passion. But eventually the police would have to know. At that point a photograph of the forger would doubtless be published, and the barman would probably remember his departure on the evening of August 1 in company with a tall blond man in a check suit and dark glasses. But it was an extremely long shot that anyone would for months come to examine the dead man's deed box, even if he had registered it in his own name.

He had exchanged no words with the barman, and the order for drinks he had given to the waiter in the same bar had been two weeks earlier. The waiter would have to have a phenomenal memory to recall the slight trace of foreign accent in the order for two beers. The police would launch a perfunctory search for a tall blond man, but even if the enquiry got as far as Alexander Duggan, the Belgian police would still have to go a long way to find the Jackal. On balance, he felt he had at least a month, which was what he needed. The killing of the forger was as mechanical as stamping on a cockroach. The Jackal relaxed, finished a second cigarette, and looked outside. It was 9:30, and a deep dusk had descended over the narrow street. He left the studio quietly, locking the outer door behind him. No one passed him as he went quietly down the street. Half a mile away he dropped the unidentifiable keys down a large drain set into the pavement and heard them splash into the water several feet down in the sewer beneath the street. He returned to his hotel in time for a late supper.

The next day, Friday, he spent shopping in one of the working-class suburbs of Brussels. From a shop specialising in camping equipment he bought a pair of hiking boots, long woollen socks, denim trousers, check woollen shirt, and a haversack. Among his other purchases were several sheets of thin foam rubber, a string shopping bag, a ball of twine, a hunting knife, two thin paint brushes, a tin of pink paint and another of brown. He thought of buying a large Honeydew melon from an open fruit stall, but decided not to, as it would probably go rotten over the weekend.

Back at the hotel he used his new driving licence, now matching his passport in the name of Alexander Duggan, to order a self-drive hire car for the following morning, and prevailed on the head reception clerk to book him a single room with shower/bath for the weekend at one of the resorts along the sea coast. Despite the lack of accommodations available in August, the clerk managed to find him a room in a small hotel overlooking the picturesque fishing harbour of Zeebrugge, and wished him a pleasant weekend by the sea.

seven

While the Jackal was doing his shopping in Brussels, Viktor Kowalski was wrestling with the intricacies of international telephone enquiries from Rome's main post office.

Not speaking Italian, he had sought the aid of the counter clerks, and eventually one of them had agreed that he spoke a little French. Laboriously Kowalski explained to him that he wished to telephone a man in Marseilles, France, but that he did not know the man's telephone number. Yes, he knew the name and address. The name was Grzybowski. That baffled the Italian, who asked Kowalski to write it down. This Kowalski did, but the Italian, unable to believe that any name could start "Grzyb . . ." spelt it out to the operator at the international exchange as "Grib . . ." thinking that Kowalski's written "z" had to be an "i." No name of Josef Gribowski existed in the Marseilles telephone directory, the operator informed the Italian at the other end of the phone. The clerk turned to Kowalski and explained that there was no such person.

Purely by chance, because he was a conscientious man anxious to please a foreigner, the clerk spelt the name out to underline that he had got it right.

"*Il n'existe pas, monsieur. Voyons: jay, air, eee—*"

"*Non, jay, air, zed . . .*" cut in Kowalski.

The clerk looked perplexed.

"Excusez moi, monsieur. Jay, air, zed? Jay, air, zed, ee-grec, bay?"

"Oui," insisted Kowalski, "G-R-Z-Y-B-O-W-S-K-I."

The Italian shrugged and presented himself to the switchboard operator once again.

"Get me international enquiries, please."

Within ten minutes Kowalski had JoJo's telephone number, and half an hour later he was through. At the end of the line the ex-legionnaire's voice was distorted by crackling, and he seemed hesitant to confirm the bad news in Kovacs's letter. Yes, he was glad Kowalski had rung, he had been trying to trace him for three months.

Unfortunately, yes, it was true about the illness of little Sylvie. She had been getting weaker and thinner, and when finally a doctor had diagnosed the illness, it had already been time to put her to bed. She was in the next bedroom at the flat from which JoJo was speaking. No it was not the same flat, they had taken a newer and larger one. What? The address? JoJo gave it slowly, while Kowalski, tongue between pursed lips, slowly wrote it down.

"How long do the quacks give her?" he roared down the line. He got his meaning over to JoJo at the fourth time of trying. There was a long pause.

"Allo? Allo?" he shouted when there was no reply. JoJo's voice came back.

"It could be a week, maybe two or three," said JoJo.

Disbelievingly, Kowalski stared at the mouthpiece in his hand. Without a word he replaced it on the cradle and blundered out of the booth. After paying the cost of the call he collected the mail, snapped the steel case on his wrist tight shut, and walked back to the hotel. For the first time in many years his thoughts were in a turmoil, and there was no one to whom he could turn for orders how to solve the problem by violence.

In his flat in Marseilles, the same one he had always lived in, JoJo also put down the receiver when he realized Kowalski had hung up. He turned to find the two men from the Action Service still where they had been, each with his Colt .45 Police Special in his hand. One was trained on JoJo, the other on his wife, who sat ashen-faced in the corner of the sofa. "Bastards," said JoJo with venom. "Shits."

"Is he coming?" asked one of the men.

"He didn't say. He just hung up on me," said the Pole.

The black, flat eyes of the Corsican stared back at him.

"He must come. Those are the orders."

"Well, you heard me. I said what you wanted. He must have been shocked. He just hung up. I couldn't prevent him doing that."

"He had better come, for your sake, JoJo," repeated the Corsican.

"He will come," said JoJo resignedly. "If he can, he will come. For the girl's sake."

"Good. Then your part is done."

"Then get out of here," shouted JoJo. "Leave us alone."

The Corsican rose, the gun still in his hand. The other man remained seated, looking at the woman.

"We'll be going," said the Corsican, "but you two will come with us. We can't have you talking about the place or ringing Rome now, can we, JoJo?"

"Where are you taking us?"

"A little holiday. A new pleasant hotel in the mountains. Plenty of sun and fresh air. Good for you, JoJo."

"For how long?" asked the Pole dully.

"For as long as it takes."

The Pole stared out of the window at the tangle of alleys and fish stalls that crouch behind the picture postcard frontage of the Old Port.

"It is the height of the tourist season. The trains are full these days. In August we make more than all the winter. It will ruin us for several years."

The Corsican laughed as if the idea amused him.

"You must consider it rather a gain than a loss, JoJo. After all, it is for France, your adopted country."

The Pole spun round. "I don't give a shit about politics. I don't care who is in power, what party wants to make a fuck-up of everything. But I know people like you. I have been meeting them all my life. You would serve Hitler, your type. Or Mussolini, or the OAS if it suited you. Or anybody. Regimes may change, but bastards like you never change . . ." He was shouting, limping towards the man with the gun whose snout had not quivered a millimetre in the hand that held it.

"JoJo," screamed the woman from the sofa. "I beg you—leave him alone!"

The Pole stopped and stared at his wife as if he had forgotten she was there. He looked round the room at the figures in it one by one. They all looked back at him, his wife imploring, the two Secret Service toughs without noticeable expression. They were used to reproaches which had no effect on the inevitable. The leader of the pair nodded towards the bedroom.

"Get packed. You first, then the wife."

"What about Sylvie? She will be home from school at four. There will be no one to meet her," said the woman.

The Corsican still stared at her husband.

"She will be picked up by us on the way past the school. Arrangements have been made. The headmistress has been told her granny is dying and the whole family has been summoned to her death bed. It's all very discreet. Now move."

JoJo shrugged, gave a last glance at his wife, and went into the bedroom to pack, followed by the Corsican. His wife continued to twist her handkerchief between her hands. After a while she looked up at the other agent on the end of the sofa. He was younger than the Corsican, a Gascon.

"What—what will they do to him?"

"Kowalski?"

"Viktor."

"Some gentlemen want to talk to him. That is all."

An hour later the family was in the back seat of a big Citroen, the two agents in the front, speeding towards a very private hotel high in the Vercors.

The Jackal spent the weekend at the seaside. He bought a pair of swimming trunks and spent the Saturday sunning himself on the beach at Zeebrugge, bathed several times in the North Sea, and wandered round the little harbour town and along the mole where British soldiers and sailors had once fought and died in a welter of blood and bullets. Some of the walrus-moustached old men who sat along the mole and threw for sea bass might have remembered forty-six years before, had he asked them, but he did not.

The English present that day were a few families scattered along the beach enjoying the sunshine and watching their children play in the surf.

On Sunday morning he packed his bags and drove leisurely through the Flemish countryside, strolling through the narrow streets of Ghent and Bruges. He lunched off the unmatchable steaks broiled over a timber fire served by the Siphon restaurant at Damm, and in the midafternoon turned the car back towards Brussels. Before turning in for the night, he asked for an early call with breakfast in bed and a packed lunch, explaining that he wished to drive into the Ardennes the following day and visit the grave of his elder brother who had died in the Battle of the Bulge between Bastogne and Malmédy. The desk clerk was most solicitous, promising that he would be called without fail for his pilgrimage.

In Rome Viktor Kowalski spent a much less relaxed weekend. He turned up regularly on time for his periods of guard duty, either as the desk man on the landing on the eighth floor, or on the roof by night. He slept little in his periods off duty, mostly lying on his bed off the main passage of the eighth floor, smoking and drinking the rough red wine that was imported by the gallon flagon for the eight ex-legionnaires who made up the guard. The crude Italian rosso could not compare for bite with the Algerian pinard that sloshes inside every legionnaire's pannikin, he thought, but it was better than nothing.

It habitually took Kowalski a long time to make up his mind on anything independently, but by Monday morning he had come to his decision.

He would not be gone long, perhaps just a day, or maybe two days if the planes did not connect properly. In any event, it was something that had to be done. He would explain to the *"patron"* afterwards. He was sure the *"patron"* would understand, even though he would be damned angry. It occurred to him to tell the colonel of the problem and ask for forty-eight hours' leave, but he felt sure that the colonel, although a good commanding officer who also stuck by his men when they got into trouble, would forbid him to go. He would not understand about Sylvie, and Kowalski knew he could never explain. He could never explain anything in words. He sighed heavily as he got up for the Monday morning shift. He was deeply troubled by the thought that for the first time in his life as a legionnaire, he was going to go A.W.O.L.

The Jackal rose at the same time and made his meticulous preparations. He showered and shaved first, then ate the excellent breakfast placed on the tray by his bedside. Taking the case containing the rifle from the locked wardrobe, he carefully wrapped each component in several layers of foam rubber, securing the bundles with twine. These he stuffed into the bottom of his rucksack. On top went the paint tins and brushes, the denim trousers and check shirt, the socks and the boots. The string shopping bag went into one of the outer pockets of the rucksack, the box of bullets into the other.

He dressed himself in one of his habitual striped shirts, a dove-grey lightweight suit as opposed to his usual check worsted ten-ounce, and a pair of light black leather loafers from Gucci. A black silk knitted tie completed the ensemble. He went down to his car, parked in the hotel lot, and locked his rucksack in the trunk. Returning to the foyer, he took delivery of his packed lunch, nodded a reply to the desk clerk's wishes for a *bon voyage*, and by 9 was speeding out of Brussels along the old E 40 highway towards Namur. The flat countryside was already basking in a warm sunshine that gave a hint of a scorching day to come. His road-map told him it was ninety-four miles to Bastogne, and he added a few more to find a quiet place in the hills and forests to the south of the little town. He estimated he would do the hundred miles by noon easily and gunned the Simca Aronde into another long, flat straight across the Walloon plain.

Before the sun had reached its zenith, he was through Namur and Marche, following the signposts that indicated Bastogne was approaching. Passing through the little town that had been torn to pieces by the guns of Hasso von Manteuffel's King Tiger tanks in the winter of 1944, he took the road southwards into the hills. The forests grew thicker, the winding road more frequently darkened by great elms and beeches and less often sliced by a single beam of sunshine between the trees.

Five miles beyond the town the Jackal found a narrow track running off into the forest. He turned the car down it and after another mile found a second trail leading away into the forest. He turned the car a few yards up this and hid it behind a clump of undergrowth. For a while he waited in the cool shade of the forest, smoking a cigarette and listening to the ticking of the engine block as it cooled, the whisper of wind through the upper branches, and the distant cooing of a pigeon.

Slowly he climbed out, unlocked the trunk, and laid the rucksack on the hood. Piece by piece he changed his clothes, folding the impeccable dove-grey suit along the back seat of the Aronde and slipping on the denim slacks. It was warm enough to do without a jacket, and he changed the collared and tied shirt for the lumberjack check shirt. Finally, the expensive town shoes gave way to the hiking boots and woollen socks into which he tucked the bottoms of the denims.

One by one he unwrapped the component parts of the rifle, fitting it together piece by piece. The silencer he slipped into one trouser pocket, the telescopic sight into the other. He tipped twenty shells from the box into one breast pocket of his shirt, the single explosive shell, still in its tissue-paper wrapper into the other.

When the rest of the rifle was assembled, he laid it on the hood of the car and went round to the trunk again and took from it the purchase he had made the previous evening from a market stall in Brussels before returning to the hotel, and which had lain in the trunk all night. It was the Honeydew melon. He locked the trunk, tipped the melon into the empty rucksack along with the paint, brushes and hunting knife, locked the car, and set off into the wood. It was just after noon.

Within ten minutes he had found a long, narrow clearing, a glade where from one end one could get a clear vision for 150 yards. Placing the gun beside a tree, he paced out 150 paces, then sought a tree from which the place where he had left the gun was visible. He tipped the contents of the rucksack out onto the ground, prised the lids off both tins of paint, and set to work on the melon. The upper and lower parts of the fruit were painted quickly brown over the dark green skin. The centre section was coloured pink. While both colours were still wet, he used his forefinger to draw crudely a pair of eyes, a nose, moustache, and mouth.

Jabbing the knife into the top of the fruit to avoid smearing the paint by finger contact, the Jackal gingerly placed the melon inside the string shopping bag. The big mesh and fine string of the bag in no way concealed either the outline of the melon or the design sketched upon it.

Lastly he jabbed the knife hard into the trunk of the tree about seven feet from the ground, and hung the handles of the shopping bag over the hilt. Against the green bark of the tree the pink and brown melon hung suspended like a grotesque autonomous human head. He stood back and surveyed his handiwork. At 150 yards it would serve its purpose.

He closed the two tins of paint and hurled them far into the forest where they crashed through the undergrowth and disappeared. The brushes he jabbed into the ground bristles foremost and stamped on them until they too were lost to view. Taking the rucksack he went back to the rifle.

The silencer went on easily, swivelling round the end of the barrel until it was tight. The telescopic sight fitted snugly along the top of the barrel. He slipped back the bolt and inserted the first cartridge into the breech. Squinting down the sight, he scoured the far end of the clearing for his hanging target. When he found it, he was surprised to find how large and clear it looked. To all appearances, had it been the head of a living man, it would have been no more than thirty yards away. He could make out the criss-cross lines of the string of the shopping bag where it restrained the melon, his own finger smears denoting the main features of the face.

He altered his stance slightly, leaned against a tree to steady his aim, and squinted again. The two crossed wires inside the telescopic sight did not appear to be quite centred, so he reached out with the right hand and twiddled the two adjusting screws until the cross in the sight appeared to be perfectly central. Satisfied, he took careful aim at the centre of the melon and fired.

The recoil was less than he had expected, and the restrained "phut" of the silencer hardly loud enough to have carried across a quiet street. Carrying the gun under his arm, he walked back the length of the clearing and examined the melon. Near the upper right hand edge the bullet had scored its path across the skin of the fruit, snapping part of the string of the shopping bag, and had buried itself in the tree. He walked back again and fired a second time, leaving the setting of the telescopic sight exactly where it had been before.

The result was the same, with half an inch of difference. He tried four shots without moving the screws of the telescopic sight until he was convinced his aim was true, but the sight was firing high and slightly to the right. Then he adjusted the screws.

This next shot was low and to the left. To make quite sure he again walked the length of the clearing and examined the hole made by the bullet. It had penetrated the lower left corner of the mouth on the dummy head. He tried three more shots with the sights still adjusted to this new position, and the bullets all went in the same area. Finally he moved the sights back by a whisker.

The ninth shot went clean through the forehead, where he had aimed it. A third time he walked up to the target, and this time he took a piece of chalk from his pockets and chalked the existing area touched by the bullets—the small cluster to the top and right, the second cluster round the left hand side of the mouth, and the neat hole through the centre of the forehead.

From then on he plugged in succession each eye, the bridge of the nose, the upper lip, and the chin. Swinging the target into a profile position he used the last six shots through the temple, ear-hole, neck, cheek, jaw and cranium, only one of them being slightly off-target.

Satisfied with the gun, he noted the positioning of the grub-screws that adjusted the telescopic sight and, taking a tube of balsa wood cement from his pocket, squirted the viscous liquid over the heads of both grub-screws and the surface of the bakelite adjacent to them. Half an hour and two cigarettes later the cement was hard, and the sights were set for his eye-sight with that particular weapon at 130 metres at spot-on accuracy.

From his other breast pocket he took the explosive bullet, unwrapped it and slid it into the breech of the rifle. He took particularly careful aim at the centre of the melon and fired.

As the last plume of blue smoke curled away from the end of the silencer, the Jackal laid the rifle against the tree and walked down the clearing towards the hanging shopping bag. It sagged, limp and almost empty, against the scarred trunk of the tree. The melon that had absorbed twenty lead slugs without coming to pieces had disintegrated. Parts of it had been forced through the mesh of the bag and lay scattered on the grass. Pips and juice dribbled down the bark. The remaining fragments of the fruit's flesh lay broken in the lower end of the shopping bag, which hung like a weary scrotum from the hunting knife.

He took the bag and tossed it into some nearby bushes. The target it had once contained was unrecognisable as anything but pulp. The knife he jerked out of the wood and put back in its sheath. He left the tree, retrieved his rifle, and strolled back to the car.

There each component was carefully wrapped in its swaddling of foam rubber sheeting and replaced in the rucksack, along with his boots, socks, shirt, and slacks. He dressed again in his city clothes, locked the rucksack in the boot, and quietly ate his lunch sandwiches.

When he had finished, he left the drive and drove back to the main road, turning left for Bastogne, Marche, Namur, and Brussels. He was back in the hotel shortly after six, and after taking his rucksack up to his room, descended to settle the charge for the hire car with the desk clerk. Before bathing for dinner, he spent an hour carefully cleaning every part of the rifle and oiling the moving parts, stacked it away in its carrying case, and locked it into the wardrobe. Later that night the rucksack, twine, and several strips of foam rubber were dumped into a corporation refuse basket, and twenty-one used cartridge cases went spinning into the municipal canal.

On the same Monday morning, August 5, Viktor Kowalski was again at the main post office in Rome seeking the help of someone who spoke French. This time he wanted the clerk to telephone the Alitalia flight enquiries office and ask the times of planes during that week from Rome to Marseilles and back. He learned that he had missed the Monday flight, for it was leaving Fiumicino in an hour and he would not have time to catch it. The next direct flight was on Wednesday. No, there were no other airlines running a direct flight to Marseilles from Rome. There were indirect flights; would the Signor be interested in that idea? No? The Wednesday flight? Certainly, it left at 11:15 a.m., arriving at Marignane Airport, Marseilles, shortly after noon. The return flight would be the next day. One booking? Single or return? Certainly, and the name? Kowalski gave the name on the papers he carried in his pocket. With passports abolished within the Common Market, the national identity card would be good enough.

He was asked to be at the Alitalia desk at Fiumicino one hour before take-off on Wednesday. When the clerk put the phone down, Kowalski took the waiting letters, locked them into his etui, and left to walk back to the hotel.

The following morning the Jackal had his last meeting with M. Goossens. He rang him over breakfast, and the armourer announced that he was pleased to say the work was finished. If Monsieur Duggan would like to call at 11 a.m.? And please to bring the necessary items for a final fitting.

He arrived again with half an hour in hand, the small attaché case inside an ordinary empty fibre suitcase that he had bought at a secondhand shop earlier in the morning. For thirty minutes he surveyed the street in which the armourer lived before finally walking quietly to the front door. When M. Goossens let him in, he went on into the office without hesitating. Goossens joined him after locking the front door, and closed the office door behind him.

"No more problems?" asked the Englishman.

"No, this time I think we have it." From behind his desk the Belgian produced several rolls of hessian sacking and laid them on the desk. As he undid them, he laid side by side a series of thin steel tubes, so polished they looked like aluminum. When the last one was laid on the desk he held out his hand for the attaché case containing the component parts of the rifle. The Jackal gave it to him.

One by one, the armourer started to slide the parts of the rifle into the tubes. Each one fitted perfectly.

"How was the target practice?" he enquired as he worked.

"Very satisfactory."

Goossens noticed as he handled the telescopic sight that the adjustment screws had been fixed into place with a blob of balsa wood cement.

"I am sorry the calibrating screws should have been so small," he said. "It is better to work off precise markings, but again it was the size of the original screw heads that got in the way. So I had to use these little grub-screws. Otherwise the sight would never have fitted into its tube." He slipped the telescope into the steel tube designed for it, and like the other components it fitted exactly. When the last of the five components of the rifle had disappeared from view, he held up the tiny needle of steel that was the trigger, and the five remaining explosive bullets.

"These, you see, I have had to accommodate elsewhere," he explained. He took the black leather padded butt of the rifle and showed his customer how the leather had been slit with a razor. He pushed the trigger into the stuffing inside and closed the slit with a strip of black insulating tape. It looked quite natural. From the desk drawer he took a lump of circular black rubber about one and a half inches in diameter and two inches long.

From the centre of one circular face a steel stud protruded upwards, threaded like a screw.

"This fits onto the end of the last of the tubes," he explained.

Round the steel stud were five holes drilled downwards into the rubber. Into each one he carefully fitted a bullet, until only the brass percussion caps showed to view.

"When the rubber is fitted, the bullets become quite invisible, and the rubber gives a touch of verisimilitude," he explained. The Englishman remained silent. "What do you think?" asked the Belgian with a touch of anxiety.

Without a word the Englishman took the tubes and examined them one by one. He rattled them, but no sound came from inside, for the interiors were lined with two layers of baize to absorb both shock and noise. The longest of the tubes was twenty inches; it accommodated the barrel and breech of the gun. The others were about a foot each, and contained the two struts, upper and lower, of the stock, the silencer, and the telescope. The butt, with the trigger inside its padding, was separate, as was the rubber knob containing the bullets. As a hunting rifle, let alone an assassin's rifle, it had vanished.

"Perfect," said the Jackal, nodding quietly. "Absolutely what I wanted." The Belgian was pleased. Although an expert in his trade, he enjoyed praise as much as the next man, and he was aware that in his field the customer in front of him was also in the top bracket.

The Jackal took the steel tubes, with the parts of the gun inside them, and wrapped each one carefully in the sacking, placing each piece into the fibre suitcase. When the five tubes, butt, and rubber knob were wrapped and packed, he closed the fibre suitcase and handed the attaché case with its fitted compartments back to the armourer.

"I shall not be needing that any more. The gun will stay where it is until I have occasion to use it." He took the remaining two hundred pounds he owed the Belgian from his inner pocket and put it on the table.

"I think our dealings are complete, M. Goossens." The Belgian pocketed the money.

"Yes, monsieur, unless you have anything else in which I may be of service."

"Only one," replied the Englishman. "You will

please remember my little homily to you a fortnight ago on the wisdom of silence."

"I have not forgotten, monsieur," replied the Belgian quietly.

He was frightened again. Would this soft-spoken killer try to silence him now, to ensure his silence? Surely not. The enquiries into such a killing would expose to the police the visits of the tall Englishman to this house long before he ever had a chance to use the gun he now carried in a suitcase. The Englishman seemed to be reading his thoughts. He smiled briefly.

"You do not need to worry. I do not intend to harm you. Besides, I imagine a man of your intelligence has taken certain precautions against being killed by one of his customers. A telephone call expected within an hour perhaps? A friend who will arrive to find the body if the call does not come through? A letter deposited with a lawyer, to be opened in the event of your death? For me, killing you would create more problems than it would solve."

M. Goossens was startled. He had indeed a letter permanently deposited with a lawyer, to be opened in the event of his death. It instructed the police to search under a certain stone in the back garden. Beneath the stone was a box containing a list of those expected to call at the house each day. It was replaced each day. For this day, the note described the only customer expected to call, a tall Englishman of well-to-do appearance who called himself Duggan. It was just a form of insurance.

The Englishman watched him calmly.

"I thought so," he said. "You are safe enough. But I shall kill you, without fail, if you ever mention my visits here or my purchase from you to anyone, anyone at all. So far as you are concerned the moment I leave this house I have ceased to exist."

"That is perfectly clear, monsieur. It is the normal working arrangement with all my customers. I may say, I expect similar discretion from them. That is why the serial number of the gun you carry has been scorched from the barrel with acid. I too must protect myself."

The Englishman smiled again. "Then we understand each other. Good day, Monsieur Goossens."

A minute later the door closed behind him, and the Belgian who knew so much about guns and gunmen but so little about the Jackal breathed a sigh of relief and withdrew to his office to count the money.

The Jackal did not wish to be seen by the staff of his hotel carrying a cheap fibre suitcase so although he was late for lunch he took a taxi straight to the mainline station and deposited the case in the left-luggage office, tucking the ticket into the inner compartment of his slim lizard-skin wallet.

He lunched at the Cygne well and expensively to celebrate the end of the planning and preparation stage in France and Belgium, and walked back to the Amigo to pack and pay his bill. When he left, it was exactly as he had come, in a finely cut check suit, wraparound dark glasses, and with two Vuitton suitcases following him in the hands of the porter down to the waiting taxi. He was also 1600 pounds poorer, but his rifle reposed safely inside an unobtrusive suitcase in the luggage office of the station and three finely forged cards were tucked into an inside pocket of his suit.

The plane left Brussels for London shortly after 4, and although there was a perfunctory search of one of his bags at London Airport, there was nothing to be found, and by 7 he was showering in his own flat before dining out in the West End.

eight

Unfortunately for Kowalski, there were no telephone calls to make at the post office on Wednesday morning; had there been he would have missed his plane. And the mail was waiting in the pigeonhole for M. Poitiers. He collected the five envelopes, locked them into his steel carrier on the end of the chain, and set off hurriedly for the hotel. By half past nine he had been relieved of both by Colonel Rodin, and was free to go back to his room for sleep. His next turn of duty was on the roof, starting at 7 that evening.

He paused in his room only to collect his Colt .45 (Rodin would never allow him to carry it on the street) and tucked it into his shoulder holster. If he had worn a well-fitting jacket the bulge of the gun and holster would have been evident at a hundred yards, but his suits were as ill-fitting as a thoroughly bad tailor could make them, and despite his bulk they hung on him like sacks. He took the roll of sticking plaster and the beret that he had bought the day before and stuffed them into his jacket, pocketed the roll of lire notes and French francs that represented his past six months savings, and closed the door behind him.

At the desk of the landing the duty guard looked up.

"Now they want a telephone call made," said Kowalski, jerking his thumb upwards in the direction of the ninth floor above. The guard said nothing, just watched him as the lift arrived and he stepped inside.

Seconds later he was in the street, pulling on the big
dark glasses.

At the cafe across the street the man with a copy of
Oggi lowered the magazine a fraction and studied
Kowalski through impenetrable sunglasses as the Pole
looked up and down for a taxi. When none came, he
started to walk towards the corner of the block. The
man with the magazine left the cafe terrace and walked
to the kerb. A small Fiat cruised out of a line of
parked cars further down the street and stopped opposite him. He climbed in and the Fiat crawled after
Kowalski at a walking pace.

On the corner Kowalski found a cruising taxi and
hailed it. "Fiumicino," he told the driver.

At the airport the SDECE man followed him quietly as he presented himself at the Alitalia desk, paid
for his ticket in cash, assured the girl on the desk that
he had no suitcases or hand luggage, and was told
passengers for the 11:15 Marseilles flight would be
called in an hour and five minutes.

With time to kill, the ex-legionnaire lounged into
the cafeteria, bought a coffee at the counter and took
it over to the plate glass windows from where he could
watch the planes coming and going. He loved airports although he could not understand how airplanes
worked. Most of his life the sound of aero engines had
meant German Messerschmitts, Russian Stormoviks,
or American Flying Forts. Later they meant air support with B-26s or Skyraiders in Vietnam, Mystères or
Fougas in the Algerian *djebel*. Now at a civilian airport he liked to watch them cruising in to land like
big silver birds, engines muted, hanging in the sky as
if on threads just before the touch-down. Although

socially a shy man, he liked watching the interminable bustle of an airport. Perhaps, he mused, if his life had been different, he would have worked in an airport. But he was what he was, and there was no going back now.

His thoughts turned to Sylvie, and his beetle brows darkened with concentration. It wasn't right, he told himself soberly, it wasn't right that she should die and all those bastards sitting up in Paris should live. Colonel Rodin had told him about them, and the way they had let France down, and betrayed the army, and destroyed the Legion, and abandoned the people in Indochina and Algeria to the terrorists. Colonel Rodin was never wrong.

His flight was called, and he filed through the glass doors and out into the burning white concrete of the apron for the hundred yard walk to the plane. From the observation terrace the two agents of Colonel Rolland watched him climb the steps into the plane. He now wore the black beret and the piece of sticking plaster on one cheek. One of the agents turned to the other and raised a weary eyebrow. As the Turbo-prop took off for Marseilles, the two men left the rail. On the way through the main hall they stopped at a public kiosk while one of them dialled a Rome local number. He identified himself to the person at the end with a Christian name and said slowly, "He's gone. Alitalia four-five-one. Landing Marignane twelve-ten. *Ciao.*"

Ten minutes later the message was in Paris, and ten minutes after that it was being listened to in Marseilles.

The Alitalia Viscount swung out over the bay of

impossibly blue water and turned onto final approach for Marignane Airport. The pretty Roman air hostess finished her smiling walk down the gangway checking that all seat belts were fastened and sat down in her own corner seat at the back to fasten her own belt. She noticed the passenger in the seat ahead of her was staring fixedly out of the window at the glaring off-white desolation of the Rhône Delta as if he had never seen it before.

He was the big lumbering man who spoke no Italian, and whose French was heavily accented from some motherland in eastern Europe. He wore a black beret over his cropped black hair, a dark and rumpled suit, and a pair of dark glasses which he never took off. An enormous piece of sticking plaster obscured one half of his face; he must have cut himself badly, she thought.

They touched down precisely on time, quite close to the terminal building, and the passengers walked across to the customs hall. As they filed through the glass doors, a small balding man standing beside one of the passport police kicked him lightly in the ankle.

"Big fellow, black beret, sticking plaster." Then he strolled quietly away and gave the other the same message. The passengers divided themselves into two lines to pass through the guichets. Behind their grilles the two policemen sat facing each other, ten feet apart, with the passengers filing between them. Each passenger presented his passport and disembarkation card. The officers were of the Security Police, the DST, responsible for all internal state security inside France, and for checking incoming aliens and returning Frenchmen.

When Kowalski presented himself, the blue-jacketed figure behind the grille barely gave him a glance. He banged his stamp down on the yellow disembarkation card, gave the proffered identity card a short glance, nodded, and waved the big man on. Relieved, Kowalski walked on towards the customs benches. Several of the customs officers had just listened quietly to the small balding man before he disappeared into a glass-fronted office behind them. The senior customs officer called to Kowalski.

"Monsieur, your baggage."

He gestured to where the rest of the passengers were waiting by the mechanical conveyor belt for their suitcases to appear from the wire-frame barrow parked in the sunshine outside.

Kowalski lumbered over to the customs officer. "I have no baggage," he said.

The customs officer raised his eyebrows. "No baggage? Well, have you anything to declare?"

"No, nothing," said Kowalski.

The customs man smiled amiably, a smile almost as broad as his sing-song Marseilles accent.

"Very well, go ahead, monsieur." He gestured towards the exit into the taxi rank. Kowalski nodded and went out into the sunshine. Not being accustomed to spending freely, he looked up and down until he caught sight of the airport bus, and climbed into it.

As he disappeared from sight, several of the other customs men gathered round the senior staffer.

"Wonder what they want him for," said one.

"He looked a surly character."

"He won't be when those bastards have finished

with him," said a third jerking his head towards the
offices at the back.

"Come on, back to work," chipped in the older one.
"We've done our bit for France today."

"For *le Grand Charlie*, you mean," replied the first
as they split up, and muttered under his breath, "God
rot him."

It was the lunch-hour when the bus stopped finally
at the Air France offices in the heart of the city, and
it was even hotter than in Rome. August in Marseilles
has several qualities, but the inspiration to great exertions is not one of them. The heat lay on the city like
an illness, crawling into every fibre, sapping strength,
energy, the will to do anything but lie in a cool room
with the jalousies closed and the fan full on.

Even the Cannebière, usually the bustling bursting
jugular vein of Marseilles, after dark a river of light
and animation, was dead. The few people and cars on
it seemed to be moving through waist-deep treacle. It
took half an hour to find a taxi; most of the drivers
had found a shady spot in a park to have their siesta.

The address JoJo had given Kowalski was on the
main road out of town heading towards Cassis. At the
Avenue de la Libération, he told the driver to drop
him, so that he could walk the rest. The driver's *"si
vous voulez"* indicated plainer than text what he
thought of foreigners who considered covering distances of over a few yards in this heat when they had
a car at their disposal.

Kowalski watched the taxi turn back into town until
it was out of sight. He found the side street named on
the piece of paper by asking a waiter at a terrace cafe
on the sidewalk. The block of flats looked fairly new,

and Kowalski thought the JoJos must have made a good thing of their station food trolley. Perhaps they had got the fixed kiosk that Madame JoJo had had her eyes on for so many years. That at any rate would account for the increase in their prosperity. And it would be nicer for Sylvie to grow up in this neighbourhood than round the docks. At the thought of his daughter, and the idiotic thing he had just imagined for her, Kowalski stopped at the foot of the steps to the apartment block. What had JoJo said on the phone? A week? Perhaps two? It was not possible.

He took the steps at a run and paused in front of the double row of letter boxes along one side of the hall. Grzybowski, read one, Apartment 23. He decided to take the stairs since it was only on the second floor.

Apartment 23 had a door like the others. It had a bell-push with a little white card in a slot beside it, with the word "Grzybowski" typed on it. The door stood at the end of the corridor, flanked by the doors of apartments 22 and 24. He pressed the bell. The door in front of him opened and the lunging pickaxe handle swung out of the gap and down towards his forehead.

The blow split the skin but bounced off the bone with a dull "thunk." On each side of the Pole the doors of apartments 22 and 24 opened inwards and men surged out. It all happened in less than half a second. In the same time Kowalski went beserk. Although slow-thinking in most ways, the Pole knew one technique perfectly, that of fighting.

In the narrow confines of the corridor his size and strength were useless to him. Because of his height the pickaxe handle had not reached the full momen-

tum of its downward swing before hitting his head.
Through the blood spurting over his eyes he discerned
there were two men in the door in front of him and
two others on each side. He needed room to move,
so he charged forward into Apartment 23.

The man directly in front of him staggered back
under the impact; those behind closed in, hands reaching for his collar and jacket. Inside the room he drew
the Colt from under his armpit, turned once and fired
back into the doorway. As he did so another stave
slammed down on his wrist, jerking the aim downwards.

The bullet ripped the kneecap off one of his assail-
ants, who went down with a thin screech. Then the
gun was out of his hand, the fingers rendered nerve-
less from another blow on the wrist. A second later he
was overwhelmed as the five men hurled themselves
at him. The fight lasted three minutes. A doctor later
estimated he must have taken a score of blows to the
head from the leather-wrapped coshes before he finally
passed out. A part of one of his ears was slashed off
by a glancing blow, the nose was broken, and the face
was a deep-red mask.

Most of his fighting was by reflex action. Twice he
almost reached his gun, until a flying foot sent it spinning to the other end of the sitting room. When he
did finally go down onto his face, there were only
three attackers left standing to put the boot in.

When they had done and the enormous body on the
floor was insensible, only a trickle of blood from the
slashed scalp indicating that it was still alive, the three
survivors stood back swearing viciously, chests heaving. Of the others, the man shot in the leg was curled

against the wall by the door, white-faced, glistening red hands clutching his wrecked knee, a long monotonous stream of obscenities coming through pain-grey lips. Another was on his knees, rocking slowly back and forward, hand thrust deep into the torn groin. The last lay face down on the carpet not far from the Pole, a dull bruise discolouring his left temple where one of Kowalski's haymakers had caught him at full force.

The leader of the group rolled Kowalski over onto his back and flicked up one of the closed eyelids. He crossed to the telephone near the window, dialled a local number, and waited.

He was still breathing hard. When the phone was answered he told the person at the other end, "We got him. . . . Fought? Of course he bloody fought. . . . He got off one bullet, Guerini's lost a kneecap. Capetti took one in the balls and Vissart is out cold. . . . What? Yes, the Pole's alive, those were the orders, weren't they? Otherwise he wouldn't have done all this damage. . . . Well, he's hurt, all right. Dunno, he's unconscious. . . . Look, we don't want a salad basket, we want a couple of ambulances. And make it quick."

He slammed the receiver down and muttered "*Cons*" to the world in general. Round the room the fragments of shattered furniture lay about like firewood, which was all they would be good for. They had all thought the Pole would go down in the passage outside. None of the furniture had been stacked in a neighbouring room, and it had got in the way. He himself had stopped an armchair thrown by Kowalski with one hand full in the chest, and it hurt. Goddamn Pole, he thought, the jerks at the head office hadn't said what he was like.

Fifteen minutes later two Citroen ambulances slid into the road outside the block, and the doctor came up. He spent five minutes examining Kowalski. Finally he drew back the unconscious man's sleeve and gave him an injection. As the two stretcher bearers staggered away towards the lift with the Pole, the doctor turned to the wounded Corsican who had been regarding him balefully from his pool of blood beside the wall.

He prised the man's hands away from his knee, took a look, and whistled.

"Right. Morphine and the hospital. I'm going to give you a knockout shot. There's nothing I can do here. Anyway, *mon petit,* your career in this line is over."

Guerini answered him with a stream of obscenities as the needle went in.

Vissart was sitting up with his hands to his head, a dazed expression on his face. Capetti was upright by now, leaning against the wall retching dry. Two of his colleagues gripped him under the armpits and led him hobbling from the flat into the corridor. The leader helped Vissart to his feet as the stretcher bearers from the second ambulance carried the inert form of Guerini away.

Out in the corridor the leader of the six took a last look back into the desolated room. The doctor stood beside him.

"Quite a mess, *hein?*" said the doctor.

"The local office can clean it up," said the leader. "It's their goddamn apartment."

With that he closed the door. The doors of apartments 22 and 24 were also open, but the interiors were untouched. He pulled the doors closed.

"No neighbours?" asked the doctor.

"No neighbours," said the Corsican, "we took the whole floor."

Preceded by the doctor, he helped the still dazed Vissart down the stairs to the waiting cars.

Twelve hours later, after a fast drive the length of France, Kowalski was lying on a cot in a cell beneath a fortress barracks outside Paris. The room had the inevitable white-washed walls, stained and musty, of all prison cells, with here and there a scratched obscenity or prayer. It was hot and close, with an odour of carbolic acid, sweat, and urine. The Pole lay face up on a narrow iron cot whose legs were embedded in the concrete floor. Apart from the biscuit mattress and a rolled-up blanket under his head, the cot contained no other linen. Two heavy leather straps secured his ankles, two more his thighs and wrists. A single strap pinned his chest down. He was still unconscious, but breathing deeply and irregularly.

The face had been bathed clean of blood, the ear and scalp sutured. A stick of plaster spanned the broken nose, and through the open mouth out of which the breath rasped could be seen the stumps of two broken front teeth. The rest of the face was badly bruised.

Beneath the thick mat of black hair covering the chest, shoulders, and belly other livid bruises could just be discerned; the results of fists, boots, and coshes. The right wrist was heavily bandaged and taped.

The man in the white coat finished his examination, straightened up, and replaced his stethoscope in his bag. He turned and nodded at the man behind him, who tapped at the door. It swung open and the pair of them went outside. The door swung to, and the gaoler slid home the two enormous steel bars.

"What did you hit him with, an express train?" asked the doctor as they walked down the passage.

"It took six men to do that," replied Colonel Rolland.

"Well, they did a pretty good job. They damn nearly killed him. If he weren't built like a bull they would have done."

"It was the only way," replied the Colonel. "He ruined three of my men."

"It must have been quite a fight."

"It was. Now, what's the damage?"

"In layman's terms: possible fracture of the right wrist—I haven't been able to do an X-ray, remember —plus lacerated left ear, scalp, and broken nose. Multiple cuts and bruising, slight internal haemorrhaging, which could get worse and kill him or could clear up on its own. He enjoys what one might call a rude good health—or he did. What worries me is the head. There's concussion all right, whether mild or severe is not easy to say. No signs of a skull fracture, though that was not the fault of your men. He's just got a skull like solid ivory. But the concussion could get worse if he's not left alone."

"I need to put certain questions to him," observed the Colonel, studying the tip of his glowing cigarette. The doctor's prison clinic lay one way, the stairs leading to the ground floor the other. Both men stopped. The doctor glanced at the head of the Action Service with distaste.

"This is a prison," he said quietly. "All right, it's for offenders against the security of the state. But I am still the prison doctor. Elsewhere in this prison what I say, concerning prisoners' health, goes. That corridor"—he jerked his head backwards in the direction from which they had come—"is your preserve. It has been most lucidly explained to me that what happens down there is none of my business, and I have no say in it. But I will say this: if you start 'questioning' that man before he's recovered, with your methods, he'll either die or become a raving lunatic."

Colonel Rolland listened to the doctor's bitter prediction without moving a muscle.

"How long?" he asked. The doctor shrugged.

"Impossible to say. He may regain consciousness tomorrow, or not for days. Even if he does, he will not be fit for questioning—medically fit, that is—for at least two weeks. At the very least. That is, if the concussion is only mild."

"There are certain drugs," murmured the Colonel.

"Yes, there are. And I have no intention of prescribing them. You may be able to get them, you probably can. But not from me. In any case, nothing he could tell you now would make the slightest sense. It would probably be gibberish. His mind is undoubtedly scrambled. It may clear, it may not. But if it does, it must happen in its own time. Mind-bending drugs now would simply produce an idiot, no use to you or anyone else. It will probably be a week before he flickers an eyelid. You'll just have to wait."

With that he turned on his heel and walked back to his clinic.

But the doctor was wrong. Kowalski opened his eyes

three days later, on August 10, and the same day had his first and only session with the interrogators.

The Jackal spent the three days after his return from Brussels putting the final touches to his preparations for his forthcoming mission into France.

With his new driving licence in the name of Alexander James Quentin Duggan in his pocket, he went down to Fanum House, headquarters of the Automobile Association, and acquired an International Driving Licence in the same name.

He bought a matching series of leather suitcases from a secondhand shop specialising in travel goods. Into one he packed the clothes that would, if necessary, disguise him as Pastor Per Jensen of Copenhagen. Before the packing he transferred the Danish maker's labels from the three ordinary shirts he had bought in Copenhagen to the clerical shirt, dog-collar, and black bib that he had bought in London, removing the English maker's labels as he did so. These clothes joined the shoes, socks, underwear, and charcoal grey light suit that might one day make up the persona of Pastor Jensen. Into the same suitcase went the clothes of American student Marty Schulberg, loafers, socks, jeans, sweat-shirts, and windbreaker.

Slitting the lining of the suitcase, he inserted between the two layers of leather that comprised the stiffened sides of the case the passport of the two foreigners he might one day wish to become. The last additions to this case-ful of clothes were the Danish book on French Cathedrals, the two sets of spectacles, one for the Dane, the other for the American, the two different sets of tinted contact lenses, carefully wrapped in tissue paper, and the preparations for hair tinting.

Into the second case went the shoes, socks, shirt, and trousers of French make and design that he had bought in the Paris Flea Market, along with the ankle-length greatcoat and black beret. Into the lining of this case he inserted the false papers of the middle-aged Frenchman André Martin. This case remained partly empty, for it would soon also have to hold a series of narrow steel tubes containing a complete sniper's rifle and ammunition.

The third, slightly smaller suitcase was packed with the effects of Alexander Duggan: shoes, socks, underwear, shirts, ties, handkerchiefs, and three elegant suits. Into the lining of this case went several thin wads of ten-pound notes to the value of a thousand pounds, which he had drawn from his private bank account on his return from Brussels.

Each of these cases was carefully locked and the keys transferred to his private key-ring. The dove-grey suit was cleaned and pressed, then left hanging in the wall cupboard of his flat. Inside the breast pocket were his passport, driving licence, international licence, and a folder containing a hundred pounds in cash.

Into the last piece of his luggage, a neat hand case, went shaving tackle, pyjamas, sponge-bag and towel, and the final pieces of his purchases—a light harness of finely sewn webbing, a two-pound bag of plaster of Paris, several rolls of large-weave lint bandages, half a dozen rolls of sticky plaster, three packs of cotton wool, and a pair of stout shears with blunt but powerful blades. The grip would travel as hand-luggage, for it was his experience that in passing customs at whatever airport an attaché case was not usually the piece of luggage selected by the customs officer for an arbitrary request to open up.

With his purchases and packing completed, he had reached the end of his planning. The disguises of Pastor Jensen and Marty Schulberg, he hoped, were merely precautionary tactics which would probably never be used unless things went wrong and the identity of Alexander Duggan had to be abandoned. The identity of André Martin was vital to his plan, and it was possible that the two others would never be required. In that event the entire suitcase could be abandoned in a left-luggage office when the job was over. Even then, he reasoned, he might need either of them for his escape. André Martin and the gun could also be abandoned when the job was over, as he would have no further use for them. Entering France with three suitcases and an attaché case, he estimated he would leave with one suitcase and the hand luggage, certainly not more.

With this task finished, he settled down to wait for the two pieces of paper that would set him on his way. One was the telephone number in Paris which could be used to feed him information concerning the exact state of readiness of the security forces surrounding the French President. The other was the written notification from Herr Meier in Zurich that 250,000 dollars had been deposited in his numbered bank account.

While he was waiting for them, he passed the time by practising walking round his flat with a pronounced limp. Within two days he was satisfied that he had a sufficiently realistic limp to prevent any observer from being able to detect that he had not sustained a broken ankle or leg.

The first letter he awaited arrived on the morning of August 9. It was an envelope postmarked in Rome and bore the message: "Your friend can be contacted at Molitor 5901. Introduce yourself with the words *'Ici Chacal.'* Reply will be *'Ici Valmy.'* Good luck."

It was not until the morning of the 11th that the letter from Zurich arrived. He grinned openly as he read the confirmation that, come what may, provided he remained alive, he was a wealthy man for the rest of his life. If his forthcoming operation was successful, he would be even richer. He had no doubts that he would succeed. Nothing had been left to chance.

He spent the rest of that morning on the telephone booking air passages, and fixed his departure for the following morning, August 12.

The cellar was silent except for the sound of breathing, heavy but controlled, from the five men behind the table, a rasping rattle from the man strapped to the heavy oaken chair in front of it. One could not tell how big the cellar was, nor what was the colour of the walls. There was only one pool of light in the whole place, and it encircled the oak chair and the prisoner. It was a standard table lamp such as is often used for reading, but its bulb was of great power and brightness, adding to the overpowering warmth of the cellar. The lamp was clipped to the left-hand edge of the table, and the adjustable shade was turned so that it shone straight at the chair six feet away.

Part of the circle of light swept across the stained wood of the table, illuminating here and there the tips

of a set of fingers, a hand and wrist, a clipped cigarette sending a thin stream of blue smoke upwards.

So bright was the light that by contrast the rest of
the cellar was in darkness. The torsos and shoulders
of the five men behind the table in a row were invisible to the prisoner. The only way he could have seen
his questioners would have been to leave his chair and
move to the side, so that the indirect glow from the
light picked out their silhouettes.

This he could not do. Padded straps pinned his
ankles firmly against the legs of the chair. From each
of these legs, front and back, an L-shaped steel bracket was bolted into the floor. The chair had arms, and
the wrists of the prisoner were secured to these also
by padded straps. Another strap ran round his waist
and a third round his massive hairy chest. The padding of each was drenched with sweat.

Apart from the quiescent hands, the top of the table
was almost bare. Its only other decoration was a slit
bordered in brass and marked along one side with
figures. Out of the slit protruded a narrow brass arm
with a bakelite knob on the top, which could be moved
backwards and forwards up and down the slit. Beside
this was a simple on/off switch. The right hand of the
man on the end of the table rested negligently close
to the controls. Little black hairs crawled along the
back of the hand.

Two wires fell beneath the table, one from the
switch, the other from the current control, towards a
small electrical transformer lying on the floor near the
end man's feet. From here a stouter, rubber-clad black
cable led to a large socket in the wall behind the
group.

In the far corner of the cellar, behind the questioners, a single man sat at a wooden table, face to the wall. A tiny glow of green came from the "on" light of the tape recorder in front of him, although the spools were still.

Apart from the breathing, the silence of the cellar was almost tangible. All the men were in shirt sleeves, rolled up high and damp with sweat. The odour was crushing, a stench of sweat, metal, stale smoke, and human vomit. Even the latter, pungent enough, was overpowered by one even stronger, the unmistakeable reek of fear and pain.

The man in the centre spoke at last. The voice was civilised, gentle, coaxing.

"*Ecoute, mon p'tit* Viktor. You are going to tell us. Not now perhaps. But eventually. You are a brave man. We know that. We salute you. But even you cannot hold out much longer. So why not tell us? You think Colonel Rodin would forbid you if he were here. He would order you to tell us. He knows about these things. He would tell us himself to spare you more discomfort. You yourself know, they always talk in the end. *N'est-ce pas*, Viktor? You have seen them talk, *hein?* No one can go on and on and on. So why not now, *hein?* Then back to bed. And sleep, and sleep and sleep. No one will disturb you. . . ."

The man in the chair raised a battered face, glistening with sweat, into the light. The eyes were closed, whether by the great blue bruises caused by the feet of the Corsicans in Marseilles or by the light, one could not tell. The face looked at the table and the blackness in front of it for a while, the mouth opened and tried to speak. A small gobbet of puke emerged

and dribbled down the matted chest to the pool of
vomit in his lap. The head sagged back until the chin
touched the chest again. As it did so the shaggy hair
shook from side to side in answer. The voice from behind the table began again.

"Viktor, *écoute-moi*. You're a hard man. We all
know that. We all recognise that. You have beaten the
record already. But even you can't go on. But we can,
Viktor, we can. If we have to, we can keep you alive
and conscious for days, weeks. No merciful oblivion
like in the old days. One is technical nowadays. There
are drugs, *tu sais*. Third degree is finished now, probably gone for good. So why not talk. We understand,
you see. We know about the pain. But the little crabs,
they do not understand. They just don't understand,
Viktor. They just go on and on. . . . You want to tell
us, What are they doing in that hotel in Rome? What
are they waiting for?"

Lolling against the chest, the great head shook slowly
from side to side. It was as if the closed eyes were examining first one and then the other of the little cop-
per crabs that gripped the nipples, or the single larger
one whose serrated teeth clipped each side of the
head of the penis.

The hands of the man who had spoken lay in front
of him in a pool of light, slim, white, full of peace. He
waited a few moments longer. One of the white hands
separated itself from the other, the thumb tucked into
the palm, the four fingers spread wide, and laid itself
on the table.

At the far end the hand of the man by the electric
switch moved the brass handle up the scale from figure

two to figure four, then took the on/off switch between finger and thumb.

The hand further along the wooden top withdrew the splayed fingers, lifted the forefinger once into the air, then pointed the fingertip downwards in the worldwide signal for "Go." The electric switch went on.

The little metal crabs fixed to the man in the chair and linked by wires to the on/off switch appeared to come alive with a slight buzzing. In silence the huge form in the chair rose as if by levitation, propelled by an unseen hand in the small of the back. The legs and wrists bulged outwards against the straps until it seemed that even with the padding the leather must cut clean through the flesh and bone. The eyes, medically unable to see clearly through the puffed flesh around them, defied medicine and started outwards, bulging into vision and staring at the ceiling above. The mouth was open as if in surprise and it was half a second before the demonic scream came out of the lungs. When it did come, it went on and on and on. . . .

Viktor Kowalski broke at 4:10 in the afternoon, and the tape recorder went on.

As he started to talk, or rather ramble incoherently between whimpers and squeaks, the calm voice from the man in the centre cut across the maunderings with incisive clarity.

"Why are they there, Viktor . . . in that hotel . . . Rodin, Montclair, and Casson . . . what are they afraid of . . . where have they been, Viktor . . . whom have they seen . . . why do they see nobody, Viktor . . . tell us, Viktor . . . why Rome . . . before Rome . . . why Vienna, Viktor . . . where in Vienna . . . which hotel . . . why were they there, Viktor . . ."

Kowalski was finally silent after fifty minutes, his last ramblings as he went into relapse being recorded on tape until they stopped. The voice behind the table continued, more gently, for another few minutes until it became clear there were going to be no more answers. Then the man in the centre gave an order to his subordinates, and the session was over.

The tape recording was taken off the spool and rushed by a fast car from the cellar beneath the fortress into the outskirts of Paris and the offices of the Action Service.

The brilliant afternoon that had warmed the friendly pavements of Paris throughout the day faded to golden dusk, and at nine the street lights came on. Along the banks of the Seine the couples strolled as always on summer nights, hand in hand, slowly as if drinking in the wine of dusk and love and youth that will never, however hard they try, be quite the same again. The open-fronted cafes along the water's edge were alive with chatter and clink of glasses, greetings and mock protests, raillerie and compliments, apologies and passes. The magic of the river Seine on an August evening. Even the tourists were almost forgiven for being there and bringing their dollars with them.

In a small office near the Porte des Lilas the insouciance did not penetrate. Three men sat round a tape recorder that turned slowly on a desk. Through the late afternoon and evening they worked. One man controlled the switches, continuously flicking the spools into playback or re-wind and then playback again on the instruction of the second. This man had a pair of earphones over his head, brow furrowed in concentration as he tried to decipher meaningful words

out of the jumble of sounds coming through the
phones. A cigarette clipped between his lips, rising
blue smoke making his eyes water, he signed with his
fingers to the operator when he wanted to hear a passage again. Sometimes he listened to a ten-second
passage half a dozen times before nodding to the
operator to hold on. Then he would dictate the last
passage of speech.

The third man, a young blond, sat behind a typewriter and waited for dictation. The questions that
had been asked in the cellar beneath the fortress were
easy to understand, coming clear and precise through
the earphones. The answers were more disjointed. The
typist wrote the transcript like an interview, the questions always on a fresh line and beginning with the
letter Q. The answers were on the next line, beginning
with the letter R. These were disjointed, involving the
use of plenty of spacing dots where the sense broke
up completely.

It was nearly twelve midnight before they had finished. Despite the open window, the air was blue with
smoke and smelt like a powder magazine.

The three men rose stiff and weary. Each stretched
in his own fashion to untwine the bunched and aching
muscles. One of the three reached for the telephone,
asked for an outside line, and dialled a number. The
man with the earphones took them off and re-wound
the tape back onto the original spool. The typist took
the last sheets out of his machine, extracted the car-
bons from between them, and began to arrange the
separate piles of paper into sets of the confession in
order of pages. The top set would go to Colonel Rolland, the second to files, and the third to mimeograph

for extra copies to be made for department heads, to be distributed if Rolland deemed fit.

The call reached Colonel Rolland at the restaurant where he had been dining with friends. As usual the elegant-looking bachelor civil servant had been his witty and gallant self, and his compliments to the ladies present had been much appreciated, by them if not by their husbands. When the waiter called him to the phone, he apologised and left. The phone was on the counter. The Colonel said simply "Rolland" and waited while his operative at the other end identified himself.

Rolland then did the same by introducing into the first sentence of his conversation the correct pre-arranged word. A listener would have learned that he had received information that his car, which had been under repair, was mended, and could be collected at the Colonel's convenience. Colonel Rolland thanked his informant, and returned to the table. Within five minutes he was excusing himself with urbanity, explaining that he faced a hard day in the morning and ought to get his ration of sleep. Ten minutes later he was alone in his car, speeding through the still crowded city streets towards the quieter faubourg of Porte des Lilas. He reached his office soon after one in the morning, took off his immaculate dark jacket, ordered coffee from the night staff, and rang for his assistant.

The top copy of Kowalski's confession came with the coffee. The first time, he read the twenty-six pages of the dossier quickly, trying to grasp the gist of what the demented legionnaire had been saying. Something in the middle caught his eye, causing him to frown, but he read on to the end without a pause.

His second reading was slower, more cautious, giving greater concentration to each paragraph. The third time, he took a black felt-nib pen from the tray in front of the blotter and read even more slowly, drawing the thick black line of ink through the words and passages relating to Sylvie, Luke-something, Indochina, Algeria, JoJo, Kovacs, Corsican bastards, the Legion. All these he understood, and they did not interest him.

Much of the wandering concerned Sylvie, some of it a woman called Julie, which meant nothing to Rolland. When all this was deleted, the confession would not have covered more than six pages. Out of the remaining passages he tried to make some sense. There was Rome. The three leaders were in Rome. Well, he knew that anyway. But why? This question had been asked eight times. By and large the answer had been the same each time. They did not wish to be kidnapped as Argoud had been in February. Natural enough, thought Rolland. Had he then been wasting his time with the whole Kowalski operation? There was one word the legionnaire had mentioned twice, or rather mumbled twice, in answering these eight identical questions. The word was "secret." As an adjective? There was nothing secret about their presence in Rome. Or as a noun. What secret?

Rolland went through to the end for the tenth time, then back again to the beginning. The three OAS men were in Rome. They were there because they did not wish to be kidnapped. They did not wish to be kidnapped because they possessed a secret.

Rolland smiled ironically. He had known better than General Guibaud that Rodin would not run for cover because he was frightened.

So they knew a secret, did they? What secret? It all seemed to have stemmed from something in Vienna. Three times the word Vienna cropped up, but at first Rolland had thought it must be the town called Vienne that lies twenty miles south of Lyon. But perhaps it was the Austrian capital, not the French provincial town.

They had a meeting in Vienna. Then they went to Rome and took refuge against the possibility of being kidnapped and interrogated until they revealed a secret. The secret must stem from Vienna.

The hours passed, and so did innumerable cups of coffee. The pile of stubs in the shell-case ashtray grew. Before the thin line of paler grey started to tip the grisly industrial suburbs that lie east of the Boulevard Mortier, Colonel Rolland knew he was on to something.

There were pieces missing. Were they really missing, gone for all time since the message by phone at three in the morning had told him Kowalski would never be questioned again because he was dead? Or were they hidden somewhere in the jumbled text that had come out of the deranged brain as the final reserves of strength failed?

With his right hand Rolland began to jot down pieces of the puzzle that had no seeming place to be there. Kleist, a man called Kleist. Kowalski, being a Pole, had pronounced the word correctly, and Rolland, knowing some German still from his wartime days, wrote it down correctly although it had been spelt wrongly by the French transcriber. Or was it a person? A place perhaps? He rang the switchboard and asked them to seek out the Viennese telephone directory and search for a person or place called Kleist. The answer was back in ten minutes. There were two columns of Kleists in Vienna, all private individuals, and two places of that name: the Ewald Kleist primary school for boys, and the Pension Kleist in the Brucknerallee. Rolland noted both, but underlined the Pension Kleist. Then he read on.

There were several references to a foreigner over whom Kowalski seemed to have mixed feelings. Sometimes he used the word *"bon,"* meaning good, to refer to this man; at other times he called him a *"fâcheur,"* an annoying or irritating type. Shortly after 5 a.m. Colonel Rolland sent for the tape and tape recorder, and spent the next hour listening to it. When he finally switched off the machine he swore quietly and violently to himself. Taking a fine pen he made several alterations to the transcribed text.

Kowalski had referred to the foreigner not as *"bon"* but as *"blond."* And the word coming from the torn lips that had been written down as *"fâcheur"* had in reality been *"faucheur,"* meaning a killer.

From then on the task of piecing together Kowalski's hazy meaning was easy. The word for jackal, which had been crossed out wherever it occurred because Rolland had thought it was Kowalski's way of insulting the men who had hunted him down and were torturing him, took on a new meaning. It became the code name of the killer with the blond hair, who was a foreigner, and whom the three OAS chiefs had met at the Pension Kleist in Vienna days before they had gone into heavily protected hiding in Rome.

Rolland could work out for himself the reason now for the wave of bank and jewel robberies that had rocked France over the preceding eight weeks. The blond, whoever he was, wanted money to do a job for the OAS. There was only one job in the world that could command that kind of money. The blond had not been called in to settle a gang fight.

At seven in the morning Rolland called his communications room and ordered the night duty operator to send off a "blitz" imperative to the SDECE office in Vienna, overriding interdepartmental protocol under which Vienna was within the district of R 3 Western Europe. Then he called in every copy of the Kowalski confession and locked them all in his safe. Finally he sat down to write a report, which had only one listed recipient and was headed "for your eyes only."

He wrote carefully in longhand, describing briefly the operation which he had personally mounted of his own initiative to capture Kowalski; relating the return of the ex-legionnaire to Marseilles, lured by the ruse of a false belief that someone close to him was ill in hospital, the capture by Action Service agents, a brief mention for the record that the man had been interrogated by agents of the Service and had made a garbled confession. He felt bound to include a bald statement that in resisting arrest the ex-legionnaire had crippled two agents but had also done himself sufficient damage in an attempt at suicide that by the time he was overcome the only possible recourse was to hospitalize him. It was here, from his sick bed, that he had made his confession.

The rest of the report, which was the bulk, concerned the confession itself and Rolland's interpretation of it. When he had finished this he paused for a moment, scanning the roof-tops now gilded by the morning sun streaming in from the east. Rolland had a reputation, as he was well aware, for never overstating his case or exaggerating an issue. He composed his final paragraph with care.

"Enquiries with the intention of establishing corroborative evidence for the existence of this plot are still under way at the hour of writing. However, in the event that these enquiries should indicate the above is the truth, the plot described above constitutes in my view the most dangerous single conception that the terrorists could possibly have devised to endanger the life of the President of France. If the plot exists as described, and if the foreign-born assassin known only by the code-name of the Jackal has been engaged for this attempt on the life of the President, and is even now preparing his plans to execute the deed, it is my duty to inform you that in my opinion we face a national emergency."

Most unusually for him, Colonel Rolland typed the final copy of the report himself, sealed it in an envelope with his personal seal, addressed it, and stamped it with the highest security classification in the Secret Service. Finally he burned the sheets of foolscap on which he had written in longhand and washed the ashes down the plug of the small hand basin in a cabinet in the corner of his office.

When he had finished he washed his hands and face. As he dried them he glanced in the mirror above the wash-stand. The face that stared back at him was, he ruefully admitted, losing its handsomeness. The lean face that had been so dashing in youth and so attractive to women in maturity was beginning to look tired and strained in middle age. Too many experiences, too much knowledge of the depths of bestiality to which man could sink when he fought for his survival against his fellow man, and too much scheming and double-crossing, sending men out to die or to kill, to scream in cellars or to make other men scream in cellars, had aged the head of the Action Service far beyond his fifty-four years. There were two lines down the side of the nose and on down beyond the corners of the mouth that, if they got much longer, would no more be distinguished but simply peasant-like. Two dark smudges seemed to have settled permanently under the eyes, and the elegant grey of the sideburns was becoming white without turning silver.

"At the end of this year," he told himself, "I really am going to get out of this racket." The face looked back at him haggard. Disbelief or simply resignation? Perhaps the face knew better than the mind did. After a certain number of years there was no getting out any more. One was what one was for the rest of one's days. From the Resistance to the security police, then the SDECE, and finally the Action Service. How many men, and how much blood in all those years? he asked the face in the mirror. And all for France. And what the hell does France care? And the face looked back out of the mirror, and said nothing. For they both knew the answer.

Colonel Rolland summoned a motorcycle despatch rider to report to him personally in his office. He also ordered fried eggs, rolls and butter, and more coffee, but this time a large cup of milky coffee, with aspirins for his headache. He handed over the package with his seal and gave the despatch rider his orders. Finishing his eggs and rolls, he took his coffee and drank it on the sill of the open window, the corner that faced towards Paris. He could make out across the miles of roofs the spires of Notre Dame and, in the already hot morning haze that hung over the Seine, the Eiffel Tower further on. It was already well after nine o'clock on the morning of August 11, and the city was busily at work, probably cursing the motorcyclist in the black leather jerkin and the wailing siren who slewed his machine through the traffic towards the eighth arrondissement.

Depending on whether the menace described in the despatch on that motorcyclist's hip could be averted, thought Rolland, might hang whether or not at the end of the year he had a job to retire from.

nine

The Minister of the Interior sat at his desk later that morning and stared sombrely out of the window into the sunlit circular courtyard beneath. At the far end of the courtyard were the beautifully wrought-iron gates, decorated on each half with the coat of arms of the Republic of France, and beyond them the Place Beauvau where streams of traffic from the Faubourg Saint Honoré and the Avenue de Marigny hooted and swirled around the policeman directing them from the centre of the square.

From the other two roads that led into the square, the Avenue de Miromesnil and the rue des Saussaies, other streams of traffic would emerge on a whistled command from the policeman to cross the square and disappear on their way. He seemed to be playing the five streams of lethal Parisian traffic as a bullfighter plays a bull, calmly, with aplomb, dignity, and mastery. M. Roger Frey envied him the ordered simplicity of his task, the assured confidence he brought to it.

At the gates of the ministry two other gendarmes watched their colleague's virtuosity in the centre of the square. They carried submachine guns slung across their backs, and looked out on the world through the wrought-iron grille of the double gates, protected from the furor of the world beyond, assured of their monthly salaries, their continuing careers, their places in the warm August sunshine. The Minister envied them too, for the uncomplicated simplicity of their lives and ambitions.

He heard a page rustle behind him and spun his swivel chair back to face the desk. The man across the desk closed the file and laid it reverently on the desk before the Minister. The two men eyed each other, the silence broken only by the ticking of the ormolu clock on the mantlepiece opposite the door and the subdued roar of traffic from the Place Beauvau.

"Well, what do you think?"

Commissaire Jean Ducret, head of President de Gaulle's personal security corps, was one of the foremost experts in France on all questions of security, and particularly as that subject relates to the protection of a single life against assassination. That was why he held his job, and that was why six known plots to kill the President of France had either failed in execution or been dismantled in preparation up till that date.

"Rolland is right," he said at length. His voice was flat, unemotional, final. He might have been giving his judgement on the probable forthcoming result of a football match. "If what he says is true, the plot is of an exceptional danger. The entire filing system of all the security agencies of France, the whole network of agents and infiltrators presently maintained inside the OAS, all are reduced to impotence in the face of a foreigner, an outsider, working completely alone, without contacts or friends. And a professional into the bargain. As Rolland puts it, it is"—he flicked over the last page of the Action Service chief's report and read aloud—"'the most dangerous single conception' that one can imagine."

Roger Frey ran his fingers through the iron-grey short-cut hair and spun away towards the window again. He was not a man easily ruffled, but he was ruffled on the morning of August 11. Throughout his many years as a devoted follower of the cause of Charles de Gaulle he had built up the reputation of a tough man behind the intelligence and urbanity that had brought him to the Minister's chair. The brilliant blue eyes that could be warmly attractive or chillingly cold, the virility of the compact chest and shoulders, and the handsome, ruthless face that had brought admiring glances from not a few women who enjoy the companionship of men of power, were no façade in Roger Frey.

In the old days, when the Gaullists had had to fight for survival against American enmity, British indifference, Giraudist ambition, and Communist ferocity, he had learned his in-fighting the hard way. Somehow they had won through, and twice in eighteen years the man they followed had returned from exile and repudiation to take the position of supreme power in France. And for the past two years the battle had been on again, this time against the very men who had twice restored the General to power—the Army. Until a few minutes before, the Minister had thought the last struggle was waning, their enemies once again sliding into impotence and helpless wrath.

Now he knew it was not over yet. A lean and fanatical colonel in Rome had devised a plan that could still bring the whole edifice tumbling down by organising the death of a single man. Some countries have institutions of sufficient stability to survive the death of a president or the abdication of a king, as Britain had shown twenty-eight years earlier and America would show before the year was out. But Roger Frey was well enough aware of the state of the institutions of France in 1963 to have no illusions that the death of his President could only be the prologue to putsch and civil war.

"Well," he said finally, still looking out into the glaring courtyard, "he must be told."

The policeman did not answer. It was one of the advantages of being a technician that you did your job and left the top decisions to those who were paid to take them. He did not intend to volunteer to be the one who did the telling. The Minister turned back to face him.

"*Bien. Merci, Commissaire.* Then I shall seek an interview this afternoon and inform the President." The voice was crisp and decisive. A thing had to be done. "I need hardly ask you to maintain complete silence on this matter until I have had time to explain the position to the President and he has decided how he wishes this affair to be handled."

Commissaire Ducret rose and left, to return across the square and a hundred yards down the road to the gates of the Elysée Palace. Left to himself, the Minister of the Interior spun the buff file round to face him and again read it slowly through. He had no doubt Rolland's assessment was right, and Ducret's concurrence left him no room for manoeuvre. The danger was there, it was serious, it could not be avoided, and the President had to know.

Reluctantly he threw down a switch on the intercom in front of him and told the plastic grille that immediately buzzed at him, "Get me a call to the Secretary General of the Elysée."

Within a minute the red telephone beside the intercom rang. He lifted it and listened for a second.

"*Monsieur Foccart, s'il vous plaît.*" Another pause, then the deceptively soft voice of one of the most powerful men in France came on the line. Roger Frey explained briefly what he wanted and why.

"As soon as possible, Jacques. . . . Yes, I know you have to check. I'll wait. Please call me back as soon as you can."

The call back came within an hour. The appointment was fixed for four that afternoon, as soon as the President had finished his siesta. For a second it crossed the Minister's mind to protest that what he had on the blotter in front of him was more important than any siesta, but he stifled the protest. Like everybody in the entourage of the President, he was aware of the inadvisability of crossing the soft-voiced civil servant who had the ear of the President at all times and a private filing system of intimate information about which more was feared than was known.

At twenty to four that afternoon the Jackal emerged from Cunningham's in Curzon Street after one of the most delicious and expensive lunches that the London sea-food specialists could provide. It was after all, he mused as he swung into South Audley Street, probably his last lunch in London for some time to come, and he had reason to celebrate.

At the same moment a black DS 19 sedan swung out of the gates of the Interior Ministry of France into the Place Beauvau. The policeman in the centre of the square, forewarned by a shout from his colleagues on the iron gates, held up the traffic from all the surrounding streets, then snapped into a salute.

A hundred metres down the road the Citroen turned towards the grey stone portico in front of the Elysée Palace. Here too the gendarmes on duty, forewarned, had held up the traffic to give the sedan enough turning room to get through the surprisingly narrow archway. The two Gardes Républicaines, standing in front of their sentry boxes on each side of the portico, smacked their white-gloved hands across the magazines of the rifles in salute, and the Minister entered the forecourt of the palace.

A chain hanging in a low loop across the inner arch of the gate halted the car while the duty inspector of the day, one of Ducret's men, briefly glanced inside the car. He nodded towards the Minister, who nodded back. At a gesture from the inspector the chain was let fall to the ground and the Citroen crunched over it. Across a hundred feet of tan-coloured gravel lay the façade of the palace. Robert, the driver, pulled the car to the right and drove round the courtyard anti-clockwise, to deposit his master at the foot of the six granite steps that lead to the entrance.

The door was opened by one of the two silver-chained, black frock-coated ushers. The Minister stepped down and ran up the steps to be greeted at the plate glass door by the chief usher. They greeted each other formally, and he followed the usher inside. They had to wait for a moment in the vestibule beneath the vast chandelier suspended on its long gilded chain from the vaulted ceiling far above while the usher telephoned briefly from the marble table to the left of the door. As he put the phone down, he turned to the Minister, smiled briefly, and proceeded at his usual majestic, unhurried pace up the carpeted granite stairs to the left.

At the first floor they went down the short, wide landing that overlooked the hallway below, and stopped when the usher knocked softly on the door to the left of the landing. There was a muffled reply of *"Entrez"* from within, the usher smoothly opened the door and stood back to let the minister pass into the Salon des Ordonnances. As the Minister entered, the door closed behind him without a sound and the usher made his stately way back down the stairs to the vestibule.

From the great south windows on the far side of the Salon the sun streamed through, bathing the carpet in warmth. One of the floor-to-ceiling windows was open, and from the palace gardens came the sound of a wood pigeon cooing among the trees. The traffic of the Champs Elysées five hundred yards beyond the windows and completely shielded from view by the spreading limes and beeches, magnificent in the foliage of full summer, was simply another murmur, not even as loud as the pigeon. As usual when he was in the south-facing rooms of the Elysée Palace, M. Frey, a townman born and bred, could imagine he was in some chateau buried in the heart of the country. The President, as he knew, adored the countryside.

The ADC of the day was Colonel Tesseire. He rose from behind his desk.

"Monsieur le Ministre . . ."

"Colonel . . ." M. Frey gestured with his head towards the closed double doors with the gilt handles on the left side of the salon. "I am expected?"

"Of course, *Monsieur le Ministre.*" Tesseire crossed the room, knocked briefly on the doors, opened one half of them, and stood in the entrance.

"The Minister of the Interior, *Monsieur le Président.*"

There was a muffled assent from inside. Tesseire stepped back, smiled at the Minister, and Roger Frey went past him into Charles de Gaulle's private study.

There was almost nothing about that room, he had always thought, that did not seem to reflect to the man who occupied it. To the right were the three tall and elegant windows, like those of the Salon des Ordonnances, that gave access to the garden. In the study also one of them was open, and the murmuring of the pigeon, muted as one passed through the door between the two rooms, was heard again coming from the gardens.

Somewhere under those limes and beeches lurked quiet men toting automatics with which they could pick the ace out of the ace of spades at twenty paces. But woe betide the one of them who let himself be seen from the windows of the first floor. The man was enraged by security measures if they obtruded on his privacy. This was one of the heaviest crosses Ducret had to bear, and no one envied him the task of protecting a man for whom all forms of personal protection were an indignity he did not appreciate.

To the left, against the wall containing the glass-fronted bookshelves, was a Louis XV table on which reposed a Louis XIV clock. The floor was covered by a Savonnerie carpet made in the royal carpet factory at Chaillot in 1615. This factory, the President had once explained to him, had been a soap factory before its conversion to carpet making, and hence the name that had always applied to the carpets it produced.

There was nothing in the room that was not simple, nothing that was not dignified, nothing that was not tasteful, and above all nothing that did not exemplify the grandeur of France. And that, so far as Roger Frey was concerned, included the man behind the desk who now rose to greet him with his usual elaborate courtesy.

The Minister recalled that Harold King, doyen of British journalists in Paris and the only contemporary Anglo-Saxon who was a personal friend of Charles de Gaulle, had once remarked to him that in all of his personal mannerisms the President was not from the twentieth but from the eighteenth century. Every time he had met his master since then Roger Frey had vainly tried to imagine a tall figure in silks and brocades making those same courteous gestures and greetings. He could see the connection, but the image escaped him. Nor could he forget the few occasions when the stately old man, really roused by something that had displeased him, had used barrack-room language of such forceful crudity as to leave his entourage or Cabinet members stunned and speechless. Security and presidential displeasure went hand in hand, and when Frey thought of the document he carried in his briefcase and the request he was going to have to make, he almost quaked.

"*Mon cher* Frey."

The tall charcoal-grey-suited figure had come round

the edge of the great desk behind which he normally
sat, hand outstretched in greeting.

"Monsieur le Président, mes respects." He took the
proffered hand. At least *le Vieux* seemed to be in a
good mood. He found himself ushered to one of the
two upright chairs covered in First Empire Beauvais
tapestry in front of the desk. Charles de Gaulle, his
duty as a host done, returned to his side and sat down,
back to the wall. He leaned back, placing the finger
tips of both hands on the polished wood in front of
him.

"I am told, my dear Frey, that you wished to see
me on a matter of urgency. Well, what have you to
say to me?"

Roger Frey breathed in deeply once and began. He
explained briefly and succinctly what had brought
him, aware that de Gaulle did not appreciate long-
winded oratory except his own, and then only for
public speaking. In private he appreciated brevity,
as several of his more verbose subordinates had discovered to their embarrassment.

While he talked, the man across the desk from him
stiffened perceptibly. Leaning back further and further, seeming to grow all the while, he gazed down
the commanding promontory of his nose at the Minister as if an unpleasant substance had been introduced
into his study by a hitherto trusted servant. Roger
Frey, however, was aware that at five yards' range his
face could be no more than a blur to the President,
who concealed his shortsightedness on all public occasions by never wearing glasses except to read
speeches.

The Interior Minister finished his monologue, which

had lasted barely more than one minute, by mentioning the comments of Rolland and Ducret, and finishing, "I have the Rolland report in my case."

Without a word the presidential hand stretched out across the desk. M. Frey slid the report out of the briefcase and handed it over.

From the top pocket of his jacket Charles de Gaulle took his reading glasses, put them on, spread the folder on his desk, and started to read. The pigeon had stopped cooing as if appreciating that this was not the moment. Roger Frey stared out at the trees, then at the brass reading lamp on the desk next to the blotter. It was a beautifully turned Flambeau de Vermeil from the Restoration, fitted with an electric light, and in the five years of the presidency it had spent thousands of hours illuminating the documents of state that passed during the night across the blotter over which it stood.

General de Gaulle was a quick reader. He finished the Rolland report in three minutes, folded it carefully on the blotter, crossed his hands over it, and asked,

"Well, my dear Frey, what do you want of me?"

For the second time Roger Frey took a deep breath and launched into a succinct recitation of the steps he wished to take. Twice he used the phrase, "in my judgement, *Monsieur le Président*, it will be necessary if we are to avert this menace . . ." In the thirty-third second of his discourse he used the phrase "the interest of France."

It was as far as he got. The President cut across him, the sonorous voice rolling the word France into that of a deity in a way no other French voice of his time could equal.

"The interest of France, my dear Frey, is that the President of France is not seen to be cowering before the menace of a miserable hireling, and"—he paused while the contempt for his unknown assailant hung heavy in the room—"of a foreigner."

Roger Frey realised that he had lost. The General did not lose his temper as the Interior Minister feared he might. He began to speak clearly and precisely, as one who has no intention that his wishes should be in any way unclear to his listener. As he spoke, some of the phrases drifted through the window and were heard by Colonel Tesseire.

"La France ne saurait accepter . . . la dignité et la grandeur assujetties aux misérables menaces d'un . . . d'un CHACAL *. . ."*

Two minutes later Roger Frey left the President's presence. He nodded soberly at Colonel Tesseire, walked out through the door of the Salon des Ordonnances and down the stairs to the vestibule.

"There," thought the chief usher as he escorted the Minister down the stone steps to the waiting Citroen and watched him drive away, "goes a man with one hell of a problem, if ever I saw one. Wonder what the Old Man had to say to him." But since he was the chief usher, his face retained the immobile calm of the façade of the palace he had served for twenty years.

"No, it cannot be done that way. The President was absolutely final on that point."

Roger Frey turned from the window of his office and surveyed the man to whom he had addressed the remark. Within minutes of returning from the Elysée he had summoned his chief of personal staff. Alexandre Sanguinetti was a Corsican, another ferocious Gaullist fanatic. As the man to whom the Interior Minister had delegated over the past two years much of the detailed work of master-minding the French state security forces, Sanguinetti had established a renown and a reputation that varied according to the beholder's personal political affiliations or concept of civil rights.

By the extreme Left he was hated and feared for his unhesitating mobilisation of the CRS anti-riot squads and the no-nonsense tactics these 45,000 para-military bruisers used when confronted with a street demonstration from either the Left or the Right.

The Communists called him a Fascist, though some of his methods of keeping public order were reminiscent of the means used in the workers' paradises beyond the Iron Curtain. The extreme Right loathed him equally, quoting the same arguments of the suppression of democracy and civil rights, but more probably because the ruthless efficiency of his public-order measures had gone a long way towards preventing the complete breakdown of order that would have helped precipitate a Right-wing coup ostensibly aimed at restoring that very order.

And the public at large disliked him, because the Draconian decrees that stemmed from his office affected them all with barriers in the streets, examinations of identity cards at most major road junctions, roadblocks on all main roads, and the much-publicized photographs of young demonstrators being bludgeoned to the ground by the truncheons of the CRS. The press had already dubbed him "Monseiur Anti-OAS" and, apart from the relatively small Gaullist press, reviled him roundly. If the odium of being the most criticised man in France affected him at all, he managed to hide it. The deity of his private religion was ensconced in an office in the Elysée Palace, and within that religion Alexandre Sanguinetti was the head of the Curia. He glowered at the blotter in front of him, on which lay the buff folder containing the Rolland report.

"It's impossible. Impossible. He is impossible. We have to protect his life, but he won't let us. I could have this man, this Jackal. But you say we are allowed to take no counter-measures. What do we do? Just wait for him to strike? Just sit around and wait?"

The Minister sighed. He had expected no less from his *chef de cabinet*, but it still made his task no easier. He seated himself behind his desk again.

"Alexandre, listen. Firstly, the position is that we are not yet absolutely certain that the Rolland report is true. It is his own analysis of the ramblings of this —Kowalski, who has since died. Perhaps Rolland is wrong. Enquiries in Vienna are still being conducted. I have been in touch with Guibaud, and he expects to have the answer by this evening. But one must agree that at this stage, to launch a nation-wide hunt for a foreigner only known to us by a code-name, is hardly a realistic proposition. To that extent, I must agree with the President.

"Beyond that, these are his instructions—no, his absolutely formal orders. I repeat them so that there will be no mistake in any of our minds. There is to be no publicity, no nation-wide search, no indication to anyone outside a small circle around us that anything is amiss. The President feels that if the secret were out the press would have a field day, the foreign na-

tions would jeer, and any extra security precautions
taken by us would be interpreted both here and abroad
as the spectacle of the President of France hiding
from a single man, and a foreigner at that.

"This he will not, I repeat, will not tolerate. In fact"
—the Minister emphasised his point with pointed forefinger—"he made quite plain to me that if in our handling of the affair the details, or even the general
impression became public knowledge, heads would
roll. Believe me, *cher ami,* I have never seen him so
adamant."

"But the public programme," expostulated the Corsican, "it must inevitably be changed. There must be
no more public appearances until the man is caught.
He must surely—"

"He will cancel nothing. There will be no changes,
not by an hour or a minute. The whole thing has got
to be done in complete secrecy."

For the first time since the dismantling of the Ecole
Militaire assassination plot in February, with the arrest of the plotters, Alexandre Sanguinetti felt he was
back where he started. In the past two months, even
though battling against the wave of bank robberies
and smash-and-grab raids, he had permitted himself
to hope that the worst was over. With the OAS apparatus crumbling under the twin assaults of the Action Service from within and the hordes of police and
CRS from without, he had interpreted the crime wave
as the death throes of the Secret Army, the last handful of thugs on the rampage trying to acquire enough
money to live well in exile.

Now the last page of Rolland's report made plain
that the scores of double agents Rolland had been

able to infiltrate into even the highest ranks of the OAS had been outflanked by the anonymity of the assassin. Only three men holed up in a hotel in Rome knew his identity. He could see for himself that the archives of dossiers on everyone who had ever been remotely connected with the OAS had been rendered useless by one simple fact: the Jackal was a foreigner.

"If we are not allowed to act, what can we do?"

"I did not say we were not allowed to act," corrected Frey. "I said we were not allowed to act publicly. The whole thing must be done secretly. That leaves us only one alternative. The identity of the assassin must be revealed by a secret enquiry, he must be traced wherever he is, in France or abroad, and then destroyed without hesitation."

". . . and destroyed without hesitation. That, gentlemen, is the only course left open to us."

The Interior Minister surveyed the meeting seated round the table of the ministry conference room to let the impact of his words sink in. There were fourteen men in the room including himself.

The Minister stood at the head of the table. To his immediate right sat his *chef de cabinet,* and to his left the Prefect of Police, the political head of France's police forces.

From Sanguinetti's right hand down the length of the oblong table sat General Guibaud, head of the SDECE, Colonel Rolland, chief of the Action Service and the author of the report lying before each man. Beyond Rolland were Commissaire Ducret of the Corps de Sécurité Présidentielle, and Colonel Saint-Clair de Villaubaun, an Air Force colonel of the Elysée staff, a fanatical Gaullist but renowned in the entourage of the President as being equally fanatical concerning his own ambition.

To the left of M. Maurice Papon, the Prefect of Police, were M. Maurice Grimaud, the Director-General of France's national crime force, the Sûreté Nationale, and in a row the five heads of the departments that make up the Sûreté.

Although beloved of novelists as a crime-busting force, the Sûreté Nationale itself is simply the very small and meagrely staffed office that has control over the five crime branches that actually do the work. The task of the Sûreté is administrative, like that of the equally mis-described Interpol, and the Sûreté does not have a detective on its staff.

The man with the national police force of France under his personal orders sat next to Maurice Grimaud. He was Max Fernet, Director of the Police Judiciaire. Apart from its enormous headquarters on the Quai des Orfèvres, vastly bigger than the Sûreté's headquarters at 11, rue des Saussaies, just round the corner from the Interior Ministry, the Police Judiciaire controls seventeen Services Régionaux headquarters, one for each of the seventeen police districts of Metropolitan France. Under these come the borough police forces, 453 in all, being comprised of seventy-four Central Commissariats, 253 Constituency Commissariats and 126 local Postes de Police. The whole network ranges through two thousand towns and villages of France. This is the crime force. In the rural areas and up and down the highways the more general task of maintaining law and order is carried out by the Gendarmerie Nationale and the traffic police, the Gendarmes Mobiles. In many areas, for reasons of efficiency, the gendarmes and the *agents de police* share the same accommodation and facilities. The total number of men under Max Fernet's command in the Police Judiciaire in 1963 was just over twenty thousand.

Running down the table from Fernet's left were the heads of the other four sections of the Sûreté: the Bureau de Sécurité Publique, the Renseignments Généraux, the Direction de la Surveillance du Territoire, and the Corps Républicain de Sécurité.

The first of these, the BSP, was concerned mainly with protection of buildings, communications, highways, and anything else belonging to the state, from sabotage or damage. The second, the RG or central records office, was the memory of the other four; in its Panthéon headquarters archives were 4,500,000 personal dossiers on individuals who had come to the notice of the police forces of France since those forces were founded. They were cross-indexed along five and a half miles of shelves in categories of the names of the persons to whom they applied or the type of crime for which the person had been convicted or merely suspected. Names of witnesses who had appeared in cases, or those who had been acquitted, were also listed. Although the system was not yet computerised, the archivists prided themselves that within a few minutes they could unearth the details of an arson committed in a small village ten years back or the names of witnesses in an obscure trial that had hardly made the newspapers.

Added to these dossiers were the fingerprints of everyone who had ever had his fingerprints taken in

France, including many sets that had never been identified. There were also 10,500,000 cards, including the disembarkation card of every tourist at every border crossing point, and the hotel cards filled in by all who stayed at French hotels outside Paris. For reasons of space alone these cards had to be cleared out at fairly short intervals to make way for the vast number of fresh ones that came in each year.

The only cards regularly filled in within the area of France that did not go to the RG were those filled in at the hotels of Paris. These went to the Préfecture de Police in the Boulevard du Palais.

The DST, whose chief sat three places down from Fernet, is the counter-espionage force of France, responsible also for maintaining a constant watch on France's airports, docks, and borders. Before going to the archives, the disembarkation cards of those entering France are examined by the DST officer at the point of entry, to keep tabs on undesirables.

The last man in the row was the chief of the CRS, the 45,000-man force of which Alexandre Sanguinetti had already made such a well publicised and heartily unpopular use over the previous two years.

For reasons of space, the head of the CRS was sitting at the foot of the table, facing down the length of wood at the Minister. There was one last seat remaining, that between the head of the CRS and Colonel Saint-Clair, at the bottom right-hand corner. It was occupied by a large stolid man whose pipe fumes evidently annoyed the fastidious colonel on his left. The Minister had made a point of asking Max Fernet to bring him along to the meeting. He was Commissaire Maurice Bouvier, head of the Brigade Criminelle of the PJ.

"So that is where we stand, gentlemen," resumed the Minister. "Now you have all read the report by Colonel Rolland which lies in front of each of you. And now you have heard from me the considerable limitations which the President, in the interests of the dignity of France, has felt obliged to impose on our efforts to avert this threat to his person. I will stress again, there must be absolute secrecy in the conduct of the investigation and in any subsequent action to be taken. Needless to say, you are all sworn to total silence and will discuss the matter with no one outside this room until and unless another person has been made privy to the secret.

"I have called you all here because it seems to me that whatever we are to do, the resources of all the departments here represented must sooner or later be called upon, and you, the departmental chiefs, should have no doubt as to the urgency of this affair. It must on all occasions require your immediate and personal attention. There will be no delegation to juniors, except for tasks which do not reveal the reason behind the requirement."

He paused again. Down both sides of the table some heads nodded soberly. Others kept their eyes fixed on the speaker or on the dossier in front of them. At the far end, Commissaire Bouvier gazed at the ceiling, emitting brief bursts of smoke from the corner of his mouth like a Red Indian sending up signals. The Air Force colonel next to him winced at each emission.

"Now," resumed the Minister, "I think I may ask for

your ideas on the subject. Colonel Rolland, have you had any success with your enquiries in Vienna?"

The head of the Action Service glanced up from his own report, cast a sideways look at the general who led the SDECE, but received neither encouragement nor a frown.

General Guibaud, remembering that he had spent half the day calming down the head of R 3 Section over Rolland's early morning decision to use the Viennese office for his own enquiries, stared straight ahead of him.

"Yes," said the Colonel. "Enquiries were made this morning and afternoon by operatives in Vienna at the Pension Kleist, a small private hotel in the Brucknerallee. They carried with them photographs of Marc Rodin, René Montclair, and André Casson. There was no time to transmit to them photographs of Viktor Kowalski, which were not on file in Vienna.

"The desk clerk at the hotel stated that he recognised at least two of the men. But he could not place them. Some money changed hands, and he was asked to search the hotel register for the days between June twelfth and eighteenth, the latter being the day the three OAS chiefs took up residence together in Rome.

"Eventually he claimed to have remembered the face of Rodin as a man who booked a room in the name of Schulze on June fifteenth. The clerk said he had a form of business conference in the afternoon, spent the night in that room, and left the next day.

"He remembered that Schulze had had a companion, a very big man with a surly manner, which was why he remembered Schulze. He was visited by two men in the morning, and they had a conference. The two visitors could have been Casson and Montclair. He could not be sure, but he thought he had seen at least one of them before.

"The clerk said the men remained in their room all day, apart from one occasion in the late morning when Schulze and the giant, as he called Kowalski, left for half an hour. None of them had any lunch, nor did they come down to eat."

"Were they visited at all by a fifth man?" asked Sanguinetti impatiently. Rolland continued his report as before, in flat tones.

"During the evening another man joined them. The clerk said he remembered because the visitor entered the hotel so quickly, heading straight up the stairs, that the clerk did not get a chance to see him. He thought he must be one of the guests, who had retained his key. But he saw the tail of the man's coat going up the stairs. A few seconds later the man was back in the hall. The clerk was sure it was the same man because of the coat.

"The man used the desk phone and asked to be put through to Schulze's room, number sixty-four. He spoke a few words in French, then replaced the phone and went back up the stairs. He spent some time there, then left without saying another word. Schulze and the other men stayed for the night, then left after breakfast in the morning.

"The only description the clerk could give of the evening visitor was: tall, age uncertain, features apparently regular but he wore wraparound dark glasses, spoke fluent French, and had blond hair left rather long and swept back from the forehead."

"Is there any chance of getting the man to help

make up an Identikit picture of the blond?" asked the Prefect of Police, Papon.

Rolland shook his head.

"My—our agents were posing as Viennese plain-clothes police. Fortunately, one of them could pass for a Viennese. But that is a masquerade that could not be sustained indefinitely. The man had to be interviewed at the hotel desk."

"We must get a better description than that," protested the head of the Records Office. "Was any name mentioned?"

"No," said Rolland. "What you have just heard is the outcome of three hours spent interrogating the clerk. Every point was gone over time and time again. There is nothing else he can remember. Short of an Identikit picture, that's the best description he could give."

"Could you not snatch him like Argoud, so that he could make up a picture of this assassin here in Paris?" queried Colonel Saint-Clair.

The Minister interjected.

"There can be no more snatches. The German Foreign Ministry is still enraged over the Argoud snatch. That kind of thing can work once, but not again."

"Surely in a matter of this seriousness the disappearance of a desk clerk can be done more discreetly than the Argoud affair?" suggested the head of the DST.

"It is in any case doubtful," said Max Fernet quietly, "whether an Identikit picture of a man wearing wrap-around dark glasses would be very helpful. Very few Identikit pictures made up on the basis of an unremarkable incident lasting twenty seconds two months before ever seem to look like the criminal when he is eventually caught. Most such pictures could be of half a million people, and some are actually misleading."

"So apart from Kowalski, who is dead, and who told everything he knew, which was not much, there are only four men in the world who know the identity of this Jackal," said Commissaire Ducret. "One is the man himself, and the other three are in a hotel in Rome. How about trying to get one of them back here?"

Again, the Minister shook his head.

"My instructions on that are formal. Kidnappings are out. The Italian Government would go out of its mind if this kind of thing happened a few yards from the Via Condotti. Besides, there are some doubts as to its feasibility. General?"

General Guibaud lifted his eyes to the assembly.

"The extent and quality of the protective screen Rodin and his two henchmen have built round themselves, according to the reports of my agents who have them under permanent surveillance, rule this out from the practical standpoint also," he said. "There are eight top-class ex-Legion gunmen round them, or seven if Kowalski has not been replaced. All the lifts, stairs, fire escape, and roof are guarded. It would involve a major gun battle, probably with gas grenades and sub-machine guns, to get one of them alive. Even then, the chances of getting the man out of the country and five hundred kilometres north to France, with the Italians on the rampage, would be very slight indeed. We have men who are some of the world's top experts in this kind of thing, and they say it would be just about impossible short of a commando-style military operation."

Silence descended on the room again.

"Well, gentlemen," said the Minister, "are there any more suggestions?"

"This Jackal must be found. That much is clear," replied Colonel Saint-Clair. Several of the others round the table glanced at each other, and an eyebrow or two was raised.

"That much certainly is clear," murmured the Minister at the head of the table. "What we are trying to devise is a way in which that can be done, within the limits imposed upon us, and on that basis perhaps we can best decide which of the departments here represented would be best suited for the job."

"The protection of the President of the Republic," announced Saint-Clair grandly, "must depend in the last resort, when all others have failed, on the Presidential Security Corps and the President's personal staff. We, I can asure you, Minister, will do our duty."

Some of the hard-core professionals closed their eyes in unfeigned weariness. Commissaire Ducret shot the colonel a glance which, if looks would kill, would have dropped Saint-Clair in his tracks.

"Doesn't he know the Old Man's not listening," growled Guibaud under his breath to Rolland.

Roger Frey raised his eyes to meet those of the Elysée Palace courtier and demonstrated why he was a minister.

"Colonel Saint-Clair is perfectly right, of course," he purred. "We shall all do our duty. And I am sure it has occurred to the Colonel that should a certain department undertake the responsibility for the destruction of this plot, and fail to achieve it, or even employ methods inadvertently capable of bringing publicity contrary to the wishes of the President, certain disapprobation would inevitably descend upon the head of him who had failed."

The menace hung above the long table more tangible than the pall of blue smoke from Bouvier's pipe. Saint-Clair's thin pale face tightened perceptibly, and the worry showed in his eyes.

"We are all aware here of the limited opportunities available to the Presidential Security Corps," said Commissaire Ducret flatly. "We spend our time in the immediate vicinity of the President's person. Evidently this investigation must be far more wide-ranging than my staff could undertake without neglecting its primary duties."

No one contradicted him, for each department chief was aware that what the Presidential Security chief said was true. But neither did anyone else wish the ministerial eye to fall on him. Roger Frey looked round the table, and rested on the smoke-shrouded bulk of Commissaire Bouvier at the far end.

"What do you think, Bouvier? You have not spoken yet?"

The detective eased the pipe out of his mouth, managed to let a last squirt of odoriferous smoke waft straight into the face of Saint-Clair, who had turned towards him, and spoke calmly as one stating a few simple facts that had just occurred to him.

"It seems to me, Minister, that the SDECE cannot disclose this man through their agents in the OAS, since not even the OAS know who he is; that the Action Service cannot destroy him since they do not know whom to destroy. The DST cannot pick him up at the border for they do not know whom to intercept, and the RG can give us no documentary information about him because they do not know what documents to search for. The Police cannot arrest him, for they do not know whom to arrest, and the CRS cannot pursue him, since they are unaware whom they are pursuing. The entire structure of the security forces of France are powerless for want of a name. It seems to me therefore that the first task, without which all other proposals become meaningless, is to give this man a name. With a name we get a face, with a face a passport, with a passport an arrest. But to find the name, and do it in secret, is a job for pure detective work."

He was silent again, and inserted the stem of his pipe between his teeth. What he had said was digested by each of the men round the table. No one could fault it. Sanguinetti, by the Minister's side, nodded slowly.

"And who, Commissaire, is the best detective in France?" asked the Minister quietly. Bouvier considered for a few seconds, before removing his pipe again.

"The best detective in France, messieurs, is my own deputy, Commissaire Claude Lebel."

"Summon him," said the Minister of the Interior.

PART TWO

Anatomy of a Manhunt

An hour later Claude Lebel emerged from the conference room dazed and bewildered. For fifty minutes
he had listened as the Minister of the Interior had
briefed him on the task that lay ahead.

On entering the room, he had been bidden to sit at
the end of the table, sandwiched between the head of
the CRS and his own chief, Bouvier. In silence from
the other fourteen men he had read the Rolland report, while aware that curious eyes were assessing him
from all sides.

When he put the report down, the worry had started
inside him. Why call him? Then the Minister started
to speak. It was neither a consultation nor a request.
It was a directive, followed by a copious briefing. He
would set up his own office; he would have unlimited
access to all necessary information; the entire resources
of the organisations headed by the men seated round
the table would be at his disposal. There were to be
no limits to the costs incurred.

Several times the need for absolute secrecy, the imperative of the Head of State himself, had been impressed on him. While he listened his heart sank. They
were asking, no, demanding the impossible. He had
nothing to go on. There was no crime—yet. There were
no clues. There were no witnesses, except three whom
he could not talk to. Just a name, a code-name, and
the whole world to search in.

Claude Lebel was, as he knew, a good cop. He had

243

always been a good cop, slow, precise, methodical, painstaking. Just occasionally he had shown the flash of inspiration that is needed to turn a good cop into a remarkable detective. But he had never lost sight of the fact that in police work ninety-nine percent of the effort is routine, unspectacular enquiry, checking and double-checking, laboriously building up a web of parts until the parts become a whole, the whole becomes a net, and the net finally encloses the criminal with a case that will not just make headlines but stand up in court.

He was known in the PJ as a bit of a plodder, a methodical man who hated publicity and had never given the sort of press conferences on which some of his colleagues had built their reputations. And yet he had gone steadily up the ladder, solving his cases, seeing his criminals convicted. When a vacancy had occurred at the head of the Homicide Division of the Brigade Criminelle three years before, even the others in line for the job had agreed it was fair that Lebel should have the job. He had a good steady record with Homicide and in three years had never failed to procure an arrest, although once the accused was acquitted on a technicality.

As head of Homicide he had come more closely to the notice of Maurice Bouvier, chief of the whole Brigade, and another old-style cop. So when Deputy Chief Hippolyte Dupuy had died suddenly a few weeks back, it was Bouvier who had asked that Lebel become his new deputy. There were some in the PJ who suspected that Bouvier, bogged down for a lot of the time with administrative details, appreciated a retiring subordinate who could handle the big, headline-making cases quietly, without stealing his superior's thunder. But perhaps they were just being uncharitable.

After the meeting at the ministry, the copies of the Rolland report were gathered up for storage in the Minister's safe. Lebel alone was allowed to keep Bouvier's copy. His only request had been that he be allowed to seek the cooperation, in confidence, of the heads of some of the Criminal Investigation forces of the major countries likely to have the identity of a professional assassin like the Jackal on their files. Without such cooperation, he pointed out, it would be impossible even to start looking.

Sanguinetti had asked if such men could be relied on to keep their mouths shut. Lebel had replied that he knew personally the men he needed to contact, that his enquiries would not be official but would be along the personal-contact basis that exists between most of the Western world's top policemen. After some reflexion, the Minister had granted the request.

And now he stood in the hall waiting for Bouvier and watching the chiefs of department file past him on their way out. Some nodded curtly and passed on; others ventured a sympathetic smile as they said good night. Almost the last to leave, while inside the conference room Bouvier conferred quietly with Max Fernet, was the aristocratic colonel from the Elysée staff. Lebel had briefly caught his name, as the men round the table were introduced, as Saint-Clair de Villauban. He stopped in front of the small and roly-poly Commissaire and eyed him with ill-concealed distaste.

"I hope, Commissaire, that you will be successful

in your enquiries, and rapidly so," he said. "We at the Palace will be keeping a very close eye on your progress. In the event that you should fail to find this bandit, I can assure you that there will be . . . repercussions."

He turned on his heel and stalked down the stairs towards the foyer. Lebel said nothing but blinked rapidly several times.

One of the factors in the make-up of Claude Lebel that had led to his successes when enquiring into crime over the previous twenty years, since he had joined the police force of the Fourth Republic as a young detective in Normandy, was his capacity to inspire people with the confidence to talk to him. He had a knack of making simple people, the humble and the lowly who normally fear and dislike policemen, unbutton their thoughts and suspicions to him. The reason he could do this was his seeming air of helplessness, of being, like them, one of the downtrodden and put-upon of this world.

He lacked the imposing bulk of Bouvier, the traditional image of the authority of the law. Nor did he have the smartness with words that exemplified so many of the new breed of young detectives now coming into the force, who could bully and browbeat a witness into tears. He did not feel the lack.

He was aware that most crime in any society is either carried out against, or witnessed by, the little people: the shopkeeper, the sales assistant, the postman, or the bank clerk. These people he could make talk to him, and he knew it.

It was partly because of his size; he was small, and resembled in many ways the cartoonist's image of a hen-pecked husband, which, although no one in the department knew it, was just what he was.

His dress was dowdy, a crumpled suit and a mackintosh. His manner was mild, almost apologetic, and in his request of a witness for information it contrasted so sharply with the attitude the witness had experienced from his first interview with the law that the witness tended to warm towards the detective as a refuge from the roughness of the subordinates.

But there was something more. He had been head of the Homicide Division of the most powerful criminal police force in Europe. He had been ten years a detective with the Brigade Criminelle of the renowned Police Judiciaire of France. Behind the mildness and the seeming simplicity was a combination of shrewd brain and a dogged refusal to be ruffled or intimidated by anyone when he was carrying out a job. He had been threatened by some of the most vicious gang bosses of France, who had thought from the rapid blinking with which Lebel greeted such approaches that their warnings had been duly taken. Only later, from a prison cell, had they had the leisure to realise they had underestimated the soft brown eyes and the toothbrush moustache.

Twice he had been subjected to intimidation by wealthy and powerful figures, once when an industrialist had wished to see one of his junior employees charged with embezzlement on the basis of a cursory glance at the auditor's evidence, and once when a society blade had wished him to drop investigations into a young actress's death from drugs.

In the first case the enquiry into the affairs of the industrialist had resulted in certain other and far bigger discrepancies being unearthed which had nothing to do with the junior accountant, but which had caused the industrialist to wish he had departed for Switzerland while he had the chance. The second time the society host had ended up with a lengthy period as a guest of the state, during which time he could regret that he had ever bothered to head a vice ring from his Avenue Victor Hugo penthouse.

Claude Lebel's reaction to the remarks of Colonel Saint-Clair was to blink like a rebuked schoolboy and say nothing.

As the last man filed out of the conference room, Maurice Bouvier joined him. Max Fernet wished him luck, shook hands briefly, and headed down the stairs. Bouvier clapped a ham-like hand on Lebel's shoulder.

"*Eh, bien, mon petit* Claude. So that's the way it is, *hein?* All right, it was me who suggested the PJ handle this business. It was the only thing to do. Those others would have talked round in circles forever. Come, we'll talk in the car." He led the way downstairs and the pair of them climbed into the back of the Citroen that waited in the courtyard.

It was past nine o'clock, and a dark purple streak lying over Neuilly was all that remained of the day. Bouvier's car swept down the Avenue de Marigny and over the Place Clemenceau. Lebel glanced out to the right and up the brilliant river of the Champs Elysées, whose grandeur on a summer night never ceased to surprise and excite him, despite the ten years that had passed since he came up from the provinces.

"You'll have to drop whatever you are doing. Everything. Clear the desk completely. I'll assign Favier and Malcoste to take over your outstanding cases. Do you want a new office for this job?"

"No, I prefer to stick to my present one."

"OK, fine, but from now on it becomes headquarters of Operation Find-the-Jackal. Nothing else. Right? Is there anyone you want to help you?"

"Yes. Caron," said Lebel, referring to one of the younger inspectors who had worked with him in Homicide and whom he had brought to his new job as Assistant Chief of the Brigade Criminelle.

"OK, you have Caron. Anyone else?"

"No thank you. But Caron will have to know."

Bouvier thought for a few moments.

"It should be all right. They can't expect miracles. Obviously you must have an assistant. But don't tell him for an hour or two. I'll ring Frey when I get to the office and ask for formal clearance. Nobody else has to know, though. It would be in the press inside two days if it got out."

"Nobody else, just Caron," said Lebel.

"*Bon*. There's one last thing. Before I left the meeting Sanguinetti suggested the whole group who were there tonight be kept informed at regular intervals of progress and development. Frey agreed. Fernet and I tried to head it off, but we lost. There's to be a briefing by you every evening at the Ministry from now on. Ten o'clock sharp."

"Oh God," said Lebel.

"In theory," continued Bouvier with heavy irony, "we shall all be available to offer our best advice and suggestions. Don't worry, Claude, Fernet and I will be there too, in case the wolves start snapping."

"This is until further notice?" asked Lebel.

"I'm afraid so. The hell of it is, there's no time schedule for this operation. You've just got to find this assassin before he gets *le grand* Charles. We don't know whether the man himself has a timetable, or what it could be. It might be for a hit tomorrow morning, maybe not for a month yet. You have to assume you are working full speed until he has been caught, or at least identified and located. From then on I think the Action Service boys can take care of things."

"Bunch of thugs," murmured Lebel.

"Granted," said Bouvier easily, "but they have their uses. We live in hair-raising times, my dear Claude. Added to a vast increase in normal crime, we now have political crime. There are some things that just have to be done. They do them. Anyway, just try and find this jackal, huh."

The car swept into the Quai des Orfèvres and turned through the gates of the PJ. Ten minutes later Claude Lebel was back in his office. He walked to the window, opened it and leant out, gazing across the river towards the Quai des Grands Augustins on the Left Bank in front of him. Although separated by a narrow strip of the Seine where it flowed round the Ile de la Cité, he was close enough to see the diners in the pavement restaurants dotted along the quay and hear the laughter and the clink of bottles on glasses of wine.

Had he been a different kind of man, it might have occurred to him that the powers conferred on him in the last ninety minutes had made him, for a spell at least, the most powerful cop in Europe; that nobody short of the President or the Interior Minister could veto his request for facilities; that he could almost mobilise the army, provided it could be done secretly. It might also have occurred to him that exalted though his powers were, they were dependent upon success; that with success he could crown his career with honours, but that in failure he could be broken, as Saint-Clair de Villauban had indicated.

Because he was what he was, he thought of none of these things. He was puzzling as to how he would explain over the phone to Amélie that he was not coming home until further notice. There was a knock on the door.

Inspectors Malcoste and Favier came in to collect the dossiers of the four cases on which Lebel had been working when he had been called away earlier that evening. He spent half an hour briefing Malcoste on the two cases he was assigning to him, and Favier on the other two.

When they had gone he sighed heavily. There was a knock on the door. It was Lucien Caron.

"I just got a call from Commissaire Bouvier's office," he began. "He told me to report to you."

"Quite right. Until further notice I have been taken off all routine duties and given a rather special job. You've been assigned to be my assistant."

He did not bother to flatter Caron by revealing that he had asked for the young inspector to be his right hand man. The desk phone rang, he picked it up and listened briefly.

"Right," he resumed, "that was Bouvier to say you have been given security clearance to be told what it is all about. For a start you had better read this."

While Caron sat on the chair in front of the desk and read the Rolland file, Lebel cleared all the remaining folders and notes off his desk and stacked them on the untidy shelves behind him. The office hardly looked like the nerve center of the biggest manhunt in France, but police offices never do look like much.

Lebel's office was no more than twelve feet by fourteen, with two windows on the south face looking out over the river towards the lively honeycomb of the Latin Quarter clustering round the Boulevard St. Michel. Through one of the windows the sounds of the night and the warm summer air drifted in. The office contained two desks, one for Lebel, which stood with its back to the window, another for a secretary, which stood along the east wall. The door was opposite the window.

Apart from the two desks and two chairs behind them, there were one other upright chair, an armchair next to the door, six large grey filing cabinets standing along almost the whole of the west wall and whose combined tops supported an array of reference and law books, and one set of bookshelves, situated between the windows and stuffed with almanacs and files.

Of signs of home there was only the framed photograph on Lebel's desk of an ample and determined-looking lady, who was Madame Amélie Lebel, and two children, a plain girl with steel-rimmed glasses and pigtails and a youth with an expression as mild and put-upon as his father's.

Caron finished reading and looked up.

"*Merde*," he said.

"As you say, *une énorme merde*," replied Lebel, who seldom permitted himself the use of strong language. Most of the top commissaires of the PJ were known to their immediate staff by nicknames like *"le Patron"* or *"le Vieux."* Claude Lebel, perhaps because he never drank more than a small aperitif, did not smoke or swear, and reminded younger detectives inevitably of one of their former school-teachers, was known within Homicide and more lately in the corridors of the Brigade chief's administrative floor as *"le Professeur."* Had he not been such a good thieftaker, he would have become something of a figure of fun.

"Nevertheless," continued Lebel, "listen while I fill you in on the details. It will be our last chance."

For thirty minutes he briefed Caron on the events of the afternoon, from Roger Frey's meeting with the President to the meeting in the ministry conference room, to his own brusque summons on the recommendation of Maurice Bouvier, to the final setting up of the office in which they now sat as the headquarters of the manhunt for the Jackal. Caron listened in silence.

"Mon Dieu," he said at last when Lebel had finished, "they *have* fixed you." He thought for a moment, then looked up at his chief with worry and concern. *"Mon commissaire,* you know they have given you this because no one else wants it? You know what they will do to you if you fail to catch this man in time?"

Lebel nodded.

"Yes, Lucien, I know. There's nothing I can do. I've been given the job. So, from now we just have to do it."

"Where on earth do we start?"

"We start by recognising that we have the widest

powers ever granted to two cops in France," replied Lebel cheerfully. "So, we use them.

"To start with, get installed behind that desk. Take a pad and note the following. Get my normal secretary transferred or given paid leave until further notice. No one else can be let into the secret. You become my assistant and secretary rolled into one. Get a camp bed in here from emergency stores, linen and pillows, washing and shaving gear. Get a percolator of coffee, some milk and sugar brought from the canteen and installed. We're going to need a lot of coffee.

"Get onto the switchboard and instruct them to leave ten outside lines and one operator permanently at the disposal of this office. If they quibble, refer them to Bouvier personally. As for any other requests from me for facilities, get straight onto the department chief and quote my name. Fortunately, this office now gets top priority from every other ancillary service—by order. Prepare a circular memorandum, copy to every department chief who attended this evening's meeting, ready for my signature, announcing that you are now my sole assistant and empowered to require from them anything that I would ask them for personally if I were not engaged. Got it?"

Caron finished writing and looked up.

"Got it, chief, I can do that tonight. Which is the top priority?"

"The telephone switchboard. I want a good man on that, the best they've got. Get on to Chief of Administration at his home, and again quote Bouvier for authority."

"Right. What do we want from them first?"

"I want, as soon as they can get it, a direct link personally to the Homicide man in seven countries. Fortunately, I know most of them personally from past meetings of Interpol. In some cases I know the Deputy-Chief. If you can't get one, get the other.

"The countries are: United States, that means the Office of Domestic Intelligence in Washington; Britain, Assistant Commissioner (Crime), Scotland Yard; Belgium; Holland; Italy; West Germany; South Africa. Get them at home or in the office.

"When you get each of them one by one, arrange a series of telephone calls from Interpol Communications Room between me and them between seven and ten in the morning at twenty-minute intervals. Better get the Americans in first because of the time difference. Get on to Interpol Communications and book the calls as each Homicide Chief at the other end agrees to be in his own Communications room at the appointed time. The calls should be person-to-person on the UHF frequency, and there is to be no listening in. Impress on each of them that what I have to say is for their ears only and of top priority not only for France but possibly for their own country. Prepare me a list by six in the morning of the schedule of the seven calls that have been booked, in order of sequence."

Caron, looking slightly dazed, glanced up from his several pages of scribbled notes.

"Yes, chief, I've got it. *Bon*, I'd better get to work." He reached out for the telephone.

Claude Lebel passed out of the office and headed for the stairs. As he did so, the clock of Notre Dame farther down the island chimed midnight, and France passed into the morning of August 12.

eleven

Colonel Raoul Saint-Clair de Villauban arrived home
just before midnight. He had spent the previous three
hours meticulously typing his report on the evening's
meeting in the Interior Ministry, which would be on
the desk of the Secretary-General of the Elysée first
thing in the morning.

He had taken particular pains over the report, tearing up two rough copies before he was satisfied, then
carefully typing out the third and final copy by himself. It was irritating to have to engage in the menial
task of typing, and he was not used to it, but it had
the advantage of keeping the facts from any secretary
—a fact that he had not hesitated to point out in the
body of the report—and also of enabling him to have
the document ready for production first thing in the
morning, which he hoped would not go unnoticed.
With luck the report would be on the President's
desk an hour after being read by the Secretary-
General, and this also would do him no harm.

He had used extra care in selecting just the right
phraseology to give a slight hint of the writer's disapproval of putting a matter so important as the security of the head of state into the sole hands of a commissaire of police, a man more accustomed by training
and experience to uncovering petty criminals of little
brains or talent.

It would not have done to go too far, for Lebel
might even find his man. But in the event that he did

not, it was as well that there was someone sufficiently on his toes to have had doubts about the wisdom of the choice of Lebel at the time.

Moreover, he had certainly not taken to Lebel. A common little man, had been his private judgement. "Possessed no doubt of a competent record," had been his phrasing in the report.

Musing over the first two copies he had written in longhand, he decided that the most advantageous position for him to take would be not to oppose the appointment outright since it had been agreed by the meeting as a whole. Also if he opposed the selection he would be asked for specific reasons. On the other hand, he determined to keep a close watch on the whole operation, on behalf of the presidential secretariat, and to be the first to point out, with due sobriety, the inefficiencies in the conduct of the investigation as and when they occurred.

His musings on how he could best keep track of what Lebel was up to were interrupted by a telephone call from Sanguinetti to inform him that the Minister had made a last-minute decision to preside over nightly meetings at ten each evening to hear a progress report from Lebel. The news had delighted Saint-Clair. It solved his problem for him. With a little background homework during the daytime, he would be able to put forceful and pertinent questions to the detective and reveal to the others that at least in the presidential secretariat they were keeping wide awake to the gravity and urgency of the situation.

Privately he did not put the assassin's chances very high, even if there were an assassin in the offing. The presidential security screen was the most efficient in the world, and part of his job in the secretariat was to devise the organisation of the President's public appearances and the routes he would follow. He had few fears that this intensive and highly planned security screen could be penetrated by some foreign gunman.

He let himself in by the front door of his flat and heard his newly installed mistress call from the bedroom.

"Is that you, darling?"

"Yes, *chérie*. Of course it's me. Have you been lonely?"

She came running through from the bedroom, dressed in a filmy black baby-doll nightie, trimmed at throat and hem with lace. The indirect light from the bedroom lamp, shining through the open door of the bedroom, silhouetted the curves of her young woman's body. As usual when he saw his mistress, Raoul Saint-Clair felt a complacent thrill of satisfaction that she was his, and so deeply in love with him.

She threw her bare arms around his neck and gave him a long open-mouthed kiss. He responded as best he could while still clutching his briefcase and the evening paper.

"Come," he said when they separated, "get into bed and I'll join you." He gave her a slap on the bottom to speed her on her way. The girl skipped back into the bedroom, threw herself on the bed, and spread out her limbs, hands crossed behind her neck, breasts upthrust.

Saint-Clair entered the room and glanced at her with satisfaction. She grinned back lasciviously.

During their fortnight together she had learned that

only the most blatant suggestiveness and carnality could arouse the courtier. Privately, Jacqueline hated him as much as on the first day they had met, but she had learned that what he lacked in virility he made up in loquacity, particularly about his importance in the scheme of things at the Elysée Palace.

"Hurry," she whispered, "I want you."

Saint-Clair smiled with genuine pleasure and took off his shoes, laying them side by side at the foot of the dumb waiter. The jacket followed, its pockets carefully emptied on to the dressing table top. The trousers came next, to be meticulously folded and laid over the protruding arm of the dumb waiter. His long thin legs protruded from beneath the shirt tails like whiskery white knitting needles.

"What kept you so long?" asked Jacqueline. "I've been waiting for ages."

Saint-Clair shook his head sombrely.

"Certainly nothing that you should bother your head with, my dear."

"Oh, you're mean." She turned over abruptly onto her side in a mock-sulk, facing away from him, knees bent. His fingers slipped on the tie-knot as he looked across the room at the chestnut hair tumbling over the shoulders and the full hips now uncovered by the shortie night-dress. Another five minutes and he was ready for bed, buttoning the monogrammed silk pyjamas.

He stretched his length on the bed next to her and ran his hand down the dip of the waist and up to the summit of her hip, the fingers slipping down towards the sheet and round the swell of the warm buttock.

"What's the matter, then?"

"Nothing."

"I thought you wanted to make love."

"You just don't give me any explanation. I can't ring you at the office. I've been lying here for hours worrying that something might have happened to you. You've never been this late before without ringing me."

She rolled over onto her back and looked up at him. Propped on his elbow, he slipped his free hand under the nightie and started to knead one of her breasts.

"Look, darling, I've been very busy. There was something of a crisis, something I had to sort out before I could get away. I'd have rung but there were people still working, popping in and out of the office the whole time. Several of them know my wife is away. It should have seemed odd for me to ring home through the switchboard."

She slipped a hand through his pyjama fly to encircle the limp penis, and was rewarded with a light tremor.

"There couldn't have been anything so big you couldn't have let me know you'd be late, darling. I was worrying all night."

"Well, there's no need to worry any more. *Suce-moi,* you know I like that."

She laughed, reached up with her other hand to pull his head down and bit him on the earlobe.

"No, he doesn't deserve it. Not yet anyway." She squeezed the slowly hardening prick in rebuke. The colonel's breathing was noticeably shallower. He started kissing her open-mouthed, his hand kneading first one and then the other nipple so hard that she wriggled.

"*Suce-moi,*" he whispered.

She shifted slightly and undid the pyjama cord. Raoul Saint-Clair watched the mane of brown hair fall forward from her head to shroud his belly, lay back, and sighed with pleasure.

"It seems the OAS are still after the President," he said. "The plot was discovered this afternoon. It's being taken care of. That's what kept me."

There was a soft "plop" as the girl withdrew her head a few inches.

"Don't be silly, darling, they were finished long ago." She went back to her task.

"They're sure as hell not. Now they've hired a foreign assassin to try to kill him. Aeeegh, don't bite."

Half an hour later Colonel Raoul Saint-Clair de Villauban lay asleep, face half-buried in the pillow, snoring gently from his exertions. Beside him his mistress lay staring up through the darkness at the ceiling, dimly lit where the lights from the street outside filtered through a tiny crack where the curtains joined.

What she had learned had left her aghast. Although she had had no previous knowledge of any such plot, she would work out for herself the importance of Kowalski's confession.

She waited in silence until the bedside clock with the luminous dials registered two in the morning. Easing herself out of the bed, she slid the plug of the bedroom telephone extension out of its socket.

Before walking to the door she bent over the colonel, and was grateful he was not the sort of man who liked to sleep in embrace with his bedmate. He was still snoring.

Outside the bedroom she quietly closed the door, crossed the sitting room towards the hall, and closed the door after her. From the phone on the hall table she dialed a Molitor number. There was a wait of several minutes until a sleepy voice answered. She spoke rapidly for two minutes, received an acknowledgement, and hung up. A minute later she was back in bed, trying to get to sleep.

Throughout the night crime chiefs of the police forces of five European countries, America, and South Africa were being disturbed or waked with long-distance calls from Paris. Most of them were irritated and sleepy. In Western Europe the time was the same as Paris, the small hours of the morning. In Washington the time was nine in the evening when the call from Paris came through, and the chief of FBI Domestic Intelligence was at a dinner party. It was only at the third attempt that Caron could get him, and then their conversation was marred by the chatter of guests and the clink of glasses from the next room, where the party was in progress. But he got the message and agreed to be in the communications room of the FBI headquarters at ten past one in the morning, Washington time, to take a call from Commissaire Lebel, who would be ringing him from Interpol at ten past seven, Paris time.

The crime chiefs of the Belgian, Italian, German, and Dutch police were all apparently good family men; each was wakened in turn and after listening to Caron for a few minutes agreed to be in his communications room at the time Caron suggested to take a person-to-person call from Lebel on a matter of great urgency.

Van Ruys of South Africa was out of town and

would not be able to get back to headquarters by sunrise, so Caron spoke to Anderson, his deputy.

The call reached Mr. Anthony Mallinson, Assistant Commissioner (Crime) for Scotland Yard, in his home at Bexley shortly before four. He growled in protest at the insistent clanging of the bell beside his bed, reached out for the mouthpiece, and muttered, "Mallinson."

"Mister Anthony Mallinson?" asked a voice.

"Speaking." He shrugged to clear the bedclothes from his shoulders, and glanced at his watch.

"My name is Inspector Lucien Caron, of the French Sûreté Nationale. I am ringing on behalf of Commissaire Claude Lebel."

The voice, speaking good but strongly accented English, was coming over clearly. Obviously line traffic at that hour was light. Mallinson frowned. Why couldn't the blighters call at a civilised hour?

"Yes?"

"I believe you know Commissaire Lebel, perhaps, Mister Mallinson?"

Mallinson thought for a moment. Lebel? Oh, yes, little fellow, had been head of Homicide in the PJ. Didn't look much but he got results. Been damn helpful over that murdered English tourist two years back. Could have been nasty in the press if they hadn't caught the killer in double-quick time.

"Yes, I know Commissaire Lebel," he said down the phone. "What's it about?"

Beside him his wife Lily, disturbed by the talking, grumbled in her sleep.

"There is a matter of very considerable urgency, which also requires a great degree of discretion, that has cropped up. I am assisting Commissaire Lebel on the case. It is a most unusual case. The Commissaire would like to place a person-to-person call to you in your communications room at the Yard this morning at nine o'clock. Could you please be present to take the call?"

Mallinson thought for a moment.

"Is this a routine enquiry between cooperating police forces?" he asked. If it were they could use the routine Interpol network. Nine o'clock was a busy time at the Yard.

"No, Mister Mallinson, it is not. It is a question of a personal request by the Commissaire to you for a little discreet assistance. It may be there is nothing that affects Scotland Yard in the matter that has come up. Most probably so. If that is the case, it would be better if there were no formal request placed."

Mallinson thought it over. He was by nature a cautious man and had no wish to be involved in clandestine enquiries from a foreign police force. If a crime had been committed or a criminal had fled to Britain, that was another matter. In that case why the secrecy? Nonetheless, Lebel wanted a bit of help on the Old Boy network and that was what Old Boy networks were for.

"All right, I'll take the call. Nine o'clock."

"Thank you so much, Mister Mallinson."

"Good night." Mallinson replaced the receiver, reset the alarm clock for six-thirty instead of seven, and went back to sleep.

In a small and fusty bachelor flat, while Paris slept towards the dawn, a middle-aged schoolmaster paced up and down the floor of the cramped bedsitter. The scene around him was chaotic; books, newspapers, magazines and manuscripts lay scattered over the table, chairs and sofa, and even on the coverlet of the narrow bed set into its alcove on the far side of the room. In another alcove a sink overflowed with unwashed crockery.

What obsessed his thoughts in his nocturnal pacings was not the untidy state of his room, for since his removal from his post as headmaster of a lycée at Sidi-bel-Abbès and the loss of the fine house with two manservants that went with it, he had learned to live as he now did. His problem lay elsewhere.

As dawn was breaking over the eastern suburbs, he sat down finally and picked up one of the papers. His eye ran yet again down the second lead story on the foreign news page. It was headlined: "OAS CHIEFS HOLED UP IN ROME HOTEL." After reading it for the last time, he made up his mind, threw on a light mackintosh against the chill of the morning, and left the flat.

He caught a cruising taxi on the nearest boulevard and ordered the driver to take him to the Gare du Nord. Although the taxi dropped him in the forecourt, he walked away from the station as soon as the taxi had left, crossed the road, and entered one of the all-night cafes of the area.

He ordered a coffee and a metal disc for the telephone, left the coffee on the counter, and went into the back of the cafe to dial. Directory Enquiries put him on to the International Exchange, and he asked them the number of a hotel in Rome. He got it within sixty seconds, replaced the receiver, and left.

At a cafe a hundred metres down the street he again used the phone, this time to ask Enquiries for the location of the nearest all-night post office from which international calls could be placed. He was told, as he had expected, that there was one round the corner from the mainline station.

At the post office he placed a call to the Rome number he had been given, without naming the hotel represented by the number, and spent an anxious twenty minutes waiting until it came through.

"I wish to speak to Signor Poitiers," he told the Italian voice that answered.

"*Signor Che?*" asked the voice.

"*Il signor francese.* Poitiers. Poitiers . . ."

"*Che?*" repeated the voice.

"*Francese, francese . . .*" said the man in Paris.

"*Ah, si, il signor francese. Un momento, per favore . . .*"

There was a series of clicks, then a tired voice answered in French.

"*Ouay . . .*"

"Listen," said the man in Paris urgently. "I don't have much time. Take a pencil and note what I say. Begins. 'Valmy to Poitiers. The Jackal is blown. Repeat. The Jackal is blown. Kowalski was taken. Sang before dying. Ends.' Got that?"

"*Ouay,*" said the voice. "I'll pass it on."

Valmy replaced the receiver, hurriedly paid his bill, and scurried out of the building. In a minute he was lost in the crowds of commuters streaming out of the main hall of the station. The sun was over the horizon, warming the pavements and the chill night air. Within half an hour the smell of morning and croissants and grinding coffee would vanish beneath the pall of exhaust fumes, body odour, and stale tobacco. Two min-

utes after Valmy had disappeared, a car drew up
outside the post office, and two men from the DST
hurried inside. They took a description from the
switchboard operator, but it could have described
anybody.

In Rome Marc Rodin was awakened at 7:55 when
the man who had spent the night on the duty desk
on the floor below shook him by the shoulder. He was
awake in an instant, half out of bed, and groping for
the gun under his pillow. He relaxed and grunted
when he saw the face of the ex-legionnaire above him.
A glance at the bedside table told him he had over-
slept anyway. After years in the tropics his habitual
waking hour was much earlier, and the August sun of
Rome was already high above the roofs. Weeks of
inactivity, passing the evening hours playing piquet
with Montclair and Casson, drinking too much rough
red wine, taking no exercise worth the name, all had
combined to make him slack and sleepy.

"A message, *mon colonel*. Someone phoned just
now, seemed in a hurry."

The legionnaire proffered a sheet from a note pad
on which were scribbled the disjointed phrases of
Valmy. Rodin read through the message once, then
leapt out of the thinly sheeted bed. He wrapped the
cotton sarong he habitually wore, a habit from the
East, round his waist, and read the message again.

"All right. Dismiss." The legionnaire left the room
and went back downstairs.

Rodin swore silently and intensely for several seconds, crumpling the piece of paper in his hands.
Damn, damn, damn, damn Kowalski.

For the first two days after Kowalski's disappearance he had thought the man had simply deserted. There had been several defections of late from the cause, as the conviction set in among the rank and file that the OAS had failed and would fail in its aim of killing Charles de Gaulle and bringing down the present government of France. He had always thought Kowalski would remain loyal to the last. Yet here was evidence that he had for some inexplicable reason returned to France, or perhaps been picked up inside Italy and abducted. Now it seemed he had talked, under pressure, of course.

Rodin genuinely grieved for his dead servitor. Part of the considerable reputation he had built up as a fighting soldier and commanding officer had been based on the enormous concern he showed for his men. These things are appreciated by fighting soldiers more than any military theorist can ever imagine. Now Kowalski was dead and Rodin had few illusions in the manner of his passing.

Still, the important thing was to try to recollect just what Kowalski had had to tell. The meeting in Vienna, the name of the hotel. Of course all of that. The three men who had been at the meeting. This would be no news to the SDECE. But what did he know about the Jackal? He had not been listening at the door, that was certain. He could tell them of a tall blond foreigner who had visited the three of them. That in itself meant nothing. Such a foreigner could have been an arms dealer, or a financial backer. There had been no names mentioned.

But Valmy's message mentioned the Jackal by his

code-name. How? How could Kowalski have told them that?

With a start of horror Rodin recalled the scene as they had parted. He had stood in the doorway with the Englishman; Viktor had been a few feet down the corridor, annoyed at the way the Englishman had spotted him in the alcove, a professional out-manoeuvred by another professional, waiting for trouble, almost hoping for it. What had he, Rodin, said? *"Bonsoir, Monsieur Chacal."* Of course, damn and blast it.

Thinking things over again, Rodin realised that Kowalski could never have got the killer's real name. Only he, Montclair, and Casson knew that. All the same, Valmy was right. With Kowalski's confession in the hands of the SDECE, it was too far blown to be retrievable. They had the meeting, the hotel, probably they had already talked to the desk clerk; they had the face and figure of a man, a code-name. There could be no doubt they would guess what Kowalski had guessed—that the blond was a killer. From then on the net around de Gaulle would tighten; he would abandon all public engagements, all exits from his palace, all chances for an assassin to get him. It was over; the operation was blown. He would have to call off the Jackal, insist on the money back, minus all expenses and a retainer for the time and trouble involved.

There was one thing to be settled, and quickly. The Jackal himself must be warned urgently to halt operations. Rodin was still enough of a commanding officer not to send a man out on his orders on a mission for which success had become impossible.

He summoned the bodyguard to whom, since the

departure of Kowalski, he had given the duties of going every day to the main post office to collect the mail and, if necessary, make telephone calls, and briefed him at length.

By nine o'clock the bodyguard was in the post office and asked for a telephone number in London. It took twenty minutes before the telephone on the other end began to ring. The switchboard operator gestured the Frenchman to a cabin to take the call. He picked up the receiver as the operator put hers down, and listened to the buzz-buzzz . . . pause . . . bzzz-bzzz of an English telephone ringing.

The Jackal rose early that morning, for he had much to do. The three main suitcases he had checked and re-packed the previous evening. Only the hand-grip remained to be topped up with his sponge bag and shaving tackle. He drank his habitual two cups of coffee, washed, showered, and shaved. After packing the remainder of the overnight toiletries, he closed up the hand luggage and stored all four pieces by the door.

He made himself a quick breakfast of scrambled eggs, orange juice, and more black coffee in the flat's small but compact kitchen, and ate it off the kitchen table. Being a tidy and methodical man, he emptied the last of the milk down the sink, broke the two remaining eggs, and poured them also down the sink. The remainder of the orange juice he drank off, junked the can in the trash basket, and the remainder of the bread, egg shells, and coffee grounds went down the disposal unit. Nothing left would be likely to go rotten during his absence.

Finally he dressed, choosing a thin silk polo-necked sweater, the dove-grey suit containing the private papers in the name of Duggan, and the hundred pounds in cash, dark grey socks, and slim black moccasin shoes. The ensemble was completed by the inevitable dark glasses.

At 9:15 he took his luggage, two pieces in each hand, closed the self-locking flat door behind him, and went downstairs. It was a short walk up Adam Mews to South Audley Street, and he caught a taxi on the corner.

"London Airport, Number Two Building," he told the driver.

As the taxi moved away, the phone in his flat began to ring.

It was ten o'clock when the legionnaire returned to the hotel off the Via Condotti and told Rodin he had tried for thirty minutes to get a reply from the London number he had been given, but had not succeeded.

"What's the matter?" asked Casson, who had heard the explanation given to Rodin and seen the legionnaire dismissed to return to his guard station. The two OAS chiefs were sitting in the drawing room of their suite. Rodin withdrew a piece of paper from his inside pocket and passed it over to Casson.

Casson read it and passed it to Montclair. Both men finally looked at their leader for an answer. There was none, Rodin sat staring out of the windows across the baking roofs of Rome, brow furrowed in thought.

"When did it come?" asked Casson eventually.

"This morning," replied Rodin briefly.

"You've got to stop him," protested Montclair. "They'll have half of France on the lookout for him."

"They'll have half of France on the lookout for a tall blond foreigner," said Rodin quietly. "In August there are over one million foreigners in France. So far as we know they have no name to go on, no face, no passport. Being a professional, he is probably using a false passport. They still have a long way to go to get him yet. There's a good chance he will be forewarned if he rings Valmy, and then he'll be able to get out again."

"If he rings Valmy, he will of course be ordered to drop the operation," said Montclair. "Valmy will order him."

Rodin shook his head.

"Valmy does not have the authority to do that. His orders are to receive information from the girl and pass it on to the Jackal when he is telephoned. He will do that, but nothing else."

"But the Jackal must realise of his own accord that it is all over," protested Montclair. "He must get out of France as soon as he rings Valmy the first time."

"In theory yes," said Rodin thoughtfully. "If he does he hands back the money. There's a lot at stake, for all of us, including him. It depends how confident he feels of his own planning."

"Do you think he has a chance now—now that this has happened?" asked Casson.

"Frankly, no," said Rodin. "But he is a professional. So am I, in my way. It is a frame of mind. One does not like to stand down an operation one has planned personally."

"Then for God's sake recall him," protested Casson.

"I can't. I would if I could, but I can't. He's gone. He's on his way. He wanted it this way and now he's got it. We don't know where he is or what he is going to do. He's completely on his own. I can't even call up Valmy and order him to instruct the Jackal to drop the whole thing. To do so would risk 'blowing' Valmy. Nobody can stop the Jackal now. It's too late."

twelve

Commissaire Claude Lebel arrived back in his office just before 6 in the morning to find Inspector Caron looking tired and strained, in shirtsleeves at his desk.

He had several sheets of foolscap paper in front of him covered with hand-written notes. In the office some things had changed. On top of the filing cabinets an electric coffee percolator bubbled, sending out a delicious aroma of freshly brewed coffee. Next to it stood a pile of paper cups, a tin of unsweetened milk, and a bag of sugar. These had come up from the basement canteen during the night.

In the corner between the two desks a single truckle bed had been set up, covered with a rough blanket. The waste-paper basket had been emptied and stored next to the armchair by the door.

The window was open still, a· faint haze of blue smoke from Caron's cigarette drifting out into the cool morning. Beyond the window the first flecks of the coming day mottled the spire of Saint Sulpice.

Lebel crossed to his desk and slumped into the chair. Although it was only twenty-four hours since he had waked from his last sleep, he looked tired, like Caron.

"Nothing," he said. "I've been through the lot over the past ten years. The only foreign political killer who ever tried to operate here was Degueldre, and he's dead. Besides, he was OAS and we had him on file as such. Presumably Rodin has chosen a man who has nothing to do with the OAS, and he's quite right. There were only four contract-hire killers who tried it in France over the past ten years—apart from the home-grown variety—and we got three. The fourth is doing life in Africa somewhere. Besides, they were all gangland killers, not of the calibre to shoot down a President of France.

"I got on to Bargeron of Central Records, and they're doing a complete double-check, but I suspect already that we don't have this man on file. Rodin would in any case insist on that before hiring him."

Caron lit up another Gauloise, blew out the smoke and sighed.

"So we have to start from the foreign end?"

"Precisely. A man of this type must have got his training and experience somewhere. He wouldn't be one of the world's tops unless he could prove it with a string of successful jobs behind him. Not presidents perhaps, but important men, bigger than mere underworld chiefs. That means he must have come to someone's attention somewhere. Surely. What have you arranged?"

Caron picked up one of the sheets of paper, showing a list of names with, in the left-hand column, a series of timings.

"The seven are all fixed," he said. "You start with the head of Domestic Intelligence, FBI, at ten past seven. That's ten past one in the morning, Washington time. I fitted him in first because of the lateness of the hour in America.

"Then Brussels at half past seven, Amsterdam at quarter to eight, and Bonn at eight-ten. The link is arranged with Johannesburg at eight-thirty and with

Scotland Yard at nine. Lastly there is Rome at nine-thirty."

"The heads of Homicide in each case?" asked Lebel.

"Or the equivalent. With Scotland Yard it's Mr. Anthony Mallinson, Assistant Commissioner (Crime). It seems they don't have a Homicide section in the Metropolitan Police. Apart from that, yes, except South Africa. I couldn't get Van Ruys at all, so you're talking to Assistant Commissioner Anderson."

Lebel thought for a moment.

"That's fine. I'd prefer Anderson. We worked on a case once. There's the question of language. Three of them speak English. I suppose only the Belgian speaks French. The others almost certainly can speak English if they have to—"

"The German, Dietrich, speaks French," interjected Caron.

"Good, then I'll speak to those two in French personally. For the other five I'll have to have you on the extension as interpreter. We'd better go. Come on."

It was ten to seven when the police car carrying the two detectives drew up outside the innocent green door in the tiny rue Paul Valéry which housed the headquarters of Interpol.

For the next three hours Lebel and Caron sat hunched over the telephone in the basement communications room talking to the world's top crime busters. From the seemingly tangled web of aerials on the roof of the building the high-frequency signals beamed out across three continents, streaming high beyond the stratosphere to bounce off the ionic layer above and home back to earth thousands of miles away to another stick of aluminum jutting from a tiled rooftop.

The wavelengths and scramblers were unintercept-able. Detective spoke to detective while the world drank its morning coffee or final nightcap.

In each telephone conversation Lebel's appeal was much the same.

"No, Commissioner, I cannot yet put this request for your assistance on the level of an official enquiry between our two police forces. . . . Certainly I am acting in an official capacity. . . . It is simply that for the moment we are just not sure if even the intent to commit an offence has been formulated or put into the preparation stage. . . . It's a question of a tip-off, purely routine for the moment. . . . Well, we are look-ing for a man about whom we know extremely little . . . not even a name, and only a poor description . . ."

In each case he gave the description as best he knew it. The sting came in the tail, as each of his for-eign colleagues asked why their help was being sought, and what clues they could possibly go on. It was at that point that the other end of the line became tensely silent.

"Simply this; that whoever this man is or may be, he must have one qualification that marks him out: he would have to be one of the world's top professional contract-hire assassins. . . . No, not a gangland trigger, a political assassin with several successful kills behind him. We would be interested to know if you have any-body like that on your files, even if he has never oper-ated in your own country. Or anybody that even springs to mind."

Inevitably there was a long pause at the other end

before the voice resumed. Then it was quieter, more concerned.

Lebel had no illusions that the heads of the Homicide departments of the major police forces of the Western world would fail to understand what he was hinting at but could not say. There was only one target in France that could interest a first-league political killer.

Without exception the reply was the same. Yes, of course. We'll go through all the files for you. I'll try and get back to you before the day is out. Oh, and Claude, good luck.

When he put down the radio-telephone receiver for the last time, Lebel wondered how long it would be before the Foreign Ministers and even Prime Ministers of the seven countries would be aware of what was on. Probably not long. Even a policeman had to report to the politicians something of that size. He was fairly certain the Ministers would keep quiet about it. There was, after all, a strong bond over and above political differences between the men of power the world over. They were all members of the same club, the club of the potentates. They stuck together against common enemies, and what could be more inimical to any of them than the activities of a political assassin? He was aware all the same that if the enquiry did become public knowledge and reached the press, it would be blasted across the world, and he would be finished.

The only people who did worry him were the English. If it could only be kept between cops, he would have trusted Mallinson.

But he knew that before the day was out it would

have to go higher than Mallinson. It was only seven months since Charles de Gaulle had brusquely rebuffed Britain's bid to the Common Market, and in the wake of the General's January 23 press conference the London Foreign Office, as even so apolitical a creature as Lebel was aware, had become almost lyrical in its campaign of words planted through the political correspondents against the French President. Would they now use this to get their revenge on the old man?

Lebel stared for a moment at the now silent transmitter panel in front of him. Caron watch him quietly.

"Come on," said the little Commissaire, rising from the stool and heading for the door, "let's get some breakfast and try to get some sleep. There's not much more we can do now."

Assistant-Commissioner Anthony Mallinson put down the telephone with a thoughtful frown and left the communications room without acknowledging the salute of a young policeman who was entering to take up his morning shift. He was still frowning as he went back upstairs to his spacious but soberly appointed office overlooking the Thames.

There was no doubt in his mind of what kind of enquiry Lebel had been making, or of his motives for making it. The French police had got some kind of tip-off that a top-class assassin was on the loose, and that it affected them. As Lebel had predicted to himself, it took very little acumen to work out who could be the only possible target in France in August 1963 for that kind of killer. He considered Lebel's predicament with the knowledge of a long-time policeman.

"Poor bastard," he said aloud as he stared down at the warm and sluggish river flowing past the Embankment beneath his window.

"Sir?" asked his Personal Aide, who had followed him into the office to put the morning mail that needed his attention on the walnut desk.

"Nothing." Mallinson continued to stare out the window as the PA left. However he might feel for Claude Lebel in his task of trying to protect his President without being able to launch an official manhunt, he too had masters. Sooner or later they would have to be told of Lebel's request to him that morning. There was the daily heads-of-department conference at ten, in half an hour's time. Should he mention it there?

On balance he decided not to. It would be enough to write a formal but private memorandum to the Commissioner himself, outlining the nature of Lebel's request. The necessity for discretion would explain later, if necessary, why the matter had not been raised at the morning meeting. In the meantime it would do no harm to put through the enquiry without revealing why it was being made.

He took his seat behind the desk and pressed one of the buttons on the intercom.

"Sir?" his PA's voice came through from the adjoining office.

"Come in here a minute, would you, John?"

The charcoal-grey-suited young detective inspector came in, notebook in hand.

"John, I want you to get on to Central Records. Speak to Chief Superintendent Markham personally. Tell him the request is from me personally, and that

I cannot explain for the moment why I am asking it. Ask him to check every existing record of known living professional assassins in this country—"

"Assassins, sir?" The PA looked as if the Assistant Commissioner had asked for a routine check on all known Martians.

"Yes, assassins. Not, repeat not, run-of-the-mill gangland thugs who either have or are known to be capable of knocking off somebody in a feud in the underworld. Political killers, John, men or a man capable of assassinating a well-guarded politician or statesman for money."

"That sounds more like Special Branch customers, sir."

"Yes, I know. I want to pass the whole thing to Special Branch. But we had better do a routine check first. Oh, and I want an answer one way or the other by midday. OK?"

"Right, sir, I'll get on to it."

Fifteen minutes later Assistant Commissioner Mallinson took his seat at the morning conference.

When he returned to his office he flicked through the mail, pushed it to one side of the desk, and ordered the PA to bring him in a typewriter. Sitting alone, he typed out a brief report for the Commissioner of Metropolitan Police. It mentioned briefly the morning call to his home, the person-to-person call over the Interpol link at nine in the morning, and the nature of Lebel's enquiry. He left the bottom of the memorandum form empty, and locked it away in his desk to get on with the day's work.

Shortly before twelve the PA knocked and entered.

"Superintendent Markham's just been on from CRO," he said. "Apparently there's no one on Criminal Records who can fit that description. Seventeen known contract-hire killers from the underworld, sir; ten in jail and seven on the loose. But they all work for the big gangs, either here or in the main cities. The Super says none would fit for a job against a visiting politician. He suggested Special Branch too, sir."

"Right, John, thank you. That's all I needed."

With the PA dismissed, Mallinson took the half-finished memo. from his drawer and re-inserted it into the typewriter. On the bottom he wrote:

"Criminal Records reported upon enquiry that no person fitting the description of type submitted by Commissaire Lebel could be traced in their files. The enquiry was then passed to the Assistant Commissioner, Special Branch."

He signed the memorandum and took the top three copies. The remainder went into the waste-paper basket for classified waste, later to be destroyed.

One of the copies he folded into an envelope and addressed to the Commissioner. The second he filed in the "Secret Correspondence" file and locked it into the wall safe. The third he folded and placed in his inside pocket.

On his desk note-pad he scribbled a message.

To: Commissaire Claude Lebel, Deputy Director-General, Police Judiciaire, Paris.

From: Assistant-Commissioner Anthony Mallinson, A.C. Crime, Scotland Yard, London.

Message: Following your enquiry this date fullest research criminal records reveals no such personage known to us stop request passing to Special Branch for further checking stop any useful information will be passed to you soonest stop Mallinson.

Time sent: . . . . . 12.8.63.

It was just gone half past twelve. He picked up the phone and, when the operator answered, asked for Assistant Commissioner Dixon, head of Special Branch.

"Hallo, Alec? Tony Mallinson. Can you spare me a minute? . . . I'd love to but I can't. I shall have to keep lunch down to a sandwich. It's going to be one of those days. No, I just want to see you for a few minutes before you go. . . . Fine, good, I'll come right along."

On his way through the office he dropped the envelope addressed to the Commissioner on the PA's desk.

"I'm just going up to see Dixon of the S.B. Get that along to the Commissioner's office, would you, John? Personally. And get this message off to the addressee. Type it out yourself in the proper style."

"Yessir." Mallinson stood over the desk while the detective inspector's eyes ran through the message. They widened as they reached the end.

"John . . ."

"Sir?"

"And keep quiet about it, please."

"Yes sir."

"Very quiet, John."

"Not a word, sir."

Mallinson gave him a brief smile and left the office. The PA read the message for Lebel a second time, thought back to the enquiries he had made with Records that morning for Mallinson, worked it out for himself, and whispered, "Bloody hell."

Mallinson spent twenty minutes with Dixon and effectively ruined the other's forthcoming club lunch. He passed over to the Head of Special Branch the remaining copy of the memorandum to the Commissioner. As he rose to leave he turned at the door, hand on the knob.

"Sorry, Alec, but this really is more up your street. But if you ask me, there's probably nothing and nobody of that calibre in this country, so a good check of records and you should be able to telex Lebel to say we can't help. I must say I don't envy him his job this time."

Assistant Commissioner Dixon, whose job among other things was to keep tabs on all the weird and crazy of Britain who might think of trying to assassinate a visiting politician, not to mention the scores of embittered and cranky foreigners domiciled in the country, felt even more keenly the impossibility of Lebel's position. To have to protect home and visiting politicians from unbalanced fanatics was bad enough, but at least they could usually be relied upon as amateurs to fail in the face of his own corps of case-hardened professionals.

To have one's own head of state the target for a native organisation of tough ex-soldiers was even worse. And yet the French had beaten the OAS. As a professional, Dixon admired them for it. But the hiring of a foreign professional was a different matter. Only one thing could be said in its favour, from Dixon's point of view; it cut the possibles down to so few that he had no doubts there would prove to be no Englishman of the calibre of the man Lebel sought on the books of the Special Branch.

After Mallinson had left, Dixon read the carbon copy of the memorandum. Then he summoned his own PA.

"Please tell Detective Superintendent Thomas I would like to see him here at"—he glanced at his watch, estimated how long a much shortened lunch-hour would take him—"two o'clock sharp."

The Jackal landed at Brussels National just after 12. He left his three main pieces of luggage in an automatic locker in the main terminal building and took with him into town only the hand-grip containing his personal effects, the plaster of Paris, pads of cotton wool, and bandages. At the main station he dismissed the taxi and went to the left-luggage office.

The fibre suitcase containing the gun was still on the shelf where he had seen the clerk deposit it a week earlier. He presented the reclamation slip and was given the case in return.

Not far from the station he found a small and squalid hotel, of the kind that seem to exist in proximity to all main line stations the world over, which ask no questions but get told a lot of lies.

He booked a single room for the night, paid cash in advance in Belgian money that he had changed at the airport, and took his case up to the room himself. With the door safely locked behind him, he ran a basin of cold water, emptied the plaster and bandages onto the bed, and set to work.

It took over two hours for the plaster to dry when he had finished. During this time he sat with his heavy foot and leg resting on a stool, smoking his filter cigarettes and looking out over the grimy array of rooftops that formed the vista from the bedroom window. Occasionally he would test the plaster with his thumb, each time deciding to let it harden a bit more before moving.

The fibre suitcase that had formerly contained the gun lay empty. The remainder of the bandages were re-packed in the hand-grip along with the few ounces of plaster that were left, in case he had to do some running repairs. When he was finally ready, he slid the cheap fibre case under the bed, checked the room for any last tell-tale signs, emptied the ashtray out of the window, and prepared to leave.

He found that with the plaster on, a realistic limp became obligatory. At the bottom of the stairs he was relieved to find the grubby and sleepy-looking desk clerk was in the back room behind the desk, where he had been when the Jackal arrived. Since it was lunchtime, he was eating, but the door with the frosted glass that gave him access to the front counter was open.

With a glance at the front door to make sure no one was coming in, the Jackal clutched his hand-case to his chest, bent onto all fours, and scuttled quickly and silently across the tiled floor. Because of the heat of summer the front door was open and he was able to stand upright on the top of the three steps that led to the street, out of the line of sight of the desk clerk.

He limped painfully down the steps and along the street to the corner where the main road ran past. A taxi spotted him inside half a minute, and he was on his way back to the airport.

He presented himself at the Alitalia counter, passport in hand. The girl smiled at him.

"I believe you have a ticket for Milan reserved two days ago in the name of Duggan," he said.

She checked the bookings for the afternoon flight to Milan. It was due to leave in an hour and a half.

"Yes indeed," she beamed at him. "Meester Duggan. The ticket was reserved but not paid for. You wish to pay for it?"

The Jackal paid in cash again, was issued with his ticket, and was told he would be called in an hour. With the aid of a solicitous porter who tut-tutted over his plastered foot and pronounced limp, he withdrew his three suitcases from the locker, consigned them to Alitalia, passed through the customs barrier, which, seeing that he was an outgoing traveller, was merely a passport check, and spent the remaining hour enjoying a late lunch in the restaurant attached to the passenger departure lounge.

Everybody concerned with the flight was very kind and considerate towards him because of the leg. He was assisted aboard the coach out to the aircraft and watched with concern as he made his painful way up the steps to the aircraft's door. The lovely Italian hostess gave him an extra wide smile of welcome and saw him comfortably seated in one of the group of seats in the centre of the aircraft that face towards each other. There was more leg room there, she pointed out.

The other passengers took elaborate pains not to knock against the plastered foot as they took their seats, while the Jackal lay back in his seat and smiled bravely.

At 4:15 the airliner was on take-off and was soon speeding southwards, bound for Milan.

Superintendent Bryn Thomas emerged from the Assistant Commissioner's office just before 3, feeling thoroughly miserable. Not only was his summer cold one of the worst and most persistent he had ever been plagued with, but the new assignment with which he had just been saddled had ruined his day.

As Monday mornings went, it had been rotten; first he had learned that one of his men had been given the slip by a Soviet trade delegate whom he was supposed to be tailing, and by mid-morning he had received an inter-departmental complaint from MI-5 politely asking his department to lay off the Soviet delegation, an unmistakable suggestion that in the view of MI-5 the whole matter had better be left to them.

Monday afternoon looked like being worse. There are few things that any policeman, Special Branch or not, likes less than the spectre of the political assassin. But in the case of the request he had just received from his superior, he had not even been given a name to go on.

"No name, but I'm afraid plenty of pack-drill," had been Dixon's bon mot on the subject. "Try and get it out of the way by tomorrow."

"Pack-drill," snorted Thomas when he reached the office. Although the short-list of known suspects would be extremely short, it still presented him and his department with hours of checking of files, records for political trouble-making, convictions, and, unlike the criminal branch, mere suspicions. All would have to be checked. There was only one ray of light in Dixon's briefings: the man would be a professional operator and not one of the numberless bee-in-the-bonnet merchants that made the Special Branch's life a misery before and during any foreign statesman's visit.

He summoned two detective inspectors whom he knew to be presently engaged on low-priority work, told them to drop whatever they were doing, as he had been, and to report to his office. His briefing to them was shorter than Dixon's had been to him. He confined himself to telling them what they were looking for, but not why. The suspicions of the French police that such a man might be out to kill General de Gaulle need have nothing to do with the search through the archives and records of Scotland Yard's Special Branch.

The three of them cleared the desks of outstanding paperwork and settled down.

The Jackal's plane touched down at Linate Airport, Milan, shortly after six. He was helped by the ever-attentive hostess down the steps to the tarmac, and escorted by one of the ground hostesses to the main terminal building. It was at customs that his elaborate preparations in getting the component parts of the gun out of the suitcases and into a less suspicious means of carriage paid dividends. The passport check was a formality but as the suitcases from the hold came rumbling through on the conveyor belt and were deposited along the length of the customs bench, the risks began to mount.

The Jackal secured a porter who assembled the three main suitcases into a line side by side. The Jackal put

his hand-grip down beside them. Seeing him limp up
to the bench, one of the customs officers sauntered
across.

"Signor? This is all your baggage?"

"Er, yes, these three suitcases and this little case."

"You have anything to declare?"

"No, nothing."

"You are on business, signor?"

"No, I've come on holiday, but it turns out it must
also include a period of convalescence. I hope to go
up to the lakes."

The customs man was not impressed.

"May I see your passport, signor?"

The Jackal handed it over. The Italian examined it
closely, then handed it back without a word.

"Please, open this one."

He gestured at one of the three larger suitcases. The
Jackal took out his key-ring, selected one of the keys
and opened the case. The porter had laid it flat on its
side to help him. Fortunately it was the case containing the clothes of the fictitious Danish pastor and the
American student. Riffling through the clothes, the
customs officer attached no importance to a dark grey
suit, underwear, white shirt, loafers, black walking
shoes, windbreaker, and socks. Nor did the book in
Danish excite him. The cover was a colourplate of
Chartres cathedral, and the title, although in Danish,
was sufficiently like the equivalent English words not
to be remarkable. He did not examine the carefully
re-sewn slit in the side lining or find the false identity
papers. A really thorough search would have found
them, but his was the usual perfunctory run-through
that would only have become intensive if he had

found something suspicious. The component parts of a complete sniper's rifle were only three feet away from him across the desk, but he suspected nothing. He closed the case and gestured to the Jackal to lock it again. Then he chalked all four cases in quick succession. His job done, the Italian's face broke into a smile.

"*Grazie, signor.* A 'appy holiday."

The porter found a taxi, was well tipped, and soon the Jackal was speeding into Milan, its usually clamorous streets made even noisier by the streams of commuter traffic trying to get home and the constant horn-honking of the drivers. He asked to be taken to the Central Station.

Here another porter was summoned, and he hobbled after the man to the left-luggage office. In the taxi he had slipped the steel shears out of the overnight case into his trouser pocket. At the left-luggage office he deposited the hand-grip and two suitcases, retaining the one containing the long French military overcoat, which also had plenty of spare room.

Dismissing the porter, he hobbled into the men's toilet, to find only one of the wash basins in the long row on the left-hand side of the urinals was in use. He dropped the case and laboriously washed his hands until the other occupant was finished. When the toilet was empty for a second he was across the room and locked into one of the cubicles.

With his foot up on the lavatory seat he chipped silently for ten minutes at the plaster on his foot until it began to drop away, revealing the cotton wool pads beneath that had given the foot the bulk of a normally fractured ankle encased in plaster.

When the foot was finally clear of the last remnants of plaster, he put back on the silk sock and the slim leather moccasin which had been taped to the inside of his calf while the foot had been in plaster. The remainder of the plaster and cotton wool he gathered up and deposited down the pan. At the first flushing half of it jammed, but it cleared at the second.

He laid the suitcase on top of the toilet and placed the series of circular steel tubes containing the rifle side by side among the folds of the coat until the case was full. When the inside straps were tight the contents of the case were prevented from banging about. Then he closed the case and cast a look outside the door. There were two people at the wash basins and two more standing at the urinals. He left the cubicle, turned sharply towards the door, and was up the steps into the main hall of the station before any had time to notice him, even if they had wished to.

He could not go back to the left-luggage office a fit and healthy man so soon after leaving it as a cripple, so he summoned a porter, explained that he was in a hurry, wished to change money, reclaim his baggage and get a taxi as soon as possible. The baggage check he thrust into the porter's hand, along with a thousand-lire note, pointing the man towards the left-luggage office. He himself, he indicated, would be getting his English pounds changed into lire.

The Italian nodded happily and went off to get the luggage. The Jackal changed the last twenty pounds that remained to him into Italian currency and was just finished when the porter returned with the other three pieces of luggage. Two minutes later he was in a taxi speeding dangerously across the Piazza Duca d'Aosta and heading for the Hotel Continentale.

At the reception desk in the splendid front hall he told the clerk, "I believe you have a room for me in the name of Duggan. It was booked by telephone from London two days ago."

Just before 8 the Jackal was enjoying the luxury of a shower and shave in his room. Two of the suitcases were carefully locked into the wardrobe. The third, containing his own clothes, was open on the bed, and the suit for the evening, a navy blue wool-and-mohair summer lightweight, was hanging from the wardrobe door. The dove-grey suit was in the hands of the hotel's valet service for sponging and pressing. Ahead lay cocktails, dinner, and an early night, for the next day, August 13, would be extremely busy.

thirteen

"Nothing."

The second of the two young detective inspectors in Bryn Thomas's office closed the last of the folders he had been allotted to read and looked across at his superior.

His colleague had also finished, and his conclusion had been the same. Thomas himself had finished five minutes before and had walked over to the window, standing with his back to the room and staring at the traffic flowing past in the dusk. Unlike Assistant Commissioner Mallinson, he did not have a view of the river, just a first-floor vista of the cars churning down Horseferry Road. He felt like death. His throat was raw from cigarettes, which he knew he should not have been smoking with a heavy cold, but could not give up, particularly when under pressure.

His head ached from the fumes, the incessant calls that had been made throughout the afternoon checking on characters turned up in the records and files. Each call-back had been negative. The man was either fully accounted for or simply not of the calibre to undertake a mission like killing the French President.

"Right, that's it, then," he said firmly, spinning round from the window. "We've done all we can, and there just isn't anybody who could possibly fit the guidelines laid down in the request we have been investigating."

"It could be that there is an Englishman who does

this kind of work," suggested one of the inspectors. "But he's not in our files."

"They're all in our files, look you," growled Thomas. It did not amuse him to think that as interesting a creature as a professional assassin existed in his "manor" without being on file somewhere, and his temper was not improved by his cold or his headache.

"After all," said the other inspector, "a political killer is an extremely rare bird. There probably isn't such a thing in this country. It's not quite the English cup of tea, is it?"

Thomas glowered back. He preferred the word "British" to describe the inhabitants of the United Kingdom, and the inspector's inadvertent use of the word "English" he suspected might be a veiled suggestion that the Welsh, Scottish, or Irish could well have produced such a man. But it wasn't.

"All right, pack up the files. Take them back to registry. I'll reply that a thorough search has revealed no such character known to us. That's all we can do."

"Who was the enquiry from, Super?" asked one.

"Never you mind, boy. Someone's got problems by the look of it, but it isn't us."

The two younger men had gathered up all the material and headed for the door. Both had families to get home to, and one was expecting to become a first-time father almost any day. He went straight to the door. The other turned back with a thoughtful frown.

"Super, there's one thing occurred to me while I was checking. If there is such a man, and he's got British nationality, it seems he probably wouldn't operate here anyway. I mean, even a man like that has to have a base somewhere. A refuge, sort of, a place to come back to. Chances are such a man is a respectable citizen in his own country."

"What are you getting at, a sort of Jekyll and Hyde?"

"Well, something like that. I mean, if there is a professional killer about, of the type we've been trying to track, and he's big enough for somebody to pull the kind of weight to get an investigation like this started, with a man of your rank leading it, well the man in question must be big. And if he's that, in his field, he must have a few jobs behind him. Otherwise he wouldn't be anything, would he?"

"Go on," said Thomas, watching him carefully.

"Well, I just thought that a man like that would probably operate only outside his own country. So he wouldn't normally come to the attention of the internal security forces. Perhaps the Service might have got wind of him once. . . ."

Thomas considered the idea, then slowly shook his head.

"Forget it, get on home, boy. I'll write the report. And just forget we ever made the enquiry."

But when the inspector was gone, the idea he had sown remained in Thomas's mind. He could sit down and write the report now. Complete negative. Drawn a blank. There could be no comebacks on the basis of the search of records that had been made. But supposing there was something behind the enquiry from France? Supposing the French had not, as Thomas suspected they had, simply lost their heads over a rumour concerning their precious President? If they really had as little to go on as they claimed, if there was no indication that the man was an Englishman, then they must be checking all over the world in a similar way. Chances were heavily odds-on there was no killer, and if there were, that he came from one of those nations with long histories of political assassinations. But what if the French suspicions were accurate? And if the man turned out to be English, even by birth alone?

Thomas was intensely proud of the record of Scotland Yard, and particularly of the Special Branch. They had never had trouble of this kind. They had never lost a visiting foreign dignitary. He personally had even had to look after that Russian bastard Ivan Serov, head of the KGB, when he came to prepare for Khrushchev's and Bulganin's visit, and there had been scores of Balts and Poles who wanted to get Serov. Not even a shooting, and the place crawling with Serov's own security men, every one packing a gun and quite prepared to use it.

Superintendent Bryn Thomas had two years to go before retirement and the journey back to the little house he and Meg had bought looking out over the green turf to the Bristol Channel. Better be safe, check everything.

In his youth Thomas had been a very fine Rugby player, and there were many who had played against Glamorgan who remembered clearly the inadvisability of making a blind-side break when Bryn Thomas was wing forward. He was too old for it now, of course, but he still took a keen interest in the London Welsh when he could get away from work and go down to the Old Deer Park at Richmond to see them play. He knew all the players well, spending time in the club house chatting with them after a match, and his reputation was enough to ensure that he was always welcome.

One of the players was known to the rest of the members simply to be on the staff of the Foreign Office. Thomas knew he was a bit more than that; the department, under the auspices of the Foreign Secretary but not attached to the Foreign Office, for which Barrie Lloyd worked was the Secret Intelligence Service, sometimes called the SIS, sometimes simply "the Service," and more usually among the public by its incorrect name of MI-6.

The two men met for a drink in a quiet pub down by the river between eight and nine. They talked Rugby for a while, as Thomas bought the drinks. But Lloyd guessed the man from Special Branch had not asked to see him at a riverside pub to talk about a season which would not start for another two months. When they had both got their drinks and given each other a perfunctory "Cheers," Thomas gestured with his head outside onto the terrace that led down to the wharf. It was quieter outside, for most of the young couples from Chelsea and Fulham were drinking up and heading off for dinner.

"Got a bit of a problem, boyo," began Thomas. "Hoped you might be able to help."

"Well . . . if I can," said Lloyd.

Thomas explained about the request from Paris and the blank drawn by Criminal Records and the Special Branch.

"It occurred to me that if there ever was such a man, and a British one at that, he might be the kind who would never get his hands dirty inside this country, see. Might just stick to operations abroad. If he ever had left a trail, maybe he came to the attention of the Service?"

"Service?" asked Lloyd quietly.

"Come on, Barrie. We have to know a lot of things, from time to time." Thomas's voice was hardly above a murmur. From the back they looked like two men in dark suits staring out over the dusky river at the lights of the south bank, talking of the day's dealings in the City. "We had to turn over a lot of files during the Blake investigations. A lot of Foreign Office people got a peek taken at what they were really up to. Yours was one, see. You were in his section at the time he came under suss. So I know what department you work with."

"I see," said Lloyd.

"Now look, I may be Bryn Thomas down at the Park. But I'm also a Superintendent of the S.B., right? You can't all be anonymous from everyone now, can you?"

Lloyd stared into his glass.

"Is this an official enquiry for information?"

"No, I can't make it that yet. The French request was an unofficial request from Lebel to Mallinson. He could find nothing in Central Records, so he replied that he couldn't help, but he also had a word with Dixon. Who asked me to have a quick check. All on the quiet, see? Mustn't get out to the press or anything. Chances are there's nothing here in Britain at all that might help Lebel. I just thought I'd cover all the angles, and you were the last."

"This man is supposed to be after de Gaulle?"

"Must be, by the sound of the enquiry. But the

French must be playing it very cagey. They obviously don't want any publicity."

"Obviously. But why not contact us direct?"

"The request for suggestions as to a name has been put through on the Old Boy network. From Lebel to Mallinson, direct. Perhaps the French Secret Service doesn't have an Old Boy network with your section."

If Lloyd had noticed the reference to the notoriously bad relations between the SDECE and the SIS, he gave no sign of it.

"What are you thinking?" asked Thomas after a while.

"Funny," said Lloyd staring out over the river. "You remember the Philby case?"

"Of course."

"Still a very sore nerve in our section," resumed Lloyd. "He went over from Beirut in January of sixty-one. Of course, it didn't get out until later, but it caused a hell of a rumpus inside the Service. A lot of people got moved around. Had to be done, he had blown most of the Arab Section and some others as well. One of the men who had to be moved very fast was our top resident in the Caribbean. He had been with Philby in Beirut six months before, then transferred to Carib.

"The same month, January, the dictator of the Dominican Republic, Trujillo, was assassinated on a lonely road outside Ciudad Trujillo. According to the reports, he was killed by partisans—he had a lot of enemies. Our man came back to London then, and we shared an office for a while until he was redeployed. He mentioned a rumour that Trujillo's car was stopped, for the ambushers to blow it open and kill the man inside, by a single shot from a marksman with a rifle. It was a hell of a shot—from one hundred and fifty yards at a speeding car. Went through the little triangular window at the driver's side, the one that wasn't of bullet proof glass. The whole car was armoured. Hit the driver through the throat and he crashed. That was when the partisans closed in. The odd thing was, there rumour had it the shooter was an Englishman."

There was a long pause as the two men, the empty beer mugs swinging from their fingers, stared across the now quite darkened waters of the Thames. Both had a mental picture of a harsh, arid landscape in a hot and distant island; of a car careering at seventy miles an hour off a bitumen strip and into the rocky verge; of an old man in fawn twill and gold braid, who had ruled his kingdom with an iron and ruthless hand for thirty years, being dragged from the wreck to be finished off with pistols in the dust by the roadside.

"This—man—in the rumour. Did he have a name?"

"I don't know. I don't remember. It was just talk in the office at the time. We had an awful lot on our plate then, and a Caribbean dictator was the last thing we needed to worry about."

"This colleague, the one who talked to you. Did he write a report?"

"Must have done. Standard practise. But it was just a rumour, understand. Just a rumour. Nothing to go on. We deal in facts, solid information."

"But it must have been filed, somewhere?"

"Suppose so," said Lloyd. "Very low priority, only a bar rumour in that area. Place abounds in rumours."

"But you could just have a look back at the files, like? See if the man on the mountain had a name?"

Lloyd pulled himself off the rail.

"You get on home," he said to the Superintendent. "I'll ring you if there's anything that might help."

They walked back into the rear bar of the pub, deposited the glasses, and made for the street door.

"I'd be grateful," said Thomas as they shook hands. "Probably nothing in it. But just on the offchance."

While Thomas and Lloyd were talking above the waters of the Thames, and the Jackal was scooping the last drops of his zabaglione from the glass in a roof-top restaurant in Milan, Commissaire Claude Lebel attended the first of the progress report meetings in the conference room of the Interior Ministry in Paris.

The attendance was the same as it had been twenty-four hours earlier. The Interior Minister sat at the head of the table, with the department heads down each side. Claude Lebel sat at the other end with a small folder in front of him. The Minister nodded curtly for the meeting to begin.

His *chef de cabinet* spoke first. Over the previous day and night, he said, every customs officer on every border post in France had received instructions to check through the luggage of tall blond male foreigners entering France. Passports particularly were to be checked, and were to be scrutinised by the DST official at the customs post for possible forgeries. (The head of the DST inclined his head in acknowledgement.) Tourists and businessmen entering France might well remark a sudden increase in vigilance at customs, but it was felt unlikely that any victim of such a baggage search would realise it was being applied across the country to tall blond men. If any enquiries were made by a sharp-eyed press man, the explanation would be that they were nothing but routine snap searches. But it was felt no enquiry would ever be made.

He had one other thing to report. A proposal had been made that the possibility be considered of making a snatch of one of the three OAS chiefs in Rome. The Quai d'Orsay had come out strongly against such an idea for diplomatic reasons (they had not been told of the Jackal plot), and they were being backed in this by the President (who was aware of the reason). This must therefore be discounted as a way out of their difficulties.

General Guibaud for the SDECE said a complete check of their records had failed to reveal knowledge of the existence of a professional political killer outside the ranks of the OAS or its sympathisers, and who could not be completely accounted for.

The head of the Renseignements Généraux said a search through France's criminal archives had revealed the same thing, not only among Frenchmen but also among foreigners who had ever tried to operate inside France.

The chief of the DST then made his report. At 7:30 that morning a call had been intercepted from a post office near the Gare du Nord to the number of the Rome hotel where the three OAS chiefs were staying. Since their appearance there eight weeks before, operators on the international switchboard had been instructed to report all calls placed to that num-

ber. The one on duty that morning had been slow on
the uptake. The call had been placed before he had
realised that the number was the one on his list. He
had put the call through, and only then rung the DST.
However, he had the sense to listen in. The message
had been, "Valmy to Poitiers. The Jackal is blown.
Repeat. The Jackal is blown. Kowalski was taken.
Sang before dying. Ends."

There was silence in the room for several seconds.

"How did they find out?" asked Lebel quietly from
the far end of the table. All eyes turned on him, except
those of Colonel Rolland, who was staring at the opposite wall deep in thought.

"Damn," he said clearly, still staring at the wall.
The eyes swivelled back to the head of the Action
Service.

The Colonel snapped out of his reverie.

"Marseilles," he said shortly. "To get Kowalski to
come from Rome we used a bait. An old friend called
JoJo Grzybowski. The man has a wife and daughter.
We kept them all in protective custody until Kowalski
was in our hands. Then we allowed them to return
home. All I wanted from Kowalski was information
about his chiefs. There was no reason to suspect this
Jackal plot at the time. There was no reason why they
should not know we had got Kowalski—then. Later of
course things changed. It must have been the Pole
JoJo who tipped off the agent Valmy. Sorry."

"Did the DST pick Valmy up in the post office?"
asked Lebel.

"No, we missed him by a couple of minutes, thanks
to the stupidity of the operator," said the man from
DST.

"A positive chapter of inefficiency," snapped Colonel Saint-Clair suddenly. A number of unfriendly glances were levelled at him.

"We are feeling our way, largely in the dark, against an unknown adversary," replied General Guibaud. "If the colonel would like to volunteer to take over the operation, all the responsibility it implies . . ."

The colonel from the Elysée Palace studiously examined his folders as if they were more important and of greater consequence than the veiled threat from the head of the SDECE. He realised it had not been a wise remark.

"In a way," mused the Minister, "it might be as well they know their hired gun is blown. Surely they must call the operation off now?"

"Precisely," said Saint-Clair, trying to recoup, "the Minister is right. They would be crazy to go ahead now. They'll simply call the man off."

"He isn't exactly blown," said Lebel quietly. They had almost forgotten he was there. "We still don't know the man's name. The forewarning might simply cause him to take extra contingency precautions. False papers, physical disguises . . ."

The optimism to which the Minister's remark had given birth round the table vanished. Roger Frey eyed the little Commissaire with respect.

"I think we had better have Commissaire Lebel's report, gentlemen. After all, he is heading this enquiry. We are here to assist him where we can."

Thus prompted, Lebel outlined the measures he had taken since the previous evening; the growing belief, supported by the check through the French files, that the foreigner could only be on the files of some foreign police force, if at all. The request to make enquiries abroad; request granted. The series of person-to-person phone calls via Interpol to police chiefs of seven major countries.

"The replies came in during the course of today," he concluded. "Here they are: Holland, nothing. Italy, several known contract-hire killers, but all in the employ of the Mafia. Discreet enquiries between the Carabinieri and the Capo of Rome elicited a pledge that no Mafia killer would ever do a political killing except on orders, and the Mafia would not subscribe to killing a foreign statesman," Lebel looked up. "Personally, I am inclined to believe that is probably true.

"Britain. Nothing, but routine enquiries have been passed to another department, the Special Branch, for further checking."

"Slow as always," muttered Saint-Clair under his breath. Lebel caught the remark and looked up again.

"But very thorough, our English friends. Do not underestimate Scotland Yard." He resumed reading.

"America. Two possibilities. One, the right-hand man of a big international arms dealer based in Miami, Florida. This man was formerly a U.S. Marine, later a CIA man in the Caribbean. Fired for killing a Cuban anti-Castroite in a fight just before the Bay of Pigs affair. The Cuban was to have commanded a section of that operation. The American then was taken on by the arms dealer, one of the men the CIA had unofficially used to supply arms to the Bay of Pigs invading force. Believed to have been responsible for two unexplained accidents that happened later to rivals of his employer in the arms business. Arms dealing, it seems, is a very cut-throat business. The man's name is Charles "Chuck" Arnold. The FBI is now checking for his whereabouts.

"The second man suggested by the FBI as a possible. Marco Vitellino, formerly personal bodyguard to a New York gangland boss, Albert Anastasia. This Capo was shot to death in a barber's chair in October fifty-seven, and Vitellino fled America in fear of his own life. Settled in Caracas, Venezuela. Tried to go into the rackets there on his own account, but with little success. He was frozen out by the local underworld. The FBI think that if he was completely broke he might be in the market for a contract killing job for a foreign organisation, if the price were right."

There was complete silence in the room. The fourteen other men listened without a murmur.

"Belgium. One possibility. Psychopathic homicide, formerly on the staff of Tshombe in Katanga. Expelled by United Nations when captured in 1962. Unable to return to Belgium because of pending charges on two counts of murder. A hired gun, but a clever one. Name of Jules Bérenger. Believed also emigrated to Central America. Belgian police are still checking on his possible present whereabouts.

"Germany. One suggestion. Hans-Dieter Kassel, former SS-Major, wanted by two countries for war crimes. Lived after the war in West Germany under an assumed name, and was a contract-killer for ODESSA, the ex-SS members' underground organisation. Suspected of being implicated in the killing of two left-wing Socialists in postwar politics who were urging a government-sponsored intensification of enquiries into war crimes. Later unmasked as Kassel, but skipped to Spain after a tip-off for which a senior police official lost his job. Believed now living in retirement in Madrid."

Lebel looked up again. "Incidentally, this man's age seems to be a bit advanced for this sort of job. He is now fifty-seven.

"Lastly, South Africa. One possible. Professional mercenary. Name: Piet Schuyper. Also one of Tshombe's top gunmen. Nothing officially against him in South Africa, but he's considered undesirable. A crack shot, and a definite penchant for individual killing. Last heard of when expelled from the Congo on the collapse of the Katanga secession early this year. Believed to be still in West Africa somewhere. The South African Special Branch is checking further."

He stopped and looked up. The fourteen men round the table were looking back at him without expression.

"Of course," said Lebel deprecatingly, "it's very vague, I'm afraid. For one thing I only tried the seven most likely countries. The Jackal could be a Swiss, or Austrian, or something else. Then three countries out of seven replied that they had no suggestion to make. They could be wrong. The Jackal could be Italian or Dutch or English. Or he could be South African, Belgian, German, or American, but not among those listed. One doesn't know. One is feeling in the dark, hoping for a break."

"Mere hoping isn't going to get us far," snapped Saint-Clair.

"Perhaps the colonel has a fresh suggestion?" enquired Lebel politely.

"Personally, I feel the man has certainly been warned off," said Saint-Clair icily. "He could never get near the President now that his plan has been exposed. However much Rodin and his henchmen have promised to pay this Jackal, they will ask for their money back and cancel the operation."

"You *feel* the man has been warned off," interposed Lebel softly, "but feeling is not far from hoping. I would prefer to continue enquiries for the present."

"What is the position of these enquiries now, Commissaire?" asked the Minister.

"Already, Minister, the police forces that have made these suggestions are beginning to send by telex the complete dossiers. I expect to have the last by noon tomorrow. Pictures will also come by wire. Some of the police forces are continuing enquiries to try to pin the whereabouts of the suspects down, so that we can take over."

"Do you think they will keep their mouths shut?" asked Sanguinetti.

"There's no reason for them not to," replied Lebel. "Hundreds of highly confidential enquiries are made each year on an unofficial person-to-person basis. Fortunately, all countries, whatever their political outlook, are opposed to crime. So we are not involved in the same rivalries as the more political branches of international relations. Cooperation among police forces is very good."

"Even for political crime?" asked Frey.

"For policemen, Minister, it's all crime. That is why I preferred to contact my foreign colleagues rather than enquire through foreign ministries. Doubtless, the superiors of these colleagues must learn that the enquiry was made, but there would be no good reason for them to make mischief. The political assassin is the world's outlaw."

"But so long as they know the enquiry was made, they can work out the implications and still privately sneer at our President," snapped Saint-Clair.

"I do not see why they should do that. It might be one of them, one day," said Lebel.

"You do not know much about politics if you are not aware how some people would be delighted to know a killer is after the President of France," replied Saint-Clair. "This public knowledge is precisely what the President was so anxious to avoid."

"It is not public knowledge," corrected Lebel. "It is extremely private knowledge, confined to a tiny handful of men who carry in their heads secrets that, if revealed, might well ruin half the politicians of their own countries. Some of these men know most of the inner details of installations that protect Western security. They have to, in order to protect them. If they were not discreet, they would not hold the jobs they do."

"Better a few men should know we are looking for a killer than they should receive invitations to attend the President's funeral," growled Bouvier. "We've been fighting the OAS for two years. The President's instructions were that it must not become press sensation and public talking point."

"Gentlemen, gentlemen," interposed the Minister. "Enough of this. It was I who authorised Commissaire Lebel to make discreet enquiries among the heads of foreign police services, after"—he glanced at Saint-Clair—"consulting with the President."

The group's amusement at the colonel's discomfiture was ill-concealed.

"Is there anything else?" asked M. Frey.

Rolland raised a hand briefly.

"We have a permanent bureau in Madrid," he said. "There are a number of refugee OAS in Spain, that's why we keep it there. We could check on the Nazi, Kassel, without bothering the West Germans about it. I understand our relations with the Bonn Foreign Office are still not of the best."

His reference to the Argoud snatch of February and the consequent anger of Bonn brought a few smiles. Frey raised his eyebrows at Lebel.

"Thank you," said the detective, "that would be most helpful, if you could pin the man down. For the rest there is nothing, except to ask that all departments continue to assist me as they have been doing over the past twenty-four hours."

"Then until tomorrow, gentlemen," said the Minister briskly and rose, gathering his papers. The meeting broke up.

Outside on the steps, Lebel gratefully drew in a lungful of the mild night air of Paris. The clocks struck 12 and ushered in Tuesday, August 13.

It was just after 12 when Barrie Lloyd rang Superintendent Thomas at his home in Chiswick. Thomas was just about to put the bedside light out, thinking the SIS man would ring in the morning.

"I found the flimsy of the report we were talking about," said Lloyd. "I was right in a way. It was just a routine report of a rumour running round the island at that time. Marked 'No action to be taken' almost as soon as it was filed. Like I said, we were pretty tied up with other things at that time."

"Was any name mentioned?" asked Thomas quietly, so as not to disturb his wife, who was asleep.

"Yes, a British businessman on the island, who disappeared around that time. He might have had nothing to do with it, but his name was linked in the gossip. Name of Charles Calthrop."

"Thanks, Barrie. I'll follow it in the morning." He put the phone down and went to sleep.

Lloyd, being a meticulous young man, made a brief report of the request and his reply to it, and despatched it to Requirements. In the small hours, the night duty man on requirements examined it quizzically for a moment, and as it concerned Paris, put it in a pouch for the Foreign Office's France Desk, the entire pouch to be delivered personally according to routine to Head of France when he came in later the same morning.

fourteen

The Jackal rose at his habitual hour of 7:30, drank the tea placed by his bedside, washed, showered, and shaved. Once dressed, he took the wad of a thousand pounds from inside the lining of his suitcase, slipped it into his breast pocket, and went down for breakfast. At nine o'clock he was on the pavement of the Via Manzoni outside the hotel and striding down the road looking for banks. For two hours he went from one to another, changing the English pounds. Two hundred were changed into Italian lire and the remaining eight hundred into French francs.

By midmorning he was finished with this task, and broke for a cup of espresso on a cafe terrace. After that he set out on his second search. After numerous enquiries, he found himself in one of the back streets off the Porta Garibaldi, a working-class area near the Garibaldi station. Here he found what he was looking for, a row of lock-up garages. One of these he hired from the proprietor who ran the garage on the corner of the street. The hire charge for two days was ten thousand lire, well above the odds, but then it was a very short let.

In a local hardware store he bought a set of overalls, a pair of metal clippers, several yards of thin steel wire, a soldering iron, and a foot of solder rod. These he packed into a canvas grip bought at the same store, and deposited the grip in the garage. Pocketing the key, he went off for lunch at a trattoria in the more fashionable centre of the city.

In the early afternoon, after making an appointment by phone from the trattoria, he arrived by taxi at a small and not too prosperous car-hire firm. Here he hired a second-hand 1962 vintage Alfa Romeo sports two-seater. He explained that he wished to tour Italy for the forthcoming fortnight, the length of his holiday in Italy, and return the car at the end of that time.

His passport, British and International driving licences were in order, and insurance was arranged within the hour from a nearby firm which habitually handled the business of the hire-car firm. The deposit was heavy, the equivalent of over a hundred pounds, but by the midafternoon the car was his, the keys in the ignition, and the proprietor of the firm wishing him a happy holiday.

Previous enquiries with the Automobile Association in London had assured him that as both France and Italy were members of the Common Market, there were no complicated formalities for driving an Italian registered car into France, provided the driving licences, car-registration hire documents, and insurance cover were in order.

From a personal enquiry at the reception desk of the Automobil Club Italiano on the Corso Venezia he was given the name of a highly respectable insurance firm close by, which specialised in offering motor insurance cover for travel in foreign countries. Here he paid cash for extra insurance cover for an expedition into France. This firm, he was assured, enjoyed a mutual relationship with a large French insurance company, and their cover would be accepted without question.

From here he drove the Alfa back to the Continentale, parked it in the hotel car-park, went up to his room, and retrieved the suitcase containing the component parts of the sniper's rifle. Shortly after tea-time he was back in the mews street where he had hired the lock-up garage.

With the door safely shut behind him, the cable from the soldering iron plugged into the overhead light socket, and a high-powered torch lying on the floor beside him to illuminate the underside of the car, he went to work. For two hours he carefully welded the thin steel tubes that contained the rifle parts into the inner flange of the Alfa's chassis. One of the reasons for choosing an Alfa had been because a search through motor magazines in London had taught him that alone among Italian cars the Alfa possessed a stout steel chassis with a deep flange on the inner side.

The tubes themselves were each wrapped in a thin sock of sacking material. The steel wire lashed them tightly inside the flange, and the places where the wire touched the chassis's edge were spot-welded with the soldering iron.

By the time he was finished the overalls were smeared with grease from the garage floor, and his hands ached from the exertions of heaving the wire tighter round the chassis. But the job was done. The tubes were almost undetectable except to a close search made from underneath the car, and would soon be coated with dust and mud.

He packed the overalls, soldering iron, and the remains of the wire into the canvas grip and dumped it under a pile of old rags in the far corner of the garage. The metal clippers went into the glove compartment set in the dashboard.

Dusk was settling again over the city when he finally emerged at the wheel of the Alfa, the suitcase shut into the trunk. He closed and locked the garage door, pocketed the key, and drove back to the hotel.

Twenty-four hours after his arrival in Milan he was again in his room, showering away the exertions of the day, soaking his smarting hands in a bowl of cold water, before dressing for cocktails and dinner.

Stopping at the reception desk before going into the bar for his habitual Campari and soda, he asked for his bill to be made up for settlement after dinner, and for a morning call with a cup of tea at 5:30 the following morning.

After a second splendid dinner he settled the bill with the remainder of his lire and was in bed asleep by shortly after eleven o'clock.

Sir Jasper Quigley stood with his back to the office, hands clasped behind him, and stared down from the windows of the Foreign Office across the immaculate acres of Horse Guards Parade. A column of Household Cavalry in impeccable order trotted across the gravel towards the Annexe and the Mall and on in the direction of Buckingham Palace.

It was a scene to delight and to impress. On many mornings Sir Jasper had stood at his window and gazed down from the ministry at this most English of English spectacles. Often it seemed to him that just to stand at this window and see the Blues ride by, the sun shine, and the tourists crane, and hear across the square the clink of harness and bit, the snort of a mettled horse, and the oooohs and aaaahs of the crowd was worth all those years in embassies in other and lesser lands. It was rare for him that, watching this sight, he did not feel his shoulders square a little squarer, the stomach draw in a trifle under the striped trousers, and a touch of pride lift the chin to iron out the wrinkles of the neck. Sometimes, hearing the crunch of the hooves on gravel, he would rise from his desk just to stand at the neo-Gothic window and see them pass, before returning to the papers of the business of the state. And sometimes, thinking back on all those who had tried from across the sea to change this scene and supplant the jingle of the spurs with the tramp of boots from Paris or jackboots from Berlin, he felt a little pricking behind the eyes and would hurry back to his papers.

But not this morning. This morning he glowered down like an avenging acid drop, and his lips were pressed so tightly together that, never full or rosy, they had disappeared completely. Sir Jasper Quigley was in a towering rage, and by a small sign here and there it showed. He was, of course, alone.

He was also the Head of France, not in the literal sense of possessing any jurisdiction over the country across the Channel towards friendship with whom so much lip-service had been paid and so little felt during his lifetime, but head of the bureau of the Foreign Office whose business it was to study the affairs, ambitions, activities, and, often, conspiracies of that confounded place and then report upon them to the Permanent Under Secretary and, ultimately, to Her Majesty's Secretary of State for Foreign Affairs.

He possessed, or he would not have got the appointment, all the essential requirements: a long and distinguished record of service in diplomacy elsewhere than in France; a history of soundness in his political judgements, which, although frequently wrong, were inevitably in accord with those of his superiors of the given moment—a fine record and one of which to be justly proud. He had never been publicly wrong or inconveniently right, never supported an unfashionable viewpoint or proffered opinions out of line with those prevailing at the highest levels of the corps.

A marriage to the virtually unmarriageable daughter of the Head of Chancery in Berlin, who had later become an Assistant Deputy Under Secretary of State, had done no harm. It had enabled an unfortunate memorandum in 1937 from Berlin, advising that German rearmament would have no real effect in political terms on the future of Western Europe, to be overlooked.

During the war, back in London, he had been for a while on the Balkan Desk and had forcefully counselled British support for the Yugoslav partisan Mikailovitch and his Chetniks. When the Prime Minister of the time had unaccountably preferred to listen to the advice of an obscure young captain called Fitzroy MacLean who had parachuted into the place and who advised backing a wretched Communist called Tito, young Quigley had been transferred to France Desk.

Here he had distinguished himself by becoming a leading advocate of British support for General Giraud in Algiers. It was, or would have been, a jolly good policy too, had it not been out-manoeuvered by that other and less senior French general who had been living in London all the while trying to put together a force called the Free French. Why Winston ever bothered with the man was something none of the professionals could ever understand.

Not that any of the French were much use, of course. No one could ever say of Sir Jasper (knighted in '61 for his services to diplomacy) that he lacked the essential qualification for a good Head of France. He had a congenital dislike of France and everything to do with the place. These feelings had become, by the close of President de Gaulle's press conference of January 23, 1963, in which he barred Britain from the Common Market and caused Sir Jasper to have an uncomfortable twenty minutes with the Minister, as nothing compared to his feelings towards the person of the French President.

There was a tap on his door. Sir Jasper swung away from the window. From the blotter in front of him he picked up a piece of blue flimsy paper and held it as though he had been reading it when the knock came.

"Enter."

The younger man entered the office, closed the door behind him, and approached the desk.

Sir Jasper glanced at him over the half-moon glasses.

"Ah, Lloyd. Just looking at this report you filed during the night. Interesting, interesting. An unofficial request lodged by a senior French police detective to a senior British police officer. Passed on to a senior superintendent of the Special Branch, who sees fit to consult, unofficially, of course, a junior member of the Intelligence Service. Mmm?"

"Yes, Sir Jasper."

Lloyd stared across at the spare figure of the diplo-

mat standing by the window studying his report as if
he had never seen it before. He had cottoned on at
least that Sir Jasper was already well versed in the
contents and that the studied indifference was probably a pose.

"And this junior officer sees fit, off his own bat and
without reference to higher authority, to assist the
Special Branch officer by passing on to him a suggestion. A suggestion, moreover, that without a shred of
proof indicates that a British citizen thought to be a
businessman may in fact be a cold-blooded killer.
Mmmmm?"

"What the hell's the old buzzard getting at?" thought
Lloyd.

He soon found out.

"What intrigues me, my dear Lloyd, is that although
this request, unofficial of course, is lodged yesterday
morning, it is not until twenty-four hours later that
the head of the department of the ministry most
closely concerned with what happens in France gets
to be informed. Rather an odd state of affairs, wouldn't
you say?"

Lloyd got the drift. Inter-departmental pique. But
he was equally aware that Sir Jasper was a powerful
man, versed in the power struggle, which exacted more
effort from the members of the hierarchy than did
state business.

"With the greatest respect, Sir Jasper, Superintendent Thomas's request to me, as you say an unofficial
one, was made at nine last night. The report was filed
at midnight."

"True, true. But I notice his request was also complied with before midnight. Now can you tell me why that was?"

"I felt the request for guidance, or possible guidance as to a line of enquiry only, came within the scope of normal inter-departmental cooperation," replied Lloyd.

"Did you now? Did you now?" Sir Jasper had dropped the pose of mild enquiry and some of his pique was coming through. "But not apparently within the scope of inter-departmental cooperation between your service and the France Desk, mmm?"

"You have my report in your hand, Sir Jasper."

"A bit late, sir. A bit late."

Lloyd decided to riposte. He was aware that if he had committed any error in consulting a higher authority before helping Thomas, it was his own chief he should have consulted, not Sir Jasper Quigley. And the head of the SIS was beloved by his staff and disliked by the mandarins of the F.O. for his refusal to allow anyone other than himself to rebuke his subordinates.

"Too late for what, Sir Jasper?"

Sir Jasper glanced up sharply. He was not going to fall into the trap of admitting it was too late to prevent the cooperation with Thomas's request from being fulfilled.

"You realise of course that a British citizen's name is concerned here. A man against whom there is not a shred of evidence, let alone proof. Don't you think it a rather odd procedure to bandy a man's name and, in view of the nature of the request, reputation about in this manner?"

"I hardly think divulging a man's name to a Superintendent of the Special Branch simply as a possible line of enquiry can be described as bandying it about, Sir Jasper."

The diplomat found his lips were pressed hard together as he sought to control his rage. Impertinent pup, but astute too. Needed watching very carefully. He took a grip on himself.

"I see, Lloyd. I see. In view of your evident desire to assist the Special Branch, a most laudable desire of course, do you think it too much to expect you to consult a little before throwing yourself into the breach?"

"Are you asking, Sir Jasper, why you were not consulted?"

Sir Jasper saw red.

"Yes, sir, I am, sir. That is exactly what I am asking!"

"Sir Jasper, with the greatest deference to your seniority, I feel I must draw attention to the fact that I am on the staff of the Service. If you disagree with my course of conduct of last night, I think it would be more seemly if your complaint went to my own superior officer rather than to me directly."

Seemly? Seemly? Was this young upstart trying to tell a Head of France what was and was not seemly?

"And it shall, sir," snapped Sir Jasper, "and it shall. In the strongest terms."

Without asking for permission Lloyd turned and left the office. He had few doubts that he was in for a roasting from the Old Man, and all he could say in mitigation was that Bryn Thomas's request had seemed urgent, with time possibly a pressing matter. If the Old Man decided that the proper channels should have been gone through, then he, Lloyd, would have to take the rap. But at least he would take it from the O.M. and not from Quigley. Oh, damn Thomas.

However Sir Jasper Quigley was very much in two minds whether to complain or not. Technically he was right, the information about Calthrop, although completely buried in long-discarded files, should have been cleared with higher authority; but not necessarily with himself. As Head of France, he was one of the customers of SIS intelligence reporting, not one of the directors of it. He could complain to that cantankerous genius (not his choice of words) who ran the SIS and probably secure a good ticking off for Lloyd, possibly damage the brat's career. But he might also get a dose of the rough edge of the SIS chief's tongue for summoning an intelligence officer without asking *his* permission, and that thought did not amuse. Besides, the head of SIS was reputed to be extremely close to some of the men at the Very Top. Played cards with them at Blades; shot with them in Yorkshire. And the Glorious Twelfth was only a month away. He was still trying to get invited to some of those parties. Better leave it.

"The damage is done now, anyway," he mused as he gazed out over Horse Guards Parade.

"The damage is done anyway," he remarked to his luncheon guest at his club just after one o'clock. "I suppose they'll go right ahead and cooperate with the French. Hope they won't work too hard, what?"

It was a good joke and he enjoyed it very much. Unfortunately he had not fully estimated his lunch guest, who was also close to some of the men at the Very Top.

Almost simultaneously a personal report from the Commissioner of Metropolitan Police and news of Sir Jasper's little *bon mot* reached the Prime Minister's eyes and ears respectively just before four when he returned to No. 10 Downing Street after questions in the House.

At ten past four the phone in Superintendent Thomas's office rang.

Thomas had spent the morning and most of the afternoon trying to track down a man about whom he knew nothing but the name. As usual when enquiring into a man of whom it was definitely known that he had been abroad, the Passport Office in Petty France had been the starting point.

A personal visit there when they opened at 9 in the morning had elicited from them photostat copies of application forms for passports from six separate Charles Calthrops. Unfortunately they all had middle names, and all were different. He had also secured the submitted photographs of each man, on a promise that they would be copied and returned to the Passport Office's achives.

One of the passports had been applied for since January 1961, but that did not necessarily mean anything, although it was significant that no records existed of a previous application by that Charles Calthrop before the one Thomas now possessed. If he had been using another name in the Dominican Republic, how come the rumours that had later linked him with Trujillo's killing had mentioned him as Calthrop? Thomas was inclined to downgrade this late applicant for a passport.

Of the other five, one seemed too old; he would be sixty-five by August of 1963. The remaining four were possibles. It did not matter whether they tallied with Lebel's description of a tall blond, for Thomas's job was one of elimination. If all six could be eliminated from suspicion of being the Jackal, so much the better. He could advise Lebel accordingly with a clear conscience.

Each application form had an address, two in London and two in the provinces. It was not enough simply to ring up, ask for Mr. Charles Calthrop, and then ask if the man had been in the Dominican Republic in 1961. Even if he had been there, he might well deny it now.

Nor were any of the four top-listed suspects marked down as "businessman" in the space for professional status. That too was not conclusive. Lloyd's report of a bar-rumour at the time might call him a businessman, but that could well be wrong.

During the morning the county and borough police, after a telephone request by Thomas, had traced the two provincial Calthrops. One was still at work, expecting to go on holiday with his family on the weekend. He was escorted home in the lunch-break and his passport was examined. It had no entry or exit visas or stamps for the Dominican Republic in 1960 or 1961. It had only been used twice, once for Mallorca and once for the Costa Brava. Moreover, enquiries at his place of work had revealed that this particular Charles Calthrop had never left the accounts department of the soup factory where he worked during

January 1961, and he had been on the staff for ten years.

The other outside London was traced to a hotel in Blackpool. Not having his passport on him, he was persuaded to authorise the police of his home town to borrow his house key off the next-door neighbour, go to the top drawer of his desk, and look at the passport. It too bore no Dominican police stamps, and at the man's place of work it was found he was a typewriter repair mechanic who also had not left his place of work in 1961 except for his summer holidays. His insurance cards and attendance records showed that.

Of the two Charles Calthrops in London one was discovered to be a greengrocer in Catford who was selling vegetables in his shop when the two quiet-spoken men in suits came to talk to him. As he lived above his own shop, he was able to produce his passport within a few minutes. Like the others it gave no indication that the possessor had ever been to the Dominican Republic. When asked, the greengrocer convinced the detectives that he did not even know where that island was.

The fourth and last Calthrop was proving more difficult. The address given in his application form for a passport four years previously was visited and turned out to be a block of flats in Highgate. The estate agents managing the block searched their records and revealed that he had left that address in December 1960. No forwarding address was known.

But at least Thomas knew his middle name. A search of the telephone directory revealed nothing, but using the authority of Special Branch Thomas learned from the General Post Office that one C. H.

Calthrop had an unlisted number in West London. The initials tallied with the name of the missing Calthrop—Charles Harold. From there Thomas checked with the registration department of the borough in which the telephone number was located.

Yes, the voice from the Borough Hall told him, a Mr. Charles Harold Calthrop was indeed the tenant of the flat at that address, and was listed on the electoral roll as a voter of that borough.

At this point a visit was made to the flat. It was locked and there was no reply to the repeated rings on the bell. Nobody else in the block seemed to know where Mr. Calthrop was. When the squad car returned to Scotland Yard, Superintendent Thomas tried a new tack. The Inland Revenue was asked to check their records for the tax returns of one Charles Harold Calthrop, private address given. Particular point of interest—who employed him, and who had been employing him over the past three years?

It was at this point that the phone rang. Thomas picked it up, identified himself, and listened for a few seconds. His eyebrows lifted.

"Me?" he asked. "What, personally? . . . Yes, of course, I'll come over. Give me five minutes? . . . Fine, see you."

He left the building and walked across to Parliament Square, blowing his nose noisily to clear the blocked sinuses. Far from getting better, his cold seemed to be worse, despite the warm summer day.

From Parliament Square he headed up Whitehall and took the first left into Downing Street. As usual it was dark and gloomy, the sun never penetrating to the inconspicuous cul-de-sac that contains the residence of the Prime Ministers of Britain. There was a small crowd in front of the door of No. 10, kept on the far side of the road by two stolid policemen, perhaps just watching the stream of messengers arriving at the door with buff envelopes to deliver, perhaps hoping to catch a glimpse of an important visage at one of the windows.

Thomas left the roadway and cut to the right across a small courtyard enclosing a little lawn. His walk brought him to the back entrance of No. 10, where he pressed the buzzer beside the door. It opened immediately to reveal a large uniformed police sergeant, who recognised him at once and saluted.

"Afternoon, sir. Mr. Harrowby asked me to show you to his room directly."

James Harrowby, the man who had telephoned Thomas in his office a few minutes before, was the Prime Minister's personal security chief, a handsome man looking younger than his forty-one years. He wore a public-school tie but had a brilliant career as a policeman behind him before he was transferred to Downing Street. Like Thomas, he had the rank of a Superintendent. He rose as Thomas entered.

"Come in, Bryn. Nice to see you." He nodded to the sergeant. "Thank you, Chalmers." The sergeant withdrew and closed the door.

"What's it all about?" asked Thomas. Harrowby looked at him with surprise.

"I was hoping you could tell me. He just rang fifteen minutes ago, mentioned you by name, and said he wanted to see you personally and at once. Have you been up to something?"

Thomas could only think of one thing he had been

up to, but he was surprised it had got so high in such a short time. Still, if the P.M. did not wish to take his own security man into his confidence for once, that was his business.

"Not that I know of," he said.

Harrowby lifted the telephone on his desk and asked for the Prime Minister's private office. The line crackled and a voice said, "Yes?"

"Harrowby here, Prime Minister. Superintendent Thomas is with me. . . . Yes, sir. Right away." He replaced the receiver.

"Straight in. Almost on the double. You must have been up to something. There are two Ministers waiting. Come on."

Harrowby led the way out of his office and down a corridor towards a green baize door at the far end. A male secretary was coming out, saw the pair of them and stepped back, holding the door open. Harrowby ushered Thomas inside, said clearly, "Superintendent Thomas, Prime Minister," and withdrew, closing the door quietly behind him.

Thomas was aware of being in a very quiet room, high-ceilinged and elegantly furnished, untidy with books and papers, of a smell of pipe tobacco and wood-panelling, a room more like the study of a university don than the office of a Prime Minister.

The figure at the window turned round.

"Good afternoon, Superintendent. Please sit down."

"Good afternoon, sir." He chose an upright chair facing the desk and perched on the edge of it. He had never had occasion to see the Prime Minister that close before, and never in private. He got the impression of a pair of sad, almost beaten eyes, drooping lids, like a bloodhound who has run a long race and taken little joy from it.

There was silence in the room as the Prime Minister walked to his desk and sat behind it. Thomas had heard the rumours round Whitehall, of course, that the P.M.'s health was not all it might be, and of the toll taken by the strain of bringing the government through the rottenness of the Keeler/Ward affair, which had just ended and was still number one talking point throughout the land. Even so, he was surprised at the look of exhaustion and sadness in the man opposite him.

"Superintendent Thomas, it has come to my attention that you are presently conducting an investigation based on a request for assistance telephoned from Paris yesterday morning by a senior detective of the French Police Judiciaire."

"Yes, sir—Prime Minister."

"And that this request stems from a fear among the French security authorities that a man may be on the loose, a professional assassin, hired, presumably by the OAS, to undertake a mission in France at some future time?"

"That was not actually explained to us, Prime Minister. The request was for suggestions as to the identity of any such professional assassin who might be known to us. There was no explanation as to why they wanted such suggestions."

"Nevertheless, what do you deduce from the fact that such a request was made, Superintendent?"

Thomas shrugged slightly.

"The same as yourself, Prime Minister."

"Precisely. One does not need to be a genius to be

able to deduce the only possible reason for the French authorities wishing to identify such a—specimen. And what would you deduce to be the eventual target of such a man, if indeed a man of this type has come to the attention of the French police?"

"Well, Prime Minister, I suppose they fear an assassin has been engaged to attempt to kill the President."

"Precisely. Not the first time such an attempt would have been made?"

"No, sir. There have been six attempts already."

The Prime Minister stared at the papers in front of him as if they might give him some clue as to what had happened to the world in the closing months of his premiership.

"Are you aware, Superintendent, that there apparently exist some persons in this country, persons occupying not obscure positions of authority, who would not be displeased if your investigations were not so energetic as they might be?"

Thomas was genuinely surprised.

"No, sir." Where on earth had the P.M. got that tidbit from?

"Would you please give me a résumé of the state of your enquiries up to the present time?"

Thomas began at the beginning, explaining clearly and concisely the trail from Criminal Records to Special Branch, the conversation with Lloyd, the mention of a man called Calthrop, and the investigations that had taken place up to that moment.

When he had finished, the Prime Minister rose and walked to the window, which gave onto the sunlit square of grass in the courtyard. For long minutes he stared down into the courtyard and there was a sag to the set of the shoulders. Thomas wondered what he was thinking.

Perhaps he was thinking of a beach outside Algiers where he had once walked and talked with the haughty Frenchman who now sat in another office three hundred miles away, governing the affairs of his own country. They had both been twenty years younger then, and a lot of things had not happened that were to come later, and a lot of things had not come between them.

Maybe he was thinking of the same Frenchman sitting in the gilded hall of the Elysée Palace eight months earlier destroying in measured and sonorous phrases the hopes of the British Prime Minister of crowning his political career by bringing Britain into the European Community before retiring into the contentment of a man who has fulfilled his dream.

Or possibly he was just thinking of the past agonising months when the revelations of a pimp and a courtesan had almost brought down the Government of Britain. He was an old man, who had been born and brought up in a world that had its standards for good or evil, and had believed in those standards and had followed them. Now the world was a different place, full of a new people with new ideas, and he was of the past. Did he understand that there were new standards now, which he could dimly recognise and did not like?

Probably he knew, looking down onto the sunny grass, what lay ahead. The surgical operation could not long be delayed, and with it retirement from the leadership. Before long the world would be handed over to the new people. Much of the world had already been handed over to them. But would it also be handed over to pimps and tarts, spies and—assassins?

From behind, Thomas saw the shoulders straighten, and the old man in front of him turned round.

"Superintendent Thomas, I wish you to know that General de Gaulle is my friend. If there is the remotest danger to his person, and if that danger would emanate from a citizen of these islands, then that person must be stopped. From now on you will conduct your investigations with unprecedented vigour. Within the hour your superiors will be authorised by me personally to accord you every facility within their powers. You will be subjected to no limits in either expenditure or manpower. You will have the authority to co-opt onto your team whomsoever you wish to assist you, and to have access to the official documentation of any department in the land which may be able to further your enquiries. You will, by my personal order, cooperate without any hint of reserve with the French authorities in this matter. Only when you are absolutely satisfied that, whoever this man may be whom the French are seeking to identify and arrest, he is not a British subject or operating from these shores, may you desist from your enquiries. At that point you will report back to me in person.

"In the event that this man Calthrop, or any other man bearing a British passport, may reasonably be considered to be the man whom the French are seeking, you will detain this man. Whoever he is, he must be stopped. Do I make myself clear?"

It could not have been clearer. Thomas knew for certain that some piece of information had come to the P.M.'s ears that had sparked off the instructions he had just given. Thomas suspected it had to do with the cryptic remark about certain persons who wished his investigations to make little progress, but he could not be sure.

"Yes, sir," he said.

The P.M. inclined his head to indicate the interview was over. Thomas rose and went to the door.

"Er—Prime Minister?"

"Yes?"

"There is one point, sir. I am not certain whether you would wish me to tell the French yet about the enquiries into the rumour about this man Calthrop in the Dominican Republic two years ago."

"Do you have reasonable grounds to believe as of now that this man's past activities justify fitting him to the description of the man the French wish to identify?"

"No, Prime Minister. We have nothing against any Charles Calthrop in the world except the rumour of two years ago. We do not yet know whether the Calthrop we have spent the afternoon trying to trace is the one who was in the Caribbean in January 1961. If he is not, then we are back to square one."

The Prime Minister thought for a few seconds.

"I would not wish you to waste your French colleagues' time with suggestions based on unsubstantiated rumours two and a half years old. Note the word 'unsubstantiated,' Superintendent. Please continue your enquiries with energy. At the moment you feel there is enough information in your possession concerning this, or any other, Charles Calthrop to add substance to the rumour that he was involved in the affair of General Trujillo, you will inform the French at once and at the same time track the man down, wherever he is."

"Yes, Prime Minister."

"And would you please ask Mr. Harrowby to come to me. I shall issue the authorities you need at once."

Back in Thomas's office, things changed quickly through the rest of the afternoon. Round him he grouped a task force of six of the Special Branch's best detective inspectors. One was recalled from leave; two were taken off their duties watching the house of a man suspected to be passing classified information from the Royal Ordinance Factory to an East European military attaché. Two of the others were the ones who had helped him the day before go through the records of the Special Branch looking for a killer who had no name. The last had been on his day off and was gardening in his greenhouse when the call came through to report to the Branch headquarters immediately.

He briefed them all exhaustively, swore them to silence, and answered a continuous stream of phone calls. It was just after 6 p.m. when the Inland Revenue found the tax returns of Charles Harold Calthrop. One of the detectives was sent out to bring the whole file back. The rest went to work on the telephone, except one who was sent to Calthrop's address to seek out every neighbour and local tradesman for information as to where the man might be. Photographs taken from the one submitted by Calthrop on his application form for a passport four years previously were printed in the photographic laboratory, and every inspector had one in his pocket.

The tax returns of the wanted man showed that for the past year he had been unemployed, and before that had been abroad for a year. But for most of the financial year 1960/61 he had been in the employ of a firm whose name Thomas recognised as belonging to one of Britain's leading manufacturers and exporters of small arms. Within an hour he had the name of the firm's managing director, and found the man at home at his country house in the stockbroker belt of Surrey. By telephone Thomas made an appointment to see him immediately, and as dusk descended on the Thames his police Jaguar roared over the river in the direction of the village of Virginia Water.

Patrick Monson hardly looked like a dealer in lethal weapons, but then, Thomas reflected, they never do. From Monson Thomas learned the arms firm had employed Calthrop for just under a year. More important, during December 1960 and January 1961 he had been sent by the firm to Ciudad Trujillo to try and sell a consignment of British Army surplus submachine guns to Trujillo's police chief.

Thomas eyed Monson with distaste.

"And never mind what they later get used for, eh boyo," he thought, but did not bother to voice his distaste. Why had Calthrop left the Dominican Republic in such a hurry?

Monson seemed surprised by the question. Well, because Trujillo had been killed, of course. The whole regime fell within hours. What could be expected from the new regime by a man who had come to the island to sell the old regime a load of guns and ammunition? Of course, he'd had to get out.

Thomas pondered. Certainly it made sense. Monson said Calthrop had later claimed he was actually sitting in the office of the dictator's police chief discussing the sale when the news came through that the General had been killed in an ambush outside the town. The Chief of Police had gone white, and left immediately for his private estate where his aircraft and pilot were permanently waiting for him. Within a few hours mobs were rampaging through the streets seeking adherents of the old regime. Calthrop had to bribe a fisherman to sail him out of the island.

Why, Thomas asked eventually, did Calthrop leave the firm? He was dismissed, was the answer. Why? Monson thought carefully for a few moments. Finally he said:

"Superintendent, the arms business is highly competitive. Cut-throat, you might say. To know what another man is offering for sale, and the price he is asking, can be vital for a rival wishing to clinch the same deal with the same buyer. Let us just say that we were not entirely satisfied with Calthrop's loyalty to the company."

In the car back into town Thomas thought over what Monson had told him. Calthrop's explanation at the time as to why he had got out of the Dominican Republic so fast was logical. It did not corroborate, indeed it tended to negate, the rumour subsequently reported by the Caribbean SIS resident that his name was linked with the killing.

On the other hand, according to Monson, Calthrop was a man who was not above playing a double cross.

Could he have arrived as the accredited representative of a small-arms company wishing to make a sale, and at the same time have been in the pay of the revolutionaries?

There was one thing Monson had said that disturbed Thomas: he had mentioned that Calthrop did not know much about rifles when he joined the company. Surely a crackshot would be an expert? But then, of course, he could have learned that while with the company. But if he was a newcomer to rifle shooting, why did the anti-Trujillo partisans want to hire him to stop the General's car on a fast road with a single shot? Or did they not hire him at all? Was Calthrop's own story the literal truth?

Thomas shrugged. It didn't prove anything or disprove anything. Back to square one again, he thought bitterly.

But back at the office there was news that changed his mind. The inspector who had been enquiring at Calthrop's address had reported in. He had found a next-door neighbour who had been out at work all day. The woman said Mr. Calthrop had left some days before and had mentioned he was going touring in Scotland. In the back of the car parked in the street outside the woman had seen what looked like a set of fishing rods.

Fishing rods? Superintendent Thomas felt suddenly chilly, although the office was warm. As the detective finished talking, one of the others came in.

"Super?"

"Yes?"

"Something has just occurred to me."

"Go on."

"Do you speak French?"

"No, do you?"

"Yes, my mother was French. This assassin the PJ are looking for, he's got the code-name Jackal, right?"

"So what?"

"Well, Jackal in French is Chacal: C-H-A-C-A-L. See? It could just be a coincidence. He must be as thick as five posts to pick a name, even in French, that's made up of the first three letters of his Christian name and the first three letters of his—"

"Land of my bloody fathers," said Thomas and sneezed violently. Then he reached for the telephone.

fifteen

The third meeting in the Interior Ministry in Paris began shortly after ten o'clock, due to the lateness of the Minister, who had been held up in the traffic on his way back from a diplomatic reception. As soon as he was seated, he gestured for the meeting to start.

The first report was from General Guibaud of the SDECE. It was short and to the point. The ex-Nazi killer, Kassel, had been located by agents of the Madrid office of the Secret Service. He was living quietly in retirement at his rooftop flat in Madrid, had become a partner with another former SS-commando leader in a prosperous business in the city, and so far as could be determined was not involved with the OAS. The Madrid office had in any case had a file on the man by the time the request from Paris for a further check came through, and was of the view that he had never been involved with the OAS at all.

In view of his age, increasingly frequent bouts of rheumatism that were beginning to affect his legs, and a remarkably high alcohol intake, Kassel in the general view could be discounted as a possible Jackal.

As the General finished, eyes turned to Commissaire Lebel. His report was sombre. During the course of the day reports had come into the PJ from the other three countries who had originally suggested possible suspects twenty-four hours earlier.

From America had come news that Chuck Arnold, the gun salesman, was in Colombia trying to clinch a deal for his American employer to sell a consignment of former U.S. Army surplus AR-10 assault rifles to the Chief of Staff. He was in any case under permanent CIA surveillance while in Bogotá, and there was no indication that he was planning anything other than to put through his arms deal, despite official U.S. disapproval.

The file on this man had, however, been telexed to Paris, as had also the file on Vitellino. This showed that although the former Cosa Nostra gunman had not yet been located, he was five feet, four inches tall, immensely broad and squat, with jet black hair and a swarthy complexion. In view of the radical difference in appearance from the Jackal as described by the hotel clerk in Vienna, Lebel felt he too could be discounted.

The South Africans had learned Piet Schuyper was now the head of the private army of a diamond mining corporation in a West African country of the British Commonwealth. His duties were to patrol the borders of the vast mining concessions owned by the company and ensure a continuous disincentive to illicit diamond poachers from across the border. No inconvenient questions were asked of him as to the methods he used to discourage poaching, and his employers were pleased with his efforts. His presence was confirmed by his employers; he was definitely at his post in West Africa.

The Belgian police had checked on their ex-mercenary. A report in the files from one of their Caribbean embassies had been unearthed, which reported the former employee of Katanga had been killed in a bar fight in Guatemala three months previously.

Lebel finished reading the last of the reports from the file in front of him. When he looked up it was to find fourteen pairs of eyes on him, most of them cold and challenging.

"*Alors, rien?*"

The question from Colonel Rolland was that of everyone present.

"No, nothing, I'm afraid," agreed Lebel. "None of the suggestions seem to stand up."

"Seem to stand up," echoed Saint-Clair bitterly. "Is that what we have come to with your 'pure detective work'? Nothing seems to stand up?" He glared angrily at the two detectives, Bouvier and Lebel, quickly aware that the mood of the room was with him.

"It would seem, gentlemen," the Minister quietly used the plural form to take in both the police commissaires, "that we are back where we started. Square one, so to speak?"

"Yes, I'm afraid so," replied Lebel. Bouvier took up the cudgels on his behalf.

"My colleague is searching, virtually without clues and without any sort of lead, for one of the most elusive types of men in the world. Such specimens do not advertise their professions or their whereabouts."

"We are aware of that, my dear Commissaire," retorted the Minister, coldly, "the question is—"

He was interrupted by a knock on the door. The Minister frowned; his instructions had been that they were not to be disturbed except in an emergency.

"Come in."

One of the ministry's porters stood in the doorway, diffident and abashed.

"*Mes excuses, Monsieur le Ministre.* A telephone call for Commissaire Lebel. From London." Feeling the hostility of the room, the man tried to cover himself. "They say it is urgent . . ."

Lebel rose.

"Would you excuse me, gentlemen?"

He returned in five minutes. The atmosphere was as cold as when he had left it, and evidently the wrangle over what to do next had continued in his absence. As he entered he interrupted a bitter denunciation from Colonel Saint-Clair, who tailed off as Lebel took his seat. The little Commissaire had an envelope in his hand with scribbled writing on the back.

"I think, gentlemen, we have the name of the man we are looking for," he began.

The meeting ended thirty minutes later almost in a mood of levity. When Lebel had finished his relation of the message from London, the men round the table had let out a collective sigh, like a train arriving at its platform after a long journey. Each man knew that at last there was something he could do. Within half an hour they had agreed that without a word of publicity it would be possible to scour France for a man in the name of Charles Calthrop, to find him, and, if deemed necessary, to dispose of him.

The fullest known details of Calthrop, they knew, would not be available until the morning, when they would be telexed from London. But in the meantime Renseignements Généraux could check their miles of shelves for a disembarkation card filled in by this man, for a hotel card registering him at a hotel anywhere in France. The Prefecture of Police could check its own records to see if he was staying at any hotel within the confines of Paris.

The DST could put his name and description into the hands of every border post, port, harbour, and air-field in France, with instructions that such a man was to be held immediately on his touching on French territory.

If he had not yet arrived in France, no matter. Complete silence would be maintained until he arrived, and when he did, they would have him.

"This odious creature, the man they call Calthrop, we have him already in the bag," Colonel Raoul Saint-Clair de Villauban told his mistress that night as they lay in bed.

When Jacqueline finally coaxed a belated orgasm from the colonel to send him to sleep the mantlepiece clock chimed twelve, and it had become August 14.

Superintendent Thomas sat back in his office chair and surveyed the six inspectors whom he had re-grouped from their various tasks after putting down the phone following the call to Paris. Outside in the still summer night Big Ben tolled midnight.

His briefing took an hour. One man was allocated to examine Calthrop's youth, where his parents now lived, if indeed he had any; where he had been to school; shooting record, if any, in the cadet corps as a schoolboy; noticeable characteristics, distinguishing marks, etc.

A second was designated to investigate his young manhood, from leaving school, through National Ser-vice—record of service and prowess at shooting—employment following discharge from the Army, right up to the time he left the employ of the arms dealers who had dismissed him for suspected double-dealing.

The third and fourth detectives were put on the trail of his activities since leaving his last known employers in October 1961. Where he had been, whom he had seen, what his income had been, from what sources. Since there was no police record and therefore presumably no fingerprints, Thomas needed every known and latest photograph of the man, up to the present time.

The last two inspectors were to seek to establish the whereabouts of Calthrop at that moment. Go over the entire flat for fingerprints, find where he bought the car, check at County Hall, London, for records of issue of a driving licence, and if there were none start checking with the provincial county licensing departments. Trace the car—make, age, colour, registration number. Trace his local garage to see if he was planning a long journey by car, check the cross-Channel ferries, go round all the airline companies for a booking on a plane, no matter what the destination.

All six men took extensive notes. Only when he had finished did they rise and file out of the office. In the corridor the last two eyed each other askance.

"Dry-clean and re-texture," said one. "The complete bloody works."

"The funny thing is," observed the other, "that the old man won't tell us what he's supposed to have done, or be going to do."

"One thing we can be sure of. To get this kind of action, it must have come down right from the top.

You'd think the bugger was planning to shoot the King of Siam."

It took a short while to wake up a magistrate and get him to sign a search warrant. By the small hours of the morning, while an exhausted Thomas dozed in the armchair in his office and an even more haggard Claude Lebel sipped black coffee in his office, two Special Branch men went through Calthrop's flat with a fine tooth comb.

Both were experts. They started with the drawers, emptying each one systematically into a bedsheet and sorting the contents diligently. When all the drawers were clean, they started on the woodwork of the drawerless desk for secret panels. After the wooden furniture came two upholstered pieces. When they had finished with these, the flat looked like a turkey farm on Thanksgiving Day. One man was working over the drawing room, the other the bedroom. After these two came the kitchen and bathroom.

With the furniture, cushions, pillows, and coats and suits in the cupboards dealt with, they started on the floors, ceilings, and walls. By six in the morning the flat was as clean as a whistle. Most of the neighbours were grouped on the landing looking at each other and then the closed door of Calthrop's flat, conversing in whispers that hushed when the two inspectors emerged from the flat.

One was carrying a suitcase stuffed with Calthrop's personal papers and private belongings. He went down to the street, jumped into the waiting squad car, and drove back to Superintendent Thomas. The other started on the long round of interviews. He began with the neighbours, aware that most would have to head for their places of work within an hour or two. The local tradesmen could come later.

Thomas spent several minutes riffling through the collection of possessions spread all over his office floor. Out of the jumble the detective inspector grabbed a small blue book, walked to the window, and started to flick through it by the light of the rising sun.

"Super, have a look at this." His finger jabbed at one of the pages in the passport in front of him. "See . . . Republica Dominicana, Aeroporto Ciudad Trujillo, Decembre 1960, Entrada. . . . He was there all right. This is our man."

Thomas took the passport from him, glanced at it for a moment, then stared out of the window.

"Oh yes, this is our man, boyo. But does it not occur to you that we're holding his passport in our hands?"

"Oh, the sod . . ." breathed the inspector when he saw the point.

"As you say," said Thomas, whose chapel upbringing caused him only very occasionally to use strong language. "If he's not travelling on this passport, then what is he travelling on? Give me the phone, and get me Paris."

By the same hour the Jackal had already been on the road for fifty minutes, and the city of Milan lay far behind him. The hood of the Alfa was down, and the morning sun already bathed the Autostrada 7 from Milan to Genoa. Along the wide straight road he pushed the car well over eighty miles an hour and kept the tachometre needle flickering just below the start of the red band. The cool wind lashed his pale hair into a frenzy around the forehead, but the eyes were protected by the dark glasses.

The road map said it was 210 kilometres to the French frontier at Ventimiglia, about 130 miles, and he was well up on his estimated driving time of two hours. There was a slight hold-up among the truck traffic of Genoa as it headed for the docks just after seven o'clock, but before 7:15 he was away on the A 10 to San Remo and the border.

The daily traffic was already thick when he arrived at 7:50 at the sleepiest of France's frontier points, and the heat was rising.

After a thirty-minute wait in the queue, he was beckoned up to the parking ramp for customs examination. The policeman who took his passport examined it carefully, muttered a brief *"Un moment, monsieur,"* and disappeared inside the customs shed.

He emerged a few minutes later with a man in civilian clothes who held the passport.

"Bonjour, monsieur."

"Bonjour."

"This is your passport?"

"Yes."

There was another searching examination of the passport.

"What is the purpose of your visit to France?"

"Tourism. I have never seen the Côte d'Azur."

"I see. The car is yours?"

"No. It's a hired car. I had business in Italy, and it has unexpectedly occasioned a week with nothing to do before returning to Milan. So I hired a car to do a little touring."

"I see. You have the papers for the car?"

The Jackal extended the international driving licence, the contract of hire, and the two insurance certificates. The plain-clothes man examined both.

"You have luggage, monsieur?"

"Yes, three pieces in the trunk, and a hand-grip."

"Please bring them all into the customs hall."

He walked away. The policeman helped the Jackal off-load the three suitcases and the hand-grip, and together they carried them to customs.

Before leaving Milan he had taken the old greatcoat, scruffy trousers and shoes of André Martin, the non-existent Frenchman whose papers were sewn into the lining of the third suitcase, and rolled them in a ball at the back of the trunk. The clothes from the other two suitcases had been divided between the three. The medals were in his pocket.

Two customs officers examined each case. While they were doing so, he filled in the standard form for tourists entering France. Nothing in the cases excited any attention. There was a brief moment of anxiety as the customs men picked up the jars containing the hair-tinting dyes. He had taken the precaution of emptying them into after-shave flasks, previously emptied. At that time after-shave lotion was not in vogue in France, it was too new on the market and mainly confined to America. He saw the two customs men exchange glances, but they replaced the flasks in the hand-grip.

Out of the corner of his eye he could see through the windows another man examining the trunk and engine hood of the Alfa. Fortunately, he did not look underneath. He unrolled the greatcoat and trousers in the trunk and looked at them with distaste, but presumed the coat was for covering the hood on winter nights and old clothes were a contingency in case repairs had to be done on the car along the road. He replaced the clothes and closed the trunk.

As the Jackal finished filling in his form, the two customs men inside the shed closed the cases and nodded to the plain-clothes man. He in turn took the entry card, examined it, checked it again with the passport, and handed the passport back.

"Merci, monsieur. Bon voyage."

Ten minutes later the Alfa was booming into the eastern outskirts of Menton. After a relaxed breakfast at a cafe overlooking the old port and yacht basin, the Jackal headed along the Corniche Littorale for Monaco, Nice, and Cannes.

In his London office Superintendent Thomas stirred a cup of thick black coffee and ran a hand over his stubbled chin. Across the room the two inspectors saddled with the task of finding the whereabouts of Calthrop faced their chief. The three were waiting for the arrival of six extra men, all sergeants of the Special Branch released from their routine duties as the result of a string of telephone calls Thomas had been making over the previous hour.

Shortly after nine o'clock, as they reported to their offices and learned of their re-deployment to Thomas's force, the men started to trickle in. When the last had arrived, he briefed them.

"All right, we're looking for a man. There's no need for me to tell you why we want him, it's not important that you should know. What is important is that we get him, and get him fast. Now we know, or think we know, that he's abroad at this moment. We are pretty certain he is travelling under a false passport.

"Here"—he passed out among them a set of photographs, blown-up copies of the portrait photo of Calthrop's passport application form—"is what he looks like. The chances are he will have disguised himself and therefore not necessarily respond to that description. What you are going to have to do is go down to the Passport Office and get a complete list of every application for a passport made recently. Start by covering the last hundred days. If that yields nothing, go back another hundred days. It's going to be a hard grind."

He continued by giving a rough description of the most common way of getting a false passport, which was in fact the method the Jackal had used.

"The important thing is," he concluded, "not to be content with birth certificates. Check the death certificates. So after you've got the list from Passport Office, take the whole operation down to Somerset House, get settled in, divide the list of names among yourselves, and get to work among those death certificates. If you can find one application for a passport submitted by a man who isn't alive any longer, the imposter will probably be our man. Off you go."

The eight men filed out, while Thomas got on to the Passport Office by phone, then the Registry of Births, Marriages and Deaths at Somerset House, to ensure that his team would get the fullest cooperation.

It was two hours later as he was shaving on a borrowed electric razor plugged into his desk lamp that the senior of the two inspectors, who was the leader of

the team, phoned back. There were, he said, 841 applications for new passports submitted in the previous
hundred days. It was the summer, he explained, holiday time. There were always more in holiday time.

Bryn Thomas hung up and snuffled into his handkerchief.

"Damn summer," he said.

Just after 11 that morning the Jackal rolled into the
centre of Cannes. As usual when he wanted something
done, he looked for one of the best hotels, and after a
few minutes cruising swept into the forecourt of the
Majestic. Running a comb through his hair, he strode
into the foyer.

Being the middle of the morning most of the guests
were out and the hall was not busy. His elegant light
suit and confident manner picked him out as an English gentleman and raised no eyebrows when he asked
a bell-hop where the telephone booths were. The lady
behind the counter that separated the switchboard
from the entry to the cloakroom looked up as he
approached.

"Please get me Paris, Molitor 5901," he asked.

A few minutes later she gestured him to a booth
beside the switchboard, and watched him close the
sound-proof door behind him.

"*Allo, ici Chacal.*"

"*Allo, ici Valmy.* Thank God you've called. We've
been trying to get hold of you for two days."

Anyone looking through the glass panel of the
booth's door would have seen the Englishman inside
stiffen and frown at the mouthpiece. For most of the
ten-minute conversation he remained silent, listening.

Occasionally his lips moved as he asked a short, terse question. But nobody was looking; the switchboard operator was busy in a romantic novel. The next thing she saw was the guest towering over her, the dark glasses staring down. From the metre on the switchboard she read off the charge for the call, and was paid.

The Jackal took a pot of coffee on the terrace looking over the Croisette and the glittering sea where brown bathers romped and screamed. Deep in thought, he drew heavily on a cigarette.

The bit about Kowalski he could follow; he remembered the hulking Pole from the hotel in Vienna. What he could not follow was how the bodyguard outside the door had known his code-name, or what he had been hired to do. Perhaps the French police had worked that out for themselves. Perhaps Kowalski had sensed what he was, for he also had been a killer, but oafish and clumsy.

The Jackal took stock. Valmy had advised him to quit and go home, but had admitted he had no direct authority from Rodin to cancel the operation. What had happened confirmed the Jackal's intense suspicions of the security slackness of the OAS. But he knew something that they did not, something that the French police could not know. It was that he was travelling under an assumed name, with a legitimate passport in that name, and three separate sets of false papers including two foreign passports and disguises to match up his sleeve.

Just what did the French police, this man Valmy had mentioned, Commissaire Lebel, have to go on? A rough description: tall, blond, foreign. There must be

thousands of such men staying in France in August.
They could not arrest every one.

The second advantage he had was that the French
police were hunting for a man carrying the passport
of Charles Calthrop. Then let them, and good luck.
He was Alexander Duggan, and could prove it.

From here on, with Kowalski dead, nobody, not
even Rodin and his henchmen, knew who he was or
where. He was on his own at last, and that was the
way he had always wanted it to be.

Nevertheless, the dangers had increased, there was
no doubt of it. With the idea of an assassination once
revealed, he would be attacking a fortress of security
that was on its guard. The question was, could his plan
for carrying out the killing beat the security screen.
On balance, he was confident that it could.

The question still remained, and it had to be answered. To go back, or to go on? To go back would
be to enter into dispute with Rodin and his bunch of
thugs over the ownership of the quarter million dollars
presently in his account in Zurich. If he refused to
hand the bulk of it back, they would not hesitate to
track him down, torture him for the signed paper that
would release the money from the account, then kill
him. To stay ahead of them would cost money, a lot of
it, probably the full extent of the money he possessed.

To go on would mean further dangers until the job
was over. It would become ever harder to pull back
at the last minute as the day approached.

The bill came, he glanced at it and winced. God,
the prices these people charged. To live this kind of
life a man needed to be rich, to have dollars and dollars and even more dollars. He looked out at the

jewelled sea and the lithe brown girls walking along the beach, the hissing Cadillacs and snarling Jaguars that crept along the Croisette, their bronzed young drivers keeping half an eye on the road and the other flicking across the pavements for a likely pick-up. This was what he had wanted for a long time, from the days when he had pressed his nose to the travel agents windows and gazed at the posters showing another life, another world, far from the drudgery of the commuter train and the forms in triplicate, the paper clips and tepid tea. Over the past three years he had almost made it; a glimpse here, a touch there. He had got used to good clothes, expensive meals, a smart flat, a sports car, elegant women. To go back meant to give it up.

The Jackal paid the bill and left a large tip. He climbed into the Alfa and headed away from the Majestic and into the heart of France.

Commissaire Lebel was sitting at his desk feeling as though he had never slept in his life and probably never would again. In the corner Lucien Caron snored loudly on the camp bed, having been up all night masterminding the search through the records for Charles Calthrop somewhere on the face of France. Lebel had taken over at dawn.

In front of him now was a pile of reports from the various agencies whose task it was to keep check on the presence and whereabouts of foreigners in France. Each one bore the same message. No man of that name had crossed any border point legally since the start of the year, the farthest back the checks had extended. No hotel in the country, either in the prov inces or Paris, had taken in a guest of that name, at least not under that name. He was not on any list of undesirable aliens, nor had he ever come to the notice of the French authorities in any way.

As each report came in, Lebel wearily told the informant to go on checking further and further back until any visit Calthrop had ever paid to France could be traced. From that, possibly, could be established whether he had a habitual place of residence, a friend's house, a favourite hotel, where he might even now be masquerading under an assumed name.

Superintendent Thomas's call of that morning had come as yet another blow to hopes of an early capture of the elusive killer. Once again the phrase "back to square one" had been used, but fortunately this time it was only between Caron and himself. The members of the evening council had not yet been informed that the Calthrop lead was probably going to prove abortive. This was something he was going to have to tell them that evening at ten o'clock. If he could not produce an alternative name to Calthrop, he could imagine once again the scorn of Saint-Clair and the silent reproach of the rest.

Two things only could comfort him. One was that at least they now had a description of Calthrop and a photograph of his head and shoulders, full-face to the camera. He had probably changed his appearance considerably if he had taken a false passport, but still, it was better than nothing. The other thing was that no one else on the council could think of anything better to do than what he was doing—checking everything.

Caron had put forward the idea that perhaps the

British police had surprised Calthrop while he was away from his flat on an errand in the town; that he had no alternative passport; that he had gone to ground and cried off on the whole operation.

Lebel had sighed.

"That would indeed be lucky," he told his adjutant, "but don't count on it. The British Special Branch reported that all his washing things and shaving gear were missing from the bathroom, and that he had mentioned to a neighbour that he was going away touring and fishing. If Calthrop left his passport behind, it was because he no longer needed it. Don't count on this man making too many errors; I'm beginning to get a feeling about the Jackal."

The man the police of two countries were now searching for had decided to avoid the agonising congestion of the Grande Corniche on its murderous way from Cannes to Marseilles, and to stay away from the southern part of the RN 7 when it turned north out of Marseilles for Paris. Both roads in August he knew to be a refined form of hell on earth.

Safe in his assumed and documented name of Duggan, he decided to drive leisurely up from the coast through the Alpes-Maritimes, where the air was cooler in the altitude, and on through the rolling hills of Burgundy. He was in no particular hurry, for the day he had set for his kill was not yet on him, and he knew he had arrived in France slightly ahead of schedule.

From Cannes he headed due north, taking the RN 85 through the picturesque perfume town of Grasse and on towards Castellane, where the turbulent Verdon river, tamed by the high dam a few miles upstream, flowed more obediently down from Savoy to join the Durance at Cadarache.

From here he pushed on to Barrême and the little spa town of Digne. The blazing heat of the Provençal plain had fallen away behind him, and the air of the hills was sweet and cool even in the heat. When he stopped he could feel the sun blazing down, but when motoring the wind was like a cooling shower and smelled of the pines and woodsmoke from the farms.

After Digne he crossed the Durance and ate lunch in a small but pretty hostelry looking down into the waters. In another hundred miles the Durance would become a grey and slimy snake hissing shallow amid the sun-bleached shingle of its bed at Cavaillon and Plan d'Orgon. But here in the hills it was still a river, the way a river should look, a cool river teeming with fish, shaded along its banks with grass growing all the greener for its presence.

In the afternoon he followed the long northward curving run of the RN 85 through Sisteron, still following the Durance upstream on its left bank until the road forked and the RN 85 headed towards the north. As dusk was falling he entered the little town of Gap. He could have gone on towards Grenoble, but decided that as there was no hurry and more chance of finding rooms in August in a small town, he should look around for a country-style hotel. Just out of town he found the brightly gabled Hôtel du Cerf, formerly a hunting lodge of one of the Dukes of Savoy, and still retaining an air of rustic comfort and good food.

There were several rooms still vacant. He had a leisurely bath, a break with his usual habit of showering, and dressed in his dove-grey suit with a silk shirt and knitted tie, while the room-maid, after receiving several winning smiles, had blushfully agreed to sponge and press the check suit he had worn all day so that he could have it back by morning.

The evening meal was taken in a panelled room overlooking a sweep of the wooded hillside, loud with the chatter of cicadas among the *pinèdes*. The air was warm, and it was only half way through the meal, when a woman diner who wore a sleeveless dress *en décolleté* commented to the maître d'hôtel that a chill had entered the air, that the windows were closed.

The Jackal turned round when he was asked if he objected to the window next to which he sat being closed, and glanced at the woman indicated by the maître as the person who had asked that they be shut. She was dining alone, a handsome woman in her late thirties with soft white arms and a deep bosom. The Jackal nodded to the maître to close the windows and gave a slight inclination of the head to the woman behind him. She answered with a cool smile.

The meal was magnificent. He chose speckled river trout grilled on a wood fire, and tournedos broiled over charcoal with fennel and thyme. The wine was a local Côtes du Rhône, full, rich, and in a bottle with no label. It had evidently come from the barrel in the cellar, the proprietor's personal choice for his vin de la maison. Most of the diners were having it, and with reason.

As he finished his sorbet he heard the low and authoritative voice of the woman behind him telling the maître that she would take her coffee in the residents' lounge, and the man bowed and addressed her as "Madame la Baronne." A few minutes later the

Jackal had also ordered his coffee in the lounge and
headed that way.

The call from Somerset House came for Superintendent Thomas at 10:15. He was sitting by the open
window of the office staring down into the now silent
street where no restaurants beckoned late diners and
drivers into the area. The offices between Millbank
and Smith Square were silent hulks, lightless, blind,
uncaring. Only in the anonymous block that housed
the offices of the Special Branch did the lights burn
late as always.

A mile away, in the bustling Strand, the lights were
also burning late in the section of Somerset House that
housed the death certificates of millions of Britain's
deceased citizens. Here Thomas's team of six detective
sergeants and two inspectors were hunched over their
piles of paper work, rising every few minutes to ac-
company one of the staff clerks, kept back at work
long after the others had gone home, down the rows
of gleaming files to check on yet another name.

It was the senior inspector in charge of the team
who rang. His voice was tired, but with a touch of
optimism, a man hoping that what he had to say
would get them all released from the grind of checking
hundreds of death certificates that did not exist because the passport holders were not dead.

"Alexander James Quentin Duggan," he announced
briefly, after Thomas had answered.

"What about him?" said Thomas.

"Born April third, nineteen-twenty-nine, in Sambourne Fishley, in the parish of Saint Mark's. Applied
for a passport in the normal way on the normal form

on July fourteenth this year. Passport issued the following day and mailed July seventeenth to the address on the application form. It will probably turn out to be an accommodation address."

"Why?" asked Thomas. He disliked being kept waiting.

"Because Alexander James Quentin Duggan was killed in a road accident in his home village at the age of two and a half, on November eighth, nineteen-thirty-one."

Thomas thought for a moment.

"How many more of the passports issued in the last hundred days remain to be checked?" he asked.

"About three hundred to go," said the voice on the phone.

"Leave the others to continue checking the remainder, just in case there is another phoney among the bunch," instructed Thomas. "Hand over the team leadership to the other fellow. I want you to check out that address to which the passport was sent. Report back to me by phone the moment you have found it. If it's an occupied premises, interview the householder. Bring me back the full details on the phoney Duggan and the file copy of the photograph he submitted with the application form. I want to have a look at this lad Calthrop in his new disguise."

It was just before eleven that the senior inspector phoned back in. The address in question was a small tobacconist and newsagent shop in Paddington, the kind that had a window full of cards advertising the addresses of prostitutes. The owner, living above the shop, had been roused and had agreed he took in mail for customers who had no fixed address. He made a charge for his services. He could not remember a regular customer named Duggan, but it could have been that Duggan only called twice, once to arrange for his mail to be received there, the second time to pick up the one envelope that he was waiting for. The inspector had showed the newsagent a photograph of Calthrop, but the man could not recognise him. He also showed him the photograph of Duggan on the application form, and the man said he thought he remembered the second man, but could not be sure. He felt the man might have worn dark glasses. Many of those who came into his shop to buy the erotic magazines displayed behind the counter wore dark glasses.

"Bring him in," ordered Thomas, "and get back here yourself."

Then he picked up the phone and asked for Paris.

A second time, the call came half way through the evening conference. Commissaire Lebel had explained that beyond a doubt Calthrop was not inside France under his own name, unless he had smuggled himself into the country in a fishing boat or across one of the land borders at an isolated spot. He personally did not think a professional would do that, because at any subsequent spot check by the police he could be caught for not having his papers in order, that is, having no entry stamp on his passport.

Nor had any Charles Calthrop checked into any French hotel in his own name.

These facts were corroborated by the head of the Central Records office, the head of the DST, and the Prefect of Police of Paris, so they were not disputed.

The two alternatives, argued Lebel, were that the man had not made any provision for obtaining a false passport, and had thought he was unsuspected. In that case, the police raid on his flat in London must have caught him short. He explained that he did not believe this, because Superintendent Thomas's men had found gaps in the wardrobe and half-empty clothes drawers, and absence of washing accoutrements and shaving tackle, indicating that the man had left his London flat for a planned absence elsewhere. This was borne out by a neighbour, who reported Calthrop as having said he was going touring by car in Scotland. Neither the British nor the French police had any reason to believe this was true.

The second alternative was that Calthrop had acquired a false passport, and this man was what the British police were presently searching for. In that event, he might either still be not in France but at some other place completing his preparations, or he might already have entered France unsuspected.

It was at this point that several of the conference members exploded.

"You mean he might be here, in France, even in the centre of Paris?" expostulated Alexandre Sanguinetti.

"The point is," explained Lebel, "that he has got his timetable, and only he knows it. We have been investigating for seventy-two hours. We have no way of knowing at which point in the man's timetable we have intervened. The one thing we can be sure of is, that apart from knowing we are aware of the existence of a plot to assassinate the President, the killer cannot know what progress we have made. Therefore we stand a reasonable chance of apprehending an unsuspecting man, as soon as we have him identified under his new name, and located under that name."

But the meeting refused to be mollified. The thought that the killer might even then be within a mile of them, and that in that man's timetable the attempt on the life of the President might be for tomorrow, caused each of them acute anxiety.

"It could be, of course," mused Colonel Rolland, "that having learned from Rodin, through the unknown agent Valmy, that the plan was exposed in principle, that Calthrop then left his flat to dispose of the evidence of his preparations. His gun and ammunition, for example, could even now be tipped into a lake in Scotland, so that he can present himself to his own police on his return as clean as a whistle. In that event it would be very difficult to bring charges."

The meeting thought over Rolland's suggestion, with increasing signs of agreement.

"Then tell us, Colonel," said the Minister, "if you had been hired for this job, and had learned that the plot was exposed, even if your own identity were still a secret, is that what you would do?"

"Certainly, *Monsieur le Ministre*," replied Rolland. "If I were an experienced assassin, I would realise that I must be on some file somewhere, and with the plot exposed it could only be a matter of time before I received a visit from the police and a search of my premises. So I would want to get rid of the evidence, and what better place than an isolated Scottish lake."

The round of smiles that greeted him from the table indicated how much those assembled approved of his speculation.

"However, that does not mean that we should just

let him go. I still think we should—take care of this Monsieur Calthrop."

The smiles vanished. There was silence for several seconds.

"I do not follow you, *mon colonel*," said General Guibaud.

"Simply this," explained Rolland. "Our orders were to locate and destroy this man. He may have dismantled his plot for the moment. But he may not have destroyed his equipment, but merely hidden it, in order to pass the scrutiny of the British police. After that, he could simply take up again where he left off, but with a new set of preparations even more difficult to penetrate."

"But surely, when the British police locate him, if he is still in Britain, they will detain him," someone asked.

"Not necessarily. Indeed I doubt it. They will probably have no proof, only suspicions. And our friends the English are notoriously sensitive about what they are pleased to call 'civil liberties.' I suspect they may find him, interview him, and then let him go for lack of evidence."

"Of course the Colonel is right," interjected Saint-Clair. "The British police have stumbled on this man by a fluke. They are incredibly foolish about things like leaving a dangerous man at liberty. Colonel Rolland's section should be authorised to render this man Calthrop harmless once and for all."

The Minister noticed that Commissaire Lebel had remained silent and unsmiling throughout the interchange.

"Well, Commissaire, and what do you think? Do

you agree with Colonel Rolland that Calthrop is even now dismantling and hiding, or destroying, his preparations and equipment?"

Lebel glanced up at the two rows of expectant faces on each side of him.

"I hope," he said quietly, "that the Colonel is right. But I fear he may not be."

"Why?" The Minister's question cut like a knife.

"Because," explained Lebel mildly, "his theory, although logical if indeed Calthrop has decided to call off the operation, is based on the theory that he has indeed made that decision. Supposing he has not? Supposing he has either not received Rodin's message or received it but decided to press ahead nevertheless?"

There was a buzz of deprecatory consternation. Only Rolland did not join in. He gazed contemplatively down the table at Lebel. What he was thinking was that Lebel was a far better brain than anyone present seemed prepared to give him credit for. Lebel's ideas, he recognised, could well be as realistic as his own.

It was at this point that the call came through for Lebel. This time he was gone for over twenty minutes. When he came back, he spoke to a completely silent assembly for a further ten minutes.

"What do we do now?" asked the Minister when he had finished. In his quiet way, without seeming to hurry, Lebel issued his orders like a general deploying his troops, and none of the men in the room, all senior to him in rank, disputed a word.

"So there we are," he concluded, "we will all conduct a quiet and discreet nation-wide search for Duggan in his new appearance, while the British police search the records of airline ticket offices, cross-Channel ferries, and so forth. If they locate him first, they pick him up if he is on British soil or inform us if he has left it. If we locate him inside France, we arrest him. If he is located in a third country, we can either wait for him to enter unsuspectingly and pick him up at the border, or . . . take another course of action. At that moment, however, I think my task of finding him will have been achieved. However, until that moment, gentlemen, I would be grateful if you would agree to do this my way."

The effrontery was so bold, the assurance so complete, that nobody could say a thing. They just nodded. Even Saint-Clair de Villauban was silent.

It was not until he was at home shortly after midnight that he found an audience to listen to his torrent of outrage at the thought of this ridiculous little bourgeois policeman having been right, while the top experts of the land had been wrong.

His mistress listened to him with sympathy and understanding, massaging the back of his neck as he lay face down on their bed. It was not until just before dawn, when he was sound asleep, that she could slip away to the hall and make a brief phone call.

Superintendent Thomas looked down at the two separate application forms for passports, and two photographs, spread out on the blotter in the pool of light thrown by the reading lamp.

"Let's run through it again," he ordered the senior inspector seated beside him. "Ready?"

"Sir."

"Calthrop: height, five feet eleven inches. Check?"

"Sir."

"Duggan: height, six feet."

"Thickened heels, sir. You can raise your height up to two and a half inches with special shoes. A lot of short people in show business do it for vanity. Besides, at a passport counter no one looks at your feet."

"All right," agreed Thomas, "thick-heeled shoes. Calthrop: colour of hair, brown. That doesn't mean much, it could vary from pale brown to chestnut brown. He looks to me here as if he had dark brown hair. Duggan also says brown. But he looks like a pale blond."

"That's true, sir. But hair habitually looks darker in photographs. It depends on the light, where it is placed and so forth. And then again, he could have tinted it paler to become Duggan."

"All right. I'll wear that. Calthrop: colour of eyes, brown. Duggan: colour of eyes, grey."

"Contact lenses, sir, it's a simple thing."

"OK. Calthrop's age is thirty-seven, Duggan's is thirty-four last April."

"He had to become thirty-four," explained the inspector, "because the real Duggan, the little boy who died at two and a half, was born in April nineteen-twenty-nine. That couldn't be changed. But nobody would query a man who happened to be thirty-seven but whose passport said he was thirty-four. One would believe the passport."

Thomas looked at the two photographs. Calthrop looked heftier, fuller in the face, a more sturdily built man. But to become Duggan he could have changed his appearance. Indeed, he had probably changed it even for his first meeting with the OAS chiefs, and remained with changed appearance ever since, including the period when he applied for the false passport. Men like this evidently had to be able to live in a second identity for months at a time if they were able to escape identification. It was probably by being this shrewd and painstaking that Calthrop had managed to stay off every police file in the world. If it had not been for that bar rumour in the Caribbean, they would never have got him at all.

But from now on, he had become Duggan, dyed hair, tinted contact lenses, slimmed down figure, raised heels. It was the description of Duggan, with passport number and photograph, that he sent down to the telex room to be transmitted to Paris. Lebel, he estimated, glancing at his watch, should have them all by 2 in the morning.

"After that, it's up to them," suggested the inspector.

"Oh no, boyo, after that there's a lot more work to be done," said Thomas maliciously. "First thing in the morning we start checking the airline ticket offices, the cross-channel ferries, the continental train ticket offices—the whole lot. We have to find out not only who he is now but where he is now."

At that moment a call came through from Somerset House. The last of the passport applications had been checked, and all were in order.

"OK, thank the clerks and stand down. Eight-thirty sharp in my office, the lot of you," said Thomas.

A sergeant entered with a copy of the statement of the newsagent, who had been taken to his local police station and interviewed there. Thomas glanced at the sworn statement, which said little more than he had told the Special Branch inspector on his own door-step.

"There's nothing we can hold him on," said Thomas. "Tell them at Paddington nick they can let him go back to his bed and his dirty photos, will you?"

The sergeant said, "Sir," and left.

Thomas settled back in the armchair to try and get some sleep.

While he had been talking it had quietly become August 15.

sixteen

Madame la Baronne de la Chalonnière paused at the door of her room and turned towards the young Englishman who had escorted her there. In the half darkness of the corridor she could not make out the details of his face; it was just a blur in that gloom.

It had been a pleasant evening, and she was still undecided whether she would or would not insist that it end at her doorway. The question had been at the back of her mind for the past hour.

On the one hand, although she had taken lovers before, she was a respectable married woman staying for a single night in a provincial hotel, and not in the habit of permitting herself to be seduced by total strangers. On the other hand, she was at her most vulnerable and was candid enough to admit it to herself.

She had spent the day at the military cadet academy at Barcelonette, high in the Alps, attending the passing-out parade of her son as a newly brevetted second lieutenant in the Chasseurs Alpins, his father's old regiment. Although she had undoubtedly been the most attractive mother at the parade, the sight of her son receiving his officer's bars and commissioned into the French Army had brought home to her with something of a shock the full realisation that she was a few months short of forty, and the mother of a grown son.

Although she could pass for five years younger, and sometimes felt ten years less than her age, the knowl-

edge that her son was twenty and probably screwing
women by now, no more to come home for the school
holidays and go shooting in the forests around the
family chateau, had caused her to wonder what she
was going to do now.

She had accepted the laborious gallantry of the
creaking old colonel who was the academy comman-
dant, and the admiring glances of the pink-cheeked
class-mates of her own boy, and had felt suddenly
very lonely. Her marriage, she had known for years,
was finished in all but name, for the Baron was too
busy chasing the teenage dollies of Paris between the
Bilboquet and Castel's to come down to the chateau
for the summer, or even to turn up at his son's com-
missioning.

It had occurred to her, as she drove the family
sedan back from the high Alps to stay overnight at a
country hotel outside Gap, that she was handsome,
female, and alone. Nothing now seemed to lie in pros-
pect but the attentions of elderly gallants like the
colonel at the academy, or frivolous and unsatisfying
flirtations with boys, and she was damned if she was
going to devote herself to charitable works. Not yet,
at any rate.

But Paris was an embarrassment and a humiliation,
with Alfred constantly chasing his teenagers and half
of society laughing at him and the other half laughing
at her.

She had been wondering about the future over
coffee in the lounge, and feeling an urge to be told she
was a woman and a beautiful one, and not simply
Madame la Baronne, when the Englishman had walked
across and asked if, as they were alone in the resi-

dents' salon, he might take his coffee with her. She had been caught unawares, and too surprised to say no.

She could have kicked herself a few seconds later, but after ten minutes she did not regret accepting his offer. He was, after all, between thirty-three and thirty-five, or so she estimated, and that was the best age for a man. Although he was English, he spoke fluent and rapid French; he was reasonably good looking and could be amusing. She had enjoyed the deft compliments and had even encouraged him to pay them, so that it was close to midnight when she rose, explaining that she had to make an early start the following morning.

He had escorted her up the stairs and at the landing window had pointed outside at the wooded hill slopes bathed in bright moonlight. They had stayed for a few moments looking at the sleeping countryside, until she had glanced at him and seen that his eyes were not on the window but on the deep divide between her breasts where the moonlight turned the skin to alabaster white.

He had smiled when detected, and leaned to her ear and murmured, "Moonlight turns even the most civilised man into a primitive." She had turned and walked on up the stairs, feigning annoyance, but inside her the unabashed admiration of the stranger caused a flutter of pleasure.

"It has been a most pleasant evening, monsieur."

She had her hand on the handle of the door and wondered vaguely whether the man would try to kiss her. In a way she hoped he would. Despite the triteness of the words, she could feel the hunger beginning in her belly. Perhaps it was just the wine, or the fiery Calvados he had ordered with the coffee, or the scene in the moonlight, but she was aware that this was not how she had forseen the evening ending.

She felt the stranger's arms slip round her back, without a word of warning, and his lips came down onto hers. They were warm and firm. "This must stop," said a voice inside her. A second later she had responded to the kiss, mouth closed. The wine made her head swim, it must have been the effect of the wine. She felt the arms round her tighten perceptibly, and they were hard and strong.

Her thigh was pressed against him below the belly and through the satin of her dress she felt the rigid arrogance of his prick. For a second she withdrew her leg, then pushed it back again. There was no conscious moment of decision-taking; the realisation came without effort that she wanted him, badly, between her thighs, inside her belly, all night.

She felt the door behind her open inwards, broke the embrace, and stepped backwards into her room.

"*Viens, primitif.*"

He stepped into the room and closed the door.

Throughout the night every archive in the Panthéon was checked again, this time for the name of Duggan, and with more success. A card was unearthed showing that Alexander James Quentin Duggan entered France on the Brabant Express from Brussels on July 22. An hour later another report from the same frontier post, the customs unit that regularly travels on the express trains from Brussels to Paris and back, doing its task while the train is in motion, was found with

Duggan's name among those passengers on the Etoile du Nord Express from Paris to Brussels on July 31.

From the Prefecture of Police came a hotel card filled out in the name of Duggan, and quoting a passport number that matched the one Duggan was carrying, as contained in the information from London, showing that he had stayed in a small hotel near the Place de la Madeleine between July 22 and 30, inclusive.

Inspector Caron was all for raiding the hotel, but Lebel preferred to pay a quiet visit in the small hours of the morning and had a chat with the proprietor. He was satisfied the man he sought was not at the hotel by August 15, and the proprietor was grateful for the Commissaire's discretion in not waking all his guests.

Lebel ordered a plain-clothes detective to check into the hotel as a guest until further notice, and to stay there without moving outside, in case Duggan turned up again. The proprietor was happy to cooperate.

"This July visit," Lebel told Caron when he was back in his office at 4:30, "was a reconnaissance trip. Whatever he has got planned, it's all laid on."

Then he lay back in his chair, gazed at the ceiling, and thought. Why did he stay in a hotel? Why not in the house of one of the OAS sympathisers, like all the other OAS agents on the run? Because he does not trust the OAS sympathisers to keep their mouths shut. He's quite right. So he works alone, trusting nobody, plotting and planning his own operation in his own way, using a false passport, probably behaving normally, politely, without raising any suspicion. The proprietor

of the hotel whom he had just interviewed confirmed
this. "A real gentleman," he had said. . . . A real gentleman, thought Lebel, and dangerous as a snake. They
are always the worst kind, for a policeman, the real
gentlemen. Nobody ever suspected them.

He glanced at the two photographs that had come
in from London, of Calthrop and Duggan. Calthrop
became Duggan, with a change of height, hair and
eyes, age, and, probably, manner. He tried to build
up a mental image of the man. What would he be like
to meet? Confident, arrogant, assured of his immunity.
Dangerous, devious, meticulous, leaving nothing to
chance. Armed of course, but with what? An automatic under the left armpit? A throwing knife lashed
against the ribs? A rifle? But where would he put it
when he went through customs? How would he get
near to General de Gaulle carrying such a thing, when
even women's handbags were suspect within twenty
yards of the President, and men with long packages
were hustled away without ceremony from anywhere
near a public appearance by the President?

Mon Dieu, and that colonel from the Elysée thinks
he's just another thug! Lebel was aware he had one
advantage: he knew the killer's new name, and the
killer did not know that he knew. That was his only
ace; apart from that, it all lay with the Jackal, and nobody at the evening conference could or would realise
it.

If he ever gets wind of what you know before you
catch him, and changes his identity again, Claude my
boy, he thought, you are going to be up against it in
a big way.

Aloud, he said "Really up against it."

Caron looked up.

"You're right, chief. He hasn't a chance."

Lebel was short-tempered with him, which was unusual. The lack of sleep must be beginning to tell.

The finger of light from the waning moon beyond the window panes withdrew slowly across the rumpled coverlet and back towards the casement. It picked out the discarded satin dress between the door and the foot of the bed, the discarded brassiere and limp nylons scattered on the carpet. The two figures on the bed were muffled in shadow.

Colette lay on her back and gazed up at the ceiling, the fingers of one hand running idly through the blond hair of the head pillowed on her belly. Her lips parted in a half-smile as she thought back over the night.

He had been good, this English primitive, hard but skilled, knowing how to use fingers and tongue and prick to bring her on five times and himself three. She could still feel the blazing heat going into her when he came, and she knew how badly she had needed a night like this for so long when she responded as she had not for years.

She glanced at the small travelling clock beside the bed. It said a quarter past five. She tightened her grip in the blond hair and pulled.

"Hey."

The Englishman muttered, half asleep. They were both lying naked among the disordered sheets, but the central heating kept the room comfortably warm. The blond head disengaged itself from her hand and slid between her thighs. She could feel the tickle of the hot breath and the tongue flickering in search again.

"No, no more."

She closed her thighs quickly, sat up and grabbed the hair, raising his face until she could look at him. He eased himself up the bed, plunged his face onto one of her full heavy breasts and started to kiss.

"I said no."

He looked up at her.

"That's enough, lover. I have to get up in two hours, and you have to go back to your room. Now, my little English, now."

He got the message and nodded, swinging off the bed to stand on the floor, looking round for his clothes. She slid under the bedclothes, sorted them out from the mess around her knees and pulled them up to the chin. When he was dressed, with jacket and tie slung over one arm, he looked down at her in the half-darkness and she saw the gleam of teeth as he grinned. He sat on the edge of the bed and ran his right hand round to the back of her neck. His face was a few inches from hers.

"It was good?"

"Mmmmmm. It was very good. And you?"

He grinned again. "What do you think?"

She laughed. "What is your name?"

He thought for a moment. "Alex," he lied.

"Well, Alex, it was very good. But it is also time you went back to your own room."

He bent down and gave her a kiss on the lips.

"In that case, good night, Colette."

A second later he was gone, and the door closed behind him.

At 7 in the morning as the sun was rising a local gendarme cycled up to the Hôtel du Cerf, dismounted, and entered the lobby. The proprietor, who was already up and busy behind the reception desk organising the morning calls and *café complet* for the guests in their rooms, greeted him.

"*Alors*, bright and early?"

"As usual," said the gendarme. "It's a long ride out here on a bicycle, and I always leave you till the last."

"Don't tell me." The proprietor grinned. "We do the best breakfast coffee in the neighbourhood. Marie-Louise, bring monsieur a cup of coffee, and no doubt he'll take it laced with a little Trou Normand."

The country constable grinned with pleasure.

"Here are the cards," said the proprietor, handing over the little white cards filled in the previous evening by the newly arrived guests. "There were only three new ones last night."

The constable took the cards and put them in the leather pouch on his belt.

"Hardly worth turning up for," he grinned, but sat on the foyer bench and waited for his coffee and Calvados, exchanging a few words of lustful banter with Marie-Louise when she brought it.

It was not until 8 that he got back to the gendarmerie and commissariat of Gap with his pouchful of hotel registration cards. These were then taken by the station inspector who flicked through them idly and put them in the rack, to be taken later in the day to the regional headquarters at Lyons, and later to the

archives of Central Records in Paris. Not that he could
see the point of it all.

As the inspector was dropping the cards into the
rack in the commissariat, Madame Colette de la Chalonnière settled her bill, climbed behind the wheel of
her car, and drove off towards the west. One floor
above, the Jackal slept on until nine o'clock.

Superintendent Thomas had dozed off when the
phone beside him gave a shrill buzz. It was the intercom phone linking his office with the room down the
corridor where the six sergeants and two inspectors
had been working on a battery of telephones since his
briefing had ended.

He glanced at his watch. Ten o'clock. Damn, not
like me to drop off. Then he remembered how many
hours sleep he had had, or rather had not had, since
Dixon had summoned him on Monday afternoon. And
now it was Thursday morning. The phone buzzed
again.

"Hello."

The voice of the senior detective inspector answered.

"Friend Duggan," he began without preliminary.
"He left London on a scheduled BEA flight on Monday morning. The booking was taken on Saturday. No
doubt about the name. Alexander Duggan. Paid cash
at the airport for the ticket."

"Where to? Paris?"

"No, Super. Brussels."

Thomas's head cleared quickly.

"All right, listen. He may have gone but come back.
Keep checking airline bookings to see if there have
been any other bookings in his name. Particularly if

there is a booking for a flight that has not yet left London. Check with advance bookings. If he came back from Brussels, I want to know. But I doubt it. I think we've lost him, although of course he left London several hours before investigations were started, so it's not our fault. OK?"

"Right. What about the search in the U.K. for the real Calthrop. It's tying up a lot of the provincial police, and the Yard's just been on to say that they're complaining."

Thomas thought for a moment.

"Call it off," he said. "I'm pretty certain he's gone."

He picked up the outside phone and asked for the office of Commissaire Lebel at the Police Judiciaire.

Inspector Caron thought he was going to end up in a lunatic asylum before Thursday morning was out. First the British were on the phone at 10:05. He took the call himself, but when Superintendent Thomas insisted on speaking to Lebel, he went over to the corner to rouse the sleeping form on the camp bed. Lebel looked as if he had died a week before. But he took the call. As soon as he had identified himself to Thomas, Caron had to take the receiver back because of the language barrier. He translated what Thomas had to say, and Lebel's replies.

"Tell him," said Lebel when he had digested the information, "that we will handle the Belgians from here. Say that he has my very sincere thanks for his help, and that if the killer can be traced to a location on the continent rather than in Britain, I will inform him immediately so that he can call his men off."

When the receiver was down, both men settled back at their desks.

"Get me the Sûreté in Brussels," said Lebel.

The Jackal rose when the sun was already high over the hills and gave promise of another beautiful summer day. He showered and dressed, taking his check suit, well pressed, from the hands of the maid, Marie-Louise, who blushed again when he thanked her.

Shortly after 10:30 he drove the Alfa down into town and went to the post office to use the long-distance telephone to Paris. When he emerged twenty minutes later, he was tight-lipped and in a hurry. At a hardware store nearby he bought a quart of high-gloss lacquer in midnight blue, a half-pint tin in white, and two brushes, one a fine-tipped camel-hair for lettering, the other a two-inch soft bristle. He also bought a screwdriver. With these in the glove compartment of the car he drove back to the Hôtel du Cerf and asked for his bill.

While it was being prepared, he went upstairs to pack and carried the suitcases down to the car himself. When the three cases were in the trunk and the hand-grip on the passenger seat, he re-entered the foyer and settled the bill. The day clerk who had taken over the reception desk would say later that he seemed hurried and nervous, and paid the bill with a new hundred-franc note.

What he did not say, because he had not seen it, was that while he was in the back room getting change for the note, the blond Englishman turned over the pages of the hotel registry that the clerk had been making up for that day's list of coming clients. Flick-

ing back one page, the Englishman had seen yesterday's inscriptions including one in the name of Mme
la Baronne de la Chalonnière, Haute Chalonnière,
Corrèze.

A few moments after settling the bill, the roar of the
Alfa was heard in the driveway, and the Englishman
was gone.

Just before midday more messages came into the
office of Claude Lebel. The Sûreté of Brussels rang to
say Duggan had only spent five hours in the city on
Monday. He had arrived by BEA from London but
had left on the afternoon Alitalia flight to Milan. He
had paid cash at the desk for his ticket, although it
had been booked on the previous Saturday by phone
from London.

Lebel at once placed another call with the Milanese
police.

As he put the phone down, it rang again. This time
it was the DST, to say that a report had been received
as normal routine that the previous morning among
those entering France from Italy over the Ventimiglia
crossing point, and filling in cards as they did so, had
been Alexander James Quentin Duggan.

Lebel had exploded.

"Nearly thirty hours," he yelled. "Over a day!" he
slammed down the receiver. Caron raised an eyebrow.

"The card," explained Lebel wearily, "has been in
transit between Ventimiglia and Paris. They are now
sorting out yesterday morning's entry cards from all
over France. They say there are over twenty-five thousand of them. For one day, mark you. I suppose I
shouldn't have yelled. At least we know one thing—

he's here. Definitely. Inside France. If I don't have something for the meeting tonight, they'll skin me. Oh, by the way, ring up Superintendent Thomas and thank him again. Tell him the Jackal is inside France, and we shall handle it from here."

As Caron replaced the receiver after the London call, the Service Régional headquarters of the PJ at Lyons came on the phone. Lebel listened, then glanced up at Caron triumphantly. He covered the mouthpiece with his hand.

"We've got him. He's registered for two days at the Hôtel du Cerf in Gap, starting last night." He uncovered the mouthpiece and spoke down it.

"Now listen, Commissaire, I am not in a position to explain to you why we want this man Duggan. Just take it from me it is important. This is what I want you to do. . . ."

He spoke for ten minutes, and as he finished, the phone on Caron's desk rang. It was the DST again to say Duggan had entered France in a hired white Alfa Romeo sports two-seater, registration MI-61741.

"Shall I put out an all-stations alert for it?" asked Caron.

Lebel thought for a moment.

"No, not yet. If he's out motoring in the countryside somewhere he'll probably be picked up by a country cop who thinks he's just looking for a stolen sports car. He'll kill anybody who tries to intercept him. The gun must be in the car somewhere. The important thing is that he's booked into the hotel for two nights. I want an army round that hotel when he gets back. Nobody must get hurt if it can be avoided. Come on, if we want to get that helicopter, let's go."

While he was speaking the entire police force at Gap was moving steel roadblocks into position on all the exits from the town and the area of the hotel and posting men in the undergrowth round the barriers. Their orders came from Lyons. At Grenoble and Lyons men armed with submachine guns and rifles were clambering into two fleets of Black Marias. At Satory camp outside Paris a helicopter was being readied for Commissaire Lebel's flight to Gap.

Even in the shade of the trees the heat of early afternoon was sweltering. Stripped to the waist to avoid staining more of his clothes than was necessary, the Jackal worked on the car for two hours.

After leaving Gap he had headed due west through Veyne and Aspres-sur-Buech. It was downhill most of the way, the road winding between the mountains like a carelessly discarded ribbon. He had pushed the car to the limit, hurling it into the tight bends on squealing tires, twice nearly sending another driver coming the other way over the edge into one of the chasms below. After Aspres he picked up the RN 93, which followed the course of the Drôme river eastwards to join the Rhône.

For another eighteen miles the road had hunted back and forth across the river. Shortly after Luc-en-Diois he had thought it time to get the Alfa off the road. There were plenty of side roads leading away into the hills and upland villages. He had taken one at random and after a mile and a half chosen a path to the right leading into the woods.

In the middle of the afternoon he finished painting and stood back. The car was a deep gleaming blue, most of the paint already dry. Although by no means a professional painting job, it would pass muster except if given a close inspection, and particularly in the dusk. The two number plates had been unscrewed and lay face down on the grass. On the back of each had been painted in white an imaginary French number of which the last two letters were 75, the registration code for Paris. The Jackal knew this was the commonest type of car number on the roads of France.

The car's hiring and insurance papers did not now match the blue French Alfa as they had the white Italian one, and if he were stopped for a road check, with improper papers, he was done for. The only question in his mind as he dipped a rag in the petrol tank and wiped the paint stains off his hands was whether to start motoring now and risk the bright sunlight, showing up the amateurishness of the paintwork on the car, or whether to wait until dusk.

He was sure that with his false name discovered, his point of entry into France and a description of his car would soon be known. He was days too early for the assassination, and he needed to find a place to lie low until he was ready. That meant getting to the department of Corrèze 250 miles across country, and the quickest way was by using the car. It was a risk, but he decided it had to be taken. Very well, then, the sooner, the better, before every speed cop in the country was looking for an Alfa Romeo with a blond Englishman at the wheel.

He screwed the new number plates on, threw away what remained of the paint and the two brushes, pulled his polo-necked silk sweater and jacket back on, and gunned the engine into life. As he swept back onto the RN 93, he checked his watch. It was 3:41 in the afternoon.

High overhead he watched a helicopter clattering on its way towards the east. It was seven miles further to the village of Die. He knew well enough not to pronounce it in the English way, but the coincidence of the name occurred to him. He was not superstitious, but his eyes narrowed as he drove into the centre of the town. At the main square near the war memorial a huge black-leather-coated motorcycle policeman was standing in the middle of the road waving him to stop and pull over to the right. His gun was still in its tubes wired to the chassis of the car. He carried no automatic or knife. For a second he hesitated, unsure whether to hit the policeman a glancing blow with the wing of the car and keep driving, later to abandon the car a dozen miles further on and try without a mirror or a washbasin to transform himself into Pastor Jensen, with four pieces of luggage to cope with, or whether to stop.

It was the policeman who made the decision for him. Ignoring him completely as the Alfa began to slow down, the policeman turned round and scanned the road in the other direction. The Jackal slid the car over to the side of the road, watched, and waited.

From the far side of the village he heard the wailing of sirens. Whatever happened, it was too late to get out now. Into the village came a convoy of four Citroen police cars and six Black Marias. As the traffic cop jumped to one side and swept his arm up in salute, the convoy raced past the parked Alfa and headed down the road from which he had come. Through the wired windows of the vans, which gave them the

French nickname of salad baskets, he could see the rows of helmeted police, submachine guns across their knees.

Almost as soon as it had come, the convoy was gone. The speed cop brought his arm down from the salute, gave the Jackal an indolent gesture that he could now proceed, and stalked off to his motorcycle parked against the war memorial. He was still kicking the starter when the blue Alfa disappeared round the corner heading west.

It was 4:50 p.m. when they hit the Hôtel du Cerf. Claude Lebel, who had landed a mile on the other side of the township and been driven to the driveway of the hotel in a police car, walked up to the front door accompanied by Caron, who carried a loaded and cocked MAT 49 submachine carbine under the mackintosh slung over his right arm. The forefinger was on the trigger. Everyone in the town knew there was something afoot by this time, except the proprietor of the hotel. The hotel had been isolated for five hours, and the only odd thing had been the non-arrival of the trout seller with his day's catch of fresh fish.

Summoned by the desk clerk, the proprietor appeared from his labours over the accounts in the office. Lebel listened to him answer Caron's questions, glancing nervously at the odd-shaped bundle under Caron's arm, and his shoulders sagged.

Five minutes later the hotel was deluged with uniformed police. They interviewed the staff, examined the bedroom, chased through the grounds. Lebel walked alone out into the drive and stared up at the surrounding hills. Caron joined him.

"You think he's really gone, Chief?" Lebel nodded.

"He's gone all right."

"But he was booked for two days. Do you think the proprietor's in this with him?"

"No. He and the staff aren't lying. He changed his mind, some time this morning. And he left. The question now is, where the hell has he gone, and does he suspect yet that we know who he is?"

"But how could he? He couldn't know that. It must be coincidence. It must be."

"My dear Lucien, let us hope so."

"All we've got to go on now, then, is the car number."

"Yes. That was my mistake. We should have put the alert out for the car. Get onto the police R/T to Lyons from one of the sound cars and make it an all-stations alert. Top priority. White Alfa Romeo, Italian, Number MI-61741. Approach with caution, occupant believed armed and dangerous. You know the drill. But one more thing, nobody is to mention it to the press. Include in the message the instruction that the suspected man probably does not know he's suspected, and I'll skin anybody who lets him hear it on the radio or read it in the press. I'm going to tell Commissaire Gaillard of Lyons to take over here. Then let's get back to Paris."

It was nearly six o'clock when the blue Alfa coasted into the town of Valence, where the steel torrent of the RN 7, the main road from Lyons to Marseilles and the highway carrying most of the traffic from Paris to the Côte d'Azur, thunders along the banks of the Rhône. The Alfa crossed the great road running south and took the bridge over the river towards the RN 533 to Saint Peray on the western bank. Below the bridge, the mighty river smoldered in the afternoon sunlight, ignored the puny steel insects scurrying southwards, and rolled at its own leisurely but certain pace towards the waiting Mediterranean.

After Saint Peray, as dusk settled on the valley behind him, the Jackal gunned the little sports car higher and higher into the mountains of the Massif Central and the province of Auvergne. After Le Puy the going got steeper, the mountains higher, and every town seemed to be a spa where the life-giving streams flowing out from the rocks of the massif had attracted those with aches and eczemas developed in the cities and made fortunes for the cunning Auvergnat peasants who had gone into the business with a will.

After Brioude the valley of the Allier river dropped behind, and the smell in the night air was of heather and drying hay in the upland pastures. He stopped to fill the tank at Issoire, then sped on through the casino town of Mont Doré and the spa of La Bourdoule. It was nearly midnight when he rounded the headwaters of the Dordogne, where it rises among the Auvergne rocks to flow south and west through half a dozen dams and spend itself into the Atlantic at Bordeaux.

From La Bourdoule he took the RN 89 towards Ussel, the county town of Corrèze.

"You are a fool, *Monsieur le Commissaire*, a fool. You had him within your grasp, and let him slip." Saint-Clair had half-risen to his feet to make his point, and glared down the polished mahogany table at the top of Lebel's head. The detective was studying the papers of his dossier, for all the world as if Saint-Clair did not exist.

He had decided that was the only way to treat the arrogant colonel from the Palace, and Saint-Clair for his part was not quite sure whether the bent head indicated an appropriate sense of shame or an insolent indifference. He preferred to believe it was the former. When he had finished and sank back into his seat, Claude Lebel looked up.

"If you will look at the mimeographed report in front of you, my dear colonel, you will observe that we did not have him in our hands," he observed mildly. "The report from Lyons that a man in the name of Duggan had registered the previous evening at a hotel in Gap did not reach the PJ until twelve-fifteen today. We now know that the Jackal left the hotel abruptly at eleven-o-five. Whatever measures had been taken, he still had an hour's start.

"Moreover, I cannot accept your strictures on the efficiency of the police forces of this country in general. I would remind you that the orders of the President are that this affair will be managed in secret. It was therefore not possible to put out an alert to every rural gendarmerie for a man named Duggan, for it would have started a hullabaloo in the press. The card registering Duggan at the Hôtel du Cerf was collected in the normal way at the normal time, and sent with due dispatch to Regional Headquarters at Lyons. Only there was it realised that Duggan was the wanted man. This delay was unavoidable, unless we wish to launch a nation-wide hue-and-cry for the man, and that is outside my brief.

"And lastly, Duggan was registered at the hotel for two days. We do not know what made him change his mind at eleven a.m. today and decide to move elsewhere."

"Probably your police gallivanting about the place," snapped Saint-Clair.

"I have already made it plain, there was no gallivanting before twelve-fifteen, and the man was already seventy minutes gone," said Lebel.

"All right, we have been unlucky, very unlucky," cut in the Minister. "However there is still the question of why no immediate search for the car was instituted. Commissaire?"

"I agree it was a mistake, Minister, in the light of events. I had reason to believe the man was at the hotel and intended to spend the night there. If he had been motoring in the vicinity, and had been intercepted by a motor patrol man for driving a wanted car, he would almost certainly have shot the unsuspecting policeman, and thus forewarned made his escape—"

"Which is precisely what he has done," said Saint-Clair.

"True, but we have no evidence to suggest that he has been forewarned, as he would have been if his car had been stopped by a single patrolman. It may well be he just decided to move on somewhere else. If so, and if he checks into another hotel tonight, he will be reported. Alternately, if his car is seen he will be reported."

"When did the alert for the white Alfa go out?" asked the director of the PJ, Max Fernet.

"I issued the instructions at five-fifteen p.m. from the courtyard of the hotel," replied Lebel. "It should have reached all major road-patrol units by seven, and the police on duty in the main towns should be informed throughout the night as they check in for night-duty. In view of the danger of this man, I have listed the car as stolen, with instructions that its presence be reported immediately to the Regional HQ, but that no approach should be made to the occupant by a lone policeman. If this meeting decides to change these orders, then I must ask that the responsibility for what may ensue be taken by this meeting."

There was a long silence.

"Regrettably, the life of a police officer cannot be allowed to stand in the way of protecting the President of France," murmured Colonel Gallon. There were signs of assent from round the table.

"Perfectly true," assented Lebel. "Providing a single police officer can stop this man. But most town and country policemen, the ordinary men on the beat and the motor patrolman, are not professional gunfighters. This Jackal is. If he is intercepted, shoots down one or two policemen, makes another getaway and disappears, we shall have two things to cope with: one will be a killer fully forewarned and perhaps able to adopt yet a new identity about which we know nothing, the other will be a nation-wide headline story in every newspaper which we will not be able to play down. If the Jackal's real reason for being in France remains a secret for forty-eight hours after the killing story breaks, I will be most surprised. The press will know within days that he is after the President. If anyone here would like to explain that to the General, I will willingly retire from this investigation and hand it over."

No one volunteered. The meeting broke up as usual around midnight. Within thirty minutes it had become Friday, August 16.

seventeen

The blue Alfa Romeo cruised into the Place de la Gare at Ussel just before one in the morning. There was one cafe remaining open across the square from the station entrance, and a few late-night travellers waiting for a train were sipping coffee. The Jackal dragged a comb through his hair and walked past the stacked-up chairs and tables on the terrace and up to the bar counter. He was cold, for the mountain air was chill as he drove at over sixty miles an hour; and stiff, with aching thighs and arms from hauling the Alfa through innumerable mountain curves; and hungry, for he had not eaten since dinner twenty-eight hours previously, apart from a buttered roll for breakfast.

He ordered two large buttered slices of a long thin loaf, sliced down the middle and known as a *tartine beurrée*, and four hard-boiled eggs from the stand on the counter. Also a large white coffee.

While the buttered bread was being prepared and the coffee was percolating through the filtre, he glanced round for the telephone booth. There was none, but a telephone stood at the end of the counter.

"Have you got the local telephone directory?" he asked the barman. Without a word, still busy, the barman gestured to a pile of directories on a rack behind the counter.

"Help yourself," he said.

The Baron's name was listed under the words "Chalonnière, M. le Baron de la . . ." and the address was the chateau at La Haute Chalonnière. The Jackal knew this, but the village was not listed on his road map. However the telephone number was given as Egletons, and he found this easily enough. It was another thirty kilometres beyond Ussel on the RN 89. He settled down to eat his eggs and bread.

It was just before two in the morning that he passed a stone by the roadside saying "Egletons, 6 km." and decided to abandon the car in one of the forests that bordered the road. They were dense woods, probably the estate of some local noble, where once boars had been hunted with horse and hound. Perhaps they still were, for parts of Corrèze seem to have stepped straight from the days of Louis XIV.

Within a few hundred metres he had found a drive leading into the forest, separated from the road by a wooden pole slung across the entrance, adorned by a placard saying "Chasse Privée." He removed the pole, drove the car into the wood, and replaced the pole.

From there he drove half a mile into the forest, the headlamps lighting the gnarled shapes of the trees like ghosts reaching down with angry branches at the trespasser. Finally he stopped the car, switched off the headlights, and took the wire cutters and torch from the glove compartment.

He spent an hour underneath the vehicle, his back getting damp from the dew on the forest floor. At last the steel tubes containing the sniper's rifle were free from their hiding place of the previous sixty hours, and he re-packed them in the suitcase with the old clothes and the army greatcoat. He had a last look round the car to make sure there was nothing left in it that could give anyone who found it a hint of who its driver had been and drove it hard into the centre of a nearby clump of wild rhododendron.

Using the metal shears, he spent the next hour cutting rhododendron branches from nearby bushes and jabbing them into the ground in front of the hole in the shrubbery made by the Alfa, until it was completely hidden from view.

He knotted his tie with one end round the handle of one of the suitcases, the other end round the handle of the second case. Using the tie like a railway porter's strap, his shoulder under the loop so that one case hung down his chest and the other down his back, he was able to grab the remaining two pieces of luggage in his two free hands and start the march back to the road.

It was slow going. Every hundred yards he stopped, put the cases down and went back over his tracks with a branch from a tree, sweeping away the light impressions made in the moss and twigs by the passage of the Alfa. It took another hour to reach the road, duck under the pole, and put half a mile between himself and the entrance to the forest.

His check suit was soiled and grimy, the polo sweater stuck to his back with greasy obstinacy, and he thought his muscles would never stop aching again. Lining the suitcases up in a row, he sat down to wait as the eastern sky grew a fraction paler than the surrounding night. Country buses, he reminded himself, tend to start early.

In fact he was lucky. A farm truck towing a trailer of hay came by at 5:50 heading towards the market town.

"Car broken down?" bawled the driver as he slowed up.

"No. I've got a weekend pass from camp, so I'm hitch-hiking home. Got as far as Ussel last night and decided to push on to Tulle. I've got an uncle there who can fix me a truck to Bordeaux. This was as far as I got." He grinned at the driver, who laughed and shrugged.

"Crazy, walking through the night up here. No one comes this way after dark. Jump on the trailer, I'll take you into Egletons, you can try from there."

They rolled into the little town at 6:45. The Jackal thanked the farmer, gave him the slip round the back of the station, and headed for a cafe.

"Is there a taxi in town?" he asked the barman over coffee.

The barman gave him the number, and he rang to call up the taxi company. There was one car that would be available in half an hour, he was told. While he waited he used the fundamental conveniences of the cold water tap offered by the cafe's lavatory to wash his hands and face, change into a fresh suit, and brush his teeth, which felt furry from cigarettes and coffee.

The taxi arrived at 7:30, an old rattletrap Renault.

"Do you know the village of Haute Chalonnière?" he asked the driver.

"Course."

"How far?"

"Eighteen kilometres." The man jerked his thumb up towards the mountains. "In the hills."

"Take me there," said the Jackal, and hefted his luggage into the roof rack, except for one case that went inside with him.

He insisted on being dropped in front of the Café de la Poste in the village square. There was no use for the taxi driver from the nearby town to know he was going to the chateau. When the taxi had driven away, he brought his luggage into the cafe. Already the square was blazing hot, and two oxen yoked to a hay-cart ruminated their cud reflectively outside while fat black flies promenaded round their gentle patient eyes.

Inside the cafe it was dark and cool. He heard rather than saw the customers shift at their tables to examine the newcomer, and there was a clacking of clogs on tiles as an old peasant woman in a black dress left one group of farm workers and went behind the bar.

"Monsieur?" she croaked.

He put down the luggage and leaned on the bar. The locals, he noticed, were drinking red wine.

"Un gros rouge, s'il vous plaît, madame."

"How far is the chateau, madame?" he asked when the wine was poured. She eyed him keenly from wily black marbles.

"Two kilometres, monsieur."

He sighed wearily. "That fool of a driver tried to tell me there was no chateau here. So he dropped me in the square."

"He was from Egletons?" she asked. The Jackal nodded.

"They are fools at Egletons," she said.

"I have to get to the chateau," he said.

The ring of peasants watching from their tables made no move. No one suggested how he might get there. He pulled out a new hundred-franc note.

"How much is the wine, madame?"

She eyed the note sharply. There was a shifting among the blue cotton blouses and trousers behind him.

"I haven't got change for that," said the old woman.

He sighed.

"If only there was someone with a van, he might have change," he said.

Someone got up and approached from behind.

"There is a van in the village, monsieur," growled a voice.

The Jackal turned with mock surprise.

"It belongs to you, *mon ami?*"

"No, monsieur, but I know the man who owns it. He might run you up there."

The Jackal nodded as if considering the merits of the idea.

"In the meantime, what will you take?"

The peasant nodded at the crone, who poured another large glass of rough red wine.

"And your friends? It's a hot day. A thirsty day."

The stubbled face split into a smile. The peasant nodded again to the woman who took two full bottles over to the group round the big table. "Benoit, go and get the van," ordered the peasant, and one of the men, gulping down his wine in one swallow, went outside.

"What appeals to me about the peasantry of the Auvergne," mused the Jackal as he rattled and bumped the last two kilometres up to the chateau, "is that they

are so surly they keep their damn mouths shut—at least
to outsiders."

Colette de la Chalonnière sat up in bed, sipped her
coffee, and read the letter again. The anger that had
possessed her on the first reading had dissipated, to
be replaced by a kind of weary disgust.

She wondered what on earth she could do with the
rest of her life. She had been welcomed home the
previous afternoon after a leisurely drive from Gap
by old Ernestine, the maid who had been in service
at the chateau since Alfred's father's day, and the
gardener, Louison, a former peasant boy who had
married Ernestine when she was still an under house-
maid.

The pair were now virtually the curators of the
chateau of which two thirds of the rooms were shut
off and blanketed in dust covers.

She was, she realised, the mistress of an empty
castle where there were neither children playing in
the park any more nor a master of the household sad-
dling his horse in the courtyard.

She looked back at the cutting from the Paris glossy
society magazine that her friend had so thoughtfully
mailed to her; at the face of her husband grinning in-
anely into the flash-bulb, eyes torn between the lens
of the camera and the jutting bosom of the girl over
whose shoulder he was peering. She was a cabaret
dancer, risen from bar hostess, quoted as saying she
hoped "one day" to be able to marry the Baron, who
was her "very good friend."

Looking at the lined face and scrawny neck of the
ageing Baron in the photograph, she wondered vaguely

what had happened to the handsome young captain of the Resistance partisans with whom she had fallen in love in 1942 and married a year later when she was expecting her son.

She had been a teenage girl, running messages for the Resistance, when she met him in the mountains. He had been in his mid-thirties, known by the code-name of Pegasus, a lean, hawk-faced, commanding man who had turned her heart. They had been married in a secret ceremony in a cellar chapel by a priest of the Resistance, and she had borne her son in her father's house.

Then after the war had come the restoration of all his lands and properties. His father had died of a heart attack when the Allied armies swept across France, and he had emerged from the heather to become the Baron of Chalonnière, cheered by the peasantry of the countryside as he brought his wife and son back to the chateau. Soon the estates had tired him, the lure of Paris and the lights of the cabarets, the urge to make up for the lost years of his youth in the colonial deserts and of his manhood in the undergrowth, had proved too strong to resist.

Now he was fifty-seven and could have passed for seventy.

The Baroness threw the cutting and its accompanying letter on the floor. She jumped out of bed and stood in front of the full-length mirror on the far wall, pulling open the laces that held the peignoir together down the front. She stood on tip-toe to tighten the muscles of her thighs as a pair of high-heeled shoes would do.

Not bad, she thought. Could be a lot worse. A full

figure, the body of a mature woman. The hips were wide, but the waist had mercifully remained in proportion, firmed by hours in the saddle and long walks in the hills. She cupped her breasts one in each hand and measured their weight. Too big, too heavy for real beauty, but still enough to excite a man in bed.

Well, Alfred, two can play at that game, she thought. She shook her head, loosening the shoulder length black hair so that a strand fell forward by her cheek and lay across one of her breasts. She took her hands away and ran them between her thighs, thinking of the man who had been there just over twenty-four hours before. He had been good. She wished now she had stayed on at Gap. Perhaps they could have holidayed together, driving round using a false name, like runaway lovers. What on earth had she come home for?

There was a clatter of an old van drawing up in the courtyard. Idly she drew the peignoir together and walked to the window that gave onto the front of the house. A van from the village was parked there, the rear doors open. Two men were at the back taking something down from the tailboard. Louison was walking across from where he had been weeding one of the ornamental lawns to help carry the load.

One of the men hidden behind the van walked round to the front, stuffing some paper into his trouser pocket, climbed into the driving seat and engaged the grinding clutch. Who was delivering things to the chateau? She had not ordered anything. The van started to pull away and she gave a start of surprise. There were three suitcases and a hand-grip on the gravel, beside them was a man. She recognised the

gleam of the blond hair in the sun and smiled wide
with pleasure.

"You animal. You beautiful primitive animal. You
followed me."

She hurried into the bathroom to dress.

When she came onto the landing, she caught the
sound of voices in the hall below. Ernestine was asking what monsieur wanted.

"Madame la Baronne, elle est là?"

In a moment Ernestine came hurrying up the stairs
as fast as her old legs would carry her. "A gentleman
has called, ma'am."

The evening meeting in the ministry that Friday
was shorter than usual. The only thing to report was
that there was nothing. For the past twenty-four hours
the description of the wanted car had been circulated
in a routine manner, so as not to arouse undue suspicion, throughout France. It had not been spotted.
Similarly, every Regional Headquarters of the Police
Judiciaire had ordered its dependent local commissariats in town and country to get all hotel registration
cards into HQ by eight in the morning at the latest.
At the Regional HQs they were immediately scoured,
tens of thousands of them, for the name of Duggan.
Nothing had been spotted. Therefore, he had not
stayed last night in a hotel, at least, not in the name
of Duggan.

"We have to accept one of two premises," explained
Lebel to a silent gathering. "Either he still believes he
is unsuspected. In other words his departure from the
Hôtel du Cerf was an unpremeditated action and a
coincidence; in which case there is no reason for him

not to use his Alfa Romeo openly and stay openly in hotels under the name of Duggan. In that case he must be spotted sooner or later. In the second case, he has decided to ditch the car somewhere and abandon it, and rely on his own resources. In the latter case, there are a further two possibilities.

"Either he has no further false identities on which to rely; in which case he cannot get far without registering at a hotel or trying to pass a frontier point on his way out of France. Or he has another identity and has passed into it. In the latter case he is still extremely dangerous."

"What makes you think he might have another identity?" asked Colonel Rolland.

"We have to assume," said Lebel, "that this man, having been offered evidently a very large sum by the OAS to carry out this assassination, must be one of the best professional killers in the world. That implies that he has had experience. And yet he has managed to stay clear of any official suspicion, and all official police dossiers. The only way he could do this would be by carrying out his assignments in a false name and with a false appearance. In other words, an expert in disguise as well.

"We know from the comparison of the two photographs that Calthrop was able to extend his height by high-heeled shoes, slim off several kilos in weight, change his eye colour by contact lenses and his hair colour with dye to become Duggan. If he can do that once, we cannot afford the luxury of assuming he cannot do it again."

"But there's no reason to suppose he suspected he would be exposed before he got close to the President," protested Saint-Clair. "Why should he take such elaborate precautions as to have one or more false identities?"

"Because," said Lebel, "he apparently does take elaborate precautions. If he did not, we should have had him by now."

"I note from Calthrop's dossier, as passed on by the British police, that he did his National Service just after the war in their parachute regiment. Perhaps he's using this experience to live rough, hiding out in the hills," suggested Max Fernet.

"Perhaps," agreed Lebel.

"In that case he is more or less finished as a potential danger."

Lebel considered for a moment.

"Of this particular person, I would not like to say that until he is behind bars."

"Or dead," said Rolland.

"If he's got any sense, he'll be trying to get out of France while he's still alive," said Saint-Clair.

On that note the meeting broke up.

"I wish I could count on that," Lebel told Caron back in the office. "But as far as I'm concerned he's alive, well, free, and armed. We keep on looking for him and that car. He had three pieces of luggage, he can't have got far on foot with all that. Find that car and we start from there."

The man they wanted was lying on fresh linen in a chateau in the heart of Corrèze. He was bathed and relaxed, filled with a meal of country pâté and jugged hare, washed down with rough red wine, black coffee, and brandy. He stared up at the gilt curlicues that writhed across the ceiling and planned the course of the days that now separated him from his assignment in Paris. In a week, he thought, he would have to move, and getting away might prove difficult. But it could be done. He would have to think out a reason for going.

The door opened and the Baroness came in. Her hair had been let down around her shoulders and she wore a peignoir held together at the throat but open down the front. As she moved, it swayed briefly open. She was quite naked beneath it, but had kept on the stockings she had worn at dinner and the high-heeled court shoes. The Jackal propped himself up on one elbow as she closed the door and walked over to the bed.

She looked down at him in silence. He reached up and slipped loose the bow of ribbon that held the night-dress closed at the throat. It swung open to reveal the breasts, and as he craned forward his hand slid the lace-edged material off her shoulder. It slid down to the floor without a sound.

She pushed his shoulder so that he rolled back onto the bed, then gripped his wrists and pinned them against the pillow as she climbed over him. He stared back up at her as she knelt above him, her thighs gripping his ribs hard. She smiled down at him, two curling strands of hair falling down to the nipples.

"*Bon, mon primitif*, now let's see you perform."

He eased his head forward as her bottom rose off his chest, and started.

For three days the trail went cold for Lebel, and at each evening meeting the volume of opinion that the

Jackal had left France secretly with his tail between his legs increased. By the meeting on the evening of the 19th he was alone in maintaining his view that the killer was still somewhere in France, lying low and biding his time, waiting.

"Waiting for what?" shrilled Saint-Clair that evening. "The only thing he can be waiting for, if he is still here, is an opportunity to make a dash for the border. The moment he breaks cover we have got him. He has every man's arm against him, nowhere to go, no one to take him in, if your supposition that he is completely cut off from the OAS and their sympathisers is correct."

There was a murmur of assent from the table, most of whose members were beginning to harden in their opinion that the police had failed, and that Bouvier's original dictum that the location of the killer was a purely detective task had been wrong.

Lebel shook his head doggedly. He was tired, exhausted by lack of sleep, by strain and worry, by having to defend himself and his staff from the constant needling attacks of men who owed their exalted positions to politics rather than experience. He had enough sense to realise that if he was wrong, he was finished. Some of the men round the table would see to that. And if he was right? If the Jackal was still on the trail of the President? If he slipped through the net and closed with his victim? He knew those round the table would desperately seek for a scapegoat. And it would be him. Either way his long career as a policeman was ended. Unless . . . unless he could find the man and stop him. Only then would they have to concede that he had been right. But he had no proof; only an odd faith, that he could certainly never divulge, that the man he was hunting was another professional who would carry out his task no matter what.

Over the eight days since this affair had landed on his lap he had come to a grudging respect for the silent, unpredictable man with the gun who seemed to have everything planned down to the last detail, including the contingency planning. It was as much as his career was worth to admit his feelings amidst the gathering of political appointees around him. Only the massive bulk of Bouvier beside him, hunching his head into his shoulders and glaring at the table, gave him a small comfort. At least he was another detective.

"Waiting for I don't know what," Lebel replied. "But he's waiting for something, or some appointed day. I do not believe, gentlemen, that we have heard the last of the Jackal yet. All the same, I cannot explain why I feel this."

"Feelings!" jeered Saint-Clair. "Some appointed day! Really, Commissaire, you seem to have been reading too many romantic thrillers. This is no romance, my dear sir, this is reality. The man has gone, that's all there is to it." He sat back with a self-assured smile.

"I hope you are right," said Lebel quietly. "In that case, I must tender to you, Monsieur le Ministre, my willingness to withdraw from the enquiry and return to the investigation of crime."

The Minister eyed him with indecision.

"Do you think the enquiry is worth pursuing, Commissaire?" he asked. "Do you think a real danger still exists?"

"As to the second question, sir, I do not know. For

the former, I believe we should go on looking until we are absolutely certain."

"Very well then. Gentlemen, it is my wish that the Commissaire continue his enquiries and that we continue our evening meetings to hear his reports—for the moment."

On the morning of August 20 Marcango Callet, a gamekeeper, was shooting vermin on the estates of his employer between Egletons and Ussel in the department of Corrèze, when he pursued a wounded wood-pigeon that had tumbled into a clump of wild rhododendron. In the centre of the clump he found the pigeon, fluttering madly on the driving seat of an open sports car that had evidently been abandoned.

At first he thought, as he wrung the bird's neck, that it must have been parked by a pair of lovers who had come into the forest for a picnic, despite the warning notice that he had nailed up on the pole at the entrance to the woods half a mile away. Then he noticed that some of the branches of shrubbery that concealed the car from view were not growing in the ground but had been jabbed into the earth. Further examination showed the cut stumps of the branches on other nearby bushes, the white cuts having been smeared over with earth to darken them.

From the bird droppings on the seats of the car he reckoned it had been there for several days at least. Taking his gun and bird he cycled back through the woods to his cottage, making a mental note to mention the car to the local village constable when he went into the village later that morning to buy some more rabbit snares.

It was nearly noon when the village policeman
wound up the hand-cranked telephone in his house
and filed a report to the commissariat at Ussel to the effect that a car had been found abandoned in the woods
nearby. Was it a white car, he was asked. He consulted
his notebook. No, it was a blue car. Was it Italian? No,
it was French-registered, make unknown. Right, said
the voice from Ussel, a towaway truck will be sent
during the afternoon, and he had better be ready waiting to guide the crew to the spot, because there was a
lot of work on and everyone was short-staffed, what
with a search going on for a white Italian sports car
that the bigwigs in Paris wanted to have a look at.
The village constable promised to be ready and waiting when the towaway truck arrived.

It was not until after four that afternoon that the
little car was towed into the pound at Ussel, and close
to five before one of the motor maintenance staff, giving the car a check over for identification, noticed that
the paintwork was appallingly badly done.

He took out a screwdriver and scratched at one of
the wings. Under the blue, a streak of white appeared.
Perplexed, he examined the numberplates, and noticed
that they seemed to have been reversed. A few minutes later the front plate was lying in the courtyard
face up, exhibiting white lettering MI-61741, and the
policeman was hurrying across the yard towards the
office.

Claude Lebel got the news just before six. It came
from Commissaire Valentin of the Regional Headquarters of the PJ at Clermont Ferrand, capital of the

Auvergne. Lebel jerked upright in his chair as Valentin's voice started talking.

"Right, listen, this is important. . . . I can't explain why it's important, I can only say that it is. . . . Yes, I know it's irregular, but that's the way it is. . . . I know you're a full Commissaire, my dear fellow, but if you want confirmation of my authority in this case I'll pass you right on to the Director-General of the PJ.

"I want you to get a team down to Ussel now. The best you can get, and as many men as you can get. Start enquiring from the spot where the car was found. Mark off the map with that spot in the centre and prepare for a square-search. Ask at every farm house, every farmer who regularly drives along that road, every village store and cafe, every hotel and woodcutter's shack.

"You are looking for a tall blond man, English by birth but speaking good French. He was carrying three suitcases and a hand-grip. He carried a lot of money in cash and is well-dressed, but probably looking as if he had slept rough.

"Your men must ask where he was, where he went, what he tried to buy. Oh, and one other thing, the press must be kept out at all costs. . . . What do you mean, they can't? . . . Well, of course the local stringers will ask what goes on. Well, tell them there was a car crash and it's thought one of the occupants might be wandering in a dazed state. . . . Yes, all right, a mission of mercy. Anything, just allay their suspicions. Tell them there's no story the national papers would bother to pay for, not in the holiday season with five hundred road accidents a day. Just play it down. . . . And one last thing, if you locate the man holed up somewhere, don't get near him. Just surround him and keep him there. I'll be down as soon as I can."

Lebel put the phone down and turned to Caron.

"Get on to the Minister. Ask him to bring the evening meeting forward to eight o'clock. I know that's supper time, but it will only be short. Then get on to Satory and get the helicopter again. A night flight, to Ussel, and they'd better tell us where they will be landing so we can get a car laid on to pick me up. You'll have to take over here."

The police vans from Clermont Ferrand, backed up by others contributed by Ussel, set up their headquarters in the village square of the tiny hamlet nearest to where the car had been found, just as the sun was setting. From the radio van, Valentin issued instructions to the scores of squad cars converging on the other villages of the area. He had decided to start with a five mile radius of the spot where the car was found, and work through the night. People were more likely to be home in the hours of darkness. On the other hand, in the twisting valleys and hillsides of the region, there was more chance that in the darkness his men would get lost, or overlook some small woodcutter's shack where the fugitive might be hiding.

There was one other factor that he could not have explained to Paris over the phone, and which he dreaded having to explain to Lebel face to face. Unbeknown to him, some of his men came across this factor before midnight. A group of them were interviewing a farmer in his cottage two miles from the spot where the car was found.

He stood in the doorway in his nightshirt, pointedly

refusing to invite the detectives in. From his hand the paraffin lamp cast flickering splashes of light over the group.

"Come on, Gaston, you drive along that road to market pretty often. Did you drive down that road towards Egletons on Friday morning?"

The peasant surveyed them through narrowed eyes. "Might have done."

"Well, did you or didn't you?"

"Can't remember."

"Did you see a man on the road?"

"I mind my own business."

"That's not what we're asking. Did you see a man?"

"I saw nobody, nothing."

"A blond man, tall, athletic, carrying three suitcases and a hand-grip?"

"I saw nothing. *J'ai rien vu, tu comprends.*"

It went on for twenty minutes. At last they went, one of the detectives making a meticulous note in his book. The dogs snarled on the ends of their chains and snapped at the policemen's legs, causing them to skip to one side and step in the compost heap. The peasant watched them until they were back on the road and jolting away in their car. Then he slammed the door, kicked an inquisitive goat out of the way, and clambered back into bed with his wife.

"That was the fellow you gave a lift to, wasn't it?" she asked. "What do they want with him?"

"Dunno," said Gaston, "but no one will ever say Gaston Grosjean helped give away another creature to them." He hawked and spat into the embers of the fire. "*Sales flics.*"

He turned down the wick and blew out the light,

swung his legs off the floor and pushed further into the cot against the ample form of his wife. "Good luck to you, friend, wherever you are."

Lebel faced the meeting and put down his papers.

"As soon as this meeting is over, gentlemen, I am flying down to Ussel to supervise the search myself."

There was silence for nearly a minute.

"What do you think, Commissaire, can be deduced from this?"

"Two things, Monsieur le Ministre. We know he must have bought paint to transform the car, and I suspect enquiries will show that if the car was driven through the night from Thursday into Friday morning from Gap to Ussel, that it was already transformed. In that case—and enquiries along these lines are proceeding—it would appear he bought the paint in Gap. If that is so, then he was tipped off. Either somebody rang him or he rang somebody, either here or in London, who told him of the discovery of his pseudonym of Duggan. From that he could work out that we would be onto him before noon, and onto his car. So he got out, and fast."

He thought the elegant ceiling of the conference room was going to crack, so pressing was the silence.

"Are you seriously suggesting," somebody asked from a million miles away, "there is a leak from within this room?"

"I cannot say that, monsieur. There are switchboard operators, telex operators, middle and junior level executives to whom orders have to be passed. It could be that one of them is clandestinely an OAS agent. But one thing seems to emerge ever more clearly. He was tipped off about the unmasking of the over-all plan to assassinate the President of France, and decided to go ahead regardless. And he was tipped off about his unmasking as Alexander Duggan. He has, after all, got one single contact. I suspect it might be the man known as Valmy whose message to Rome was intercepted by the DST."

"Damn," swore the head of the DST, "we should have got the bastard in the post office."

"And what is the second thing we may deduce, Commissaire?" asked the Minister.

"The second thing is that when he learned he was blown as Duggan, he did not seek to quit France. On the contrary, he headed right into the centre of France. In other words, he is still on the trail of the head of state. He has simply challenged the whole lot of us."

The Minister rose and gathered his papers.

"We will not detain you, Monsieur le Commissaire. Find him. Find him, and tonight. Dispose of him if you have to. Those are my orders, in the name of the President."

With that he stalked from the room.

An hour later Lebel's helicopter lifted away from the take-off pad at Satory and headed through the purpling-black sky towards the south.

"Impertinent pig. How dare he? Suggesting that somehow we, the topmost officials of France, were at fault. I shall mention it of course in my next report."

Jacqueline eased the thin straps of her slip from her shoulders and let the transparent material fall to settle in folds round her hips. Tightening her biceps to push the breasts together with a deep cleavage down the middle, she took her lover's head and pulled it towards her bosom.

"Tell me all about it," she cooed.

eighteen

The morning of August 21 was as bright and clear as the previous fourteen of that summer heat wave had been. From the windows of the Château de la Haute Chalonnière, looking out over a rolling vista of heather-clad hills, it looked calm and peaceful, giving no hint of the tumult of police enquiries that was even then enveloping the town of Egletons eighteen kilometres away.

The Jackal, naked under his dressing gown, stood at the windows of the Baron's study making his routine morning call to Paris. He had left his mistress asleep upstairs after another night of ferocious lovemaking.

When the connection came through, he began as usual, *"Ici Chacal."*

"Ici Valmy," said the husky voice at the other end. "Things have started to move again. They have found the car . . ."

He listened for another two minutes, interrupting only with a terse question. With a final *"merci,"* he replaced the receiver and fumbled in his pockets for cigarettes and lighter. What he had just heard, he realised, changed his plans whether he liked it or not. He had wanted to stay on at the chateau for another two days, but now he had to leave, and the sooner, the better. There was something else about the phone call that worried him, something that should not have been there.

418

He had thought nothing of it at the time, but as he drew on his cigarette it niggled at the back of his mind. It came to him without effort as he finished the cigarette and threw the stub through the open window onto the gravel. There had been a soft click on the line soon after he had picked up the receiver. That had not happened during the phone calls over the past three days. There was an extension phone in the bedroom, but surely Colette had been fast asleep when he left her. Surely. . . . He turned and strode briskly up the stairs on silent bare feet and burst into the bedroom.

The phone had been replaced on its cradle. The wardrobe was open and the three suitcases lay about the floor, all open. His own key-ring with the keys that opened the suitcases lay nearby. The Baroness, on her knees amid the debris, looked up with wide staring eyes. Around her lay a series of slim steel tubes, from each of which the hessian caps that closed the open ends had been removed. From one emerged the end of a telescopic sight, from another the snout of the silencer. She held something in her hands, something she had been gazing at in horror when he entered. It was the barrel and breech of the gun.

For several seconds neither spoke. The Jackal recovered first.

"You were listening."

"I—wondered who you were phoning each morning like that."

"I thought you were asleep."

"No. I always wake when you get out of bed. This —thing; it's a gun, a killer's gun."

It was half-question, half-statement, but as if hoping he would explain that it was simply something else, something quite harmless. He looked down at her, and for the first time she noticed that the grey flecks in the eyes had spread and clouded over the whole expression, which had become dead and lifeless like a machine staring down at her.

She rose slowly to her feet, dropping the gun barrel with a clatter among the other components.

"You want to kill him," she whispered. "You are one of them, the OAS. You want to use this to kill de Gaulle."

The lack of any answer from the Jackal gave her the answer. She made a rush for the door. He caught her easily and hurled her back across the room onto the bed, coming after her in three fast paces. As she bounced on the rumpled sheets, her mouth opened to scream. The back-handed blow across the side of the neck into the carotid artery choked off the scream at source, then his left hand was tangled in her hair, dragging her face downwards over the edge of the bed. She caught a last glimpse of the pattern of the carpet when the forehanded chop with the edge of the palm came down on the back of the neck.

He went to the door to listen, but no sound came from below. Ernestine would be preparing the morning rolls and coffee in the kitchen at the back of the house and Louison should be on his way to market shortly. Fortunately, both were rather deaf.

He re-packed the parts of the rifle in their tubes and the tubes in their third suitcase with the Army great-coat and soiled clothes of André Martin, patting the lining to make sure the papers had not been disturbed. Then he locked the case. The second case, containing the clothes of the Danish pastor Per Jensen, was unlocked but had not been searched.

He spent five minutes washing and shaving in the bathroom that adjoined the bedroom. Then he took his scissors and spent a further ten minutes carefully combing the long blond hair upwards and snipping off the last two inches. Next he brushed into it enough of the hair tint to turn it into a middle-aged man's iron-grey. The effect of the dye was to dampen the hair, enabling him finally to brush it into the style shown in Pastor Jensen's passport, which he had propped on top of the bathroom shelf. Finally he slipped on the blue-tinted contact lenses.

He wiped every trace of the hair tint and washing preparations off the wash basin, collected up the shaving things, and returned to the bedroom. The naked body on the floor he ignored.

He dressed in the undershirt, shorts, socks, and shirt he had bought in Copenhagen, fixed the black bib round his neck, and topped it with the parson's dog-collar. Finally he slipped on the black suit and conventional walking shoes. He tucked the gold-rimmed glasses into his top pocket, re-packed the washing things in the hand-grip, and put the Danish book on French cathedrals in there as well. Into the inside pocket of his suit he transferred the Dane's passport, and a wad of money.

The remainder of his English clothes went back into the suitcase from which they had come, and this too was finally locked.

It was nearly eight o'clock when he finished, and Ernestine would be coming up shortly with the morning coffee. The Baroness had tried to keep their affair

from the servants, for both had doted on the Baron
when he had been a small boy and later the master
of the house.

From the window he watched Louison cycle down
the broad path that led towards the gates of the
estate, his shopping panier jolting along behind the
bicycle. At that moment he heard Ernestine knock at
the door. He made no sound. She knocked again.

"*Y a vot' café, madame,*" she shrilled through the
closed door. Making up his mind, the Jackal called
out in French, in a tone half asleep.

"Leave it there. We'll pick it up when we're ready."

Outside the door Ernestine's mouth formed a perfect O. Scandalous. Whatever were things coming to
—and in the Master's bedroom. She hurried downstairs
to find Louison, but as he had left had to content herself with a lengthy lecture to the kitchen sink on the
depravity of people nowadays, not at all like what the
old Baron had been used to. So she did not hear the
soft thud as four cases, lowered from the bedroom
window on a looped sheet, plumped into the flower-
bed on the front of the house.

Nor did she hear the bedroom door locked from the
inside, the limp body of her mistress arranged in a
natural sleeping position on the bed with the clothes
tucked up to the chin, the snap of the bedroom window
as it shut behind the grey-haired man crouching outside on the sill, nor the thud as he dropped in a clean
fall down to the lawn.

She did hear the roar as Madame's Renault was
gunned into life in the converted stable at the side
of the chateau, and peering through the scullery window she caught a glimpse as it swung round into the

driveway leading to the front courtyard and away down the drive.

"Now what is that young lady up to?" she muttered as she scuttled back upstairs.

In front of the bedroom door the tray of coffee was still luke-warm but untouched. After knocking several times, she tried the door but it would not open. The gentleman's bedroom was also locked. Nobody would answer her. Ernestine decided there were goings-on, the sort of goings-on that had not happened since the Boche came to stay as guests of the unwilling Baron back in the old days and ask him silly questions about the Young Master.

She decided to consult Louison. He would be at market, and someone in the local cafe would go to fetch him. She did not understand the telephone, but believed that if you picked it up people spoke to you and went and found the person you really wanted to speak to. But it was all nonsense. She picked it up and held it for ten minutes but no one spoke to her. She failed to notice the neat slice through the cord where it joined the skirting board of the library.

Claude Lebel took the helicopter back to Paris shortly after breakfast. As he said later to Caron, Valentin had been doing a first-class job, despite the obstructions of those damned peasants. By breakfast time he had traced the Jackal to a cafe in Egletons where he had had breakfast, and was looking for a taxi driver who had been summoned. Meanwhile he had arranged for roadblocks to be erected in a twenty-kilometre radius around Egletons, and they should be in place by midday.

Because of the calibre of Valentin, he had given him a hint of the importance of finding the Jackal, and Valentin had agreed to put a ring round Egletons, in his own words "tighter than a mouse's asshole."

From Haute Chalonnière the little Renault sped off through the mountains heading south towards Tulle. The Jackal estimated that if the police had been enquiring since the previous evening in ever-widening circles from where the Alfa had been found, they must have reached Egletons by dawn. The cafe barman would talk, the taxi driver would talk, and they would be at the chateau by the afternoon, unless he had a lucky break.

But even then they would be looking for a blond Englishman, for he had taken good care that no one had seen him as a grey-haired priest. All the same, it was going to be a close-run thing. He whipped the little car through the mountain byways, finally emerging onto the RN 89 eighteen kilometres southwest of Egletons on the road to Tulle, which lay another twenty kilometres ahead. He checked his watch: 9:40.

As he vanished round a bend at the end of a stretch of straight, a small convoy came buzzing down from Egletons. It comprised a police squad car and two closed vans. The convoy stopped in the middle of the straight, and six policemen started to erect a steel roadblock.

"What do you mean, he's out?" roared Valentin to the weeping wife of a taxi driver in Egletons. "Where did he go?"

"I don't know, monsieur. I don't know. He waits every morning at the station square when the morning train comes in from Ussel. If there are no passengers he comes back here to the garage and gets on with some repair work. If he does not come back it means he has picked up a fare."

Valentin looked around gloomily. It was no use bawling out the woman. It was a one-man taxi business run by a fellow who also did a bit of repair work on cars.

"Did he take anyone anywhere on Friday morning?" he asked, more patiently.

"Yes, monsieur. He had come back from the station because there was no one there, and a call came from the cafe that somebody there wanted a taxi. He had got one of the wheels off, and was worried in case the customer should leave and go in another taxi. So he was cussing all through the twenty minutes it took to put the wheel back on. Then he left. He got the fare, but he never said where he took him." She snuffled. "He doesn't talk to me much," she added by way of explanation.

Valentin patted her on the shoulder.

"All right, madame. Don't upset yourself. We'll wait till he gets back." He turned to one of the sergeants. "Get a man to the main station, another to the square, to the cafe. You know the number of that taxi. The moment he shows up I want to see him—fast."

He left the garage and strode to his car.

"The commissariat," he said. He had transferred the headquarters of the search to Egletons police station, which had not seen activity like it in years.

In a ravine six miles outside Tulle the Jackal dumped the suitcase containing all his English clothes and the passport of Alexander Duggan. It had served him well. The case plummeted over the parapet of the bridge and vanished with a crash into the dense under-growth at the foot of the gorge.

After circling Tulle and finding the station, he parked the car unobtrusively three streets away and carried his two suitcases and grip the half mile to the railway booking office.

"I would like a single ticket to Paris, second class, please," he told the clerk. "How much is that?" He peered over his glasses and through the little grille into the cubbyhole where the clerk worked.

"Ninety-seven new francs, monsieur."

"And what time is the next train, please?"

"Twelve-fifty. You've got nearly an hour to wait. There's a restaurant down the platform. Platform 1 for Paris, *je vous en prie*."

The Jackal picked up his luggage and headed for the barrier. The ticket was clipped, he picked up the cases again and walked through. His path was barred by a blue uniform.

"*Vos papiers, s'il vous plaît*."

The CRS man was young, trying to look sterner than his years would allow. He carried a submachine carbine slung over his shoulder. The Jackal put down his luggage again and proffered his Danish passport. The CRS man flicked through it, not understanding a word.

"*Vous êtes Danois?*"

"*Pardon?*"

"*Vous—Danois.*" He tapped the cover of the pass-port.

The Jackal beamed and nodded in delight.

"*Dansk—ja, ja.*"

The CRS man handed the passport back and jerked his head towards the platform. Without further inter-est he stepped forward to bar passage to another traveller coming through the barrier.

It was not until nearly one o'clock that Louison came back, and he had had a glass of wine or two. His distraught wife poured out her tale of woe. Louison took the matter in hand.

"I shall," he announced, "mount to the window and look in."

He had trouble with the ladder to start with. It kept wanting to go its own way. But eventually it was propped against the brickwork beneath the window of the Baroness's bedroom, and Louison made his un-steady way to the top. He came down five minutes later.

"Madame la Baronne is asleep," he announced.

"But she never sleeps this late," protested Ernestine.

"Well, she is doing today," replied Louison, "one must not disturb her."

The Paris train was slightly late. It arrived at Tulle on the dot of one o'clock. Among the passengers who boarded it was a grey-haired Protestant pastor. He took a corner seat in a compartment inhabited only by two middle-aged women, put on a pair of gold-rimmed reading glasses, took a large book on churches and cathedrals from his hand-grip, and started to read.

The arrival time in Paris, he learned, was 8:10 that evening.

Charles Bobet stood on the roadside next to his immobilised taxi, looked at his watch, and swore. Half past one, time for lunch, and here he was stuck on a lonely stretch of road between Egletons and the hamlet of Lamazière. With a busted half-shaft. *Merde* and *merde* again. He could leave the car and try to walk to the next village, take a bus into Egletons, and return in the evening with a repair truck. That alone would cost him a week's earnings. But then again, the car doors had no locks, and his fortune was tied up in the rattletrap taxi. Better not leave it for those thieving village kids to ransack. Better to be a little patient and wait until a truck came along that could (for a consideration) tow him back to Egletons. He had had no lunch, but there was a bottle of wine in the glove compartment. Well, it was almost empty now. Crawling around under taxis was thirsty work. He climbed into the back of the car to wait. It was extremely hot on the roadside and no trucks would be moving until the day had cooled a little. The peasants would be taking their siesta. He made himself comfortable and fell fast asleep.

"What do you mean he's not back yet? Where's the bastard gone?" roared Commissaire Valentin down the telephone. He was sitting in the commissariat at Egletons, ringing the house of the taxi driver and speaking to his own policeman. The babble of the voice on the other end was apologetic. Valentin slammed the phone down. All morning and through the lunch hour radio reports had come in from the squad cars manning the roadblocks. No one remotely resembling a tall blond Englishman had left the twenty-kilometre radius circle round Egletons. Now the sleepy market town was silent in the summer heat, dozing blissfully as if the two hundred policemen from Ussel and Clermont Ferrand had never descended upon it.

It was not until four o'clock that Ernestine got her way.

"You must go up there again and wake Madame," she urged Louison. "It's not natural for anyone to sleep through the day."

Old Louison, who could think of nothing better than to be able to do just that, and whose mouth tasted like a vulture's crotch, disagreed but knew there was no use in arguing with Ernestine when her mind was made up. He ascended the ladder again, this time more steadily than before, eased up the window, and stepped inside. Ernestine watched from below.

After a few minutes the old man's head came out of the window.

"Ernestine," he called hoarsely, "Madame seems to be dead."

He was about to climb back down again when Ernestine screamed at him to open the bedroom door from the inside. Together they peered over the edge of the coverlet at the eyes staring blankly at the pillow a few inches away from the face.

Ernestine took over.

"Louison."

"Yes, my dear."

"Hurry down to the village and fetch Doctor Mathieu. Hurry now."

A few minutes later Louison was pedalling down the drive with all the force his frightened legs could muster. He found Doctor Mathieu, who had tended the ills of the people of Haute Chalonnière for over forty years, asleep under the apricot tree at the bottom of his garden, and the old man agreed to come at once. It was 4:30 when his car clattered into the courtyard of the chateau and fifteen minutes later when he straightened up from the bed and turned round on the two retainers who stood in the doorway.

"Madame is dead. Her neck has been broken," he quavered. "We must fetch the constable."

Gendarme Caillou was a methodical man. He knew how serious was the job of an officer of the law, and how important it was to get the facts straight. With much licking of his pencil he took statements from Ernestine, Louison, and Doctor Mathieu as they sat around the kitchen table.

"There is no doubt," he said, when the doctor had signed his statement, "that murder has been done. The first suspect is evidently the blond Englishman who has been staying here, and who has disappeared in Madame's car. I shall report the matter to headquarters in Egletons."

And he cycled back down the hill.

Claude Lebel rang Commissaire Valentin from Paris at 6:30.

"*Alors*, Valentin?"

"Nothing yet," replied Valentin. "We've had roadblocks up on every road and track leading out of the area since midmorning. He must be inside the circle somewhere, unless he moved far away after ditching the car. That thrice damned taxi driver who drove him out of Egletons on Friday morning has not turned up yet. I've got patrols scouring the roads around here for him—Hold it a minute, another report just coming in."

There was a pause on the line, and Lebel could hear Valentin conferring with someone who was speaking quickly. Then Valentin's voice came back on the line.

"Name of a dog, what's going on round here? There's been a murder."

"Where?" asked Lebel with quickened interest.

"At a chateau in the neighbourhood. The report just came in from the village constable."

"Who's the dead person?"

"The owner of the chateau. A woman. Hold on a moment. . . . The Baroness de la Chalonnière."

Caron watched Lebel go pale.

"Valentin, listen to me. It's him. Has he got away from the chateau yet?"

There was another conference in the police station at Egletons.

"Yes," said Valentin, "he drove away this morning in the Baroness's car. A small Renault. The gardener discovered the body, but not until this afternoon. He thought she must have been sleeping. Then he climbed through the window and found her."

"Have you got the number and description of the car?" asked Lebel.

"Yes."

"Then put out a general alert. There's no need for secrecy any more. It's a straight murder hunt now.

I'll put out a nation-wide alert for it, but try and pick up the trail near the scene of the crime if you can. Try to get his general direction of flight."

"Right, will do. Now we can really get started."

Lebel hung up.

"Dear God, I'm getting slow in my old age. The name of the Baronne de la Chalonnière was on the guest list at the Hôtel du Cerf the night the Jackal stayed there."

The car was found in a back street in Tulle at 7:30 by a policeman on the beat. It was 7:45 before he was back in the police station at Tulle and 7:55 before Tulle had contacted Valentin. The Commissaire of Auvergne rang Lebel at 8:05.

"About five hundred metres from the railway station," he told Lebel.

"Have you got a railway timetable there?"

"Yes, there should be one here somewhere."

"What was the time of the morning train to Paris from Tulle, and what time is it due at the Gare d'Austerlitz? Hurry, for God's sake hurry."

There was a murmured conversation at the Egletons end of the line.

"Only two a day," said Valentin. "The earlier train left at about one and is due in Paris at . . . here we are, ten past eight . . ."

Lebel left the phone hanging and was half way out of the office yelling at Caron to follow him.

The 8:10 express steamed majestically into the Gare d'Austerlitz precisely on time. It had hardly stopped when the doors down its gleaming length were flung open and the passengers were spilling out onto the platform, some to be greeted by waiting relatives, others to stride towards the series of arches that led from the main hall into the taxi rank. One of these was a tall grey-haired parson in a dog-collar. He was one of the first at the taxi-rank, and humped his three bags into the back of a Mercedes diesel.

The driver slammed the meter over and eased away from the entrance to slide down the incline towards the street. The forecourt had a semi-circular driveway, with one gate for coming and one for going out. The taxi rolled down the slope towards the exit. Both driver and passenger became aware of a wailing sound rising over and above the clamour of passengers trying to attract the attention of taxi drivers before their turn had arrived. As the taxi reached the level of the street and paused before entering the traffic, three squad cars and two Black Marias swept into the entrance and drew to a halt before the main arches leading to the station hall.

"Huh, they're busy tonight, the pricks," said the taxi driver. "Where to, Monsieur l'Abbé?"

The parson gave him the address of a small hotel on the Quai des Grands Augustins.

Claude Lebel was back in his office at nine o'clock, to find a message asking him to ring Commissaire Valentin at the commissariat in Tulle. He was through in five minutes. While Valentin talked, he took notes.

"Have you fingerprinted the car?" asked Lebel.

"Of course, and the room at the chateau. Hundreds of them, all matching."

"Get them up here as fast as you can."

"Right, will do. Do you want me to send the CRS man from Tulle railway station up as well?"

"No, thanks, but he can't tell us more than he already has. Thanks for trying, Valentin. You can stand your boys down now. He's in our territory now. We'll have to handle it from here."

"You're sure it is the Danish pastor?" asked Valentin. "It could be coincidence."

"No," said Lebel, "it's him all right. He's junked one of the suitcases, you'll probably find it somewhere between Haute Chalonnière and Tulle. Try the rivers and ravines. But the other three pieces of luggage match too closely. It's him all right."

He hung up.

"A parson this time," he said bitterly to Caron, "a Danish parson. Name unknown, the CRS man couldn't remember the name on the passport. The human element, always the human element. A taxi driver goes to sleep by the roadside, a gardener is too nervous to investigate his employer's oversleeping by six hours, a policeman doesn't remember a name in a passport. One thing I can tell you, Lucien, this is my last case. I'm getting too old. Old and slow. Get my car ready, would you. Time for the evening roasting."

The meeting at the ministry was strained and tense. For forty minutes the group listened to a step-by-step account of the trail from the forest clearing to Egletons, the absence of the vital taxi driver, the murder in the chateau, the tall grey Dane boarding the Paris express at Tulle.

"The long and the short of it," said Saint-Clair icily, when he had finished, "is that the killer is now in

Paris, with a new name and a new face. You seem to have failed once again, my dear Commissaire."

"Let us save the recriminations for later," interposed the Minister. "How many Danes are there in Paris to-night?"

"Probably several hundreds, Monsieur le Ministre."

"Can we check them?"

"Only in the morning, when the hotel registration cards come in to the Prefecture," said Lebel.

"I will arrange to have every hotel visited at midnight, two o'clock, and four o'clock," proposed the Prefect of Police. "Under the heading of 'Profession' he will have to put 'Pastor' or the hotel clerk will be suspicious."

The room brightened.

"He will probably wrap a scarf round his dog-collar, or take it off, and register as 'Mister Whatever-his-name-is,'" said Lebel. Several people glowered at him.

"At this point, gentlemen, there is only one thing left to do," said the Minister. "I shall ask for another interview with the President and ask him to cancel all public appearances until this man is found and disposed of. In the meantime, every Dane registering in Paris tonight will be checked personally first thing in the morning. I can rely on you for that, Commissaire? *Monsieur le Préfet de Police?*"

Lebel and Papon nodded.

"Then that is all, gentlemen."

"The thing that sticks in my craw," said Lebel to Caron later in their office, "is that they insist on thinking it's just his good luck and our stupidity. Well, he's had good luck, but he's also devilishly clever. And we've had bad luck, and we've made mistakes. I've made them. But there's another element. Twice we've missed him by hours. Once he gets out of Gap with a repainted car in the nick of time. Now he leaves the chateau and kills his mistress into the bargain within hours of the Alfa Romeo being found. And each time it's the morning after I have told that meeting at the ministry that we have him in the bag, and his capture can be expected within twelve hours. Lucien, my dear fellow, I think I'm going to use my limitless powers, and organise a little wire-tapping."

He was leaning against the window ledge, looking out through and across the softly flowing Seine towards the Latin Quarter where the lights were bright and the sound of laughter floated over the floodlit water.

Three hundred yards away another man leaned over his window sill in the summer night and gazed pensively at the bulk of the Police Judiciaire lying to the left of the spot-lit spires of Notre Dame. He was clad in black trousers and walking shoes, with a polo-necked silk sweater covering a white shirt and black bib. He smoked a king-size English filter cigarette, and the young face belied the shock of iron-grey hair above it.

As the two men looked towards each other unknowingly above the waters of the Seine, the varied chimes of the churches of Paris ushered in August 22.

PART THREE

Anatomy of a Kill

nineteen

Claude Lebel had a bad night. It was 1:30, and he had barely got to sleep when Caron shook him awake.

"Chief, I'm sorry about this, but I've had an idea. This chap, the Jackal. He's got a Danish passport, right?"

Lebel shook himself awake.

"Go on."

"Well he must have got it from somewhere. Either he had it forged, or he stole it. But as carrying the passport has entailed a change of hair colouring, it looks as if he stole it."

"Reasonable. Go on."

"Well, apart from his reconnaissance trip to Paris in July, he has been based in London. So the chances are he stole it in one of those two cities. Now what would a Dane do when his passport was lost or stolen? He'd go to his Consulate."

Lebel struggled off the cot.

"Sometimes, my dear Lucien, I think you will go far. Get me Superintendent Thomas at his home, then the Danish Consul-General in Paris. In that order."

He spent another hour on the phone and persuaded both men to leave their beds and get back to their offices. Lebel went back to his cot at nearly three o'clock in the morning. At four he was woken by a call from the Préfecture de Police to say that over 980 hotel registration cards filled in by Danes staying in Paris hotels had been brought in by the collections at

midnight and 2 a.m., and sorting of them into categories of "probable," "possible," and "others" had already started.

At 6 he was still awake and drinking coffee when
the call came from the engineers at the DST, to whom
he had given his instructions just after midnight. There
had been a catch. He took a car and drove down
through the early morning streets to their headquarters
with Caron beside him. In a basement communications laboratory they listened to a tape recording.

It started with a loud click, then a series of whirrs
as if someone were dialling seven figures. Then there
was the long buzz of a telephone ringing, followed
by another click as the receiver was lifted.

A husky voice said, "*Allo?*"

A woman's voice said, "*Ici Jacqueline.*"

The man's voice replied, "*Ici Valmy.*"

The woman said quickly, "They know he's a Danish
parson. They're checking through the night the hotel
registration cards of all Danes in Paris, with card collections at midnight, two, and four o'clock. Then
they're going to visit every one."

There was a pause, then the man's voice said,
"*Merci.*" He hung up, and the woman did the same.

Lebel stared at the slowly turning tape spool.

"You know the number she rang?" Lebel asked the
engineer.

"Yes. We can work it out from the length of the
delay while the dialing disc spins back to zero. The
number was Molitor fifty-nine-o-one."

"You have the address?"

The man passed him a slip of paper. Lebel glanced
at it.

"Come on, Lucien. Let's go and pay a call on Monsieur Valmy."

The knock came at seven o'clock. The schoolmaster was brewing himself a cup of breakfast coffee on the gas-ring. With a frown he turned down the gas and crossed the sitting room to open the door. Four men were facing him. He knew who they were and what they were without being told. The two in uniform looked as if they were going to lunge at him, but the short, mild-looking man gestured for them to remain where they were.

"We tapped the phone," said the little man quietly. "You're Valmy."

The schoolmaster gave no sign of emotion. He stepped back and let them enter the room.

"May I get dressed?" he asked.

"Yes, of course."

It took him only a few minutes, as the two uniformed policemen stood over him, to draw on trousers and shirt, without bothering to remove his pyjamas. The younger man in plain-clothes stood in the doorway. The older man wandered round the flat, inspecting the piles of books and papers.

"It'll take ages to sort through this little lot, Lucien," he said, and the man in the doorway grunted.

"Not our department, thank God."

"Are you ready?" the little man asked the schoolmaster.

"Yes."

"Take him downstairs to the car."

The Commissaire remained when the other four had left, riffling through the papers on which the schoolmaster had apparently been working the night before. But they were all ordinary school examination papers being corrected. Apparently the man worked from his flat; he would have to stay in the flat all day to remain on the end of the telephone in case the Jackal called. It was 7:10 when the telephone rang. Lebel watched it for several seconds. Then his hand reached out and picked it up.

"*Allo?*"

The voice on the other end was flat, toneless.

"*Ici Chacal.*"

Lebel thought furiously.

"*Ici Valmy,*" he said. There was a pause. He did not know what else to say.

"What's new?" asked the voice at the other end.

"Nothing. They've lost the trail in Corrèze."

There was a film of sweat on his forehead. It was vital the man stay where he was for a few hours more. There was a click and the phone went dead. Lebel replaced it and raced downstairs to the car at the kerb-side.

"Back to the office," he yelled at the driver.

In the telephone booth in the foyer of a small hotel by the banks of the Seine the Jackal stared out through the glass perplexed. Nothing? There must be more than nothing. This Commissaire Lebel was no fool. They must have traced the taxi driver in Egletons, and from there to Haute Chalonnière. They must have found the body in the chateau, and the missing Renault. They might have found the Renault in Tulle, and questioned the staff at the station. They must have . . .

He strode out of the telephone booth and across the foyer.

"My bill, if you please," he told the clerk. "I shall be down in five minutes."

The call from Superintendent Thomas came in as Lebel entered his office at 7:30.

"Sorry to have been so long," said the British detective. "It took ages to wake the Danish consular staff and get them back to the office. You were quite right. On July fourteenth a Danish parson reported the loss of his passport. He suspected it had been stolen from his room at a West End hotel, but could not prove it. Did not file a complaint, to the relief of the hotel manage. Name of Pastor Per Jensen, of Copenhagen. Description, six feet tall, blue eyes, grey hair."

"That's the one, thank you, Superintendent." Lebel put the phone down. "Get me the Prefecture," he told Caron.

The four Black Marias arrived outside the hotel on the Quai des Grands Augustins at eight-thirty. The police turned Room 37 over until it looked as if a tornado had hit it.

"I'm sorry, *Monsieur le Commissaire*," the proprietor told the rumpled-looking detective who led the raid, "Monsieur Jensen checked out an hour ago."

The Jackal had taken a cruising taxi back towards the Gare d'Austerlitz where he had arrived the previous evening, on the grounds that the search for him would have moved elsewhere. He deposited the suitcase containing the gun and military greatcoat and clothes of the fictitious Frenchman André Martin in

the left-luggage office, and retained only the suitcase
in which he carried the clothes and papers of American student Marty Schulberg, and the hand-grip with
the articles of make-up.

With these, still dressed in the black suit but with
a polo sweater covering the dog-collar, he checked
into a poky hotel round the corner from the station.
The clerk let him fill in his own registration card, being too idle to check the card against the passport on
the visitor, as regulations required. As a result the
registration card was not even in the name of Per
Jensen.

Once up in his room, the Jackal set to work on his
face and hair. The grey dye was washed out with the
aid of a solvent, and the blond reappeared. This was
tinted with the chestnut brown colouring of Marty
Schulberg. The blue contact lenses remained in place,
but the gold-rimmed glasses were replaced by the
American's heavy-rimmed executive spectacles. The
black walking shoes, socks, shirt, bib, and clerical suit
were bundled into the suitcase, along with the passport of Pastor Jensen of Copenhagen. He dressed
instead in the loafers, socks, jeans, T-shirt, and windbreaker of the American college boy from Syracuse,
New York.

By midmorning, with the American's passport in one
breast pocket and a wad of French francs in the other,
he was ready to move. The suitcase containing the last
remains of Pastor Jensen went into the wardrobe, and
the key of the wardrobe went down the flush of the
bidet. He used the fire escape to depart, and was no
more heard of in that hotel. A few minutes later he
deposited the hand-grip in the left-luggage office at

the Gare d'Austerlitz, stuffed the docket for the second case into his back pocket to join the docket of the first suitcase, and went on his way. He took a taxi back to the Left Bank, got out at the corner of Boulevard St. Michel and the rue de la Huchette, and vanished into the crowds of students and young people who inhabit the rabbit warren of the Latin Quarter of Paris.

Sitting at the back of a smoky dive for a cheap lunch, he started to wonder where he was going to spend the night. He had few doubts that Lebel would have exposed Pastor Per Jensen by this time, and he gave Marty Schulberg no more than twenty-four hours.

"Damn that man Lebel," he thought savagely, but smiled broadly at the waitress and said, "Thanks, honey."

Lebel was back on to Thomas in London at ten o'clock. His request caused Thomas to give a low groan, but he replied courteously enough that he would do everything he could. When the phone went down, Thomas summoned the senior inspector who had been on the investigation the previous week.

"All right, sit down," he said. "The Frenchies have been back on. It seems they've missed him again. Now he's in the centre of Paris, and they suspect he might have another false identity prepared. We can both start as of now ringing round every consulate in London asking for a list of passports of visiting foreigners reported lost or stolen since July first. Forget Negroes and Asiatics. Just stick to Caucasians. In each case I want to know the height of the man. Everybody above five feet, eight inches is suspect. Get to work."

The daily meeting at the ministry in Paris had been brought forward to two o'clock in the afternoon.

Lebel's report was delivered in his usual inoffensive monotone, but the reception was icy.

"Damn the man," exclaimed the Minister half way through, "he has the luck of the devil."

"No, *Monsieur le Ministre*, it hasn't been luck. At least, not all of it. He has been kept constantly informed of our progress at every stage. This is why he left Gap in such a hurry, and why he killed the woman at la Chalonnière and left just before the net closed. Every night I have reported my progress to this meeting. Three times we have been within hours of catching him. This morning it was the arrest of Valmy and my inability to impersonate Valmy on the telephone that caused him to leave where he was and change into another identity. But the first two occasions he was tipped off in the early morning after I had briefed this meeting."

There was a frigid silence round the table.

"I seem to recall, Commissaire, that this suggestion of yours has been made before," said the Minister coldly. "I hope you can substantiate it."

For answer Lebel lifted a small portable tape recorder onto the table, and pressed the starter button. In the silence of the conference room the conversation tapped from the telephone sounded metallic and harsh. When it finished the whole room stared at the machine on the table. Colonel Saint-Clair had gone ashen grey, and his hands trembled slightly as he shuffled his papers together into his folder.

"Whose voice was that?" asked the Minister finally.

Lebel remained silent. Saint-Clair rose slowly, and the eyes of the room swivelled onto him.

"I regret to have inform you—*Monsieur le Ministre* —that it was the voice of—a friend of mine. She is staying with me at the present time. . . . Excuse me."

He left the room to return to the Palace and write his resignation. Those in the room stared at their hands in silence.

"Very well, Commissaire." The Minister's voice was very quiet. "You may continue."

Lebel resumed his report, relating his request to Thomas in London to trace every missing passport over the previous fifty days.

"I hope," he concluded, "to have a short list by this evening of probably no more than one or two who fit the description we already have of the Jackal. As soon as I know, I shall ask the countries of origin of these tourists in London who lost their passports to provide photographs of those people, for we can be sure the Jackal will by now look more like his new identity than like either Calthrop or Duggan or Jensen. With luck I should have these photographs by noon tomorrow."

"For my part," said the Minister, "I can report on my conversation with President de Gaulle. He has refused point blank to change an item of his itinerary for the future to shield himself from this killer. Frankly, it was to be expected. However I was able to obtain one concession. The ban on publicity may now be lifted, at least in this respect. The Jackal is now a common murderer. He has slain the Baronne de la Chalonnière in her own home in the course of a burglary of which the objective was her jewelry. He is believed to have fled to Paris and to be hiding here. All right, gentlemen?

"That is what will be released for the afternoon papers, at least the last editions. As soon as you are quite certain as to the new identity, or choice of two or three alternative identities, under which he is now masquerading, Commissaire, you are authorised to release that name or those names to the press. This will enable the morning papers to update the story with a new lead.

"When the photograph of the unfortunate tourist who lost his passport in London comes through tomorrow morning, you can release it to the evening papers, radio, and television for a second up-date to the murder-hunt story.

"Apart from that, the moment we get a name, every policeman and CRS man in Paris will be on the street stopping every soul in sight to examine their papers."

The Prefect of Police, chief of the CRS, and Director of the PJ were taking furious notes. The Minister resumed.

"The DST will check every sympathiser of the OAS known to them, with the assistance of the Central Records Office. Understood?"

The heads of the DST and the RG office nodded vigorously.

"The Police Judiciaire will take every one of its detectives off whatever he is on, and transfer them to the murder hunt."

Max Fernet of the PJ nodded.

"As regards the Palace itself, evidently I shall need a complete list of every movement the President intends to take from now on, even if he himself has not been informed of the extra precautions being taken in his interest. This is one of those occasions when we must risk his wrath in his own interest. And, of course, I can rely on the Presidential Security Corps to tighten up the ring round the President as never before. Commissaire Ducret?"

Jean Ducret, head of de Gaulle's personal bodyguard, inclined his head.

"The Brigade Criminelle"—the Minister fixed Commissaire Bouvier with his eye—"obviously has a lot of underworld contacts in its pay. I want every one mobilised to keep an eye out for this man, name and description to be supplied. Right?"

Maurice Bouvier nodded gruffly. Privately, he was disquieted. He had seen a few manhunts in his time, but this was gigantic. The moment Lebel provided a name and a passport number, not to mention a description, there would be nearly 100,000 men from the security forces to the underworld scanning the streets, hotels, bars, and restaurants for one man.

"Is there any other source of information that I have overlooked?" asked the Minister.

Colonel Rolland glanced quickly at General Guibaud, then at Commissaire Bouvier. He coughed.

"There is always the Union Corse."

General Guibaud studied his nails. Bouvier looked daggers. Most of the others looked embarrassed. The Union Corse, brotherhood of the Corsicans, descendants of the Brothers of Ajaccio, sons of the vendetta, was and still is the biggest organised crime syndicate in France. They already ran Marseilles and most of the South Coast. Some experts believed them to be older and more dangerous than the Mafia. Never having emigrated like the Mafia to America in the early years of this century, they had avoided the publicity that had since then made the Mafia a household word.

Twice already Gaullism had allied itself with the Union, and both times found it valuable but embarrassing. For the Union always asked for a kickback, usually in a relaxation of police surveillance of their crime rackets. The Union had helped the Allies to invade the south of France in August 1944, and had owned Marseilles and Toulon ever since. It had helped again in the fight against the Algerian settlers and the OAS after April 1961, and for this had spread its tentacles far north and into Paris.

Maurice Bouvier, as a policeman, hated their guts; but he knew Rolland's Action Service used Corsicans heavily.

"You think they can help?" asked the Minister.

"If this Jackal is as astute as they say," replied Rolland, "then I would reckon that if anyone in Paris can find him the Union can."

"How many of them are there in Paris?" asked the Minister dubiously.

"About eighty thousand. Some in the police, customs officers, CRS, Secret Service, and of course the underworld. And they are organised."

"Use them," said the Minister.

There were no more suggestions.

"Well, that's it then. Commissaire Lebel, all we want from you now is one name, one description, one photograph. After that I give this Jackal six hours of liberty."

"Actually, we have three days," said Lebel who had

been staring out of the window. His audience looked startled.

"How do you know that?" asked Max Fernet.

Lebel blinked rapidly several times.

"I must apologise. I have been very silly, not to see it before. For a week now I have been certain that the Jackal had a plan, and that he had picked his day for killing the President. When he quit Gap, why did he not immediately become Pastor Jensen? Why did he not drive to Valence and pick up the express to Paris immediately? Why did he arrive in France and then spend a week killing time?"

"Well, why?" asked someone.

"Because he has picked his day," said Lebel. "He knows when he is going to strike. Commissaire Ducret, has the President got any engagements outside the Palace today, or tomorrow, or Saturday?"

Ducret shook his head.

"And what is Sunday, August twenty-fifth?" asked Lebel.

There was a sigh round the table like wind blowing through corn.

"Of course," breathed the Minister, "Liberation Day. And the crazy thing is, most of us were here with him on that day, the Liberation of Paris, 1944."

"Precisely," said Lebel. "He is a bit of a psychologist, our Jackal. He knows there is one day of the year that General de Gaulle will never spend elsewhere than here. It is, so to speak, his great day. That is what the assassin has been waiting for."

"In that case," said the Minister briskly, "we have got him. With his source of information gone, there is no corner of Paris where he can hide, no single com-

munity of Parisians that will take him in, even un-
wittingly, and give him protection and shelter. We
have him. Commissaire Lebel, give us that man's
name."

Claude Lebel rose and went to the door. The others
were rising and preparing to leave for lunch.

"Oh, there is one thing," the Minister called after
Lebel, "how did you know to tap the telephone line
of Colonel Saint-Clair's private apartment?"

Lebel turned in the doorway and shrugged.

"I didn't," he said, "so last night I tapped all your
telephones. Good day, gentlemen."

At 5 that afternoon, sitting over a beer at a cafe
terrace just off the Place de l'Odéon, his face shielded
from the sunlight by dark glasses such as everyone
else was wearing, the Jackal got his idea. He got it
from watching two men stroll by in the street. He paid
for his beer, got up, and left. A hundred yards down
the street he found what he was looking for, a woman's
beauty shop. He went in and made a few purchases.

At 6 that evening papers changed their headlines.
The late editions carried a screaming banner across
the top: "ASSASSIN DE LA BELLE BARONNE SE REFUGIE A
PARIS." There was a photo beneath it of the Baronne
de la Chalonnière, taken from a society picture of her
five years ago at a party in Paris. It had been found
in the archives of a picture agency and the same photo
was in every paper. At 6:30, with a copy of *France-
Soir* under his arm, Colonel Rolland entered a small
cafe off the rue Washington. The dark-jowled bar-

man glanced at him keenly and nodded towards another man in the back of the hall.

The second man came over and accosted Rolland. "Colonel Rolland?"

The head of the Action Service nodded.

"Please follow me."

He led the way through a door at the back of the cafe and up to a small sitting room on the first floor, probably the owner's private dwelling. He knocked, and a voice inside said, *"Entrez."*

As the door closed behind him, Rolland took the outstretched hand of the man who had risen from an armchair.

"Colonel Rolland? *Enchanté*. I am the Capo of the Union Corse. I understand you are looking for a certain man. . . ."

It was eight o'clock when Superintendent Thomas came through from London. He sounded tired. It had not been an easy day. Some consulates had cooperated willingly. Others had been extremely difficult.

Apart from women, Negroes, Asiatics, and short men, eight foreign male tourists had lost or had stolen their passports in London during the previous fifty days, he said. Carefully and succinctly he listed them all, with names, passport numbers, and descriptions.

"Now let's start to deduct those whom it cannot be," he suggested to Lebel. "Three lost their passports during periods when we know that the Jackal, alias Duggan, was not in London. We've been checking airline booking and ticket sales right back to July first as well. It seems on July eighteenth he took the evening flight to Copenhagen. According to BEA, he bought a ticket at their counter in Brussels, paying cash, and flew back to England on the evening of August sixth."

"Yes, that checks," said Lebel. "We have discovered that part of that journey out of London was spent in Paris. From July twenty-second until July thirty-first."

"Well," said Thomas, his voice crackling on the London line, "three of the passports were missing while he was not here. We can count them out, yes?"

"Right," said Lebel.

"Of the remaining five, one is immensely tall, six feet six inches, that's over two metres in your language. Besides which, he's Italian, which means that his height on the fly-leaf of his passport is given in metres and centimetres, which would be immediately understood by a French customs officer, who would notice the difference, unless the Jackal is walking on stilts."

"I agree, the man must be a giant. Count him out. What of the other four?" asked Lebel.

"Well, one is immensely fat, two hundred and forty-two pounds, or well over a hundred kilos. The Jackal would have to be so padded he could hardly walk."

"Count him out," said Lebel. "Who else?"

"Another is too old. He's the right height, but over seventy. The Jackal could hardly look that old unless a real expert in theatrical make-up went to work on his face."

"Count him out too," said Lebel. "What about the last two?"

"One's Norwegian, the other American," said Thomas. "Both fit the bill. Tall, wide-shouldered, between twenty and fifty; there are two things that militate against the Norwegian being your man. For one thing he is blond; I don't think the Jackal, after being exposed as Duggan, would go back to his own hair-colouring, would he? He would look too much like Duggan. The other thing is, the Norwegian reported to his consul that he is certain his passport slipped out of his pocket when he fell fully clothed into the Serpentine while boating with a girl-friend. He swears the passport was in his breast pocket when he fell in, and was not there fifteen minutes later when he climbed out. On the other hand, the American made a sworn statement to the police at London Airport to the effect that his hand-grip with the passport inside it was stolen while he was looking the other way in the main hall of the airport building. What do you think?"

"Send me," said Lebel, "all the details of the American. I'll get his photograph from the Passport Office in Washington. And thank you again for all your efforts."

There was a second meeting in the ministry at 10 that evening. It was the briefest so far. Already an hour previously every department of the apparatus of the security of state had received mimeographed copies of the details of Marty Schulberg, wanted for murder. A photograph was expected before morning, in time for the first editions of the evening papers that would be appearing on the streets by 10 in the morning.

The Minister rose.

"Gentlemen, when we first met, we agreed to a suggestion by Commissaire Bouvier that the identification of the assassin known as the Jackal was basically a task for pure detective work. With hindsight, I would not disagree with that diagnosis. We have been fortunate in having had, for these past ten days, the services of Commissaire Lebel. Despite three changes of identity by the assassin, from Calthrop to Duggan, Duggan to Jensen, and Jensen to Schulberg, and despite a constant leak of information from within this room, he has managed both to identify and, within the limits of this city, to track down our man. We owe him our thanks." He inclined his head towards Lebel, who looked embarrassed.

"However, from now on the task must devolve upon us all. We have a name, a description, a passport number, a nationality. Within hours we shall have a photograph. I am confident that, with the forces at your disposal, within hours after that, we shall have our man. Already every policeman in Paris, every CRS man, every detective, has received his briefing. Before morning, or at latest tomorrow noon, there will be no place to hide for this man.

"And now let me congratulate you again, Commissaire Lebel, and remove from your shoulders the burden and the strain of this enquiry. We shall not be needing your invaluable assistance in the hours to come. Your task is done, and well done. Thank you."

He waited patiently. Lebel blinked rapidly several times and rose from his seat. He bobbed his head at the assembly of powerful men who commanded thousands of underlings and millions of francs. They smiled back at him. He turned and left the room.

For the first time in ten days, Commissaire Claude Lebel went home to bed. As he turned the key in the lock and caught the first shrill rebuke of his wife, the clock chimed midnight and it was August 23.

twenty

The Jackal entered the bar an hour before midnight. It was dark and for several seconds he could hardly make out the shape of the room. There was a long bar running down the left hand wall, with an illuminated row of mirrors and bottles behind it. The barman stared at him with unveiled curiosity as the door swung closed.

The shape of the room was long and narrow down the length of the bar, with small tables set on the right-hand wall. At the far end the room broadened into a salon, and here there were larger tables where four or six could sit together. A row of bar stools were against the bar counter. Most of the chairs and stools were occupied by the night's habitual clientele.

The conversation had stopped at the tables nearest the door while the customers examined him, and the hush spread down the room as others further away caught the glances of their companions and turned to study the tall athletic figure by the door. A few whispers were exchanged, and a giggle or two. He spotted a spare bar stool at the far end and walked between the tables on the right and the bar on the left to reach it. He swung himself onto the bar stool. Behind him he caught a quick whisper.

"Oh, *regarde-moi ça!* Those muscles, darling, I'm going out of my mind."

The barman slipped down the length of the bar to

stand opposite him and get a better look. The carmined lips widened in a coquettish smile.

"Bonsoir—monsieur." There was a chorus of giggles from behind, most of them malicious.

"Donnez-moi un Scotch."

The barman waltzed away delighted. A man, a man, a man. Oh there was going to be such a row tonight. He could see the *petites folles* on the far side of the corridor sharpening their claws. Most were waiting for their regular "butches," but some were without a date and had turned up on spec. This new boy, he thought, was going to create an absolute sensation.

The client next to the Jackal turned towards him and gazed with unconcealed curiosity. The hair was a metallic gold, meticulously groomed down onto the forehead in a series of pointed spikes like a young Greek god on an ancient frieze. There the likeness ended. The eyes were mascaraed, the lips a delicate coral, the cheeks dusted with powder. But the make-up could not conceal the tired lines of an ageing degenerate, nor the mascara the arid hungry eyes.

"Tu m'invites?" The voice was a girlish lisp.

The Jackal slowly shook his head. The drag shrugged and turned back to his companion. They went on with their conversation in whispers and squeaks of mock dismay. The Jackal had taken off his windbreaker and as he reached for his drink, proffered by the barman, the muscles down the shoulders and back rippled under the T-shirt.

The barman was delighted. A "straight"? No, he couldn't be, he wouldn't be here. And not a butch looking for a nance, or why had he snubbed poor little

Corinne when she asked for a drink. He must be . . .
how marvellous. A handsome young butch looking for
an old queen to take him home. What fun there was
going to be tonight.

The butches started homing in just before midnight,
sitting at the back, surveying the crowd, occasionally
beckoning the barman for a whispered conversation.
The barman would return to the bar and signal to one
of the "girls."

"Monsieur Pierre wants to have a word with you,
darling. Try and look your best, and for God's sake
don't cry like you did last time."

The Jackal made his mark shortly after midnight.
Two of the men at the back had been eyeing him for
several minutes. They were at different tables and
occasionally shot each other venomous glances. Both
were in late middle age; one was fat, with tiny eyes
buried in obese lids and rolls on the back of his neck
that flowed over his collar. He looked gross and pig-
gish. The other was slim, elegant, with a vulture's
neck and balding pate across which the few strands
of hair were elaborately plastered. He wore a beautifully tailored suit with narrow trousers and a jacket
whose sleeves showed a hint of lace at the cuffs. There
was a flowing silk foulard artfully knotted at the
throat. Something to do with the world of the arts,
fashion, or hair-styling, the Jackal thought.

The fat one beckoned to the barman and whispered
in his ear. A large note slipped into the barman's tight
trousers. He returned across the bar floor.

"The monsieur wonders if you would care to join
him for a glass of champagne," whispered the barman, and regarded him archly.

The Jackal put down his whisky.

"Tell the monsieur," he said clearly, so the pansies round the bar could hear, "that he does not attract me."

There were gasps of horror, and several of the flick-knife thin young men slipped off their bar stools to come nearer so that they would not miss a word. The barman's eyes opened wide with horror.

"He's offering you champagne, darling. We know him, he's absolutely loaded. You've made a hit."

For reply the Jackal slid off his bar stool, took his glass of whisky, and sauntered over to the other old queen.

"Would you permit that I sit here?" he asked. "One is embarrassing me."

The arty one almost fainted with pleasure. A few minutes later the fat man, still glowering from the insult, left the bar, while his rival, his bony old hand indolently placed across that of the young American at his table, told his new-found friend what absolutely, absolutely shocking manners some people had.

The Jackal and his escort left the bar after one o'clock. Several minutes before, the man, whose name was Jules Bernard, had asked the Jackal where he was staying. With a show of shamefacedness the Jackal admitted that he had nowhere to stay, and that he was flat broke, a student down on his luck. As for Bernard, he could hardly believe his good fortune. As chance would have it, he told his young friend, he had a beautiful flat, very nicely decorated, and quite quiet. He lived alone, no one ever disturbed him, and he never had anything to do with the neighbours in the block, because in the past they had been terribly, terribly rude. He would be delighted if young Martin would stay with him while he was in Paris. With another show, this time of intense gratitude, the Jackal had accepted. Just before they left the bar he had slipped into the lavatory (there was only one) and had emerged a few minutes later with his eyes heavily mascara'ed, powder on his cheeks, and lipstick on his mouth. Bernard looked very put out, but concealed it while they were still in the bar.

Outside on the pavement he protested, "I don't like you in that stuff. It makes you look like all those nasty pansies back in there. You're a very good-looking young boy. You don't need all that stuff."

"Sorry, Jules, I thought it would improve things for you. I'll wipe it all off when we get home."

Slightly mollified, Bernard led the way to his car. He agreed to drive his new friend first to the Gare d'Austerlitz to pick up his bags, before going home. At the first cross-roads a policeman stepped into the road and flagged them down. As the policeman's head came down to the driver's side window, the Jackal flicked the inside light on. The policeman stared for a minute, then his face drew back with an expression of revulsion.

"*Allez*," he commanded without further ado. As the car rolled away he muttered, "*Sales pédés.*"

There was one more stop, just before the station, and the policeman asked for papers. The Jackal giggled seductively.

"Is that all you want?" he asked archly.

"Fuck off," said the policeman and withdrew.

"Don't annoy them like that," protested Bernard *sotto voce.* "You'll get us arrested."

The Jackal withdrew his two suitcases from the left-luggage office without more than a disgusted glance from the clerk in charge, and hefted them into the back of Bernard's car.

There was one more stop on the way to Bernard's flat. This time it was by two CRS men, one a sergeant and the other a private, who flagged them down at the street junction a few hundred metres from where Bernard lived. The private came round to the passenger door and stared into the Jackal's face. Then he recoiled.

"Oh my God. Where are you two going?" he growled.

The Jackal pouted. "Where do you think, sweetie?"

The CRS man screwed up his face in disgust.

"You fucking queers make me sick. Move on."

"You should have asked to see their identity papers," said the sergeant to the private as the tail-lights of Bernard's car disappeared down the street.

"Oh, come on, Sarge," protested the private, "we're looking for a fellow who screwed the arse off a baroness and did her in; not a couple of raving fairies."

Bernard and the Jackal were inside the flat by two o'clock. The Jackal insisted on spending the night on the studio couch in the drawing room and Bernard quelled his objections, although he peeked through the bedroom door as the young American undressed It was evidently going to be a delicate but exciting chase to seduce the iron-muscled student from New York.

In the night the Jackal checked the refrigerator in the well-appointed and effeminately decorated kitchen, and decided there was enough food for one person for three days, but not for two. In the morning Ber-

nard wanted to go out for fresh milk, but the Jackal
detained him, insisting that he preferred tinned milk
for his coffee. So they spent the morning indoors talking. The Jackal insisted on seeing the midday television news.

The first item concerned the hunt for the killer of
Madame la Baronne de la Chalonnière forty-eight
hours earlier. Jules Bernard squealed with horror.

"Oooh, I can't stand violence," he said.

The next second the screen was filled with a face;
a good-looking young face, with chestnut brown hair
and heavy-rimmed glasses, belonging, so the announcer
said, to the killer, an American student by the name
of Marty Schulberg. Would anybody having seen this
man, or having any knowledge . . .

Bernard, who was sitting on the sofa, turned round
and looked up. The last thing he thought was that the
announcer had not been right, for he had said Schulberg's eyes were blue; but the eyes looking down at
him from behind the steel fingers that gripped his
throat were grey . . .

A few minutes later the door of the hall coat-
cupboard closed on the staring distorted features, hair
awry and tongue protruding, of Jules Bernard. The
Jackal took a magazine out of the rack in the drawing
room and settled down to wait for two days.

During those two days Paris was searched as it
never had been before. Every hotel from the smartest
and most expensive to the sleaziest whorehouse was
visited and the guest-list checked; every pension,
rooming house, flophouse, and hostel was searched.
Bars, restaurants, night-clubs, cabarets, and cafes were

haunted by plainclothesmen, who showed the picture of the wanted man to waiters, barmen, and bouncers. The house or flat of every known OAS sympathiser was raided and turned over. More than seventy young men bearing a passing resemblance to the killer were taken for questioning, later to be released with routine apologies, even these only because they were all foreigners and foreigners have to be more courteously treated than natives.

Hundreds of thousands in the streets, in taxis, and on buses were stopped, and their papers examined. Roadblocks appeared on all the major access points for Paris, and late-night strollers were accosted several times within the space of a mile or two.

In the underworld the Corsicans were at work, silently slipping through the haunts of pimps, prostitutes, hustlers, pickpockets, hoodlums, thieves, and conmen, warning that anyone withholding information would incur the wrath of the Union, with all that that could entail.

A hundred thousand men in the employ of the state, in various capacities from senior detectives to soldiers and gendarmes were on the look-out. The estimated 50,000 of the underworld and its fringe industries vetted the passing faces. Those making a living off the tourist industry by day or night were briefed to keep their eyes open. Students' cafes, bars and talking clubs, social groups and unions were infiltrated with youthful-looking detectives. Agencies specialising in placing foreign-exchange students with French families were visited and warned.

It was on the evening of August 24 that Commissaire Claude Lebel, who had spent the Saturday afternoon pottering about his garden in a cardigan and patched trousers, was summoned by telephone to report to the Minister in his private office. A car came for him at six o'clock.

When he saw the Minister, he was surprised. The dynamic chief of the whole of France's internal security apparatus looked tired and strained. He seemed to have grown older inside forty-eight hours, and there were lines of sleeplessness round the eyes. He gestured Lebel to a chair opposite his desk, and seated himself in the swivel chair in which he liked to be able to spin round from the window with its view of the Place Beauvau back to the desk. This time he did not look out of the window.

"We can't find him," he said briefly. "He's vanished, just disappeared off the face of the earth. The OAS people, we are convinced, just don't know where he is any more than we do. The underworld hasn't had sight nor sound of him. The Union Corse reckons he can't be in town."

He paused and sighed, contemplating the little detective across the desk, who blinked several times but said nothing.

"I don't think we ever really had any idea what kind of a man you have been pursuing these past two weeks. What do you think?"

"He's here, somewhere," said Lebel. "What are the arrangements like for tomorrow?"

The Minister looked as if he was in physical pain.

"The President won't change a thing or permit any of his planned itinerary to be altered. I spoke to him this morning. He was not pleased. So tomorrow remains the same as published. He will rekindle the

Eternal Flame under the Arc de Triomphe at ten. High Mass in Notre Dame at eleven. Private meditation at the shrine of the martyred resistants at Montvalérien at twelve-thirty, then back to the Palace for lunch and siesta. One ceremony in the afternoon, presentation of Médailles de la Libération to a group of ten veterans of the Resistance whose services to the Resistance are being rather belatedly recognised.

"That's at four o'clock on the square in front of the Gare de Montparnasse. He chose the place himself. If construction goes ahead according to plan, it may be the last Liberation Day that the old façade of the station remains untouched."

"What about crowd control?" asked Lebel.

"Well, we've all been working on it. Crowds are to be kept back at every ceremony further than ever before. Steel crowd barriers go up several hours before each ceremony, then the area inside the barrier-ring is searched from top to bottom, including the sewers. Every house and apartment is to be searched. Before each ceremony and during it there will be watchers with guns on every nearby roof-top surveying the opposite roofs and windows. Nobody gets through the barriers except officials, and those taking part in the ceremonies.

"We've gone to some extraordinary lengths this time. Even the cornices of Notre Dame, inside and out, will be infiltrated by policemen, right up to the roof and among the spires. All the priests taking part in Mass will be searched for concealed weapons, and the acolytes and choirboys. Even the police and CRS are having special lapel badges issued tomorrow morning at dawn, in case he tries to masquerade as a security man.

"We've spent the past twenty-four hours secretly slipping bulletproof windows in the Citroen the President will ride in. Incidentally, don't breathe a word of that; not even the President must know. He'd be furious. Marroux will drive him as usual, and he's been told to speed up the pace faster than usual, in case our friend tries for a snap shot at the car. Ducret has drafted in a posse of especially tall officers and officials to try and hedge the General round without him noticing.

"Apart from that, everybody who comes within two hundred metres of him is going to be frisked—no exceptions. It will create havoc with the Diplomatic Corps, and the press is threatening a revolt. All press and diplomatic passes are going to be suddenly changed at dawn tomorrow in case the Jackal tries to slip in as one of them. Obviously, anyone with a package or a lengthy-looking object will be hustled away as soon as spotted. Well, have you any ideas?"

Lebel thought for a moment, twisting his hands between his knees like a schoolboy trying to explain himself to his headmaster. In truth he found some of the workings of the Fifth Republic rather overpowering for a cop who had started on the beat and had spent his life catching criminals by keeping his eyes open a bit wider than anyone else.

"I don't think," he said at length, "that he will risk getting killed himself. He is a mercenary, he kills for money. He wants to get away and spend his money. And he has worked out his plan in advance, during his reconnaissance trip here in the last eight days of July.

If he had any doubts, either about the success of the operation or of his chances of getting away, he would have turned back before now.

"So he must have something up his sleeve. He could work out for himself that on one day of the year, Liberation Day, General de Gaulle's pride would forbid him staying at home, no matter what the personal danger. He could probably have worked out that the security precautions, particularly after his presence had been discovered, would be as intensive as you describe, Monsieur le Ministre. And yet he didn't turn back."

Lebel rose and, despite the breach of protocol, paced up and down the room.

"He didn't turn back. And he won't turn back. Why? Because he thinks he can do it, and get away. Therefore, he must have hit on some idea that nobody else has ever thought of. It has to be a bomb triggered by remote control, or a rifle. But a bomb could well be discovered, and that would ruin everything. So it's a gun. That was why he needed to enter France by car. The gun was in the car, probably welded to the chassis or inside the panelling."

"But he can't get a gun near de Gaulle," cried the Minister. "Nobody can get near him, except a few, and they are being searched. How can he get a gun inside the circle of crowd barriers?"

Lebel stopped pacing and faced the Minister. He shrugged.

"I don't know. But he thinks he can, and he's not failed yet, despite having some bad luck and some good. Despite being betrayed and tracked by two of the best police forces in the world, he's here. With a gun, in hiding, perhaps with yet another face and identity card. One thing is certain, Minister. Wherever he is, he must emerge tomorrow. When he does, he must be spotted for what he is. And that comes down to one thing—the old detective's adage of keeping your eyes open.

"There's nothing more I can suggest as regards the security precautions, Minister. They seem perfect, indeed overwhelming. So may I just wander round each of the ceremonies and see if I can spot him? It's the only thing left to do."

The Minister was disappointed. He had hoped for some flash of inspiration, some brilliant revelation from the detective whom Bouvier had described a fortnight earlier as the best in France. And the man had suggested he keep his eyes open. The Minister rose.

"Of course," he said coldly. "Please do just that, Monsieur le Commissaire."

Later that evening the Jackal laid out his preparations in Jules Bernard's bedroom. On the bed were the pair of scuffed black shoes, grey woollen socks, trousers and open-necked shirt, long military greatcoat with a single row of compaign ribbons, and black beret of the French war veteran André Martin. He tossed on top the false papers, forged in Brussels, that gave the wearer of the clothes his new identity.

Beside these he laid out the light webbing harness he had had made in London, and the five steel tubes that looked like aluminum and which contained the stock, breech, barrel, silencer, and telescopic sight of his rifle. Lying beside them was the black rubber stud into which were stuffed five explosive bullets.

He took two of the bullets out of the rubber, and using the pliers from the tool-box under the kitchen sink carefully removed the noses from them. From inside each he slid the small pencil of cordite they contained. These he kept; the cases of the now useless cartridges he threw in the ash-can. He still had three bullets left, and these would suffice.

He had not shaved for two days, and a light golden stubble covered his chin. This he would shave off badly with the cut-throat razor he had bought on his arrival in Paris. Also lying on the bathroom shelf were the flasks of after-shave that in fact contained the grey hair-tint he had once used already for Pastor Jensen, and the solvent spirit. He had already washed out the chestnut brown tint of Marty Schulberg, and sitting in front of the bathroom mirror he cut his own blond hair shorter and shorter, until the tufts stuck up from the top of the head in an untidy brush-cut.

He made one last check to see that all the preparations for the morning were in order, then cooked himself an omelette, settled in front of the television, and watched a variety show until it was time for bed.

Sunday, August 25, 1963, was scorching hot. It was the height of the summer heat wave, as it had been just one year and three days previously when Lieutenant Colonel Jean-Marie Bastien-Thiry and his men had tried to shoot Charles de Gaulle at the roundabout at Petit-Clamart. Although none of the plotters of that evening in 1962 realised it, their action had set off a chain of events that were only to terminate once and for all on the afternoon of the summer Sunday that now blazed down on a city on holiday.

But if Paris was on holiday to celebrate its own liberation from the Germans nineteen years earlier, there were 75,000 among them who sweated in blue-serge blouses and two-piece suits trying to keep the rest in order. Heralded by ecstatic columns of press publicity, the ceremonies to mark the day of liberation were massively attended. Most of those who came, however, hardly had a glimpse of the Head of State as he stalked through solid phalanxes of guards and policemen to officiate at the commemorations.

Apart from being boxed in from public view by a cohort of officers and civil servants who, although delighted to be asked to be in attendance, failed to notice that their one common characteristic was their height and that each in his way served as a human shield for the President, General de Gaulle was also surrounded by all four of his bodyguards.

Fortunately, his short-sightedness, accentuated by his refusal to wear glasses in public, prevented him from noting that behind each elbow and flanking him on each side were the huge bulks of Roger Tessier, Paul Comiti, Raymond Sasia, and Henri d'Jouder.

They were known to the Press as "gorillas," and many thought this was simply a tribute to their looks. In fact, there was a practical reason for their manner of walking. Each man was an expert in combat of all forms, with heavily muscled chests and shoulders. With muscles tensed, the dorsals forced the arms out from the sides so that the hands swung well away from the body. To add to this, each man carried his favourite automatic under his left armpit, accentuating the gorilla-like stance. They walked with hands half-open, ready to sweep the gun out from its shoulder-holster and start firing at the first hint of trouble.

But there was none. The ceremony at the Arc de Triomphe went off exactly as planned, while all along the great amphitheatre of roofs that overlook the Place de l'Etoile hundreds of men with binoculars and rifles crouched behind chimney stacks, watched, and guarded. As the presidential motorcade finally swept down the Champs Elysées towards Notre Dame, they all breathed a sigh of relief and started to come down again.

At the cathedral it was the same. The Cardinal Archbishop of Paris officiated, flanked by prelates and clergy, all of whom had been watched as they robed. In the organ loft two men perched with rifles (not even the Archbishop knew they were there) and watched the gathering below. The worshippers were heavily infiltrated by plain-clothes police, who did not kneel or close their eyes, but who prayed as fervently as the rest the old policeman's prayer: "Please, dear Lord, not while I'm on duty."

Outside, several bystanders, even though they were two hundred metres from the door of the cathedral, were hustled away when they reached inside their jackets. One had been scratching his armpit, the other going for a cigarette case.

And still nothing happened. There was no crack of a rifle from a roof-top, no muffled crump of a bomb. The police even scanned each other, making sure that their colleagues had the indispensable lapel-badge issued that very morning so that the Jackal could not copy it and masquerade as a policeman. One CRS man who lost his badge was arrested on the spot and bustled to a waiting van. His submachine carbine was taken from him, and it was not until the evening that he was released. Even then, it took twenty of his colleagues who personally recognised the man and vouched for him to convince the police that he was who he said he was.

At Montvalérien the atmosphere was electric, although if the President noticed it he gave no sign. In this working-class suburb, the security man had estimated that while actually inside the ossuary the General would be safe. But while his car was wending its way through the narrow streets approaching the prison, slowing down for the corners, the assassin might make his attempt.

In fact, at that moment, the Jackal was elsewhere.

Pierre Valrémy was fed up. He was hot, his blouse was sticking to his back, the strap of his submachine carbine chafed his shoulder through the soaking material, he was thirsty, and it was just lunchtime, which he knew he was going to miss. He was beginning to regret joining the CRS at all.

It had been all very well when he was laid off redundant from his factory job at Rouen and the clerk at the Labour Exchange had pointed to the poster on the wall of a beaming young man in the uniform of the CRS who was telling the world that he had a job with a future and prospects of an interesting life. The uniform in the picture looked as if it had been tailored by Balenciaga himself. So Valrémy had enlisted.

No one had mentioned the life in the barracks that looked like a prison, which was just what it had once been. Nor the drill, nor the night exercises, nor the

itchy serge blouse, nor the hours of waiting on street
corners in bitter cold or blazing heat for the Great
Arrest that never took place. People's papers were
always in order, their missions inevitably mundane
and harmless, and it was enough to drive anyone to
drink.

And now Paris, the first trip out of Rouen he had
ever made. He had thought he might see the City of
Light. Not a hope, not with Sergeant Barbichet in
charge of the squad. Just more of the same. See that
crowd barrier, Valrémy. Well, stand by it, watch it,
see it don't move, and don't let nobody through it
unless they're authorised, see? Yours is a responsible
job, my lad.

Responsible indeed! Mind you, they had gone a bit
wild over this Paris Liberation Day, bringing in thousands from the provinces to supplement the Paris
troops. There had been men from ten different cities
in his barracks last night, and the Paris men had a
rumour someone was expecting something to happen,
else why all the fuss. Rumours, there were always
rumours. They never came to anything.

Valrémy turned round and looked back up the rue
de Rennes. The crowd barrier he was guarding was
one of a chain stretched across the street from one
building to the other, about two hundred and fifty
metres up the street from the Place du 18 Juin. The
façade of the railway station was another two hundred
metres beyond the square, fronted by the forecourt
in which the ceremony was to take place. In the distance he could see some men inside the forecourt,
marking out the places where the old veterans would
stand, and the officials, and the band of the Garde

Républicaine. Three hours to go. Jesus, would it never end?

Along the line of barriers the first of the public were beginning to assemble. Some of them had fantastic patience, he thought. Fancy waiting in this heat for hours just to see a crowd of heads three hundred metres away and know that de Gaulle was in the middle of that lot, somewhere. Still, they always came when Charlot was about.

There were about a hundred or two hundred scattered along the barriers when he saw the old man. He was hobbling down the street looking like he was never going to make it another half mile. The black beret was stained with sweat and the long greatcoat swished below his knee. There was a row of medals dangling and clinking on his chest. Several of the crowd by the barrier cast him glances full of pity.

These old codgers always kept their medals, Valrémy thought, like it was the only thing they had in life. Well, may it *was* the only thing left for some of them. Especially when you had one of your legs shot off. Maybe, thought Valrémy, watching the old man hobbling down the street, he had run around a bit when he was young, when he had two legs to run on. Now he looked like a smashed up old seagull the CRS man had seen once on a visit to the seaside at Kermadec.

Christ, fancy having to spend the rest of your days limping about with one leg, propping yourself up on an aluminum crutch. The old man hobbled up to him.

"*Je peux passer?*" he asked timidly.

"Come on, Dad, let's have a look at your papers."

The old war veteran fumbled inside his shirt, which

could have done with a wash. He produced two cards which Valrémy took and looked at. André Martin, French citizen, aged fifty-three, born at Colmar, Alsace; resident in Paris. The other card was for the same man. Written across the top of it were the words: "Mutilé de Guerre."

"Well, you're mutilated all right, pal," thought Valrémy.

He studied the photographs on each card. They were of the same man, but taken at different times. He looked up.

"Take off your beret."

The old man took it off and crumpled it in his hand. Valrémy compared the face in front of him with those in the photograph. It was the same. The man in front of him looked sick. He had cut himself shaving, and small bits of toilet paper were stuck on the cuts where specks of blood still showed. The face was grey-coloured and greasy with a film of sweat. Above the forehead the tufts of grey hair stuck up at all angles, disarranged by the act of sweeping off the beret. Valrémy handed the cards back.

"What do you want to go down there for?"

"I live there," said the old man. "I'm retired on my pension. I have an attic."

Valrémy snatched the cards back. The identity card gave his address at 154, rue de Rennes, Paris 6ème. The CRS man looked at the house above his head. Written over the door was the number 132. Fair enough, 154 must be further down the road. No orders against letting an old man go home.

"All right, pass through. But don't get into no mischief. Charlot's going to be along in a couple of hours."

The old man smiled, putting away his cards and nearly stumbling on his one leg and crutch, so that Valrémy reached out to steady him.

"I know. One of my old pals is getting his medal. I got mine two years ago"—he tapped the Médaille de la Libération on his chest—"but only from the Minister of the Armed Forces."

Valrémy peered at the medal. So that's the Liberation Medal. Hell of a small thing to get a leg shot off for. He remembered his authority and nodded curtly. The old man hobbled away down the street. Valrémy turned to stop another chancer who was trying to slip through the barrier.

"All right, all right, that's enough of that. Stay back behind the barrier."

The last thing he saw of the old soldier was the flash of the greatcoat disappearing into a doorway at the far end of the street next to the square.

Madame Berthe looked up startled as the shadow fell over her. It had been a trying day, what with policemen looking in all the rooms, and she didn't know what the tenants would have said if they had been there. Fortunately all but three were away for the August holidays.

When the police had gone she had been able to settle back in her usual place in the doorway for a bit of quiet knitting. The ceremony due to take place a hundred yards away across the square in the station forecourt in two hours interested her not in the slightest.

"*Excusez-moi, madame*—I was wondering—perhaps a glass of water. It is terribly hot waiting for the ceremony . . ."

She took in the face and form of an old man in a greatcoat such as her long-dead husband had once worn, with medals swinging below the lapel on the left breast. He leaned heavily on a crutch, one single leg protruding from beneath the greatcoat. His face looked haggard and sweaty. Madame Berthe bundled up her knitting and stuffed it into the pocket of her apron.

"Oh, *mon pauv' monsieur*. Walking around like that —and in this heat. The ceremony is not for two hours yet. You are early. . . . Come in, come in . . ."

She bustled off towards the glass-fronted door of her parlour at the back of the hall to get a glass of water. The war veteran hobbled after her.

Above the running of the water from the kitchen tap she did not hear the door close on the outer lobby; she hardly felt the fingers of the man's left hand slide round her jawbone from behind. And the crash of the bunched knuckles under the mastoid bone on the right side of her head just behind the ear was completely unsuspected. The image of the running tap and the filling glass in front of her exploded into fragments of red and black, and her inert form slid soundlessly to the floor.

The Jackal opened the front of his coat, reached for the waist, and unbuckled the harness that kept his right leg strapped up under his buttocks. As he straightened the leg and flexed the cramped knee, his face tightened with pain. He spent several minutes allowing the blood to flow back into the calf and ankle of the leg before putting any weight on it.

Five minutes later Madame Berthe was trussed up hand and foot with the clothesline from beneath the sink, and her mouth was covered with a large square of sticking plaster. He put her in the scullery and shut the door.

A search of the parlour revealed the keys of the flat in the table drawer. Re-buttoning the coat, he took up the crutch, the same on which he had hobbled through the airports of Brussels and Milan twelve days earlier, and peered outside. The hall was empty. He left the parlour, locked the door after him, and loped up the stairs.

On the sixth floor he chose the flat of Mademoiselle Béranger and knocked. There was no sound. He waited and knocked again. From neither that flat nor the next door one of M. and Mme Charrier came a sound. Taking the keys he searched for the name Béranger, found it and entered the flat, closing and locking the door after him.

He crossed to the window and looked out. Across the road, on the rooftops of the blocks opposite, men in blue uniforms were moving into position. He was only just in time. At arm's length he unclipped the window lock and swung both halves of the frame quietly inwards until they came back against the inside of the living room wall. Then he stepped well back. A square shaft of light fell through the window onto the carpet. By contrast, the rest of the room appeared darker.

If he stayed away from that square of light, the watchers opposite would see nothing.

Stepping to the side of the window, keeping to the shadows of the withdrawn curtains, he found he could look downwards and sideways into the forecourt of the station 130 metres away. Eight feet back from the window and well to one side, he set up the living room table, removing the table-cloth and pot of plastic flowers and replacing them with a pair of cushions from the armchair. These would form his firing rest.

He stripped off his greatcoat and rolled up his sleeves. The crutch came to pieces section by section. The black rubber ferrule on the end was unscrewed and revealed the shining percussion caps of his three remaining shells. The nausea and sweating inspired by eating the cordite out of the other two was only beginning to leave him.

The next section of the crutch was unscrewed, and from it slid the silencer. The second section came away to disgorge the telescopic sight. The thickest part of the crutch, where the two upper supports merged into the main stem, revealed the breech and barrel of the rifle.

From the Y-shaped frame above the join, he slid the two steel rods which, when fitted together, would become the frame of the rifle's stock. Lastly the padded armpit-support of the crutch; this alone concealed nothing except the trigger of the rifle embedded in the padding. Otherwise the armpit-support slid onto the stock of the gun as it was, to become the shoulder-guard.

Lovingly and meticulously he assembled the rifle—breech and barrel, upper and lower component of the stock, shoulder-guard, silencer, and trigger. Lastly he slid on the telescopic sight and clipped it fast.

Sitting on a chair behind the table, leaning slightly forward with the gun barrel resting on top of the upper cushion, he squinted through the telescope. The sunlit square beyond the windows and fifty feet down leapt into focus. The head of one of the men still marking out the standing positions for the forthcoming ceremony passed across the line of sight. He tracked the target with the gun. The head appeared large and clear, as large as a melon had looked in the forest glade in the Ardennes.

Satisfied at last, he lined the three cartridges up on the edge of the table like soldiers in a row. With finger and thumb he slid back the rifle's bolt and eased the first shell into the breech. One should be enough, but he had two spare. He pushed the bolt forward again until it closed on the base of the cartridge, gave a half-twist, and locked it. Finally he laid the rifle carefully among the cushions, and fumbled for cigarettes and matches.

Drawing hard on his first cigarette, he leant back to wait for another hour and three quarters.

twenty-one

Commissaire Claude Lebel felt as if he had never had a drink in his life. His mouth was dry and the tongue stuck to the roof of it as though it were welded there. Nor was it just the heat that caused this feeling. For the first time in many many years he was really frightened. Something, he was sure, was going to happen during that afternoon, and he still could find no clue as to how or when.

He had been at the Arc de Triomphe that morning, and at Notre Dame and at Montvalérien. Nothing had happened. Over lunch with some of the men from the committee, which had met for the last time at the ministry that day at dawn, he had heard the mood change from tenseness and anger to something almost of euphoria. There was only one more ceremony to go, and the Place du 18 Juin, he was assured, had been scoured and sealed off.

"He's gone," said Rolland as the group who had lunched together at a brasserie not far from the Elysée Palace while General de Gaulle lunched inside it, emerged into the sunlight. "He's gone, fucked off. And a very wise thing too. He'll surface somewhere, sometime, and my boys will get him."

Now Lebel prowled disconsolately round the edge of the crowd held two hundred metres down the Boulevard Montparnasse, so far away from the square that no one could see what was going on. Each policeman and CRS man he spoke to on the barriers had the

same message. No one had passed through since the
barriers went up at twelve.

The main roads were blocked, the side roads were
blocked, the alleys were blocked. The rooftops were
watched and guarded, the station itself, honeycombed
with offices and attics racing down onto the forecourt,
was crawling with security men. They perched atop
the great engine sheds, high above the silent platforms
from which all trains had been diverted for the afternoon to the Gare Saint-Lazare.

Inside the perimeters every building had been
scoured from basement to attic. Most of the flats were
empty, their occupants away on holiday at the seaside
or the mountains.

In short, the area of the Place du 18 Juin was sealed
off, as Valentin would say, "tighter than a mouse's asshole." Lebel smiled at the memory of the language of
the Auvergnat policeman. Suddenly the grin was wiped
off. Valentin had not been able to stop the Jackal
either.

He slipped through the side streets, showing his
police pass to take a short cut, and emerged in the
rue de Rennes. It was the same story. The road was
blocked off two hundred metres from the square, the
crowds massed behind the barriers, the street empty
except for the patrolling CRS men. He started asking
again.

Seen anyone? No, sir. Anyone been past, anyone at
all? No, sir. Down in the forecourt of the station he
heard the band of the Garde Républicaine tuning their
instruments. He glanced at his watch. The General
would be arriving any time now. Seen anybody pass,

anyone at all? No, sir. Not this way. All right, carry on.

Down in the square he heard a shouted order, and from one end of the Boulevard de Montparnasse a motorcade swept into the Place du 18 Juin. He watched it turn into the gates of the station forecourt, police erect and at the salute. All eyes down the street were watching the sleek black cars. The crowd behind the barrier a few yards from him strained to get through. He looked up at the rooftops. Good boys. The watchers on the roof ignored the spectacle below them; their eyes never stopped flickering across the rooftops and windows across the road from where they crouched on the parapets, watching for a slight movement at a window.

He had reached the western side of the rue de Rennes. A young CRS man stood with his feet planted squarely in the gap where the last steel crowd barrier abutted the wall of Number 132. He flashed his card at the man, who stiffened.

"Anybody passed this way?"

"No, sir."

"How long have you been here?"

"Since twelve o'clock, sir, when the street was closed."

"Nobody been through that gap?"

"No, sir. Well . . . only the old cripple, and he lives down there."

"What cripple?"

"Oldish fellow, sir. Looked sick as a dog. He had his I.D. card, and Mutilé de Guerre card. Address given as 154, rue de Rennes. Well, I had to let him through, sir. He looked all in, real sick. Not surprised with him in that greatcoat, and in this weather and all. Crazy, really."

"Greatcoat?"

"Yessir. Great long coat. Military, like the old soldiers used to wear. Too hot for this weather though."

"What was wrong with him?"

"Well, he was too hot, wasn't he, sir?"

"You said he was war-wounded. What was wrong with him?"

"One leg, sir. Only one leg. Hobbling along he was, on a crutch."

From down in the square the first clear peals from the trumpets sounded. "*Allons, enfants de la patrie, le jour de gloire est arrivé. . . .*" Several of the crowd took up the familiar chant of the "Marseillaise."

"Crutch?" To himself, Lebel's voice seemed a small thing, very far away. The CRS man looked at him solicitously.

"Yessir. A crutch, like one-legged men always have. An aluminum crutch . . ."

Lebel was taking off down the street yelling at the CRS man to follow him.

They were drawn up in the sunlight in a hollow square. The cars were parked nose to tail along the wall of the station façade. Directly opposite the cars, along the railings that separated the forecourt from the square, were the ten recipients of the medals to be distributed by the Head of State. On the east side of the forecourt were the officials and diplomatic corps, a solid mass of charcoal grey suiting, with here and there the red rosebud of the Legion of Honour.

The western side was occupied by the serried red plumes and burnished casques of the Garde Républicaine, the bandsmen standing a little out in front of the guard of honour itself.

Round one of the cars up against the station façade clustered a group of protocol officials and Palace staff. The band continued to play the "Marseillaise."

The Jackal raised the rifle and squinted down into the forecourt. He picked the war veteran nearest to him, the man who would be the first to get his medal. He was a short, stocky man, standing very erect. His head came clearly into the sight, almost a complete profile. In a few minutes, facing this man, about one foot taller, would be another face, proud, arrogant, topped by a khaki kepi adorned with the two gold stars on the front.

"*Marchons, marchons, qu'un sang impur . . .*" Boomba-boom. The last notes of the national anthem died away, replaced by a great silence. The roar of the Commander of the Guard echoed across the station yard. "General Salute . . . Prese-e-ent ARMS." There were three precise crashes as white-gloved hands smacked in unison across rifle butts and magazines, and heels came down together. The crowd around the car parted, falling back into halves. From the centre a single tall figure emerged and began to stalk towards the line of war veterans. At fifty metres from them the rest of the crowd stopped, except the Minister of Veterans' Affairs, who would introduce the veterans to their President, and an official carrying a velvet cushion with a row of ten pieces of metal and ten coloured ribbons on it. Apart from these two, Charles de Gaulle marched forward alone.

"This one?"

Lebel stopped, panting, and gestured towards a doorway.

"I think so, sir. Yes, this was it, second from the end. This was where he came in."

The little detective was gone down the hallway, and Valrémy followed him, not displeased to be out of the street, where their odd behaviour in the middle of a serious occasion was attracting disapproving frowns from some of the higher brass standing at attention against the railing of the station yard. Well, if he was put on the carpet, he could always say that the funny little man had posed as a Commissaire of Police, and that he had been trying to detain him.

When he got into the hall, the detective was shaking the door of the concierge's parlour.

"Where's the concierge?" he yelled.

"I don't know, sir."

Before he could protest the little man had smashed the frosted glass panel with his elbow, reached inside, and opened the door.

"Follow me," he called, and dashed inside.

"You're damned right I'm going to follow you," thought Valrémy. "You're off your chump."

He found the little detective at the door of the scullery. Looking over the man's shoulder he saw the concierge tied up on the floor, still unconscious.

"Shit." Suddenly it occurred to him the little man was not joking. He *was* a police commissaire, and they *were* after a criminal. This was the big moment he had always dreamed of, and he wished he was back in barracks.

"Top floor," shouted the detective, and was gone up the stairs with a speed that surprised Valrémy, who pounded after him, unslinging his carbine as he ran.

The President of France passed before the first man in the line of veterans and stooped slightly to listen to the Minister explain who he was and what was his citation for valour shown on that day nineteen years before. When the Minister had finished, he inclined his head towards the veteran, turned towards the man with the cushion, and took the proffered medal. As the band began a softly played rendering of "La Marjolaine," the tall General pinned the medal onto the rounded chest of the elderly man in front of him. Then he stepped back for the salute.

Six floors up and 130 metres away the Jackal held the rifle very steady and squinted down the telescopic sight. He could see the features quite clearly, the brow shaded by the peak of the kepi, the peering eyes, the prow-like nose. He saw the raised saluting hand come down from the peak of the cap, the crossed wires of the sight were spotted on the exposed temple. Softly, gently, he squeezed the trigger. . . .

A split second later he was staring down into the station forecourt as if he could not believe his eyes. Before the bullet had passed out of the end of the barrel, the President of France had snapped his head forward without warning. As the assassin watched in disbelief, he solemnly planted a kiss on each cheek of the man in front of him. As he himself was a foot taller, he had had to bend forward and down to give the traditional kiss of congratulation that is habitual among the French and certain other nations, but which baffles Anglo-Saxons.

It was later established the bullet had passed a fraction of an inch behind the moving head. Whether the President heard the whipcrack of the bullet is not known. He gave no sign of it. The Minister and the official heard nothing; neither did those fifty metres away.

The slug tore into the sun-softened tarmacadam of the forecourt, its disintegration taking place harmlessly inside more than an inch of tar. "La Marjolaine" played on. The President, after planting the second kiss, straightened up and moved sedately on towards the next man.

Behind his gun, the Jackal started to swear, softly, venomously. He had never missed a stationary target at 150 yards in his life before. Then he calmed down; there was still time. He tore open the breech of the rifle, ejecting the spent cartridge to fall harmlessly onto the carpet. Taking the second one off the table he pushed it home and closed the breech.

Claude Lebel arrived panting on the sixth floor. He thought his heart was going to burst from his chest. There were two doors leading towards the front of the building. He looked from one to the other as the CRS man joined him, submachine carbine held on his hip, pointing forward.

As Lebel hesitated in front of the two doors, from

behind one of them came a low but distinct "phut." Lebel pointed at the door lock with his forefinger.

"Shoot it off," he ordered, and stepped back. The CRS man braced himself on both feet and fired. Bits of wood and metal, and spent, flattened slugs flew in all directions. The door buckled and swung drunkenly inwards. Valrémy was first into the room, Lebel on his heels.

Valrémy could recognise the grey tufts of hair, but that was all. The man had two legs, the greatcoat was gone, and the forearms that gripped the rifle were on a strong young man. The gunman gave him no time; rising from his seat behind the table, swinging in one smooth motion at a half-crouch, he fired from the hip. The single bullet made no sound; the echoes of Valrémy's gunburst were still ringing in his ears. The slug from the Jackal's rifle tore into his chest, struck the sternum, and exploded. There was a feeling of tearing and ripping and of great sudden stabs of pain; then even they were gone. The light faded as if summer had turned to winter. A piece of carpet came up and smacked him on the cheek, except that it was his cheek that was lying on the carpet. The loss of feeling swept up through the thighs and belly, then the chest and neck. The last thing he remembered was a salty taste in the mouth, like he had had after bathing in the sea at Kermadec, and a one-legged old gull sitting on a post. Then it was all dark.

Above his body Claude Lebel stared into the eyes of the other man. He had no trouble with his heart; it did not seem to be pumping any more.

"Chacal," he said. The other man said simply, "Lebel." He was fumbling with the gun, tearing open the breech. Lebel saw the glint of the cartridge case as it dropped to the floor. The man swept something off the table and stuffed it into the breech. His grey eyes were still staring at Lebel.

"He's trying to fix me rigid," thought Lebel with a sense of unrealism. "He's going to shoot. He's going to kill me."

With an effort he dropped his eyes to the floor. The boy from the CRS had fallen sideways; his carbine had slipped from his fingers and lay at Lebel's feet. Without conscious thought he dropped to his knees, grabbed the MAT 49, swinging it upwards with one hand, the other clawing for the trigger. He heard the Jackal snap home the breech of the rifle as he found the trigger of the carbine. He pulled it.

The roar of the exploding ammunition filled the small room and was heard in the square. Later press inquiries were met with the explanation that it had been a motorcycle with a faulty silencer which some ass had kicked into life a few streets away at the height of the ceremony. Half a magazine full of nine-millimetre bullets hit the Jackal in the chest, picked him up, half-turned him in the air, and slammed his body into an untidy heap in the far corner of the room. As he fell, he brought the standard lamp with him. Down below, the band struck up *"Mon Régiment et Ma Patrie."*

Superintendent Thomas had a phone call at 6 that

evening from Paris. He sent for the senior inspector of his staff.

"They got him," he said. "In Paris. No problems, but you'd better get up to his flat and sort things out."

It was eight o'clock when the inspector was having a last sort-through of Calthrop's belongings that he heard someone come into the open doorway. He turned. A man was standing there scowling at him. A big-built, burly man.

"What are you doing here?" asked the inspector.

"I might ask you just the same thing. What the hell do you think you're doing?"

"All right, that's enough," said the inspector. "Let's have your name."

"Calthrop," said the newcomer, "Charles Calthrop. And this is my flat. Now what the hell are you doing to it?"

The inspector wished he carried a gun.

"All right," he said quietly, warily, "I think you'd better come down to the Yard for a little chat."

"Too bloody right," said Calthrop. "You've got a bit of explaining to do."

But in fact it was Calthrop who did the explaining. They held him for twenty-four hours, until three separate confirmations came through from Paris that the Jackal was dead, and five landlords of isolated taverns in the far north of Sutherland County, Scotland, had testified that Charles Calthrop had indeed spent the previous three weeks indulging his passion for climbing and fishing, and had stayed at their establishments.

"If the Jackal wasn't Calthrop," said Thomas after

Calthrop had finally walked out of the door a free man, "then who the hell was he?"

"There can be no question, of course," said the Commissioner of Metropolitan Police the next day to Assistant Commissioner Dixon and Superintendent Thomas, "of Her Majesty's Government ever conceding that this Jackal fellow was an Englishman at all. So far as one can see there was a period when a certain Englishman came under suspicion. He has now been cleared. We also know that for a period of his—er—assignment in France, the Jackal feller masqueraded as an Englishman under a falsely issued English passport. But he also masqueraded as a Dane, an American, and a Frenchman, under two stolen passports and one set of forged French papers. As far as we are concerned, our enquiries established that the assassin was travelling in France under a false passport in the name of Duggan, and in this name he was traced to—er—this place Gap. That's all. Gentlemen, the case is closed."

The following day the body of a man was buried in an unmarked grave at Père Lachaise cemetery in Paris. The death certificate showed the body to be that of an unnamed foreign tourist, killed on Sunday August 25, 1963, in a hit-and-run accident on the motorway outside the city. Present were a priest, a policeman, a registrar, and two gravediggers. Nobody present showed any interest as the plain deal coffin was lowered into the grave, except the single other person who attended. When it was all over he turned round, declined to give his name, and walked back down the cemetery path, a solitary little figure, to return home to his wife and children.

The day of the Jackal was over.

RELAX!
SIT DOWN
and Catch Up On Your Reading!

WHODUNIT?

Bantam did! By bringing you these masterful tales of murder, suspense and mystery!

- ☐ THE MYSTERIOUS AFFAIR AT STYLES
  by Agatha Christie   2215 $1.75
- ☐ THE DROWNING POOL
  by Ross Macdonald   2284 $1.50
- ☐ PENHALLOW
  by Georgette Heyer   2924 $1.50
- ☐ THE LEVANTER
  by Eric Ambler   7603 $1.50
- ☐ THE UNDERGROUND MAN
  by Ross Macdonald   7910 $1.50
- ☐ THE SPY WHO CAME IN FROM THE COLD
  by John LeCarre   8888 $1.75
- ☐ DEATH ON THE NILE
  by Agatha Christie   10022 $1.75
- ☐ THE SECRET ADVERSARY
  by Agatha Christie   10025 $1.75
- ☐ POIROT INVESTIGATES
  by Agatha Christie   10026 $1.75
- ☐ POSTERN OF FATE
  by Agatha Christie   10066 $1.75
- ☐ THE SILENT SPEAKER
  by Rex Stout   10067 $1.50

Buy them at your local bookstore or use this handy coupon for ordering:

Don't Forget These Other Famous Leon Uris Novels

WE DELIVER!
And So Do These Bestsellers.

BOOKS BEHIND THE LINES:

The side of war you will never read about in the history books

☐	THE HOUSE ON GARIBALDI STREET Isser Harel	2501	●	$1.95
☐	THE WAR AGAINST THE JEWS Lucy S. Dawidowicz 1933-1945	2504	●	$2.50
☐	THE WALL John Hersey	2569	●	$2.25
☐	HIROSHIMA John Hersey	2827	●	$1.25
☐	THE UPSTAIRS ROOM Johanna Reiss	2858	●	$1.25
☐	THE HIDING PLACE Corrie ten Boom	7903	●	$1.75
☐	THE PAINTED BIRD Jerzy Kosinski	8257	●	$1.75
☐	FAREWELL TO MANZANAR Jeanne Wakatsuki Houston and James D. Houston	8507	●	$1.25
☐	SUMMER OF MY GERMAN SOLDIER Bette Greene	10192	●	$1.50
☐	THE LAST OF THE JUST Andre Schwarz-Bart	10469	●	$1.95

Buy them at your local bookstore or use this handy coupon for ordering:

"HITLER'S WAR"

From the German point of view and secret Nazi documents never before revealed to the public, here is the whole gigantic drama of the most crucial days of World War II. Bantam now presents the books that individually capture the major personalities and events of the war.

Bantam Book Catalog

It lists over a thousand money-saving best-sellers originally priced from $3.75 to $15.00 —bestsellers that are yours now for as little as 60¢ to $2.95!

The catalog gives you a great opportunity to build your own private library at huge savings!

So don't delay any longer—send us your name and address and 25¢ (to help defray postage and handling costs).